PRAISE FOR JO

"For anyone who has ever had to find their voice in a crowd shouting to be the same as everyone else, Sadie Fremd will be your hero. With lush gardens so generously described that one feels as if they can pick the flowers, *All the Pretty Places* is immersive, engaging, and full of wonder."

—PATTI CALLAHAN HENRY, *NEW YORK TIMES*
BESTSELLING AUTHOR OF *SURVIVING SAVANNAH*

"Joy Callaway's *All the Pretty Places* is a fascinating, heartwarming story that brings to light a time and place where only the wealthy had access to the beauty and restorative power of gardens. Callaway draws us into Sadie's world with gorgeous prose (you can practically feel the rich, damp soil and smell the sweet lilacs) that transports readers to the lush landscapes that Sadie will go to any lengths to protect."

—ADELE MYERS, AUTHOR OF *THE TOBACCO WIVES*

"Masterfully written with elegant prose and exquisite detail, Joy Callaway crafts a story as sumptuous and colorful as the Gilded Age gardens she transports readers to. *All The Pretty Places* is the story of a young woman fighting for personal and professional integrity and freedom, as well as a searing social commentary on poverty, privilege, and class discrepancy. I found myself cheering for Sadie with each page and tearing up at the emotional and nuanced ending."

—YVETTE MANESSIS CORPORON, INTERNATIONAL BESTSELLING
AUTHOR OF *WHERE THE WANDERING ENDS*

"*All the Pretty Places* is a verdant, gorgeous novel, filled with lush scenery, fascinating characters, and engaging drama. Callaway skillfully transports her readers into the Gilded Age gardens of the late-twentieth century, where the yearnings of the heart come into conflict with the economic realities of the time. I was instantly swept away and stayed enraptured by the story to its very last page."

—LAUREN EDMONDSON, AUTHOR OF *WEDDING OF THE SEASON*

"If you yearn for a more gracious era, when natural beauty was a human birthright, you'll adore Joy Callaway's *All the Pretty Places*. Sadie's struggle to be taken seriously in an age when women are considered as ornamental as roses and her desire to freely pursue both her talents and her heart create a warm and engaging novel. And the fact that the story is based on Callaway's real-life ancestors only makes *All the Pretty Places* an even more satisfying read!"

—KIM WRIGHT, AUTHOR OF *LAST RIDE TO GRACELAND*

"Callaway's dialogue captures the cadences and concerns of the American upper crust, and the society drama is sure to please fans of such aristocratic historicals as *The House of Mirth* and *The Gilded Age*."

—PUBLISHERS WEEKLY FOR *THE GRAND DESIGN*

"A treat for historical fiction fans."

—BOOKLIST FOR *THE GRAND DESIGN*

"The story is a thoroughly enjoyable read with the characters, including The Greenbrier, coming vividly to life."

—HISTORICAL NOVEL SOCIETY FOR *THE GRAND DESIGN*

"A beautifully written historical romance novel. Joy Callaway has impeccably researched the life of Dorothy Draper from her days as 'Greenbrier' debutante to her return as the hotel's decorator. Five Stars!"

—CARLETON VARNEY, PRESIDENT OF DOROTHY DRAPER & COMPANY, INC., FOR *THE GRAND DESIGN*

"*The Grand Design* is a spellbinding tale of a woman's quest to escape the confines of upper-crust society and make her own way in the world. With vivid characters, illuminating prose, and perfect pacing, this novel is as captivating and confident as the heroine at its center."

—KRISTY WOODSON HARVEY, NEW YORK TIMES BESTSELLING AUTHOR OF *THE WEDDING VEIL*

"Joy Callaway's *The Grand Design* is a sumptuous look at the complicated life of famous interior designer Dorothy Draper."

—AIMIE K. RUNYAN, BESTSELLING AUTHOR OF *THE SCHOOL FOR GERMAN BRIDES*

ALL THE PRETTY PLACES

ALSO BY JOY CALLAWAY

The Grand Design: A Novel of Dorothy Draper
The Fifth Avenue Artists Society
Secret Sisters

ALL THE PRETTY PLACES

A NOVEL OF THE GILDED AGE

JOY CALLAWAY

HARPER MUSE

All the Pretty Places

Published by Harper Muse, an imprint of HarperCollins Focus LLC.

Any internet addresses (websites, blogs, etc.) in this book are offered as a resource. They are not intended in any way to be or imply an endorsement by HarperCollins Focus LLC, nor does HarperCollins Focus LLC vouch for the content of these sites for the life of this book.

Library of Congress Cataloging-in-Publication Data

Names: Callaway, Joy, author.
Title: All the pretty places : a novel of the Gilded Age / Joy Callaway.
Description: [Nashville] : Harper Muse, [2023] | Summary: "Joy Callaway returns with a captivating story of a strong woman in a striking setting, examining the life-changing effects of the beauty of nature and how that splendor is restricted to the rich and privileged in the Gilded Age"-- Provided by publisher.
Identifiers: LCCN 2022051784 (print) | LCCN 2022051785 (ebook) | ISBN 9781400234400 (TP) | ISBN 9781400234417 (epub) | ISBN 9781400234424 (audiobook)
Classification: LCC PS3603.A4455 A55 2023 (print) | LCC PS3603.A4455 (ebook) | DDC 813/.6--dc23
LC record available at https://lccn.loc.gov/2022051784
LC ebook record available at https://lccn.loc.gov/2022051785

Printed in the United States of America

23 24 25 26 27 LBC 5 4 3 2 1

*For my mom, Lynn, the personification of
joy and the best gardener in the world*

*For my dad, Fred, the epitome of steadfast love and
the ultimate role model in business and compassion*

*For my grandma, Lee, my BFF and keeper
and sharer of magical family stories*

CHAPTER 1

APRIL 1893
RYE, NEW YORK

Charles was leaving. At long last. *Si longtemps*, Charles! *Abschied*, dearest brother! *Tot ziens!* I loved him fiercely—more than I loved anyone, really—but I was glad to see him go.

Come 11:14 p.m., the rail cars would screech and lurch and he'd wave from the wrought iron caboose railing in his new champagne duster jacket, his fist full of the Bells of Ireland sprigs I'd shove into his hand for good luck. The clouds of his farewell shouts would mingle with thick rail steam in the chilly evening air. By Tuesday he'd be standing 1,300 miles away in the construction shadow of Mr. Flagler's latest lavish hotel, boots sinking into the veritable beach the structure was built upon. Charles would think, of course, that he'd have no problem whatsoever transforming the barrenness into a lush utopia of viburnums and palms and, most importantly, royal poinciana—a scarlet flowering beauty for which the hotel was named. Never mind that the royal poinciana was native to Madagascar and had never been grown in Florida. Charles had achieved enough success cultivating foreign species from Japan and Germany and Italy and Israel with Father that he would believe the task an easy one. We all did.

I hoped he would love Florida. That he'd be so enraptured by the aquamarine sea, the prestige of being Mr. Flagler's premiere landscape man, and the gorgeous fortune hunters—bless them—that he'd stay. Perhaps he'd even find a suitable girl who wouldn't mind the oppressive heat akin to that of a boiler room or the way even the finest silks swallowed the humidity and stuck to her limbs as though they'd been bathed in maple sap. Surely a girl of that fortitude could persevere in her pursuit of Charles despite his obsessive love of plants. Charles and I were afflicted with the same curse—a curse that drove me to celebrate his going and that of my younger brother, Freddie, two years ago when he went to work for Uncle Teddy's friend Mayor Carter Harrison in Chicago.

My brothers had been my greatest supporters and my greatest obstructions. Until Mr. Flagler's offer, I'd thought Charles would succumb to Father's plan to make him successor and never leave. But Charles had been an adventurer from birth, always wanting the opportunity to travel, to make his mark apart from Father's accomplishments.

Mr. Flagler had kept us as the primary gardeners at his Mamaroneck estate for nearly a decade. One day, when Charles was replacing a Countess of Oxford in his rose garden, Mr. Flagler came downstairs from his office, interrupted Charles, and asked him to take his talents to Florida. Before that fateful day only a month ago, I'd considered my life all but lost to the doom of a debutante's marital duty—a practice I found altogether disgusting.

I was no commodity, no acquisition to be considered due to the success of my parents and for the diversification of a gentleman's holdings. Despite my ardent study of horticulture, despite a mastery of it that exceeded both Charles's and Freddie's, Father refused to see me as a viable successor. Instead, he paraded suitable men in and out of our home as though he thought my utopia would be found in a handsome face and pockets as deep as the Mariana Trench. Or perhaps he thought I might be satisfied with love. What he didn't know was that I'd been in love, desperately in love, and had let it go for the only utopia I'd ever seen—the one I'd been looking at my whole life: the nurseries Father started.

I took one last minute to stare at my paradise—at the four rows of glass-paned greenhouses sparkling in the crescent moonlight, at the fields of roses and larkspur and phlox and hyacinth beyond them, at the groves of rare trees and shrubs to my right, at the whitewashed roofs of the barns in the distance beyond the railroad tracks, at the streams of chimney smoke from the gardeners' village.

Just this morning, I'd been elbow-deep in potting soil, cultivating cut-leaf weeping birch seedlings that would one day grow tall and strong and stately. Though life was difficult at times, nature was perpetually hopeful. I'd always taken refuge among the green—some of my earliest memories were of running to my father with fists full of wild roses and dandelions, amazed that they'd sprung up spontaneously. After Mother's death, I'd practically absorbed myself into the plants. The nurseries were my passion and always had been. Soon Father would notice.

Soon he would realize that *I* was his true successor, that I knew our customers—from the Iselins to the Chapmans to the Vanderbilts—like the back of my hand, that there was a reason I had studied his horticulture books from the moment I learned to read.

I turned away from the view and snatched the poem I'd written for Charles off my desk and glanced at the mirror. The gown was ambitious for a farewell fete—a triple skirt of ciel-blue satin edged in silver bead trimming with a corsage of silver embroidered chiffon—but my lady's maid, Agnes, had insisted I look my best. Who knew when I'd see my brother again, she'd said. I supposed that was true.

Below me the house was alive with over one hundred guests for Charles's send-off—nearly all of Rye and a few choice men from around Westchester County whom Father was hoping would catch my eye. I could hear Mr. Wright, who dealt in spirits, bellowing loudly about the quality of Father's brandy while Maribelle McRae struck the piano keys with a desperate fervor, as though playing every waltz she'd ever danced with Charles would convince him to stay and marry her.

I glanced out the window one last time, wishing I could disappear into the quiet of the flower field rather than enter the roaring rollick below, but my absence would be noticed. I turned, patted the intricate figure-eight hairstyle Agnes had spent nearly an hour crafting and waving with curling tongs, and stepped into the hall. I ran my hand along the mahogany wainscot and locked eyes with the portrait of my mother as a young girl hanging on the wall between Charles's and Freddie's quarters. Mother had been a saint. She'd taught Father English and gladly moved from the city to a tiny one-room house in Rye so Father could start the nurseries, not minding whatsoever that Father hadn't a cent to his name.

Suddenly footsteps pounded up the stairs and Charles appeared in the hall.

"Sadie, come quick. Father's leaned into the bottle quite a bit and I'm afraid he's cornered Harry Brundage about his intentions with you."

I sighed. Harry Brundage was nice enough and of decent appearance, but he was an iron heir who did nothing on his own. I'd even heard rumors that one of his servants steamed his newspapers. Spoiled men were demanding and entitled, and I absolutely wouldn't subject myself to that. A true gentleman handled success with humility. My parents, their union forged in the city slums, had always been clear that our wealth was a gift won by hard work and providence and that we were always to be grateful for the endowment given to us.

"Father should be more concerned with mine," I said.

"For your sake, I wish you didn't have them," Charles said, looping my arm through his as we made our way down the stairs. "I know you want the run of this place, but despite your pointed hints, you have never plainly expressed your interest to Father for a reason. You know he would rather dig his own grave than let our peers believe he's subjected his only daughter to the perils of commerce. Especially now. Marry well—a man who enjoys plants like you do. That would satisfy you, would it not?"

"Whatever do you mean, 'especially now'? And my gowns have already been soiled by 'the perils of commerce,' as you say. I'm just as involved as you are, Charles."

He looked down at the steps as we descended, a short tendril of light brown hair coming loose from his pomade.

"That may be the case, Sadie, but you're involved in the natural work, in the work of the soil, while I know the figures and read the papers and keep an eye on the state of the economy. Wall Street is sinking. Has been for two months since the Philadelphia and Reading Rail collapse. Surely you know it too. You've heard the whispers. The Shorts, the Adamses, the McCluskys have all gone bankrupt, their fortunes vanished by the collapse of the market or the collapse of others' fortunes who can no longer afford the fine furniture and linens their businesses offered."

I could hear the phrase he refused to say, that perhaps the luxury of fine gardens was next. I'd thought those families had left town solely because they were heavily invested in the market—something Father was not. I'd thought we were safe. Perhaps Charles hadn't been lured to Florida by the promise of adventure, fame, and philandering after all. Perhaps he knew something I didn't. The fear of it was paralyzing.

"Look around tonight," he went on, his voice low. "The LeBlanc family is gone as of this morning."

"What?" The news shocked me and I stopped on the landing, clutching the baluster and feeling at once like I might faint. Charles turned and grasped my other arm.

"Are you all right?"

The heavy scents of hyacinth and magnolia mingled with imperial crab and duck confit. Minutes ago I had smiled with the warmth of the combination, but now it made my stomach weak.

"I just saw Sylvie yesterday in the village."

"Mr. LeBlanc was hoping the Patterson account would be paid and buy him some time, but he found out last night that the funds weren't going to be deposited. The Pattersons should be ashamed, truly. Obviously they're a railroad family and their fortunes are greatly diminished, which is why they're halting construction on their country place in Port Chester, but they're not in danger of losing their Fifth Avenue townhome."

Charles's jaw hardened. He had a horrid temper to begin with, but his chiseled features and narrow eyes always made him look fiercer.

"They should have paid the LeBlancs, but they did not. Now there's no business coming in. LeBlanc Stoneworks has to close, and George and Marian and Sylvie are moving to the city for work. I suppose he'll have to go into the factories. This crash has wrecked us all, and if it keeps on, nothing will be left of this town in the coming years save a few summer estates." Charles squeezed my hand. "That's why I have to go."

"You told me you were taking the post for the adventure of it all, to make a name for yourself on your own terms. What do you mean nothing will be left of this town? We're still here and thriving. Or am I mistaken? Are we in peril?" I looked up at him, sure I could see the truth in his eyes.

"Not yet," he said, letting go of my hands. "I wasn't being dishonest when I said that. I'm following the adventure and the independence too. But it's the responsibility of a businessman to think of the worst and prepare for it. In case the nurseries begin to falter, I'll have obtained a sizable income. My funds could assist us—at least for a short while. And that's another reason you should choose someone to marry—a good someone, Sadie. Father is worried every suitable man in town will wind up like the LeBlancs, or heaven forbid, we might. He wants you connected to a stable fortune that will keep you safe, an old fortune that won't fold with this downturn. Don't you suppose Sylvie wishes she'd accepted Aden Blankenship or Vic Griffin rather than face the city slums?"

The question struck me. Sylvie had been my friend since childhood, a girl envied by most for her delicate looks and sizable fortune. Just last month she'd turned down two proposals because she barely knew either of the men and refused to settle for anything less than love. Marriage declarations were made to heiresses as often as business propositions were made to their fathers. Sylvie passed these over without much thought—as I often did—assuming there would be more and that someday one of them might come with love attached.

"It's time to forget about your fantasies, sister. This is reality. I'm certain you'll be allowed to have a garden wherever you end up."

"'Allowed,'" I muttered. Despite the fear gripping me at the thought of facing poverty and ruin, the idea of giving up and going the way of safety to avoid it was equally harrowing. Father had been poor once and he'd found his way out of it. Even in poverty, there was a chance, however slim, that misfortune lasted a moment, not a lifetime. I'd clung to that idea once—when I'd almost chosen poverty for love. But marriage to someone like Harry Brundage wouldn't be merely a moment. It would be for the rest of my life.

"Why don't *you* marry rich then, dearest brother? Forget your silly little notion of making a mark on this world and settle for a society darling who will give you a square of her estate in which to bury your dreams."

"I only want you to be protected," he said, meeting my gaze. His brown eyes were solemn. Fiercely loyal to me ever since Mother asked him to look after me as a baby, Charles had always been my defender. Ordinarily, I was thankful for it, but in this instance his counsel was an irritation.

"Think what you will about my ambitions, but I'll not give them up and I'll be fine," I said, fire igniting my veins. "After you're gone, Father will see. He already respects other women in industry—Anna Bissell and Rebecca Lukens, just to name two, and I'm no different from them. I'm just as capable at the helm here as you would be. Despite the dire nature of things, we will grow and thrive. I'll see to that. We will not sink. And I'll say it again—until you're willing to surrender yourself to matrimony, don't advise the same to me."

"Very well," Charles said. "If anyone can do it, I believe you can, Sadie, and I'll be hoping my hardest for you." He clutched my hand and smiled. For as much as he refused to concede an argument with nearly anyone else, he always did so for me.

We made our way down the remaining steps and into the crush occupying our drawing room. Uncle Teddy Fremd, the current mayor of Rye, still wore his fireman's coat from a scare earlier today and stood by the white marble mantel with a group of employees from his meat market he'd started upon moving to Rye twenty years ago. William Robson, the town physician, and John Whittaker, the town lawyer, were detaining our butler, Mr. Cooper, with his tray full of a selection of Charles's favorite foods.

"Dear boy, come tell us all about your latest adventure," Mr. Hazelhurst said as he pulled Charles into a group of older men whose grandfathers had settled the town.

"Sorry." Charles glanced at me apologetically. "Find Father."

I wandered into the room and past a group of my friends gathered around the old Bechstein grand piano that Maribelle was still playing with vigor, and spotted Jonathan Severs and

Stephen Bishop among them. Of course Father would take every opportunity to invite potential suitors into our home. Perhaps they would both be taken with someone else—Susan, possibly. She was beautiful and from a *Mayflower* family. Or Juliana. She had the fairest hair and was poised to inherit her grandfather's estate on the Long Island Sound.

Despite Jonathan's humor and wit and Stephen's beautiful face and Harry Brundage's deep pockets, I couldn't fathom marriage to any of them. It wasn't only about the nurseries, though I couldn't pretend it wasn't mostly so. It was also about a pair of ocean-blue eyes in the moonlight; strong, work-worn hands on my waist; the feel of midnight hair threading through my fingers; the way he saw my soul laid bare; and the look he gave me when I promised I'd go with him, that I'd love him forever. I only lied about half of that.

I forced the memory away and walked toward the foyer. Father wasn't among the group gathered there either. I turned back around, sure that he'd materialize in the drawing room somewhere, when I heard his voice coming from the hall that led to the back of the house. My father had thankfully retreated to his study—or it was possible Harry had encouraged them to retire there to have a private word. Either way, I could hear Father shouting in German and wondered if Harry even spoke the language. Most society men spoke French. It was thought to be more refined, more delicate. Father spoke French too. Spanish as well. But German was his native tongue.

I walked down the hallway toward the sound, the electric lights from the study casting a punctuating beam on a landscape painting on the adjacent wall of a field of English poppies in bloom.

"What did you expect, Charles?" Father's voice boomed, still in German. I wondered how Charles had broken free of Mr. Hazelhurst so quickly. The man was known to deliver lengthy monologues on his father's conquests against the British during the War of 1812 anytime he had an audience. The conquests became greater and greater each time they were recounted.

"We need the accounts and since you're a practical turn-coat now—leaving me alone to run this enterprise that I built for *you*, for Freddie, to one day operate—I have no choice. We employ sixty people and more will be knocking on my door with LeBlanc's closure. Do you suppose I should admit defeat now and let the nurseries crumble with so many in my care?" Father's voice was shaking. I hoped Harry—if he was in fact tangled in this conversation—couldn't speak German.

"Of course not," Charles said. "I understand the position you're in. But to ask the man for both his life's love and his business in the space of a breath is poor form. If you hadn't taken so much bourbon, you would see it clearly."

Something clattered on Father's desktop. I started to walk into the room, to tell him he wasn't alone without Charles, that he had me and discounting my capability was insulting, but I stopped when I heard Harry's voice.

"Gentlemen," Harry said in English. "If you'll excuse me. I'd like to find Miss Fremd and have a word."

"Yes, yes. Very well." Father's temper was now alleviated by what he doubtless considered progress on resolving one of his chief concerns.

I spun away, nearly tripping over the hem of my gown, and walked quickly down the hall. Perhaps if I was fast enough I could evade his company. He always made flirtatious gestures that I chose to ignore, but now, having returned permanently from his studies at Yale, I had a feeling he was keen to settle down, and I had no interest in nesting with him.

"I'd know that silhouette anywhere." His voice echoed over me, but I kept walking, hoping he'd think the crowd's noise and the piano had simply drowned him out.

"Miss Fremd." He caught my arm as the hall gave way to the drawing room.

"Oh, hello there, Mr. Brundage," I said. "Lovely to see you again. If you don't mind terribly, I must go say hello to our guests. I've just come down, you know, and I—"

"I know, and I understand that my request will therefore be terribly inconvenient, but I'm afraid I must ask it of you all the same. Your father has just now been reminding me of the vast array of rare varieties you offer an estate such as mine. I'd like to see these rarities for myself before I employ his company. My current nurseryman is a longtime peer of my father's. I'd hate to disrupt the relationship if it won't be worthwhile for us."

He smiled. As average as his pale skin and brown hair made him, I'd always thought he could be attractive with the right sort of personality and charm. One couldn't do anything to alter that, though. Even so, I knew I'd have to accept his tour request if I was to prove to Father that I was a proper partner in industry and not just a daughter with a love of plants.

"Of course, Mr. Brundage. I'm confident you'll be most impressed," I said. "This way, if you please." I exited the drawing room and proceeded toward the front door, very aware of how closely he was following me.

The night air still held a nip of winter and the smell of woodsmoke. Harry extended his arm to me, and I reluctantly took it as we crossed the whitewashed porch boards and made our way down the steps.

"I shouldn't have asked you outside in this weather. Especially with you wearing the ensemble you have on. It's quite unsuitable."

"Don't think anything of it," I said, trying my best to be polite. "I've been out here in much harsher temperatures and enjoy the feel of my hands in the dirt no matter the weather. Plants are a balm to my soul." I'd spoken intentionally, hoping whatever fondness he had toward me might be dissolved by the notion of a woman whose fingernails—and frock, for that matter—would always be stained with earth.

"But you're shivering. I can feel it."

Harry ran his free palm over my arm and I bristled, silently cursing the little bumps that gave me away.

"Here, take my jacket at least."

Before I could tell him no, he'd edged out of his gray tweed jacket and settled it over my shoulders. The garment smelled of a heavy bergamot cologne that I suspected was imported from somewhere in France. Despite the gesture being completely unwanted, I had to admit that the silk lining felt like butter against my skin.

"Right this way," I said as I quickly crossed the well-worn dirt drive in front of him, hoping the distance would prevent him from offering his arm again. Ahead, the twenty-four greenhouses beckoned. I knew I couldn't go inside any of them to check on the plants while the party was in full swing, yet my fingers itched. There was always so much to do.

"Your father tells me the estate is about seventy-five acres," Harry said as he caught up to me. "I'm ashamed to say I haven't taken much notice of it before." I turned to look at him. I'd never heard anyone call the nurseries an estate. If anything, it was a working farm. He stopped to survey the field of greenhouses and then looked back at our home, a hulking structure of three-story white wood shrouded in part by my father's favorite shrubs and trees on both sides—the andromeda, or Sorrell, shrub with its narrow, glossy leaves and small white flowers and the Carya, or hickory, that produced father's favorite nuts and fall foliage.

"Yes, we have seventy-five acres, though seventy of them are engaged in the planting business."

I started down the middle aisle between the greenhouses. With another man, a night like this would be romantic—the moonglow making stars twinkle on the glass panes all around us, the soft crunch of our tandem steps on the frosty grass.

"The first row of greenhouses, just over there, is dedicated to seed growth. We source seeds from England, Japan, Italy—really all over the world. The second row right here"—I pointed to my right—"is dedicated to tropical varieties like lilliums, Easter and tiger lilies, and azaleas—especially the Chinese and Indian sort—and orchids and palms of all kinds."

I stopped in front of a greenhouse boasting an array of palms. Harry stopped beside me. "We cultivate tropical species year-round for greenhouse gardens at estates like the Goulds' Lyndhurst. This one here is our palm house. In one corner are the areca lutescens with broad glossy fronds and yellow stems, and closer here are Cocos weddeliana, which is one of my favorites. They're light and feathery and somewhat fern-like in their—"

Harry was staring at me, not at all interested in anything I was saying.

"You weren't speaking in jest when you said you enjoy

these plants. You're impassioned when you speak of them, Miss Fremd." He shoved his hands in his pockets and looked at the ground. I hoped this motion indicated disapproval of my chosen pastime.

"Quite." I smiled. "There's much to see. Let's keep on."

"Surely your service is not required by the business. Your father said he employs in the area of sixty gardeners and hands with most living on the property in homes he provides."

"Is that an inquiry or a statement, Mr. Brundage?" I didn't know what he was after, but it clearly wasn't an assessment of our natural offerings. He hadn't taken notice of a single bloom, and we'd passed the combined varieties of four countries already.

"I suppose it's a question, Miss Fremd," he said, and his brows rose as though he were a lawyer examining me.

"Then why do you ask? My involvement in my father's affairs has little to do with your need for a fine garden." I gestured to my left. "The greenhouses occupying this side are used for new varieties of roses and evergreens and hydrangeas and any sort of plant we choose to cross-pollinate, really. We've cultivated some lovely new breeds in the last several years that are especially suited to our part of the country. The fourth row is reserved for arrangements—bouquets and floral gifts for Easter and wreaths and the like for Christmas."

"The Severses have lost their fortune," Harry said abruptly as he fell in step with me. I thought of Jonathan standing among our peers in the drawing room. He hadn't appeared to be in distress. Still, hearing the news tonight of two families losing their livelihoods was shocking.

"They had to shut down the little factory in Port Chester and are now only selling the wallpapers in their inventory here in town. I imagine they've spent through Mr. Severs's trust fund. If they hadn't, they wouldn't have shut down the factory. I do wonder what will become of this town if Wall Street's dip continues. There have been too many closures. The LeBlancs have also been affected, as I'm sure you've heard."

I despised idle gossip and didn't understand why Harry wanted to discuss Jonathan's presumed misfortune. I also couldn't bear the thought of Rye, my home, going extinct. Then I heard the echo of Charles's words. *"In case the nurseries begin to falter . . ."* It terrified me to think we could be next. I wouldn't let it happen.

"I'm sorry to hear it if that's the case. The Severses are a fine family. Perhaps they will spring back." We cleared the greenhouses and stood looking over the fields of roses and evergreens and trees of all sorts and the barns beyond, washed in silvery moonlight.

"They're acting as though nothing is amiss, but it assuredly is. Terribly so," Harry went on, ignoring my attempt to end that line of conversation.

"As you can see here"—I swept my hand across the panorama—"we grow all of our climate-appropriate varieties to maturity in this field. When someone such as yourself selects a landscaper—either us or one of our peers, such as Platt or Vaux or Olmsted—we are more than prepared to deliver excellence to our clients."

Harry suddenly pivoted to face me and took my hand in his.

"Miss Fremd, it's not polite conversation, and I don't desire to mingle business affairs with talk of love, but I must ask regardless. Do you suppose your family as financially stable as your father has promised you are?"

I gasped and tried to pull my hand away as I stepped back, but he held tighter.

"Please don't take offense, dearest. You must know I've always found you enchanting. I know the more delicate sex is often not subject to the particulars of economy, but if you've had any hints of calamity, if you've overheard anything troublesome, please tell me. I cannot bear the betrayal I would feel if I was lied to." He ran his fingers gently across my knuckles and I yanked my hand free.

"I am keenly aware of our books, Mr. Brundage." It was the second time in a matter of hours I'd been accused of knowing nothing of finances, and despite the allegation being mostly accurate, I would not appear as a damsel in distress. I prayed I was not one.

"I participate in the nurseries because horticulture is my passion, the sole captor of my heart. Our more than sixty employees are stable, and we have had to let none of them go. I—" I'd planned to say that I had no interest in being his dearest and that I didn't need to defend myself or my family to him, but he interrupted.

"I must say I'm relieved. It's only that my father has dictated quite pointedly that any match I make must not be a charitable one. In this harsh time in the world, one must secure his own lifeboat first and give the papers no bait with which to make his name a laughingstock."

"Your options for a match must be considerably small then," I said.

"On the contrary, I could have anyone I want. You must know how ardently generational fortunes such as mine are sought." He smiled as though I would positively faint at the idea that he could choose me. In truth, I wanted to slap him. "But, Miss Fremd, Sadie, if you will allow it, I am enraptured by your beauty and your poise. I must admit, most nights I find myself awake at night thinking of the possibility of you lying beside me."

I feared I would vomit on his shoes. I know my face reflected as much. Despite knowing of his interest in me, I'd never heard him expressing it so openly.

"Darling," he whispered, and before I could step away, he drew me into his arms and kissed me. I stiffened, my mouth pinched tight, then pulled free of his embrace.

"Mr. Brundage, I don't—"

"Don't say anything now. I will propose properly someday soon, and—"

"Miss Fremd. Mr. Brundage." A deep voice came from behind me.

I whirled around and my body flushed with goose bumps, my chest clenching. Surely I was seeing things. Surely this was an apparition.

A man filled the doorway of one of the greenhouses wearing a white linen shirt and work trousers, his hand gripping a galvanized watering can. His black hair was cropped short and he'd grown a bit of facial hair, but the broad shoulders, the way his mouth ticked up even when his eyes were somber, were all the same.

"Sam . . . What are you doing here? Mr. Jenkins, I mean." The words barely escaped my lips. I thought I'd never see him again.

"Finishing up the watering for Ward. Christina had their baby tonight." His eyes were steady, trained on mine. I swallowed, hoping the lump in my throat would dissipate.

"I meant . . . back here," I said.

18

"Did you not get the note?" His voice was low, as if there was a chance Harry wouldn't hear him. "Agnes said she'd give it to you." He walked out of the greenhouse and shut the door behind him.

"No," I said when his gaze fell on mine again.

"That would explain your expression then, I suppose." He smiled at that and the white teeth, the dimples, transformed his face. I'd fallen in love with that grin. It wrung my heart to bits. Seeing him here, this close, yet being unable to go to him was at once the most excruciating torture.

Harry slipped his arm around my waist and I edged away. Sam glanced at him, then back at me.

"It comes down to I didn't have a choice but to return," Sam said as he wandered over to the well tap. "Your father was kind enough to take me on again." Of course Father would take him on again. Sam's father had been the superintendent of the town cemetery grounds, so Sam had grown up around plants as well. After my brothers and me, he'd been the one Father counted on most to manage the other employees. He'd been a promising geneticist, too, and had created three new fir varieties and a rhododendron that were still in high demand for their hardiness.

"Well, good for you, my man," Harry said. "I'm not sure, however, why Miss Fremd would need a note of explanation on the occasion of your second employment. Did you offend her in some way or other? In that case her father's hiring you would seem unwise and I will advise him as such."

Sam shook his head and laughed under his breath as he twisted the nozzle. Naturally Harry would never assume the message would have any sort of romantic bent. It was an unspoken rule among men like Harry and my father and Charles that romantic entanglements with employees were forbidden and shameful.

"Offense would offer some explanation, Mr. Brundage, though if that was the case, I certainly didn't intend it," Sam said. His eyes were fixed on Harry, who was now leaning closer to me, his hand on the small of my back.

Sam didn't know why I hadn't come to the station that night. I always assumed he knew deep down why I couldn't, why I'd let him go. For two years I'd conjured an image of him alone on the platform as he realized I wouldn't be going with him to Newport, realized our love wasn't strong enough to pull me away from the nurseries and the expectations of my father, who had never known anything about us.

That image shattered me each time I thought of it, but now registering that he'd gone without knowing why I stayed made it even worse. I suppose, given what I'd said before, the confusion made sense. I'd sworn I was ready to go, that with my brothers as heirs I would never have the nurseries and all I needed was him. I hadn't intended to lie. I hadn't thought I was lying to begin with, but when I went to place a farewell note on my father's desk in the middle of the night and saw an unfinished letter to my uncle in Germany, hope like I'd never allowed before had suddenly blossomed and rooted me where I was.

Sadie has the ingenuity of Rebecca Lukens, that industrialist woman I had occasion to meet in the city once, who served as the head of Brandywine Iron Works. At times I worry it will undo her. If she were born a boy, she and Charles would be neck and neck.

My father had spoken positively about Mrs. Lukens, a woman in industry. Surely he could come around to seeing me in the same way. I'd hurried out of the study to get to the station on time, hoping to find Sam and convince him to return with me, to tell him that finally Father was seeing my worth and I was certain that in time we would be able to tell him about our love, too, but a light beneath Father's bedroom door delayed me. By the time it was extinguished and I made it to the station, the platform was empty. I'd missed the train by six minutes.

"Mr. Jenkins did nothing untoward, Mr. Brundage, and even if he had, my father hardly needs advising on the subject of those he finds qualified to work here," I said, pulling myself out of the memory. I looked at Sam. I wanted to tell him more. I desperately wanted to explain. "Mr. Jenkins and I were friends. I was surprised to see him because I was certain I'd never see him again."

"I apologize for startling you," Sam said. He glanced at me as he tightened the nozzle, cutting off the water. Perhaps he thought his presence unwelcome, that I'd wanted him to disappear forever. In truth my tardiness that night at the station was my greatest regret.

"I'm glad you're here," I said.

"Friendship with those in one's employ is quite unique, Sadie. My father has always frowned upon it," Harry said. "Then again, I suppose you must find yourself conversing with those working these grounds fairly often if you're so keen to roll up your sleeves yourself."

"I am friendly with whomever I wish, Mr. Brundage. And I am proud of my proficiency in horticulture. If you can't overcome your horror of it, then I'm afraid—"

"Oh my dear, you know nothing could sway my affection away from you. You are the loveliest portrait in human form." I wished he would stop talking. I could feel my soul shrivel and my cheeks redden.

"Mr. Brundage, I don't feel that I am—"

"Don't you think so, too, Mr. Jenkins? That she's the crown jewel of this county? The papers have even said so multiple times."

Sam didn't respond but tipped the brim of his bowler at us, his gaze lingering on mine as he started toward the next greenhouse.

"Have a lovely evening, Miss Fremd, Mr. Brundage," he said. "Give my best to Mr. Fremd on his next adventure."

Three hours later I was standing on the rail platform choking down coal smoke. For a late train, the area was fairly crowded, and Father, Charles, and I huddled together as the porters took his luggage and begged passengers to leave their loved ones and board.

I couldn't get Sam out of my mind. He was back. Here. Again.

We'd planned to go to Newport first. Sam was going to work for his uncle on the electric rail until we could save enough to travel to Minneapolis and beg a post from Horace Cleveland—one of the only renowned landscape architects without a close relationship with Father. I wondered if Sam had done those things. I wondered what had gone wrong and how long he'd been here.

I wondered if he still loved me.

"I'll miss you both," Charles said, eyeing the train as a

whistle rang out. "Thank you for the perfect send-off, Father." He clapped Father's shoulder. "My only regret is that I didn't see Sadie engaged tonight. I thought for sure Harry Brundage would propose."

"I don't regret it a bit. I hope that buffoon never comes back." I shoved the Bells of Ireland into his hand and adjusted my hat. Though I'd just had it made, the egret feathers were already drooping over my eyes. "Well, that's not quite true. I want his business, so he can come knocking with his check-book. Otherwise, he can disappear for all I care."

"Sadie," Father said quietly, his earlier liquor-induced vibrance now reduced to a vague sense of fatigue. "We don't confer about business in public and I do wish you'd reconsider Mr. Brundage, but we'll discuss it later."

"He is a bit conceited; I'll give Sadie that," Charles said. "In any case what matters most is Sadie's happiness—and yours, Father, and mine too. And with that, I'd better board lest they leave me." He shook Father's hand and kissed my head, then pushed through the crowd in his champagne suit.

"Don't forget to send me the spring catalog posthaste, Father," he shouted when he reached the train door.

"It's a nice thought, but it's too far. Flagler will use St. Augustine Nurseries," Father muttered. I wasn't sure if he was addressing me or himself.

"Write every day, Charles!" I yelled. He extracted his hand-kerchief and waved, then disappeared into the train.

Father and I stood silently as the doors closed and the whistle whistled and the "All aboards" ended. The train's wheels began rolling and the coal smoke billowed over us, and then Charles was officially gone.

"I suppose we should go home," I said to Father. When he looked at me, tears filled his eyes, and as he extracted his handkerchief to dab his nose, I noticed his hands were shaking. "Father," I whispered.

"When we came here and built the nurseries, I envisioned generations of Fremds at the helm," he said softly, then shook his head and slowly led the way to the waiting carriage, leaving me to wonder whether his emotion marked a dream departing or fear approaching.

Either way, I was here. Alone. My ship had come in at last. My eyes were fixed on our triumph.

CHAPTER 2

Rain struck the panes and the spring chill seeped through the windows, displaying inky early morning light. I pulled my mink robe tighter around me and moved the oil lamp closer to Charles's ledgers.

This couldn't be correct. Strikes crossed out at least twenty names of patrons we'd worked with forever—the Myerses, who only last year had us plant an English rose garden, the Perrys, who maintained a wisteria garden in their breakfast room, and the Hatchers, who always boasted about the tropical varieties we provided for their conservatory. And then there were the zeros, the unpaid balances from even our wealthiest clients—people with fortunes that could impact Wall Street with a single transaction.

I ran my finger down the short list of remaining accounts and upcoming work. We had a project with Charles Platt, who'd been hired to build a bird sanctuary at the Osborns' waterfront estate, and a consultation with the Olmsted brothers, who were constructing a summer garden at the Rockefellers'. Father was half finished with a boxwood garden at the Iselins'. According to the ledger, those were our only large commissions. Sure, there was a handful of orders for house plants from people around town, but that income would hardly pay one employee for a week.

I flipped to the expenses section. All of our employees were listed with their salaries due monthly. Payments were due to our sources in England and Japan. Charges were listed for pesticides, tools, and wagons. The costs were daunting against the numbers on the income page.

I closed the book and placed my palm on the leather. Twenty-three other ledgers just like it were stacked in the bottom drawer of Charles's desk, each representing the years Rye Nurseries had been in business. Those ledgers looked different. Those ledgers boasted open account lines well into the two hundreds. Those ledgers showed growth.

I placed the book in the drawer and shut it, then leaned back in the tufted leather chair. At once, the nurseries' future felt hopeless. Father and Charles had kept the true state of the business from me. I hated that they had. Ignorance helped nothing. It only made me feel delicate, as though the others believed I couldn't handle the knowledge, and then, when the truth was revealed, the burden felt like an avalanche. I would have much rather felt the earthquake.

Outside the window the sun was rising in deep shades of red. *"Red sky in morning, sailor take warning."* The rain would continue all day. Regardless, I needed to go to the greenhouses and think through our situation. I couldn't bear news like this and not have my hands in the soil. There had to be a solution.

I wondered when I would see Sam again. It was odd that

I knew nothing of his life since he left. He'd been with me the first time I came undone after Mother passed away. I had run to the greenhouses after the funeral—my hands full of the white rosa rugosa alba clippings we used in the arrangements at her service—determined to propagate them, as though doing so would somehow bring my mother back. Sam had been in the same greenhouse fertilizing seedlings and simply began working beside me, never questioning or trying to make my pain go away. Our souls united that day, both of us sharing our grief over the loss of our mothers while surrounded by the determined hope of nature.

Sam had seen me cry on more occasions than my family had. He'd sustained me again when my father brought Robert Whitley, my first suitor, home for luncheon and described my lifelong love of plants simply as an interesting pastime to benefit Mr. Whitley should we marry. I'd had no warning, no idea his visit was for me. That was the moment I realized my fate. Unlike the lives of my brothers or parents, my life wouldn't be allowed passion or love. It was also then, right after I declined Mr. Whitley's request for a solitary outing, that I realized I loved Sam.

He had been in the horse barn that day, saddling Gene and Admiral for a delivery, when I walked in, my face streaked with tears. I'd never told him of my affection for him, that the sight of him made me weak, that his steady presence was the epitome of my peace. He'd never dared step over that threshold with me. But that day in the barn, the words came quickly. They had to, lest I stop myself. I told him if I married Mr. Whitley I would positively die from heartbreak, that all I wanted was Sam and the flowers. He'd set the saddle gently atop Admiral and then walked toward me.

"Are you certain?" he'd whispered when we were face-to-face. The only response I could muster was a nod as I held his gaze. His hands rose to caress each side of my head and he wiped my tears away with his thumbs before one thumb drifted down across my lips.

"I love you," he'd said, and before I could reply, his mouth found mine. In that moment my heart was entirely his. All the misery had departed.

But he couldn't take the despair from me this time, just like he couldn't the last time when I thought I'd lost him forever. The moment I returned from the empty train station, I'd absorbed fully into the nurseries, the love I still had, spending my days inventing new fertilizers, new varieties of flowers, designing gardens, anything to keep my mind occupied and away from the memory of Sam that ached and bled with each passing thought.

I glanced out the study window again, toward the sunrise over the gardeners' village, and wondered if he was awake. Even if he still loved me, even if his love could be the balm to my fear, he wouldn't comfort me again. Even if I explained myself, even if I told him I'd thought about him every moment since he left, it wouldn't matter. Sam wasn't the sort who got riled or held grudges, but once a book ended, he didn't feel compelled to reread it—especially if the ending was a sad one.

"Miss Sadie?" Agnes appeared in the doorway holding a tray. Coffee in the delicate bone china set Mother's family brought over from Cheshire. "I thought I heard someone in here. Are you all right?" Her tone was soft this morning, making her Irish accent sound lyrical.

"Yes, of course." I smiled at her, at the perfect coil of her copper-gray hair and the pressed fit of her uniform that matched the confident trim of her shoulders, and I attempted to straighten my posture. I was sure I looked a fright. My hair was half out of its braid, hanging about my waist, and my under eyes were doubtless smudged with gray—they were always first to give away a sleepless night.

"When you're ready, I'd be happy to dress you. Miss Margaret sent Johann over with a card first thing this morning hoping you would be available to call for an hour or two while the architect visits. She would like your opinion. Said she can't decide on the shine of a gilded ceiling or the patina of a mural from an English manor house for her drawing room."

Margaret Monroe Ridgeway, my best friend from primary school, had recently married Tempy Ridgeway, a society man who inherited his money from his great-uncle, a copper baron of the West. They'd returned from their wedding tour a month ago and I hadn't yet seen her. Given that my flair for plants didn't translate to interiors, I hoped her request was a ruse to catch up—Tempy was known to be possessive of her time.

Then again, she, like the rest of the women in my social circle, seemed unable to make any sort of decorating decision without consulting someone else, lest the outcome be deemed in poor taste by another woman in the group. Recently, it seemed everyone had gone the way of covering their ceilings and lining their trim in gold plate. I suppose to indicate that they had the pockets to do so and that their lives were just as bright as ever. Of course for most it was a lie. The gilded trappings were installed over foundational fissures, over long cracks in the plaster, over misery masquerading as joy.

"I suppose I can spare an hour this morning, so long as the

carriage idles nearby. I can't be gone too long. There's the rest of the seedlings to plant," I said, rising from the desk.

Agnes pursed her lips. I knew what she was thinking—that it would get done regardless of my involvement. She was right. The workers would carry on without me. Father wasn't always about the greenhouses or the fields. Sometimes he didn't appear among the plants for an entire week if he was on-site at one garden or another or if he had meetings in town. Still, my involvement pertained to my emotions, and I knew that without seeing evidence of hope blooming in front of me, I'd be liable to forget it existed. Especially today. Unlike gold plate that was used to conceal, natural beauty had the power to heal.

I walked down the hall to my room and Agnes followed. Father's door was still closed when I passed by. It was peculiar for him to sleep past six o'clock.

"If I may impart a word, Miss Sadie?" Agnes paused after we stepped through my doorway. I glanced back and nodded for her to go on. "Please stay as long as it takes for Miss Margaret to settle on something. Johann said when the architect came yesterday she couldn't make a decision, and Mr. Ridgeway became quite irritable, going on about how the home is the wife's jurisdiction and how he wants a fine home but doesn't want to be involved in the beautification of it."

Her words resonated and suddenly I knew what I'd do—how I'd save the nurseries.

"I could kiss you, Agnes!" I flung open the doors to my wardrobe. "I'll have the white frock today. The one with the Brussels lace on the bodice."

"Are you certain? You're always in white, Miss Sadie, and you have so many new spring gowns. *Harper's* said kelly green is the ladies' color this spring."

"White is more easily cleaned." I sat on the bench at my dressing mirror and she poured my coffee. "However, I do think I'll take your other advice and spend the day out after all. You're right; ladies make the decisions for the beautification of their homes, and I plan to call on at least a dozen neighbors today."

Father and Charles always approached men for their business, but men were the scarcest occupants of a garden. It was the women who held tea parties and lawn fetes and wandered the garden for fresh air and to read. It was women who truly took pride in the careful manicuring of a fine lawn. Men held the paper, that much was true, but merely a word from a wife that Edith down the street had a new formal garden, and the husband—keen to keep up appearances and status—would relinquish the needed funds.

Despite the businesses folding in Rye and the whole of Westchester County crippled by the market crash, some families were impacted less or not at all. I would approach those women—at least five each week. I would sip tea and gossip and eventually make a beautiful landscape sound as necessary to their social status as a closet full of Worth gowns. It was, after all.

"Would you at least agree on color in your hat today?" Agnes asked, surveying my armoire.

"I suppose," I said after taking a sip of the coffee. I heard her sigh softly and watched her retrieve the dress, then weed through my things to locate a wide royal-blue hat with pluming ostrich feathers. I wondered if she found me exhausting, and then I remembered Sam mentioning he'd given her a note for me.

"I saw Mr. Jenkins yesterday."

"Oh?" she said, opening a drawer to extract hat pins.

"He said he gave you a note for me, but I didn't receive one." Despite having already selected my frock, the hat, and the pins, too, she pretended to busy herself in my wardrobe.

"Agnes."

She finally turned to face me.

"I didn't give it to you because I know what happened," she said finally. "As much as you two attempted to disguise it, we all knew."

"Whatever do you mean?" I pretended to laugh. If news of my affair with Sam got back to my father, I'd never see him again. I'd thought him gone forever just days ago, but now I wouldn't let that happen again. I couldn't. Even if we were never to be as we were, I could at least be close to him.

"Mr. Jenkins and I became friends and—"

"I cannot betray your father's wishes by playing the part of messenger between former lovers," she said, her Irish lilt exaggerated by her defensiveness.

I gasped.

"Your father employs me, Miss Sadie, and I am grateful. He wants you well matched with a man of your own status who can protect you."

"We were never . . . lovers," I said, choking the word out while my cheeks reddened.

"I suppose I only meant you were in love," she said as she placed the dress, the hat, and the pins on the foot of my bed.

I busied myself with stirring my coffee while Agnes returned to the wardrobe for my corset.

"Even if I wasn't in your father's employ, I would have kept the note to myself all the same. The minute I saw Mr. Jenkins back here I told him to leave. No one knows why he returned in the first place, and I was hoping he'd heed our advice and go before you noticed him. It seems he chose not to listen."

"Why would you tell him to leave?" I stood and removed my robe. Agnes fastened my corset around me and did up the laces.

"When he told us he was going away that night two years ago, we all suspected he was going with you. He'd shown Ward a gold wedding band he bought for a woman he said he intended to marry, and the way the two of you spent days alone together doing one task or another in the greenhouses, the way you looked at each other? All of us knew, even if your father and brothers didn't. Some people don't see what they don't want to see."

I'd never seen a ring. I was about to burst into tears but gritted my teeth to keep them at bay. Agnes reached for my dress.

"Please don't tell Father," I said.

Agnes unbuttoned the bodice of the dress and slipped it over my head.

"What would I tell? I know there's no danger of you leaving this place for the likes of Sam now," she said. "You already had the chance. But if you have any sort of affection for him, urge him to go. Hearts like ours run with red blood—blood that loves unbidden by expectation unless mingled with blue blood like yours. In that case, it is fatal."

"He's been away for two years," I whispered as she did up the buttons at my back. "I don't believe his heart as soft toward me as you might assume. He may have found someone along the way." The thought shattered my heart. I had no idea what had transpired in the years Sam had been gone and was now desperate to know it. Had he been happy? Had he found success working with Horace Cleveland, the landscape architect he loved, creating new varieties for his gardens? "I loved him.".

"You still do," Agnes said, and of course she was right. "Love itself isn't the conundrum. It's that you love more than one thing, and when that happens you must inevitably select the course you love more."

She was right, and there was nothing left to say. I couldn't have both Sam and the nurseries. Father had made it clear early on that relationships with our staff were not to be tolerated, when Freddie's childhood friendship with our maid's daughter became a flirtation. They hadn't been in love, not like Sam and me, but I could still hear the way Father reprimanded Freddie, banging his fist on the desk in anger, saying he'd worked too hard to elevate the Fremd name to have it dashed by a poor match. He'd even threatened to send Freddie to Germany to live with Oma and Opi if he couldn't control himself, and we all knew he meant it.

Agnes finished buttoning at the nape of my neck and motioned for me to have a seat on my silk dressing bench.

"A soft pompadour finished with a knot today, please," I said.

Agnes pursed her lips. Clearly she didn't approve of my decisions. I was certain of it by the way she avoided my eyes in the mirror and bristled as she jammed the curling tongs into the electrical outlet we'd had installed five years back. Father still held a general suspicion about using electric indoors; reports of the wires causing blazes all about the country were reported in the papers daily. I supposed the convenience outweighed the fear, at least for me.

Agnes brushed a strand of my hair and twirled it round the tongs with vigor.

"Is there something else you would like to say to me?" I asked as I watched the reflection of her face in the glass. "Please speak freely. I'm not Queen Victoria or Caroline Astor, and I'm not going to ask Father for your head on a platter if you offend me."

She released the strand from the tongs and our eyes met in the mirror.

"Very well, but I do hope you'll excuse my frankness," she sighed. "Your father is a kind man, a fine man of business and of moral fortitude. Heaven knows we all appreciate his generosity and employment, especially now."

She brushed another strand of hair, then wound it around and pinched it, gently this time, in the tongs. "However, he is a man of tradition, a man who was taught the roles of fine men and women of high breeding, of which you are such a woman."

I couldn't help but laugh at that.

"Agnes, my mother was an English immigrant seamstress at the Triangle Waist Company factory, and my father descended upon New York as a penniless German immigrant without knowing a hint of English and took employ as a simple planter for Mr. Vaux," I said. "We're hardly the blue bloods you make us out to be."

"Your family may have begun as common working folk, but you are not any longer. Your father has made a success of himself and will do anything he can to uphold that standard for his three children. I don't blame him for it. But seeing you today in Charles's study confirmed what I suspected."

She paused, glanced away, and then placed her hand on my shoulder and squeezed. "Miss Sadie, I want your happiness, but surely you must see that you won't get what you want. Mr. Fremd would never further involve you in the business, even if you are the most qualified. It is against what he sees as natural for a woman of your status."

"I'm not sure I know what you're implying, Agnes," I said. "I was simply completing a request from Charles this morning."

I loathed the practice of lying. At once I felt both embarrassed and furious. It was easier to pretend I had no aspirations with the nurseries until Father came to his senses, until he saw how valuable I was. Everyone would soon see; I'd save us all with my ingenuity. I'd visit the women around the county and acquire at least two accounts each week until everyone who was anyone required a garden sourced by Rye Nurseries.

If we were commissioned to design it as well, all the better. *That* would be a contribution that couldn't be ignored. I plastered on a smile and reached for the tube of pink rouge everyone loathed and thought belonged solely to ladies of the night. I liked the way it made my cheeks look. It also disguised how often someone's words had the ability to drain the life from both my soul and my countenance.

"Miss Sadie, not for today, surely—" Agnes reached to take the tin from my hand, but I edged away and unscrewed the top.

"I like it," I said, dabbing a bit onto my cheeks.

Agnes sighed.

"I'm relieved you aren't hoping to contend for the nurseries now that your brothers have gone different routes. I know you love working with the plants. I see the same fire in your eyes that your father has, the same passion that spills over and enlivens the workers too. It worried me terribly to think you were hoping you'd someday become mistress of the nurseries when it isn't to be." She removed the curling tong's prongs from the outlet and wound the cord around the handle.

I busied myself with replacing the rouge lid. Anything I said that was true would give me away, making me such a laughing-stock to every employee that I'd be unable to face them in the fields or the greenhouses. It was easier to feign indifference, to pretend horticulture was simply my wealthy debutante amusement, my version of piano or painting.

Agnes laughed. "I'm going to be able to breathe again, Miss Sadie, knowing that what kept you from going with Mr. Jenkins wasn't the plants but simply the desire for a proper match."

The way her mood brightened with the assumption that I was nothing more than a shallow fortune hunter keen to make my future comfortable, rather than a woman with intellectual aspirations, made my hands fist. Doubtless that was how Father felt too. It was much easier to marry me off.

"Do you suppose you'll accept a proposal from Mr. Brundage then? I had occasion to visit their Newport estate with your mother when you were but a babe. It is a stunning property with a lovely view of the sea."

I closed my eyes for a moment before replying. "Occupying a seaside estate as Mrs. Sadie Brundage would be enough to make me throw myself in."

Agnes met my gaze in the mirror once more.

"Mr. Brundage's appearance isn't so offensive," she said, her lips gripping my hairpins. She pushed a few against the back of my head as she continued working. "If I may, Miss Sadie, sometimes the attention of a man so handsome and kind and smart as Mr. Jenkins might skew one's perception of the qualities of another man more suited to one's lifestyle."

I thought of Sam—the tan of his skin in the summertime,

the body of a Roman sculpture, the perfection of his face, the combination of fierce bone and gentle eyes. The idea that there was a more handsome man alive was implausible. The idea that there was another man more suited to loving me was absolutely unfeasible. No one would ever understand me like Sam had. He made my soul laugh. He fascinated me with his imagination and intelligence. He'd been my home. Perhaps, somehow, we could find our way back to each other again.

"After breakfast I'd like the single Kingston carriage brought around. I'll call on Margaret and then be out until dinner. I don't need Mr. Green to spend his whole day driving me to and fro." This conversation had to conclude. I couldn't bear more talk of possible matches. I had no interest in conversing about Sam or the nurseries either. They were both doomed loves according to Agnes. Perhaps she was right. Regardless, I couldn't think of that right now. When one made up one's mind that something would fail, it would. I refused to tether my mind to that anchor.

"Of course, Miss Sadie." Agnes helped me up, handed me my hat, and glanced at the grandmother clock in the corner of my room. "Heavens. I didn't realize it was nearly eight. Hurry lest you keep your father waiting. Cold oatmeal is quite unfortunate."

Even in the midst of a dismal rain, the breakfast room was bright. Tall windows without drapes occupied most of the space along three walls and the room had been painted a cheery robin's-egg blue. Even the teak breakfast table gave off the feel of sunny Florida instead of April showers New York.

Father was dressed in his work suit, a tailored gray ensemble with brass buttons that somehow always maintained the illusion that he'd been locked away in a boardroom instead of out wandering in gardens. He was reading the *Port Chester Enterprise* and didn't look up when I walked in.

"Good morning, Miss Sadie," Mr. Cooper said as he pulled out my chair and scooted it in upon my sitting. "Would you like a cup of coffee?"

"Yes, please," I said, trying my hardest to sound cheery. Mr. Cooper lifted the silver Tiffany coffee carafe with a shaking arm. He'd been Father's butler for as long as I could recall and was easily twenty years Father's senior, which would imply his age was at least seventy-three.

He poured the coffee into one of Father's family's one-hundred-year-old willow pattern china cups and then turned to the buffet to ready my oatmeal. I always took it with a lump of sugar, cream, and blueberries. One of the many advantages of owning greenhouses was fresh spring and summer fruit year-round.

"What's the news today, Father?" I asked, extracting my white linen napkin from its Tiffany ring.

Mr. Cooper deposited my oatmeal in front of me and took his leave into the kitchen.

"Anything of note?" I asked again, assuming he'd been so engaged in an article he hadn't heard me.

He lowered the paper and crumpled it to the side of his breakfast. His eyes were glassy. My whole body froze.

"Is something wrong?"

His gaze met mine and he shook his head before turning his face away to wipe his eyes.

"This isn't how it's supposed to be, my Lily girl," he said

softly. He'd always called me Lily after his favorite flower, the lily of the valley. "You've heard of the LeBlancs' misfortune . . . the others too. I was always told that if a man worked hard, he'd be protected. What will happen to Andrew?" Mr. LeBlanc was one of Father's best friends. "He won't help me here. I've offered and he's refused. And what of his employees? Several have already come calling before sunrise today, and I can only afford to hire ten additional workers. He had more than forty on his roll." Father was weeping now, his tears flowing unbidden down his face into his white beard. "My greatest worry is that we'll be next. It keeps my eyes open at night and my heart pounding all day."

"We'll be all right, Father. Perhaps Mr. LeBlanc will go work for one of the larger stonework businesses in the city and then come back and reopen when the panic concludes. His customers would be loyal; I'm certain of it." The sight of Father weeping into his oatmeal was shocking. It wasn't that he never cried. He cried often when confronted with anything sentimental, but this was different.

"His fortune has vanished. Sylvie will spend her life toiling in a factory somewhere. She will spend her nights packed in a tenement home with at least one other family, likely two or three. It is a horrendous, filthy life. I know because I lived it." He picked his spoon up as if he might eat and then set it down again. "And when, if, she marries, her life will be the same, only there also will be children to feed. They could have come here. They could have lived down in the village there." He gestured out the window in the general vicinity of the little community of homes he'd built for our employees and their families.

"Why won't Mr. LeBlanc agree to it?" I asked. "We have three empty bedrooms in this house alone. I would love to have Sylvie here with me."

"Pride. The same reason the Shorts refused—the McCluskys too," he said. "They'd rather leave town altogether than labor here. It is a peculiar sort of melancholy, I've heard, like begging for scraps in the shadow of your abandoned mansion."

He took a labored breath and looked out the window. The nurseries were waking up. The Sylvester family made its way up from the village and into the greenhouses, followed by the Bruins. The morning watering began promptly at eight.

"I want you to marry," Father said suddenly. "Well and quickly, for your own sake. I want to be clear that unlike other fathers who marry off their daughters for their own advantage, I desire nothing from the match." He kept his gaze fixed out the window as he spoke. "I don't wish to alarm you, Lily, but we are suffering, too, like the rest, and though I will do everything in my power to hold on to this place, despite your brothers' clear disregard for it, my greatest fear is what will happen to you if we fail."

He sipped his coffee. "What will happen to those families?" he whispered, watching Elise, the smallest of the Sylvester children, fill a tiny watering can and run after her mother. The weight of his responsibility was palpable.

"I'm not worried," I said evenly. "I'm not afraid of poverty or bankruptcy. I'm not afraid of losing my luxuries."

"You should be." He turned back to me, his face suddenly stony. "It is a trauma of both soul and body, a life of endless fear that I will give my last breath to prevent you from experiencing. You've never had to decide which child will eat or if you can afford to have a doctor set your broken arm. You have no idea what it's like to live in such peril." He was speaking of my mother's life and his own before they met. My mother often talked about how she and her sister had alternated meals. Father had broken his left arm when a marble planting urn fell atop it. He hadn't had the money to have it repaired and the bones grew back together crooked.

"I know you believe I'll—"

"I'll not back down on this," he said. "You will marry. There is still a handful of fine men with stable fortunes. You'll be safe and settled."

The carriage was being brought around. Mr. Green swung down from the box seat and gave Admiral, our old Percheron, a pat.

"We're going to be fine, Father." I took a bite of oatmeal. If I could help the nurseries thrive again, if I could solidify our fortune, perhaps his worry over my future would cool, and he would slow his pushing me to the altar. I didn't want to disappoint Father—I knew that would only strain our rapport while I was trying to win him to my side—but at the same time, I couldn't marry, perhaps ever, unless my intended was Sam and my home was the nurseries. Marriage otherwise would be a prison, ripping me away from everything I loved.

"If you'll excuse me, I'm going out. I'm to call on Margaret, then Mrs. Fink, Mrs. Crowe, and Mrs. Biddle. I'll be home for dinner."

"Whatever do you need with all of them?" Father asked.

I thought I'd make some quip about inquiring after any suitable bachelors willing to marry me but chose to fall on virtuous honesty instead.

"They're all in need of fine gardens this season. Their fortunes haven't been touched by this downturn and they are more than able to hire us to source and possibly design new landscapes."

"Absolutely not," Father said. "Imagine. Sending my daughter out to fish for accounts. What would people say?"

"Nothing. You underestimate me. They won't know they've been sold at all, Father. I'll only go to say hello and then happen to mention the fine gardens we're doing for the Goulds or the Iselins. You know it's the ladies who make the decisions about the house and its furnishings. The moment I leave they'll be ringing for their husbands, asking them to make a visit here at once."

I rose from my chair.

"And if they ask you particulars? Do you know the details of our offerings?" I was shocked he didn't continue arguing with me.

"Quiz me if you doubt my proficiency, Father. Surely you know that I understand the minutiae of every single variety we source and how they are to be used in design. Unlike Freddie and Charles, I have read your entire library and have taken to heart everything I've heard you say. Would you like me to recite the most recent catalog? Or perhaps describe the design of the Walworths' red garden?" I tipped my chin up, daring him.

He sighed and set his napkin on the table.

"I don't doubt your intellect, Sadie. I don't doubt that you are as quick and bright as your brothers. But this isn't the course of a lady. This is the business of a man."

"I disagree," I said. "What of Rebecca Lukens and Anna Bissell—both women in commerce I know you respect? And in any case, calling on my friends is quite a ladylike activity indeed. I will not pitch formally as you and Charles are apt to do.

Mentioning the designs of their peers is simply conversation. If it works to win us accounts, however, I would think it a worthy endeavor."

"Fine," he said. "But know this—as much as I respect her legacy, you are not Mrs. Lukens and you will never be Mrs. Bissell. They are widows who were left with no choice but to take on their husbands' affairs. I will permit your involvement on this one occasion—with one condition. You must include in your discussion a mention of the men you're considering—Brundage and Bishop, especially. Ensure neither are brutes. A fortune alone isn't good enough for you, but a fortune is needed."

"I'll not ask about either. I will not marry them," I said as I breezed out of the room, ignoring his insistence that I wouldn't be like the businesswomen he held in high esteem. His admiration for them at all, when most men in industry turned up their noses, indicated his progressive spirit. My contributions to our nurseries' business would change his mind and he'd find he wasn't so opposed to my participation in commerce after all. "Brundage is pompous and Bishop's teeth are horrendous."

"Don't concern yourself with his teeth," Father called. "If he loses them, he can replace them with diamonds should he so choose. Worry instead about a man who cannot replace them at all."

CHAPTER 3

The sun peeked through the clouds as soon as Mrs. Fink's gatekeeper heaved the heavy wrought iron gate wide enough for me to fit through. The Kingston cart was the perfect choice for such a lovely day. Completely open to the elements, just a seat atop a set of wheels, really. I nodded in thanks to the man and encouraged Admiral to walk through.

As the gold rays danced on the mansion's copper roof, I couldn't help but smile. The estate was considered one of America's showplaces, and I had to agree. It was built in the Spanish Renaissance style—a gray stucco with terraces in the back of the house leading down to a grassy lawn and the Long Island Sound.

I'd loved being at Margaret's place—a large Craftsman on a hill with a view of what was left of town—because in the matter of a walk or short ride, one could be at the library or the meat market or the church, but on the drive down the peninsula to the Finks' place at Milton Point, one instantly understood the allure of living with the sea outside the window. Everything was different here. The air smelled fresh and a bit salty, the breeze making one feel as if she'd been transported somewhere like Cornwall.

"Good afternoon, Miss Fremd!" the Finks' butler, Mr. Wilson, called from the porch.

I waved and pulled the reins, slowing Admiral. His feet crunched along the crushed-shell path lined with old boxwoods that appeared as if they were catching some sort of blight. The landscaping wasn't completely horrible—a fine family couldn't maintain the notion of being a fine family without at least a tidy design—but it was simply boring. I wondered if the back of the house looked the same.

"I'm glad the sun's peeked out, aren't you? I've tired of April showers," Mr. Wilson said as he took my reins and helped me down.

"I admit I was feeling rather dreary with the rain." I smiled at him. "Is Mrs. Fink about?"

"I believe she is. If you'll follow me in, I'll situate you in the drawing room and ring her to see. I know Mr. Fink is in the city today."

I had no doubt Mr. Fink was a busy man these days. I read the paper enough to know that his firm financed the Hudson Tubes and was creating a new locomotive company. With the fresh crash of two important rail systems, I had a feeling he was either checking the allocations of his own holdings or taking advantage of the available rail space.

Mr. Wilson led me through the heavy wood doors carved in an ornate scroll pattern and into the foyer, which boasted a grand, curved limestone staircase with cherubim perched on the posts, a row of leather receiving chairs on either side of the room, and an ancient Oriental rug.

"Right through here," he said. I followed him through a hall beneath the stairs and into the drawing room adorned with floral chintz and silver that overlooked the terraces and the Sound. "If you'd like to have a seat, I'll tell her you've come to call."

I sat on the hardest fainting sofa I'd ever encountered and studied the white cut roses in the vase on the tea table in front of me. They were an ordinary sort—perhaps even wild—nothing like the Kaiserin Augusta Victoria or The Bride—two white varieties we grew that boasted the most exquisite large buds and delicate fragrance. I squinted out of the windows toward the terraces. The green simplicity I'd found at the front of the home was indeed duplicated at the back. I had much to recommend to Mrs. Fink.

"I'm so sorry to keep you waiting, Miss Fremd." Mary Fink breezed into the room looking the picture of spring in a gown of green and cream brocaded taffeta with embroidered steel jewels. "The children have a new au pair and are quite uncertain about her." She turned back to the doorway. "May we have some tea, Mr. Wilson?"

Though Mrs. Fink was ten years my senior, she looked seventeen at most. She yawned and sat across from me on a chintz-covered sofa. Margaret had seemed similarly exhausted and given me a skeletal description of her wedding tour while we talked about her ceiling decoration. I'd thought it strange. She'd been my liveliest friend, the one always scolded for talking too much in our finishing courses. I wondered if the life of a society wife was truly that tiresome or if the lack of mental stimulation was the cause. Either way, it seemed dreadful.

"Thank you for taking the time to see me," I said. "To be frank, I don't have a particular reason to call other than to say hello. The rain was making me feel claustrophobic, so I thought I'd make the rounds and catch up with everyone. We haven't seen each other since the Iselins' St. Valentine's soiree, and—"

"Wasn't that the most fun? I'll never be able to look at Orion again without seeing that ridiculous Cupid ensemble he wore." She laughed, a dainty tinkling sound.

Orion Aisling, a distant cousin of the Iselins, had arrived in a ridiculous costume—a gigantic diaper affixed to his waist with diamond-encrusted gold pins, a wreath of roses he'd asked Father to create, and a bow and arrow he swore had belonged to Robin Hood. The whole soiree was dramatic, with caged pigeons dressed in cherub ensembles and the fountain colored red with beet juice. Then again, the Iselins were the Fifth Avenue sort and anyone associated with the city had been inadvertently stuck in the middle of the Astor and Vanderbilt feud, a feud that required balls and soirees to be more elaborate than any that was ever held at Buckingham Palace.

"I know," I said, laughing. "I admit, I was quite embarrassed for him."

"He is nearly sixty-five and his skin is not as taut as I'm sure it once was," she said, at once falling into a fit of hilarity. "All the same, it was a lovely occasion. There's nothing like St. Valentine's Day to help an old biddy like me recall the way her husband looked at her when she was the one to catch." Mrs. Fink smoothed her gown.

"You're hardly an old biddy, Mrs. Fink. You're one of the beauties of this county and look younger than I do."

"Yet you call me Mrs. Fink." She rolled her eyes. "I'll accept the title from schoolchildren and servants, but surely not from you. Please call me Mary."

Just then Mr. Wilson entered with the tea in a silver service and steaming scones fresh from the oven.

"Thank you," I said after he settled the tray before us.

"Speaking of St. Valentine's Day and debutantes"—Mary accepted a cup of tea from Mr. Wilson and nodded at him to depart—"you are quite the emerald in a pile of diamonds. I saw the number of gentlemen on your dance card that evening."

"I've known most of them since we were babies. They're my friends." The realization that two of the men, David Short and Thomas McClusky—who had occupied me for three dances each—would never again haunt the halls of any great home or Rye at all because of their families' economic misfortune, was strange and devastating.

"That might be so, but not all of them are so familiar, and I imagine they view you quite differently even if they are. I would hate to embarrass them, but I will . . . I have heard your name so many times in this exact room from Stephen Bishop and Harry Brundage that I'm surprised you aren't engaged yet."

Mary took a tiny bite of scone and looked at me, waiting. Perhaps she thought I'd swoon.

"That's kind of you to say." Knowing the Finks were close with both men, I couldn't very well say I thought them both average at best.

"But you don't fancy either of them. Interesting. Many a young lady would positively die to have their attention. They are the heirs of the most suitable—and stable—fortunes in the area," she said before taking another bite.

"I'm aware," I said. I sipped my tea, an Earl Grey with a heavy bergamot. "Mr. Brundage was by the nurseries for my brother's send-off the other day."

"Oh, that's right. Your brother has gone to work with Mr. Flagler in Florida, has he not?"

I nodded.

"And Freddie is still in Chicago pulling the political strings for Mayor Harrison?"

"Yes. Much to the horror of my father," I said.

"I'm sure your father misses them so much." Mary took another bite of her scone. "Did Harry say anything to you? Did he voice any intention or interest?"

I recalled his hand on the small of my back, the possessive manner in which he'd treated me—especially when he realized I had some kind of connection to Sam—and could feel my nose wrinkle in disgust.

"I suppose. Yes, he did. He said he would like to propose soon. However, we were mostly discussing his plans for new landscaping. He's quite envious of what we've done at Lyndhurst in conjunction with Ferdinand Mangold. Miss Helen Gould is eager to continue her father's legacy of fine gardens, and Harry would like the same."

I stirred a lump of sugar into my tea. "I had to tell him that we've already scheduled Margaret Ridgeway's place, which we will also design, and Mrs. Walworth's, designed by Mr. Olmsted, so it would be a few weeks before we could get to the Brundages'. You know how it is. With spring here and summer approaching, everyone is keen to begin entertaining out of doors."

"I have heard of more garden fetes over the last few years. The Goelets' reveal of their blue garden in Newport was quite the party last summer, and the Starins' summer solstice soiree was gorgeous—the full moon and the fragrance of all of those roses." Mary had a dreamy, faraway look in her eyes. I was hoping this meant she'd taken the bait and that she, too, was dreaming of hosting something just as lovely that would require a garden fit for the papers.

"You know, the funny thing about the Goelets' garden is that there's actually no such thing as a blue flower. It simply doesn't exist. We manipulated the color a bit in the greenhouses to produce a purple that appears blue, but it will never truly be blue. Isn't that interesting?" I took a bite of scone. "We sent Olmsted grape hyacinths, bachelor's buttons, delphiniums, irises, agapanthus, and butterfly bushes, among other things."

"I had no idea the flowers at the Goelets' were your family's doing," Mary said. "Then again, I shouldn't be surprised. I heard your nurseries are the largest on this coast now. Did you source the Starins' as well?"

"Yes, but Father also designed theirs." I didn't elaborate. Nothing was worse than coming off as pompous or desperate. "Have you ever considered hosting an outdoor party? You have such a grand entry and a tremendous view from the back. I swear I think I'm in Ireland every time I see it."

"You know, I did consider the possibility of it briefly only a month ago. A fellow came by . . . Oh, you may know him as he said he'd done work for your father. His father has passed, but he was superintendent of the Greenwood Union Cemetery."

The blood drained from my face. I nodded and tried to smile to cover it up. Sam had come to the Finks looking for employment first. When he said he'd had no choice but to come back, perhaps he was right. Perhaps he hadn't come back to see me. If he'd come knocking on the Finks' door, he'd likely knocked on them all.

"I recognized him, actually, because when my father-in-law

passed away nearly a decade ago, Mother was in such a state at the graveside that she could barely stand," Mary went on. "The young man hastened to her side. His father had just taken the position at the cemetery, I believe. But he held her up, encouraging her to breathe in a bit of some herb he had on hand to calm her nerves."

I remembered this occasion too. My whole family had been there to mourn with the Finks. It was the first time I'd ever seen Sam. I'd been young, twelve or so, and he was fifteen. With that one kind gesture, he'd made an impression on me—and on everyone else for that matter. When he came to our door four years ago seeking employment, his reputation as a promising horticulturist and man of high moral character was well established. Father had hired him on the spot.

"It was lemon balm. And I believe you're referring to Mr. Jenkins," I said.

"Yes!" she said, snapping at me as though I'd just won a prize. "He said he could serve as our head gardener, that he had much proficiency in plants and could help us transform our green spaces into something quite stunning—using your beautiful plants, of course. I dreamed about hosting an outdoor affair for some time after that, but admit I'd forgotten all about it until now."

"He's one of our best," I said. "He managed the rest of our employees and was quite a skilled horticulturist and geneticist as well. We were so grieved when he left us and are heartened to have him back."

"I'm sure you are. To be honest, I'm uncertain why he didn't go back to your father straightaway. But perhaps the hardships he experienced these past years made him feel like he couldn't return to a place he once loved because he isn't the same person anymore. In a way, I understand it. No one wants people who know you asking why you seem different, why you're so broken."

A dull ache stretched across my chest. Sam had been shattered, somehow, by someone. My hand tensed around the teacup. I knew I could be the cause.

I cleared my throat.

"Do you know the nature of his hardship?" I asked. At once my skin prickled with fury at myself. I'd left him. I'd let him go. I'd tried writing several times, to Newport and to Mr. Cleveland, but the letters were returned unopened. I'd begged to accompany Father on his business trip to the Goelets' home in Newport just a week after Sam's departure, feigning a meeting with a friend so I could ask after him in town, but my inquiries came up short. For months I looked for him each time I had occasion to visit, but eventually I gave up hope. All of it was my fault. And now here I was, sitting with a practical stranger asking if she knew what had crushed the man I loved.

"No, of course not. He didn't even mention a difficulty. I only knew because I recognized the despair in his eyes, the same sort I'd had right before I met Phin, when my mother died and everything I knew in this whole world seemed to die with her. I couldn't stand being around anyone who knew my mother. I wanted to go far away and never return."

I swallowed hard and turned away from her to look out the glass doors so she wouldn't see my eyes fill.

"In any case, despite my begging to hire him, Phin declined. He said he'd be happy to oblige my want for beautification but that he was sure your father or Vaux or Olmsted would be a better investment and that our groundsmen could handle the day-to-day needs of such a design. And then, like I said, I suppose I forgot about the thought of gardens at all. It's hard to think about tulips when the ground is ice and you venture outside only once per week."

I couldn't imagine the state of my mind if I only left the house once each week.

"I know what you mean," I said. "And of course we're always available to design a garden so wonderful all of Rye would envy it."

"Between us, I think the real reason Phin declined was because Mr. Jenkins is so handsome." Mary had lowered her voice to a whisper, as though her husband could materialize from the city at any moment, as though she hadn't heard my offer. "Everyone's husband is rattled after that fiasco with Daniel Thornton's wife and their butler. She still got half of his fortune, you know."

"I suppose I could understand Mr. Fink's concern." It wasn't only husbands who were worried about the women in their lives falling into the arms of someone as unsuitable and majestic as Sam; it was also fathers—like mine—though given Father's employment of Sam, he must think me immune.

"Of course you understand. You've seen the man," Mary whispered again. "Is it terrible if I like it that Phin gets a little jealous sometimes?"

"Not at all," I said. "It just proves he still wants you for himself. Everyone should hope for a love like that." I wondered if Sam had been jealous when he saw me with Harry. If he had, he hadn't let on.

"Perhaps you will find one too . . . at my garden party. You've inspired me, Sadie. Would you mind having your father come around in about a week's time, when Phin is back, to work out the particulars?"

I smiled, but inside I was positively squealing with excitement. It had worked. The Ridgeways and the Finks were both engaging us—in the matter of a day. Father would be elated.

"It would be his honor and mine too. I want to assure you that we have the largest variety in the country. Your new garden will be exceptional—and completely unique."

"I want it to be romantic, whimsical. Do you know what I mean?"

"Yes. It absolutely must match the landscape—feathery ferns and roses and weeping Russians and hydrangeas and clematis . . . I could go on forever." I laughed.

"I don't know half of what you just said, but I'm sure it will be lovely." In the faraway caverns of the house, a baby's cry sounded. "Oh, I hate to be rude and depart so soon after you've arrived, but I must check on the children. As I said, we've just asked a new nanny into our employ and I'm afraid Archie is giving her a fright."

She stood and I did as well.

"Do have your father call next week. Come as well, if you're able. It's clear you understand what I want," she said, smiling.

"Very well," I said, returning her warm expression. "It's been so nice catching up, Mary."

"And with you, Sadie." She clutched my hand. "I hope you'll have a fine home to play gardener with soon." She winked and I grinned, wanting so badly to say I already had one.

CHAPTER 4

"D o you like what you see so far?" Mrs. Brundage asked. I nodded. We were situated on the front terrace of the Brundages' English baroque mansion. The home was enormous, a limestone and redbrick structure that Harry always boasted was modeled after England's Hampton Court Palace. Below us on the front lawn, half of my father's employees were laying out English boxwoods and hundreds of rose varieties—from the rich pink American Beauty to the Wichuriana, a new Japanese trailing rose—and situating them around the newly poured circular reflecting pond.

"It's quite lovely, is it not?" Mrs. Brundage pressed. I glanced at her, wondering if this question was different from the first. Perhaps she hadn't seen me nod, or perhaps she was now referring to the grounds. As it was, the front entry looked like a desert with a pond in the middle. Beyond the estate's wrought iron gates, the Boston Post Road boasted an uneventful handful of carriages and travelers on foot coming or going to the Bronx or to Greenwich every hour. I assumed she meant the house.

"Yes, it is," I said politely. "You should be proud."

Mrs. Brundage likely thought my visit personal, but it was not. Charles had often gone with our gardeners to the sites to see the design orchestrated properly, and I now stood in his place—in a way. Charles had often worked alongside our men, his hands in the soil. My supervisory duties today were won only because Father was occupied with incoming shipments. Even then, he'd barely allowed it, requiring that I remain with Mrs. Brundage and appear to be calling socially. As angry as I was at being confined to the terrace in a gown entirely unsuitable for gardening of any sort—a moss-green silk covered with embroidered black chiffon and beaded tulle insertions—at least I was here.

"Do you prefer our home to the Bishops'?" she asked, avoiding my eyes, her hands poised on her teaspoon. "I know it's quite forward of me to ask, but Harry says Stephen has been making advances as well, and . . . I saw your carriage there four days past on my way to call on Mrs. Straten." Her cheeks pinkened at the confession.

I'd visited the Crowes after Mary Fink to seek their business as well, and I'd secured it. The Crowes, however, happened to live next to the Bishops on Stuyvesant Avenue heading back toward town. The Crowes' footman must have deposited my carriage in a place that appeared to be on the Bishops' property. I hadn't been aware.

"Oh, I think all Rye homes are lovely," I said, knowing my answer wasn't at all what she wanted to hear. I shielded my eyes from the sun and gazed down at Donato Sigallis, easily the largest man I'd ever seen, lugging an entire pallet of boxwoods from the carriage on his own, while his brothers, Roceo and Joseph, cursed each other in Italian.

"As do I," Mrs. Brundage said. She sighed and set her crystal glass, still half filled with lemonade, on the rattan table and adjusted her yellow brocaded skirt.

"Your garden will look spectacular," I said. "Not to say it wasn't lovely before, but I have a particular fondness for this new design." I smiled. Father had let me create this one—the first garden I'd been allowed to craft alone for a client. I knew in part it was because he hoped I would accept Harry's eventual proposal. Regardless, I was proud of my work and chose to see his faith in me as progress. Pieces of my ideas had been used in countless gardens. If time allowed, our designs were collaborative efforts and had been since I was a child, but if we were rushed, the work fell to my brothers or Father while I gathered and fertilized the correct plants and recruited extra gardener assistance.

For as long as I could remember, I'd been treated as an esteemed part of the process by Father, so my early assumption that I was being taught and groomed in commerce for a reason was Father's fault really. I'd thought I was different from my peers, that my parents weren't apt to follow the rules of society when it came to my future. The truth of my fate as a debutante had come as a tremendous shock. There had been no hint of it from my parents until I was presented. I could still recall Mother's gentle but stern tone as she scrubbed my fingernails clean of soil before the ceremony.

"We are proud of the way you've taken to the nurseries, dearest. It has been the most wonderful childhood pastime, has it not? But now you must be encouraged to lean away, to focus your nurturing talents on a husband, on a home apart from it."

Her words had upset me so deeply that I'd been unable to respond.

I forced my mind away from the memories. I should be thankful. I was here now, being useful in the way I'd always desired. Before, the Brundages' lawn had been pretty but ordinary, arrayed with the spring bulbs every gardener of any fine home planted. Now it would be a showpiece, equally as magnificent as the ornate Italianate design we'd done for the Carrolls down the street.

"The morning after your brother's send-off soiree, Harry came down to breakfast adamant that we have a new rose garden installed at once," she said. "I know your family's reputation is unmatched, but I also know that a large part of his insistence on the matter was due to his affection for you. I believe he hopes you'll be here as mistress someday soon to oversee your family's design."

"I'm glad he saw the importance of a fine garden. It truly elevates any beautiful home." I took a sip of my lemonade, hoping she'd stop attempting to discuss my involvement with Harry—or lack thereof. The lemons for our drinks had been grown proudly by the Brundages' lawn man and I had to admit they were luscious.

"Do you love him—my Harry?" The question came quickly and sounded strangled. I choked on the lemonade and looked up from my glass to find Mrs. Brundage leaning toward me, her face ablaze with embarrassment yet desperate for an answer.

"We've tried to match him with a dozen women, Miss Fremd, all of fine face and breeding, all of a fortune that matches ours. He is not interested. He insisted he knew who he wanted and that when he returned home after his studies were over, he would pursue her in earnest. He refused to tell us her name, but I knew it was you. Of course it was you." Her voice was rising, her words coming faster as she spoke.

"I see why he burns for you. Your beauty is unmatched. It is almost unfair." She flipped her hand my direction. "Skin like porcelain, hair as black as a raven, large mossy eyes, a figure made for the fashion magazines. He says you possess intellect as well, that you challenge him."

I took a breath at her pause and tried to figure out what to say. Despite her tone, I knew she wasn't angry with me, only frantic, worried she wouldn't see her son settled. My father, though he articulated his desperation differently, was of the same mind.

"He said when he returns from the city on Monday he's going straight to you, and . . . well, I can't say I suppose, but you've given me no indication that you want him, and we've been sitting here together—a possible mother-in-law and her new daughter—for two hours."

By the end of her statement, she was practically yelling and her voice ricocheted through the terrace's channel. I could feel eyes on my face and looked down to find our employees staring up at me—including Sam, who had just arrived with another carriage full of roses. The moment our eyes met he looked away. I hadn't seen him since the last time I'd been in Harry's company. He was avoiding me. There was no other explanation.

"Mrs. Brundage, I wish I could say that I loved him," I said quietly, hoping my tone would dictate hers. Father was going to have my head for this, for ruining another chance at a match, but it would have been futile anyway. Even if he'd proposed, I would have declined. "In my defense, I haven't given him any reason to believe I—"

"Who could possibly be better suited for you?" she snapped under her breath. "Stephen Bishop might boast a handsome face, but he is as dull as an ox. My Harry isn't close to a blot on the landscape. He is in possession of an attractive appearance, an intelligence far beyond that of myself or his father, and a wit that keeps one merry. Not to mention his fortune." She swept her hands across the tableau of their estate. "Mr. Brundage and I will be moving to our townhome in the city when Harry marries, and this estate will be his wife's alone."

It was stunning to me that despite my saying I didn't love him she continued to discuss the matter.

"You shouldn't want me for him, Mrs. Brundage. Even if he loves me, I don't love him. I intend to be deliriously happy with the man I marry, and Harry should require the same. Surely a person cannot be satisfied with a match knowing the other loves only the situation of their funds and not the situation of their heart."

Mrs. Brundage sat back in her chair and sighed.

"You would grow to love him," she said. "There's no possibility you would remain cold to him after you see how he provides for you, how he loves you."

Harry was a proud man, a man who didn't seem to understand failure or compromise. A man like that could never comprehend his wife's aspirations stretching beyond children and a house. That alone would prevent my love for any man.

"Perhaps I would become fond of him, but fondness and love are two different feelings," I said.

"And you believe you know the difference? At your age?" She scoffed. "Twenty-two is still young enough to recall the fairy tales nannies read. That sort of love is a cruel fiction, my dear."

It was not. So many women settled for fondness, women who had been tricked into believing that love didn't exist. I glanced below. Sam was crouched in front of a rose, his back to me, instructing the rest of the men on how to plant the different varieties. A warmth spread through me, and at once I wanted to brush my hands along his broad shoulders.

"This conversation has tired and grieved me," Mrs. Brundage said. "I'm afraid I must retire for a bit."

"I'm sorry I cannot offer you joy," I said as she stood. She gripped the back of the chair before she took her first step, as though the news of my indifference had thoroughly stolen her strength.

"I fear he's let so many pass by on account of you. Mr. Brundage worries he'll never see grandchildren." Her voice was barely louder than a whisper. "Lydia!" she called to her maid, her voice breaking. "Come and bring my cane."

By the time I made it down the spiral staircase and onto the lawn, my hands were shaking. This sort of thing didn't happen to Charles or Freddie. They could laugh off talk of marriage and children with mention of a thriving business. Men had time. Men weren't considered an hourglass running out of sand by the time they were twenty. Men weren't considered a commodity to be secured the moment they were on the market. They could settle at fifty if they so chose. Women, however, were seen as fading flowers. If one was beautiful and perfect, it needed to be plucked at its prime before another could pick it. The desperation to secure such a flower made people quite insane.

"Remember, a foot of grass before the boxwoods, please," I said as I stepped onto the crushed limestone path that threaded through the garden in a T-shape from the top of the fountain.

Mike Rich looked up at me, his hands pressed into the earth at the base of a boxwood.

"It's a bit too narrow," I said, gesturing to the row behind him.

"It's in line," Mike said.

Felicio and Luis were placing roses behind the boxwoods in perfect rows exactly like I'd designed—white blooms that would give way to blush behind them and deep pink behind them, until the colors deepened to Prince Camille de Rohan's velvety crimson, marking the final edge of the quartered circle. Behind the formed circle would be another walkway and beyond the walk, crawling white roses that Sam and Nick were installing and which would eventually overtake the estate's brick wall.

"Move it in a hair, please, Mr. Rich," I said firmly. Mike nodded and jerked the boxwood up too swiftly, causing the root ball to detach. The plant was ruined.

"Get me another one," I said. "I'll show you the correct placement." Mike immediately rose and went to the pallet to retrieve a new plant.

I knelt on the soft grass and dug my hands into the soil, filling the hole. Then I gestured to Mr. Gibson who was standing across the garden with a shovel. The moment he saw me, his eyes widened and he hustled over.

"Miss Sadie, get up. You'll ruin your gown." Mr. Gibson had come over from Italy only a month before and his accent was heavy.

"I don't mind if I do." I took the shovel from his hands and pushed it into the ground. "I'm working, the same as all of you. I don't care if Father forbids it or prefers I pretend I'm only here for polite conversation with the lady of the house. This is where I belong and where I want to be."

He stood there silently until I handed him the shovel, then dropped back down to the grass to clear the remaining soil. This had to be perfect. Not an inch out of line. Father needed to see I could do this, that I was just as capable as Charles.

"Here." Sam materialized beside me, a new boxwood in his hand. His white linen shirt was nearly translucent with exertion and smudged with dirt and he'd rolled up his sleeves. "Tony was planting them backward on the other side. I told him to try again."

"Thank you," I said. Our fingers brushed as I reached up to take the plant, and at once my breath caught. He started to turn away but then stopped and dropped to his knees beside me.

"It's occurred to me that my coming back here might have confused things," he whispered.

I placed the boxwood in the ground and pushed a lump of soil over the roots. Sam did the same and seemed not to notice our hands touching as we moved the earth. If we had been alone, I would have grasped his fingers in mine. I would have told him why I hadn't come with him, that I still loved him, that I was sorry. But we were here, surrounded by thirty people.

"Not at all. I—"

"I've tried to keep my distance," he said under his breath. "But I couldn't refuse your father when he assigned me here today." He stopped moving the soil for a moment and looked at me. I could barely hold his gaze. "We all heard Mrs. Brundage earlier, and after I saw the two of you the other night . . . Sadie, please don't alter your plans on account of thinking you'll maim me in some way."

"I don't want Mr. Brundage. I don't love him and I—"

"My presence cannot interfere with the sort of life you could have with him," Sam said.

"What do you mean?" I asked, my voice rising. "I've never wanted riches," I whispered, wishing I could scream. Of course he assumed I'd let him go because I didn't want to walk away from my luxuries. "I was honest when I told you all I've ever wanted was to work with plants and—" *Be with you.* I'd almost said it. He could tell. I said those words before, the night I told him I loved him.

"I don't want me working here to stop you from whatever it is you want," he said. "I know you and your kindness. If you thought anyone's well-being in peril in any way, you would alter your plans." He paused. "I don't want you to think I came back for you. You and I are in the past. We're not in love anymore. Perhaps we never were. I've gone on with my life."

Before I could reply, he stood and walked away. I tried to ignore the tension in my throat but couldn't stop my eyes from filling with tears. I patted the soil and stretched my hands into a line, measuring the distance from the shrub I'd just planted to the two next to it, busying myself so he wouldn't see the stake he'd driven through my heart.

Then again, it was obvious he thought me indifferent to any affection he may have for me, save a sort of pity for unrequited feelings. I couldn't blame him for that assumption. I had assumptions of my own, namely, that he'd never forgive me, that he hated me for abandoning him, that he thought me dishonest and spineless. In a way I was glad he'd never received my letters begging him to return, to put his dream of us on hold, to hope someday Father would approve of us and I could realize both of my aspirations. It was shameful to admit it, but I'd never realized until now how selfish the request was. How could I presume my heartache welcome to him when I'd been the one to cause both his and mine, when I knew I wouldn't alter my plans and follow him if he asked again?

I wiped my eyes and stood, brushing the dirt from my skirt.

"Are you all right, Miss Fremd?" Felicio asked, his hand poised on a bare-root Francois Levet.

"Yes, thank you, Felicio. I only got a bit of dirt in my eyes."

He dug into the pocket of his trousers and extracted a hand-kerchief, which he handed to me.

"Thank you," I said, accepting it and dabbing the corners of my eyes. I took a long breath and walked toward the gates where a pallet of Paul Neyron roses waited. Feeling horrid wouldn't help me outfit this garden properly. I couldn't do my task as architect with anguish walking alongside. I would have to shut off my feelings. I would have to learn to work with Sam without thinking of our tragedy and all we'd left unsaid.

I circled the pallet, examining the roses. Mrs. Shoemacker had done an excellent job selecting them. She always did. None of the canes were brittle or exhibited signs of dieback. Inevitably we'd have to come out and replace a few roses in a month or two, but only a couple dozen or so out of the four hundred we were planting.

"Is it roses they're planting?" A voice from behind the gate startled me and I whirled around.

"Yes," I said, smiling at the man in filthy duck overalls.

He grinned, exhibiting rows of missing teeth, and adjusted the pack he must have made out of scraps of linen. I wondered how old he was. He could be my age or seventy; he was the sort of person who wore his hardship on his body.

"Mighty glad to hear that, miss," he said. "Are any bloom-ing yet?"

"No. None of these anyway, though there are a few mature varieties we planted in those limestone urns at the edges of the walkways just there." I gestured to the tall planters that marked the four ends of the crushed limestone path. I'd chosen the Eugene Verdier for the containers—a silvery pink and fawn variety with large, exquisite blossoms.

The man edged closer to the gate to peer inside.

"Ah. Those are lovely." He closed his eyes and inhaled a deep breath. Then he looked at me and smiled. "I walk this road every day, and most days I come back from where I've been with nothing but despair in my heart. It's easy to think today's troubles will be tomorrow's and the next day's, too, and that nothing but hunger and death await."

"What—" I wanted to ask the cause of his misery, but he kept speaking.

"Then I look inside the gates of one of these places, and I see the flowers coming out of the ground that was dead and frozen a few weeks before, and I start to think that maybe my life's just in winter right now and in a while I'll bloom again too."

"Nature is the most hopeful of all creation," I said. "I don't know how I could possibly fare without being completely surrounded by it."

"You'd despair the moment hardship came to call," he said. "I am so easily desolate. I had it all a year ago. I was a switchman on the rail in the city. I had a wife I loved. When I lost my post to the crash, I lost my wife too. Left me for my friend, a brakeman who was kept on." He looked at the ground.

"I'm sorry." When his gaze again met mine, tears were streaming down his face.

"I got hired on the Westchester & Putnam on the night shift

last week. I'm saving all I can, but she won't come back to me. Can't say I blame her. Right now all I have left is the old barn my parents left me up the way. Oftentimes I wonder if I'll die there." He paused and glanced beyond me. "But then I see the beauty of that flower right there"—he pointed toward the potted roses—"and I find the strength to keep on." He cleared his throat. "Those people must be brimming with hope." He gestured to the Brundages' mansion.

"I'm afraid they've never required much of it," I said. It was the truth. I knew a handful of wealthy families who'd never experienced an ounce of hardship at all. The Brundages were one of them.

"When I make it in the world, when I get my girl back, I'm going to hire you folks to build me a garden." He chuckled. "Until then, I'll just have to linger awhile when I walk past here."

"I'm glad there will be someone to appreciate it. I doubt the Brundages will regard it much." Most of the grounds we beautified were cared for by a team of workers and never received a minute of attention from the families who so adamantly made the gardens a requirement.

"So do I," he said. "Well, I better get going. Still a mile to go."

"Are you out by the rail?" I asked. There was a bit of land occupied by only ramshackle barns and crumbling houses beyond the railroad. It had become a haven for those made homeless since the crash.

"Yes," he said. "Which is why I must hurry. I've hidden a bit of bread in the barn, but everyone's hungry. It wouldn't surprise me at all if it's gone by the time I get back."

He walked away, his belongings strapped to his back. I glanced at the roses, wishing I could give him a few dozen. I was fortunate; I was able to bury my gloom in beauty anytime I wanted. So could my peers. They could simply say a word, draft a check, and their land would overflow with the hope of nature.

But it wasn't so for people like this man. He would have to wait at the gates for the buds to blossom, never allowed to walk among them or smell the resinous scent of boxwoods mingled with the honey-clove of the roses. Something about the reality of that deprivation felt terribly wrong—some folk who needed the healing of wild beauty the most were barred from it.

CHAPTER 5

I woke in a sweat and threw the swan-feather duvet from my body. In the dark my bed posters looked eerily like the shadowy cell bars in my dream.

I'd been locked in a prison with the railman from the Brundages'. Beyond the bars were Sam and the man's wife and the nurseries and light, but where we stood was dark and muddy and desperate. I could still feel my heart pounding and my stomach gnawing with hunger. I could still hear my screams for someone to let us out. The dream wasn't a fantasy, one that was so implausible it was forgotten. The filth, the dread were a reality for so many, and for a few moments, I'd felt their grip.

I got out of bed and walked over to my armoire. I hadn't been able to get the man out of my mind all day yesterday. He'd seemed to be in such a horrible state, yet he was so enlivened by the idea that his life could improve, that there was hope to be found despite it all. I should have given him a few roses. We always had a dozen or more left over after a project that we'd planned to use but didn't. Instead, I'd let him walk away, let him return empty-handed to whatever unfortunate shelter his barn provided. I had to correct my mistake.

The grandmother clock read 12:25 a.m. I slipped my nightgown over my head and pulled one of my white visiting gowns off its clips. I pulled the shirtwaist on and buttoned it, not concerning myself with a corset, and then stepped into the skirt. It would be frosty out. I reached in the back of my armoire and found a jacket from three seasons ago—a tight-fitting dark blue with Persian lamb trim and buttons. It would be warm at least.

The thought of going beyond the railroad tracks alone in the middle of the night gave me pause. I'd heard rumors of drunken fights and stabbings and fields set afire for a wrong done. I was never to go—that's what Father would say. Fortunately he'd never know.

I tiptoed out of my room and down the hall and the stairs, avoiding the eighth step that creaked terribly. When the front door clicked shut behind me, I finally breathed.

I descended the porch steps and looked up as I walked across the lawn toward the greenhouses. The stars were out and the sky was barely streaked with wispy clouds. Owls called to each other, their hoots like shouts in the otherwise silent night. I snaked through the greenhouses and down to the fields where we grew our varieties to maturity. The men had dug at least fifty mature roses today to be distributed to the Goulds' tomorrow for their indoor planters. The Nicoli family always prepared the root balls in burlap and soaked them in water in the front room of the horse barn. Surely they wouldn't miss a few of the plants.

I pushed the barn door open and found a match to strike against the flint on the wall. I lit the oil lamp we'd kept on an old barrel inside the door for as long as I could remember. The flame flickered and caught, washing the dim in gold. The horses continued snoring in the back of the barn, not at all startled by the sound of the door or the lamp's light.

The roses were gathered on the left in the large carriage room. Carriages and carts were stored on the right. I'd only need the smallest cart. Its shafts were laid out in front with the leather reins and traces, the crupper and the wrap straps, the breastplate and the girth hanging on a hook to the side.

It occurred to me just then that I hadn't any idea how to harness a horse to the contraption. I'd never even watched anyone do it. Perhaps I could simply carry the roses on Gene's back. He was the oldest and most docile of our horses. But I'd only be able to transport two bushes at most that way and I wanted to plant enough for a sitting area.

I sighed and walked down the aisle of stalls. Gene was in the last one. He was a huge Appaloosa who'd been bred on a Kansas ranch. I lifted his bridle from its hook on the stall door and went in, running a hand down his mane to reassure him. He blinked at me and nickered. I pulled the leather band over his nose, eased the bit into his mouth, and secured the headpiece.

"Come on," I murmured, leading him out of his stall. "Let's see if we can figure this out together."

I edged the back door to the barn open and led him out. Fifty yards away, the small village of clapboard homes was silent. A few chimneys billowed woodsmoke, but otherwise no one seemed to be about.

"Miss Fremd?" someone on the porch closest to me whispered into the silent night. "It's me, Vincenzo Pratte. Do—"

"What in the world are you doing, Sa—Miss Fremd?" Sam appeared from around the side of the house. He'd withdrawn a cigar from his mouth and started toward me. I'd never known him to smoke.

"No need to help me, fellows," I called quietly. "I'm just going to see a friend who's in a bit of trouble. Carry on." I tried to hurry around the side of the barn, but before I could, Sam reached me and Vincenzo stepped off the porch to follow.

"It's past midnight," Sam said, breathing hard from his sprint to my side. "What are you doing out here?"

"I could ask the same of you and Mr. Pratte." I tightened my fingers on Gene's reins.

"We can't sleep. After you've been in the city for some time, you have to reacclimate to the quiet." He ran a hand through his hair, then patted Gene's side.

"That's right," Vincenzo said as he joined us. "When you're in the city packed together with thirteen people in one flat, it's never quiet. Not to mention the shouts from the streets, the rumble of the streetcars at all hours, and the ringing of the factory in your ears hours after you've gone home."

"The city?" I asked, meeting Sam's gaze. How had he ended up in the city?

"Yes."

"But I thought you—" He shook his head slightly before I could ask how he'd ended up in New York, what he'd been doing there. Clearly he wasn't interested in discussing it in front of Vincenzo.

"What are you really doing, Sadie?" Sam asked. "I know no one's in trouble. If that were the case, your father would be out here in the middle of the night."

I didn't have to lie to Sam or ask that he not tell my father. I'd never had to mince words around him or worry that he'd betray me, but I didn't have the same confidence in Vincenzo. I'd only met him a few weeks ago.

"One of my friends needs me," I said simply.

Sam nodded.

"Vin, would you mind taking Gene around front and start tacking him for Miss Fremd? I'll be right around to help," he said.

"I'll need the harness leather, I'm afraid. And the small cart too," I said.

Vincenzo's eyebrows rose in question, but he didn't ask.

"Certainly, but you might have to come quick. Gene doesn't like me. Last time I tried to tack him, he bit me," Vincenzo said before leading Gene around to the front of the barn.

"What's the truth?" Sam whispered. He stepped toward me, leaving less than a foot of space between us. I could feel his warmth, smell the sweet cigar smoke on his clothes.

"You might think I'm crazy, but I'm going over to the rail-road village. I need to plant a little rose garden. There was a man who came to the gate at the Brundages', and he . . . I know it may not make sense, Sam, but he needs the roses." I looked up at him.

Sam's eyes flashed with something and he ran a hand across his face.

"It makes more sense than you know," he said. "You can't go alone, though. I'll come with you. If anyone catches us, perhaps we say you were summoned by Margaret for some reason or other—I recall her always having some sort of supposed crisis—and that I was about, unable to sleep, and thought you shouldn't go by yourself at this hour?"

"Yes, that's a sensible story." He was right about Margaret. She had always been dramatic. He'd heard all about her antics over the years. "I'd appreciate your company. And I thank you and Mr. Pratte both for helping me. I admit I don't think I would have been able to figure out harnessing the cart to Gene."

I followed Sam around to the front. Vincenzo had already harnessed Gene and was hoisting the cart onto his back.

"Hold on a minute, man. I'll get the other side," Sam said.

They lifted the cart and fitted the tug strap, then stood back.

"All set, Miss Fremd," Vincenzo said. "Be mindful of the potholes in the road this late at night. I'll stay up until your return in case you fall into trouble."

"I appreciate your kind offer more than you know, but Mr. Jenkins will accompany me," I said.

"Get some rest, Vin," Sam said, clapping him on the back. "Don't fret if I'm not back in my room at daybreak. I'll likely stay up and bag the weeping birch seeds Mr. Fremd and I just cross-pollinated."

"Always working," Vincenzo said. "Then again, I suppose we're used to it. I sure don't miss enduring the boiling steam off those presses for fifteen hours at a time."

Sam laughed and seemed to purposely avoid my gaze. Moving to the city hadn't been our plan. Working in a factory certainly hadn't.

"The soil doesn't burn the skin off my hands, that's for sure," Sam said. "And anyway, I love working with plants. It's—"

"It's what he was meant to do," I said. It was the truth. Sam was brilliantly inventive. He'd created some of our best varieties of firs and other trees, varieties that withstood both the winter cold and diseases that often mutilated a grove. He only walked away from it so we could be together. We'd figured he could get on with another nursery eventually, doing the same sort of thing.

That was the plan. But despite his willingness to risk it all for me, I hadn't been willing to do the same, and my staying had clearly resulted in hardship for him.

"Well, good night then," Vincenzo said. He tipped his head to me and wandered back toward his porch.

Silence fell over Sam and me in his absence, a thousand questions hanging in the air.

"I'm going to take five of those rosebushes over there," I said, gesturing to the Goulds' order. "I'll dig more to replace them when I return, but I want two of the John Hopper, one of the La Reine, and—"

"The Madame Cusin would look beautiful with those," Sam said. The rose he suggested was violet, tinged yellow.

"I agree." I lifted one of the John Hoppers and Sam didn't stop me. He picked up the Madam Cusins instead. Sam had never thought me too fragile to do the work of the nurseries.

"I'm glad you're doing this," he said after he set the roses in the cart.

"I just couldn't bear his despair. I wanted to help," I said before going back for the last rose.

"It shouldn't be this way, you know. Natural beauty being reserved only for the wealthy. It is a true balm to the mind, and to keep it restricted is a sort of greed I know too well." He spoke softly, but his face hardened.

"I suppose I didn't realize that some were deprived of flowers until today." I set the last rose in the cart.

"How could you? You've never had to live without them. But there are so many robbed of even an inch of grass, people dying in filth and dim and disease. If they could just see . . . If they could just see even one bloom, they would know they could go on, that there's something better." He paused and swallowed hard. His eyes held a heaviness I'd never seen.

"Sam," I whispered. "What happened?"

He shook his head and forced a smile.

"Let's go."

I climbed onto the cart seat and Sam followed. We hadn't been this close in years, but it still felt familiar. It felt right.

He reached for the reins and his hand brushed mine. I grasped it.

"Sam," I whispered. "I . . . I want to explain why I didn't come."

He looked at me and shook his head, then pulled his hand from mine.

"It's okay, Sadie. It's been years. There's no need." He tapped the reins against Gene's back, and we were off. The cart lurched and I grasped the iron bar at my side to steady myself. We rode up the path that snaked around the side of the greenhouses and down the tree-lined entrance to the nurseries.

"Yes, there is," I said. "I need you to know that it wasn't because I didn't love you."

The trees dropped away as we approached North Street. On the other side of the road, the cemetery stretched out in front of us, the headstones poised like silent gray soldiers on the rolling hills. My mother was beyond the second row of them, her monument a tower I could see from the road.

Sam turned the cart left onto the street, toward the railroad track, and I looked at him, his face aglow with starlight. He was the most handsome man I'd ever seen.

"I know you loved me," he said finally. "You just didn't love me enough. No matter the reason, when it comes down to it, that's my answer. That's all I need to know."

I wasn't sure what to say, but I couldn't bear the idea that he assumed I remained to find a wealthy husband.

"It was the nurseries," I blurted. "I couldn't leave them. It's my legacy. I want to take over someday. I want Father to know it's me, that I'm the one he can count on to keep it going. I . . . I was on my way out; my trunk was packed. I went to leave my farewell letter on Father's desk and saw an unfinished note to my uncle. Father wrote that I had the ingenuity of Rebecca Lukens, that if I had been born a boy, my aptitude would rival Charles's. It gave me hope that he was on his way to seeing me as a viable successor and I realized I couldn't leave. I couldn't abandon my dream if there was truly a chance." My voice sounded choked. "I went to the station to find you, to ask you to stay with me, but I was too late. The nurseries are the only thing that kept me here. It wasn't that I wanted riches or a different man. I wanted the nurseries and I wanted you."

Sam was silent for a moment.

"You never told me you were looking for a reason to stay and contend for this place," he said at last, an edge to his voice. "You always said winning the successorship was a lost cause, that it was completely off the table, a closed book. I thought you'd made peace with it."

He looked at me then. "Why didn't you tell me it was something you still wanted, Sadie? If you had, I never would have asked you to leave it." He turned back to the road but continued. "I never would have asked you to marry me. I know you love it here; we both do. Surely you know I would never put you in a position to choose between disobeying your father to marry me and retaining this place you love. I knew you couldn't have both . . . And you said you wanted to go. You said you were ready. Then . . . you didn't come, Sadie." His jaw bulged and his hands fisted around the reins. "You should have been honest. I could have endured it."

He was right. We'd talked countless times about my wanting to run the nurseries, but we both always agreed that despite my desire for Father to see my talent and passion for it, he wouldn't. Father's letter had given me hope that perhaps I'd been wrong.

"I'm so sorry, Sam." It seemed like the only thing I could say.

The path ahead narrowed and curved inland, breaking from the rail line that curved over a stream in the opposite direction.

"There's no need to apologize. I put us in the past long ago. To be frank, I never thought I'd see you again. I moved on with my life."

I swallowed hard and pushed my fingers into the rough wooden seat to dull the pain. His love for me was gone. It was natural for love to fade after years away, especially when it was thought extinct, but the moment I'd seen him again, I realized mine hadn't faded at all. I'd been naive to think separation from the nurseries was the only reason I hadn't accepted any of the men Father attempted to pair me with. My love for Sam would always fill my heart. There wasn't room for anyone else.

"Where did you go? Where have you been all this time? What happened to Newport?" I asked. "I wrote to you at your uncle's address and my letters were returned. I went up to Newport with Father and asked after you everywhere, several times, and no one had heard of you—or your uncle."

"My uncle was a liar," he said. "When I got there, there was no house and there was no job. He's a homeless drunk. He attempted to lure us there so we would find work and take compassion on him and house him with us, though he is just as able-bodied as me. I knew then there was a greater reason you weren't with me. We would have ended up living . . . Sadie, there are some things you wish you could forget. I would have torn you away from your family and ruined your life. You would have come around to loathing me."

We reached a clearing, and at once the stench made me want to vomit. The decay of raw sewage and discarded meals hung heavy in the air. Tumbledown lean-tos crammed the acreage on both sides of the path, and dirty linens flapped from clotheslines. The ground was almost entirely mud from the recent rain and the number of feet trampling upon it daily. A few goats bleated from a pen I couldn't see.

"This is awful," I whispered. I was shivering. Not from cold but because I was terrified our intrusion wouldn't be welcome, that we'd wake the whole village.

Sam's hand found mine and squeezed, then let go.

"You may think so, but this is paradise," he said.

"Why were you in the city, Sam? What happened? We planned to go to Horace Cleveland after Newport, and you were going to find work with him—"

"Life doesn't always turn out the way we expect. Mr. Cleveland didn't have a job for me either. I was homeless and hungry, so when his secretary said her cousin owned a tenement in the city and was looking for an eviction officer, I went."

I'd read about the horror of the factories and the tenements that housed those in their employ, but I'd never seen them. We were only thirty miles from the city, but things like that seemed a world away. I couldn't imagine Sam in the midst of the desolation and disease.

"I can't fathom what you saw—what you endured," I said. "I'm so sorry. I wish I could have spared you from it all."

We were passing a small pond now, and judging by the buckets set out beside it, these people were drinking the filthy water—water that doubtless contained building contaminants and sewage.

"I'm not sorry and I'm glad you weren't there. I don't think you would have survived it. I realize now I needed to see it. I've never been wealthy like you, but I was always comfortable. There, you live in a tiny apartment, five or six or more to a room. During the day you're inside a factory with a thousand people and only two windows. There are rats and bugs, and outside the sky is always filled with gray ash even when the sun is out. There is no grass, no flowers, and even when you're desperate to breathe clean air or wander on a bit of grass, you are escorted out of the 'people's park' by security officers. I learned that park was partially won by claiming eminent domain of an entire village of African American landowners.

"I realized more than ever before that natural beauty and health are only available to those who can afford them. Central Park is used solely as a promenade by those of your ilk. It is not a public park. Those of a certain pedigree work quite vigilantly to keep the rest of us out. I'm sure your father would agree that nothing soils a garden more than a man in filthy dress."

"That is horrific, but my father is far from the Fifth Avenue set. Don't lump him in with them, please." Despite the shock of the existence he'd just described, I couldn't help but react in offense that he thought my family so vain, so unfeeling. "I've never heard him make any sort of comment about opposing the working class's enjoyment of a garden, considering we are the working class."

Sam laughed. "Hardly. I know you love your father. I do, too, in a way. But how many gardens has he planted for those whose lives are in peril, those who need a bit of beauty in their desolation? People I knew, people I loved, became sick and died because they had no place to go to breathe. Many were Irish, from vast farms where they were surrounded by fresh air and open space."

He paused. "And then there's the matter of us. Your father would rather ship you off to Germany to learn your lesson than have you marry a man with a status beneath yours. That's why we had to hide and ultimately run away if we wanted to be married. He'd never allow a match like ours. You must admit, he's quite pompous."

"Yet he employs and houses five dozen," I said. "Of course I wish he would see that marriage to whoever I love would be the best route, but he worries for me."

"It would be unnatural if he didn't," Sam said. "Let's stop discussing it."

Up ahead, I saw a small channel of dirt and then a small barn.

"There it is." I pointed.

Sam stopped Gene in the middle of the path and hopped down.

"Just something simple," I said as he came around the cart. "Perhaps we plant them in a circle with a little space for an entrance. He can walk in the middle and sit, surrounded by the blooms."

Sam lifted me down from the cart, but when my feet hit the ground, we lingered.

"To be clear, I don't think you pretentious," he said, his arms still encircling my waist.

"Oh, but I am," I said, startling myself with the confession. I had fine things—fine carriages and horses and dresses and servants. I'd never gone without any sort of luxury. Even if I had no intention of being pompous, I had never truly considered lives that were different from mine, lives mired in poverty so all-encompassing that it arrested both body and mind.

We carried the roses closer to the barn and then went back for our shovels. The barn was nothing more than thick timber boards propped atop a frame. The structure couldn't possibly keep out animals or the elements. It offered no privacy. I knew if we drew close enough, we would see the man sleeping.

We started digging and planted side by side, silently, listening to the frogs croaking. The soil was damp and cold in my hands. By the time we finished with the last rose, my fingers had long since gone numb.

"Do you suppose he'll be surprised?" I whispered as I pushed a final bit of dirt over the roots. I wiped my brow, trickling with either sweat or dew, and Sam smiled before reaching over to push a strand of hair from my eyes.

"In the years I was away, the image that always came to mind when I thought of you was the way you looked with your hair slightly unbound, your hands covered in dirt. You're happiest like that. Knowing what I do now, I suppose I should've been more jealous of the plants." He smiled. "You chose them instead of me, and I have no doubt that if we were still in love, you'd do it over again."

His fingers lingered on my cheek and I thought he might kiss me. My heart pounded the same way it had when I first told him I loved him, but then his touch faded and he stepped back, extending his hand to me.

"If we were still in love, I'd want you both, the same as I always have." It was a terrible misery to speak of us this way, in the past, when my love for him was perennial.

"That's why it's best that we've moved on. We can never be," Sam said as he helped me into the cart and then hoisted himself up. "You know having both is impossible."

I glanced at the little garden, at the hopeful blooms in the starlight, and I knew Sam was right.

"He's going to love it," Sam whispered. "You've done a beautiful thing, Sadie."

Then he tapped Gene and we were gone, and a sense of peace washed through me.

CHAPTER 6

-I waved to Leonardo Vicchialla—one of our most seasoned employees, going on eighty—as he walked back from the growing field to the potting greenhouse, his arms full of empty clay planters. I placed the last just-sprouted English boxwood on the rack in the corner of the greenhouse and dusted my dirty hands on my frock, then emerged from the humidity to a perfectly crisp yet warm spring day.

The nurseries were always busiest when the weather was fair. Today was moving day. Workers hauled seedlings from the greenhouses to the growing fields and varieties grown for pots were harvested.

"Good morning, Vincenzo," I said as I walked down the hill beyond the greenhouses toward the field and barn. He was struggling under the weight of a wheelbarrow full of horse manure. An enormous pile outside the horse barn showed that the Mirani children had shoveled stalls before sunup. Moving plants required fertilizing them too.

Vincenzo lifted his shoulder up to his cheek to wipe a bit of sweat away and smiled. "Lovely day, isn't it, Miss Fremd?"

He had no idea where Sam and I went last night, and I hoped he'd keep quiet about seeing me in the first place.

"Vincenzo," Father called. He appeared from around the back of the barn where he'd just deposited the farrier to reshoe the horses. "If there's any left when you're done spreading it over the new roses, put the residual on the purple barberry roots. They're down the sixteenth row, all the way to the right, on the barn side. I don't like the way they're growing."

"Yes, sir," Vincenzo said, then continued wheeling toward the roses.

"Sadie, would you mind staying down here in case the farrier needs anything?" Father asked. "I've got to see how many John Hopper roses still need transporting from the greenhouse. Looks like Ward's running out of room over there." He gestured to the far-right edge of the field where Ward was planting the carmine-pink variety.

"Of course," I said.

I watched him walk away and then stop for a moment on the hill between the greenhouses and the field. He shoved his hands into his suit pockets and squinted at the small square designated for the roses before continuing toward the greenhouses.

While I waited for Father to return, I watched Tony and his brother Luis digging up a dozen Andromeda floribunda for the Crowes' new garden to be installed next week. The boys' blue-jeaned dungarees were stained brown. Floribunda was one of my favorite springtime shrubs. The beautiful dark green myrtle-like leaves and pure white flowers presenting in sprays like lilies of the valley made a lovely addition to any garden design, and Father used them often.

Mitzy walked through a grove of trees in the field, making her way to the well on the side of the hay barn with an empty basin.

"Mitzy! The nettle trees will need water today as well, please," I shouted loud enough for her to hear.

"Yes, Miss Fremd!" Mitzy shouted back.

"Speaking of nettles, Olmsted needs four and seven floribundas at the Crowes'," Father called to me as he made his way back down from the greenhouses. I extracted the notebook that outlined the particulars of their garden design from the bag at my waist and wrote down the amounts.

I glanced at Father. He'd aged of late. His normally rosy countenance looked ashen and the few wrinkles he had only weeks ago seemed to have multiplied.

"I got a letter from Charles yesterday," he said when he reached me, his gaze still fixed on the activity in the fields.

"Why didn't you tell me? I've been eager to hear how he's getting on." I yanked at the duchesse lace on my bodice despite knowing full well the action would do nothing to relieve the constraints of the Cleopatra—a new corset Agnes had ordered me from H. O'Neill & Co. She'd told me I had to wear it, that it was the talk of every ladies' magazine this season, and that I needed to break it in before I attended any sort of fine occasion.

"I suppose I forgot," Father replied. Just then the farrier emerged from the barn and declared he was finished, climbed on his cart, and was gone.

"Charles only said that Flagler has him situated in a little bungalow on the beach and that they're sourcing plants from

Jacksonville, though he hopes to convince Flagler it's worth the trouble to obtain better varieties from us."

I knew the news wasn't at all what Father wanted to hear. Despite the distance, projects like Flagler's new Royal Poinciana Hotel commanded at least $100,000—a sum that would ensure Rye Nurseries' existence and success for the next several years. Father hadn't said so outright, but I knew he believed Flagler owed him the business. He'd wooed Father's successor away, and granting us the nursery bid was the least he could do to make up for it.

"You were out all day attending to the Brundages' project, in any case. I heard Mrs. Brundage was well pleased with your design." I waited for him to mention that I'd upset her, that I'd dashed another chance at a match, but he didn't. Perhaps she hadn't said anything in hopes I would alter my opinion.

"It's going to be gorgeous, Father, and so beautifully fragrant when the roses are all in bloom." I intended to think of the Brundages' new garden, but my mind flashed instead to the little circle of roses outside the tumbledown barn. I wondered how the man felt when he saw it. I smiled.

"I'm happy to go to the Crowes' next week as well. I quite enjoyed being there, and you must admit—"

"It is not right for me to rely on you this way, Lily," Father said. "I know it's only been a week since Charles left, but I know he's not returning, and now I find myself depending on my daughter to obtain new accounts." He shook his head. "I do appreciate you securing the Finks, the Brundages, and the Crowes. That is quite a feat indeed, but it's time for me to seek a successor. I can't operate all of this on my own. I have a few men in mind with the experience I require. They'll apprentice under me until I am ready to take a rest in a few years. I want to ensure they will carry this place on as I do."

"What about me?" The question was asked before I could consider if this was the right time to gamble my future.

Silence hung in the air between us. I suddenly felt as though I might faint.

Finally, Father shook his head.

"You will be married soon. Don't worry, my dear. Even if this place withers, we will sustain until then. Nothing will alter my plans for you," he said, completely misinterpreting my vying to take his place as concern for my well-being. "Come along to the tropical section. Mrs. Crowe would like a small palm court in her atrium."

"Father"—I caught him by the arm—"I mean to say, why not me as your successor? No one loves this place the way I do, not even Charles or Freddie, and I'm good at running it. I'm quite a natural at design work too. This is all I've ever wanted."

He laughed.

"The run of this place would drive you to an early grave," he said. "Business affairs are not the concern of the fairer sex. It's not that I don't respect women who have little choice but to involve themselves with commerce, but it's rumored Mrs. Lukens died from an illness caused by stress. Mrs. Ayer of Recamier Toilet Preparations is now mad, and the inventor, Mrs. Kies, became homeless.

"You are my daughter, under my charge. I will not subject you to a life like theirs. Concern for figures and expenses and worries therein would ruin you. I love you too much to allow you to gamble your fate. Your proper place is by the side of a good and decent husband, and with your hands in the soil of a small garden, if you so choose."

"My mental fortitude is strong and so is my ability." My heart pounded as my shoulders tightened with tension. I wanted to remind him that Mother hadn't been involved in commerce, that illness befell everyone in equal measure, but I knew he'd come apart at the mention of her. Instead, I said, "Not every woman in business faces such calamity."

"I understand that well, Lily." He resumed his walk to the palms and nodded at the Santorini family having an early luncheon outside one of the seeding houses. When we passed them, he continued.

"However, I'll say it again. The affairs of business aren't the affairs of women. Even if it was possible that you could avoid illness or madness or poverty, even if these nurseries would thrive in your care—if we make it out of this downturn at all— eventually, you would not. I can't fathom the plight of you as both an old maid and a businesswoman. Your struggles would be great. And in any case, sooner or later you will want a husband and children. It is the natural desire of a woman."

"I could have both," I said as we entered the greenhouse, then closed the door behind us.

"Five Kentia belmoreanas, seven royal palms, ten Latania borbonicas," Father said, wandering the circular path inside the greenhouse. I scribbled them in my notebook. "Men of stable fortunes have business affairs of their own. No bachelor suitable for you will have an interest in a wife whose preference is to tend to the plants before him."

"Perhaps I won't marry a man with great wealth," I said. "Perhaps I will marry a man whose passions align with mine. A true partner in both life and business could make the nurseries tremendously successful."

Father stopped in the aisle in front of me.

"I still don't think you understand," he said sternly before turning to face me. "These nurseries are not a fortune to inherit, especially now. You are not Gertrude Vanderbilt, and though I don't want to alarm you, perhaps I must. We have not been immune to this downturn. Right now we are swimming in the midst of an undertow that threatens to drown us. It is one thing for Charles or Freddie to fail at the helm of this place. It is one thing for my sons to have to find work as a skilled planter with Olmsted or Vaux and work their way back up. It is another thing entirely for my *daughter* to sink with this ship." His face was red with fury by the time he took a breath.

"You would be ruined. You would have nowhere to go. I have worked too hard to elevate the Fremd name to have it dashed by poverty or a poor match and you with it. The door to America's finest families has been unlatched for you. You will concede to a suitable match. We won't discuss this further. You will choose someone by the end of this season. You will accept someone's hand in case the nurseries don't recover. And I will find a successor."

His last word deadened in the damp greenhouse air. I stared at him, waiting for him to realize he was wrong, but he only ran a hand over his face before continuing to dictate various palms.

I expected myself to cry, but instead, I felt numb. Perhaps I'd been a fool to think his respect for businesswomen and his words about my proficiency meant he would change his mind about my leadership here. In the last years, I'd become well aware that my greatest strength and my fatal flaw were one and the same—my resilient optimism, my tendency to alter a hint of hope into near surety. I recalled how swiftly I'd decided to stay after reading Father's letter. In reality his words had likely meant nothing. I realized that now, yet I'd clung to them like a life raft that would inevitably lift me into my purpose. And I'd lost Sam in the process.

"Perhaps you will fall in love at Edith Gould's ball tonight." His face brightened. "If you aren't satisfied with the men of this county, you may become enchanted with a man in the city. Several of the Goulds' contemporaries from London will be there as well, I hear."

With Charles recently gone and the nurseries being in peril and Sam back, I'd forgotten all about Mrs. Gould's annual birthday ball. Last year I'd faked being sick. I supposed it was too late to do that again.

"The event will take place on the rooftop garden this year," Father said. "I anticipate the gardeners have kept the design in good taste."

"I'm sure they have," I said. Father and Charles had designed an elaborate azalea garden for the George Jay Goulds'—Jay Gould's eldest son and his wife, Edith—rooftop two years back. I'd walked through it only once, but it had been quite magical— banks of rhododendron in an array of colors on each side of a long reflecting pool that boasted a smattering of water lilies and stretched to a terrace overlooking the city. "Perhaps we should think about the same sort of variety for the Finks', without the reflecting pool, of course."

I'd dipped my toe in the water on purpose. As long as Father didn't forbid me from helping him now, there was still a chance he'd come around. I realized how futile my hope likely was, but something inside me refused to give up.

A tap on the door interrupted us before Father could answer. Mr. McCrane, the manager of Griffith's Department Store, stood outside with his bowler pressed to his chest, his face pale.

"Good morning, Christopher," Father said after he walked over and opened the glass door. The cool outside air mingled with the greenhouse humidity, and for a moment, it felt like winter again. "How can I help? Has Mrs. Griffith sent you to place some tulip orders for the Easter display?"

I looked from Father to Mr. McCrane and back again. How could Father possibly think the man had come on ordinary business? He looked like he was about to collapse. Then again, women were more perceptive. And despite society saying otherwise, that fact alone proved that women belonged in business. Perception built relationships and had the power to guide customers to the exact product they didn't know they wanted. It was why I knew I could successfully convince my peers that fine gardens were societal necessities.

"No, not exactly," Mr. McCrane said as Father and I exited the greenhouse. "I've come because I'm hoping you have need for a man like me. I've got good managerial experience and can get along with about anyone. My references are unmatched if I'm being honest, and—"

"What happened to your post at Griffith's?" Father asked. At once everything seemed to pause. Griffith's couldn't have gone under. It was a staple of the town, a place where everyone went to select a Christmas gift or have a new hat made or meet a friend at the tearoom.

"The bank came to close us down this morning," Mr. McCrane said, his voice shaking. "I hadn't been paid in a few months, so I knew we were in trouble, but Mrs. Griffith always said she was good for the money, that Mr. Cyrus would pay me. The bank took Mrs. Griffith's house too."

"No." The word whispered from my lips and Mr. McCrane's gaze drifted across mine before settling back on Father.

Father clutched Mr. McCrane's hands, then let them go. "I can't believe it."

"All the business went to the five-and-dime, and the wealthy are sourcing their goods from the city. No one is shopping with us anymore. Can you take me?" Mr. McCrane asked.

A bit of a crowd was gathering around us. Not that they would actively intend to eavesdrop, but the moment word came of something unusual happening, everyone seemed to busy themselves in the vicinity.

Father stayed silent for a moment too long. He patted Mr. McCrane's shoulder.

"You know I wish I could," Father said softly. "But if I take on anyone else, we will be next. I'm sorry, Christopher."

Mr. McCrane broke then. His body careened into Father's and he sobbed.

"I don't know what I'll tell the children," he said.

My heart filled with dread. We had never turned anyone away. I diverted my gaze from Mr. McCrane embracing my father like his own and glanced up the aisle to our house. The lawn held at least twenty of Griffith's former employees. I knew all of them and their families. In the matter of a morning, their security was dashed and we couldn't do anything to stop it. I remembered what Sam had said about tenement housing. The thought of people I'd known my whole life wasting away in disease-ridden factories was enough to make me weep with grief.

"Where is Mrs. Griffith?" I asked, suddenly remembering Mr. McCrane's remark that she'd been turned out of her home. Mrs. Griffith was nearing eighty years old. The store was left to her upon her husband's passing twenty years ago, though she hadn't been the one to run it. Her husband's best friend, Mr. Lyons, had done all of that. Still, regardless of who was to blame for the store's demise, Mrs. Griffith was suffering the consequences.

"Someone said she'd be moving into the little apartment down from the meat market in town. Mr. Griffith bought it for storage some time ago, and it's the only property she's able to keep since it was actually held in her sister's name." Mr. McCrane straightened and put his bowler back on.

"Godspeed, Christopher," Father said, clapping Mr. McCrane once more on the back. "If something turns up here, I'll be the first to write."

"Thank you kindly," he said. "I'll tell the others."

I watched him walk away, his once proud shoulders slumped in defeat. He had been the face of Griffith's, the manager for thirty-one years. Another Rye staple, gone. Perhaps Charles hadn't been wrong. Perhaps this town was disappearing.

Father sniffed.

"Please understand that I'm not overreacting," he said under his breath. "Now, Sadie. Before the ground crumbles beneath our feet."

The train into the city had taken what felt like hours. I hadn't endured the ride since the last time I attended Mrs. Gould's birthday ball two years ago, and sitting in my new Driscoll gown, with the Cleopatra constricting my every breath, was torture.

Father and I stood in the Grand Central Depot as the evening light faded through the long channels of glass and iron on the ceiling. The place was jammed with passengers, most dressed in fine clothing—it cost a pretty penny to ride by rail, after all—and the crush coupled with the screech of the train brakes and the chatter and shouting of the railway employees made my skin itch with the need to get out of doors.

"Say, man." Father tapped the arm of a New York Central railman passing by us. The man stopped and wiped a filthy towel across his soot-stained face.

"How can I help you?"

"How do we access the elevated rail?" Father asked.

The man looked at me and shook his head. "Out the front doors and down the block to the right, though I don't believe you should access that line at all, sir," he said. "The engines expel coal gas, soot, and ash. Your daughter's fine dress would be ruined. A horse carriage would be my recommendation."

"Thank you," Father said, then turned to me. "George Gould is always after me to try his father's rail. I haven't once. I know he'll ask again, so I don't believe I can avoid it this time."

"I've never been one to cry over my silks," I said, but the truth was that I'd chosen the wrong dress to wear to the city. The base was white silk with four panels of white lace embroidered with pearls and gold spangles along the skirt, and the sleeves were puffs of white tulle, Brussels lace, and ribbon. The only bit of color came from the John Hopper pink roses adorning the left side of my décolleté.

"I suppose you're right, but I can't very well have you arriving at the Goulds' looking as though you've just come from a shift in the mines," Father said. "Perhaps you should simply lift your skirts a bit as we walk. Not enough to cause scandal, of course, but just so the hem won't skim the ground."

"That suits me." I didn't care if I did arrive at the Goulds' looking a fright. Father's only purpose in dragging me there was to find a match. For the first time, however, I understood his concern. I hadn't been able to get Mrs. Griffith and the others out of my mind. I couldn't imagine how she felt—ripped from her lavish chalet on the Sound, told her fortune was gone. She wasn't young. She couldn't start again or claw her way out of poverty. She wasn't likely to find another man of means to support her.

We stepped onto the street and into the full glory of gold evening light. Horse carriages idled in the narrow pedestrian walkway and a restaurant sign loomed over them. The smell of some sort of gravy momentarily overtook the offensive odor of burning coal.

I followed Father through the crowded path, past the carriages, to where the streets opened on Third Avenue. Here, the hint of red sunset was extinguished by the overhead rail tracks stretching over almost the entirety of the road six stories high. I pitied the people who lived below them as if trapped in a perpetual desert night. No rain or snow could fall directly on the street below, which would explain the expectation that one might be swallowed in the heavy layer of dirt atop the cobblestone street.

"This way, it appears," Father said. We followed the channel of limestones and brownstones boasting ornaments of folded metal stairs to a stationary set of steps leading to a steel platform. A slight man with an impressively bushy mustache stood in a small shack that had originally been constructed of a light wood—oak or maple, most likely—but was now tarnished nearly black. When he saw us, he lifted the small windowpane.

"Two tickets to Fifth Avenue and Sixty-Seventh Street, please," Father said.

"There is no such train that will get you there, sir," the man said. He eyed my father's hatter's plush silk top hat and tuxedo jacket with satin lapels and then turned his gaze to me.

"Your peers on the park are not fond of the elevated train and its effects. I'm sorry to tell you that you'll need to go back to the depot and procure a carriage unless you'd like to ride this rail down to the Third Avenue and Fifty-Ninth station, where you would then need to secure a carriage up to Fifth and down to Sixty-Seventh."

"We'll do just that," Father said cheerily. The ticket man seemed taken aback by his joy. I had no doubt that a ride on the elevated train wasn't the thrill Father was anticipating.

"Very well. Two tickets will cost you five cents at this hour." He withdrew a pocket watch and clicked it open. "The next train headed north will arrive in three minutes and depart in five. Miss, I advise you to stand behind my booth here until it arrives. Otherwise your white gown will be made into gray."

"Surely not in the instance of a moment," I said as Father handed him a nickel for our fare.

His eyebrows rose.

"Have you ever been doused with a pail of water?" he asked.

I nodded. "Unfortunately, yes. It was entirely by accident though, and—"

"The smoke is as dense and as quick to shower as the water," he said. "Good evening."

And with that he closed the window. Father and I moved to stand next to the booth.

"You must admit this is an impressive venture," Father said. "When I lived here, it took over three hours to transport anything from the peninsula to the depot. Now you can zip about anywhere without trouble. Much has improved." He pinched the edges of his mustache and twisted to form the upward curl so many men were fond of these days. I did not prefer it whatsoever. Keeping the pomade tacky through the day was impossible, and the inevitable drooping of the mustache's wisps was unfortunate indeed.

"I wonder how often Mr. and Mrs. Gould find themselves zipping to and fro on this project they're so proud of," I said. Mrs. Gould, and every other lady like her, barely lifted a water glass to her lips on her own. I doubted the Goulds would make the effort to refuse their brougham carriages in order to climb the dirty stairs to reach the trains.

"Likely little, if ever, but George's pride in the rail has to do with his father's influence on the city and its improvements— and it *is* much improved," Father said. Perhaps it was only Father's station that had improved. Upon his entrance to this country, he wouldn't have occupied the Goulds' carriage house as a stablehand, let alone been permitted to enter their drawing rooms.

"Here comes the gilded transport now," I said, moving behind the booth with Father. Even from a distance the clanging and screeching and whistling of the train was so loud it rattled my ears. Steam plumed in a robust black cloud from the smokestack of a regular steel engine pulling three cars.

The train came to a halt and as the doors were hauled open, people poured out quickly and scattered down the stairs.

"Let's go before we're left," Father said, taking my hand. He gave our tickets to the conductor and stepped inside. The car was unimpressive to say the least, boasting only five rows of thin metal chairs and windows, nothing more. We sat in the first two seats.

"I don't suppose you'll be telling Gould he should sell his carriages," I said.

Father laughed under his breath.

"No, but this is not about luxury, Sadie. This is about transport."

A disheveled man in patched denim dungarees came aboard, followed by more of the same. A few women joined them in the same sort of unkempt dress. The smell of acrid sweat and soiled linen arrested the air.

Another train stopped on our other side and I waved at the passengers through the window, wondering if they, too, would have given anything to submerge their noses into hyacinth blossoms.

The last call was shouted, and a final passenger was deposited into our car. Half of his face was blistered red and his right eye was swollen shut.

"What happened to you, Boyd?" one of the women breathed with a heavy Irish lilt, her shock palpable.

"We was asked to mix the varnish, but it wasn't mixed proper and splashed me," he said. He shrugged and took a seat behind us. Nothing else was said.

At once I was embarrassed for my elaborate ball gown. It

marked me as a woman of luxury among people who had not a mite of it.

Father kept his gaze fixed out the window.

"The tired eyes," he muttered. "I remember them well."

I looked around the car at these people. It was no surprise there hadn't been more conversation about the state of this Boyd. No one had the energy to speak.

The train lurched forward and in an instant we were whipping around buildings at nearly twenty miles per hour.

"This isn't right," Father said under his breath after a few moments. The stone townhomes and stately limestone businesses had given way to broken windows and laundry flapping from windowsills. The buildings were closer and closer together and the wash of sunset that had been present only minutes ago was now completely absent. I looked up at what I could see of the sky but found only a towering brick smokestack streaming black smoke twice as heavy as that of the train.

"Where are we?" I whispered.

"We must have boarded the wrong train," he said. "That's Hobbs's wallpaper factory there—the one that caught fire last year. Do you recall reading about it?"

I nodded and swallowed hard. People had died in that fire. Seventy families had been made homeless because of the flames' spread.

"Over there, closer to the river, are the Young Molding Factory and Mill Factory and Gigham's Shoes," Father whispered. "When I first arrived, I stayed with a family in a tenement there. I shall never go back."

The train's brakes screeched and the whistle blew, and we came to a halt.

Our fellow passengers, who had spoken not another word the entire ride, filed out in silence. We waited until the last had gone before disembarking. The platform here in the lower part of the city was thick with filth.

"Let me go speak to the ticket man. Stay here," Father said.

I nodded and walked over to the railing overlooking the street. Down below, the unpaved road was crowded, in part because it seemed that many families had claimed a space to live on the sides, narrowing the thoroughfare. The aisle for commerce was riddled with manure and garbage and the stench of it permeated the dense, gray air. Overhead, linens clipped to lines affixed from one building to another barely moved. A stagnancy permeated the air as though a breeze simply couldn't fight its way through the concentration of ash and smoke.

Sam had lived here. If not here exactly, somewhere just like it. The thought of him toiling in a place like this made my soul wither and my eyes water. He'd said he was glad I hadn't been with him, that I wouldn't have survived. Despite desperately wishing I could have prevented his coming here in the first place, my horror at the sight of it meant he was right. I would have expired one way or another and pulled him down with me.

Suddenly it was hard to breathe. I looked over the people lying in filth on the streets, their hands empty, their eyes tired. In the alley a family was huddled inside a discarded piano box. Sam hadn't been exaggerating. There was no hope here. There was no green, no chance that a flower could spring forth from the earth. The sort of existence found here matched the atmosphere.

"I have our tickets," Father said as he climbed the stairs toward me. "The next train, the right train, will be bound for the park. I asked twice to be sure." He dug in his pocket and handed me a silk handkerchief imported from Austria. "Cover your mouth or your throat will be raw for days."

He extracted a second handkerchief and covered his own mouth. I didn't move to cover mine. It didn't seem right, protecting myself, when in a matter of minutes I would be able to breathe again. The thought that I would soon be whisked away from this place filled me with both relief and guilt.

"I'm sorry. I never intended for you to see this," Father said through the handkerchief.

A woman walked past carrying two babies. I tapped her arm.

"Please take this," I said, holding out the handkerchief. "For your children. You can put it over their mouths."

She laughed and shook her head. "They won't abide something like that," she said. "They'll grow strong lungs that will withstand it. They have no choice."

I watched her walk away. She had no way out. She knew she'd live here her whole life, that her children would grow up here. I wanted to stand on the platform and scream that only thirty miles away were green fields and clean air, that they could leave—but for what? As the rest of the country seemed to collapse, at least there were jobs here.

"Mr. Jenkins told me he was living here," I said. My voice sounded weak. I felt it, too, as though at any moment my knees could buckle. I gripped the rail in front of me.

"Yes," Father said. "Poor boy. I do hope he'll be able to forget it someday."

"Have you?" I asked. Father had been gone from the city

for thirty years, and there were still occasions that triggered his memories.

"No," he said. "But the memories have mostly faded like a nightmare. I don't know if it will be the same for Mr. Jenkins, though. He didn't tell me the particulars of his life here, only that he'd lived in the tenements for some time and decided to leave after losing someone—to calamity or disease he didn't say. I suppose that bit makes our experiences rather different. I didn't lose anyone."

Half an hour later we were riding along Fifth Avenue in a rented carriage among the shadows of imported brick and limestone and wrought iron, passing William Henry Vanderbilt's Italian Renaissance Triple Palace followed by William and Alva Vanderbilt's Petit Chateau and then Cornelius Vanderbilt's brick-and-limestone palace. The streetlights glittered gold light on the wide, clean street, and out the other window stretched Central Park. Even in the dark I could see the cherry blossoms. The smell of fresh grass and flowers permeated the air.

Despite our escape from the filth and grime, the knowledge that thousands of people breathed under ash-ridden skies, walked in excrement, and lived with ten in a one-bedroom flat broke my heart. Father's comment about Sam losing someone in the midst of it made my mind race. Who had he lost and how?

"Those people near the factories should have access to this sort of beauty. Everyone should," I said to Father. I gestured out the window at the wide walkway beside the park. "Think of what a balm it would be to their souls. Even near us, Father, people are living in squalor without a single flower to cheer them."

"I agree, but some are satisfied with factory life, Lily," he said.

As we continued down the street, the Vanderbilt bit of the neighborhood was replaced by the Astors', their demure brownstone meant to signify that they didn't need to prove their place in New York City. Descended from the first settlers, they *were* New York City.

"I hardly think that's true," I said. "Who would possibly choose that life?"

Father shrugged and ran his hand along the gold-plated window trimming.

"The moment I arrived here, I knew I had to leave or I'd die. I met your mother and she felt the same. I didn't know any English, but I learned it, and when I saw the call for planters for Vaux, I went after that post as diligently as I could," he said. "Even when they told me they'd filled their quota, I kept coming back to the office until they tired of me and gave me employment. Anyone can get out, but they must hate it enough to make escaping an obsession. They must never accept that life."

"Suppose Vaux hadn't hired you. Suppose you'd worked in the factories for years, hardly seeing the sun, never seeing green grass or blue sky. Wouldn't it deplete you? Wouldn't you begin to think of everything as hopeless? Perhaps the miracle of a few flowers would extend hope. If a tulip can emerge from a dead bulb, these people, too, can keep on," I said. It was clear to me that despair was the true disease, that though cholera and dysentery ravaged the body, despair ravaged the mind.

"Of course you know how much I believe in the therapy of nature, and perhaps you're right. But I wouldn't have allowed my attentions to fixate on despair. I would have pressed on until I got out," Father said. "In regard to men in general, there aren't many eager to better themselves. How many of our workers do you suppose have asked to apprentice under me?"

"I don't know, but I imagine it can't be many. When Freddie and Charles were still here, their training occupied most of your time." I didn't bother to remind him that I, too, had been there for all of it.

"That's not an excuse. I have always encouraged them to come to me. There has only ever been one," Father said. "Sam Jenkins. And then he ran off for some reason and abandoned his post before obtaining the knowledge." Father shook his head.

I knew of Sam's intelligence and his interest, but I never knew he'd asked to apprentice under Father.

"Perhaps our workers are simply happy working with the plants in the capacity they already are," I said. "Even so, no matter what someone does, don't you feel that fresh air and flowers are a basic human right?"

Father sighed.

"Everything costs something, Lily. Flowers included. Someone has to pay for them."

I didn't know how to respond. I knew the truth of his words, and yet the vision of the tenements just five miles south of these lavish mansions, the memory of the settlement next to the railroad tracks only a mile and a half from the nurseries, the idea of an old woman ripped from her home and placed in a drafty room made for her store's storage, made me feel ill. It was true that hard work should award much, but at the same time, no human being should be subjected to the sorts of living conditions I'd seen.

The carriage slowed. Up ahead other coaches idled for nearly a block. Mrs. Gould's birthday party was always well attended, in part because of the wildlife. Four years ago Mr. Gould ordered ten thousand Brazilian butterflies released in her honor. Three years ago they set several swans afloat in the reflecting pond, and two years ago they'd hired a monkey to roam about the party in a tuxedo.

"I read in the papers that the Honorable Lionel Reynolds will be in attendance tonight," Father said. "I met him a few months ago at the Whitneys'. Rumor is that he's come back to New York looking for a match. He's quite taken with horticulture and told me when we last spoke that he grew his first garden at the age of five."

He paused. "You know, Brundage is on business in the South and won't be in attendance this evening. And Bishop is occupied in the country, so there would be no damage to your other prospects if you were to connect with Mr. Reynolds."

I ignored him. Of course he'd waited until I was already in the city to tell me he'd insisted I come to this party to meet another potential match.

"Word has it Reynolds is interested in purchasing the Mitfords' Exbury House in Hampshire for his new bride," Father continued. "It's one of their family homes that has fallen into the hands of his father's cousins."

"I'm not moving to England," I snapped. "It rains a great deal."

Father straightened and fidgeted with his silver filigree cuff links. He always did things like this when he was angry. I supposed it was to stop himself from punching the coach door or screaming.

"Every time we discuss our situation, I am hopeful that you

will take it to heart," he said. "I cannot make you. Still, I wish I could. I beg you to consider it."

"I will consider it," I said, primarily to make peace. I had no interest in anyone who would take me away from my home prematurely. Despite Father's assurance otherwise, I had every confidence that if I continued to win new accounts and plan beautiful gardens and assist our employees with the daily needs of the nurseries, he would eventually see my capability.

Our carriage lurched forward and stopped in front of the Goulds' entrance. The neo-Gothic mansion was a cacophony of gables and balustrades, the corner of the estate punctuated by a turret wrapped with stone balconies and finished with a conical roof.

The carriage door clicked open and a footman dressed in black silk held his hand out for me.

"Good evening, Miss Fremd," he said. I wondered how he knew who I was. Perhaps Mrs. Gould had given him cards to study. I'd heard of the Astors doing such things. "Mr. Fremd," the footman said. "Do make haste to the drawing room on your way up to the rooftop. Mrs. Gould has called on the cast of *La Basoche* to perform a few songs from the opéra comique. It is quite lovely."

Mrs. Gould was an actress herself, something she had continually mentioned throughout her marriage, despite some of the older set seeing the profession as beneath a proper woman of society.

I looped my gloved hand through Father's and started up the steps.

"I'm glad this is an evening affair," Father whispered. "Your dress has a bit of ash on it, but nothing noticeable in the dim."

"I don't mind if they do notice. Surely some of these folks go below Twentieth Street from time to time."

"I doubt it," he said. We made our way into the entry hall and across the Oriental rug toward the drawing room. Father tipped his head at a few women lingering under Corinthian pillars on the side of the hall that separated the main thoroughfare from a sort of palm court. Two large crystal chandeliers glistened overhead, casting a bit of light on Wedgwood urns held by ceramic scrolled planters along the walls.

We turned the corner and ran smack into a crowd gathered in the drawing room listening to the opera singers. Their vibrato echoed through the cavernous home as we bypassed them and made our way up the limestone steps to the second floor and then the third. The entrance to the rooftop garden was through the third-floor drawing room, and as we neared, the low roar of guests' laughter and chatter overtook the songs from below.

"Say, glad you made it, Charlie." Mr. Gould was standing right outside the door with his wife beside him.

"We just had occasion to ride your father's elevated train," Father said, and Mr. Gould smiled.

"Finally. And your thoughts?"

"It is swift indeed and quite a ride through the sky. A great asset to the city," Father said.

"Indeed. Indeed. Did you spot anything that could be improved?" Mr. Gould asked.

I turned my attention to Mrs. Gould while Father and Mr. Gould discussed the train.

"Lovely to see you again, Mrs. Gould. Happy birthday. Thank you for having us." I extended my hand to her. She looked lovely in a pretty costume of finely figured challis. The skirt was a bell silhouette with a full flounce of lace around the bottom caught with bowknots of challis.

"Thank you for being here, dear," she said. "I've been telling all of you young debutantes to make sure to marry a man who will throw you a bash as wonderful as mine every year."

"I'm simply glad to be invited to yours."

She pulled me close. "Do go over and meet my friend Lionel Reynolds," she whispered. "He's over by the end of the reflecting pool if he hasn't moved since I saw him last. He's quite taken by my little garden, and when I told him the family who designed it would be here, he positively lit up. He adores your father. And I must mention, he's a bachelor and quite handsome."

"I shall introduce myself," I said. "Heaven knows I can discuss plants all night."

Mrs. Gould's nose scrunched as she likely thought my plant obsession was the reason I wasn't yet married. No one found the topic of horticulture a subject for wooing a man. Art, certainly. Music, acceptable. But the science of growing things was too technical for the brain of a proper woman.

"Make sure to snatch a cobbler from one of the trays on the way. I've ordered two varieties—one with fresh peaches and the other with rose blossoms. You've never tasted anything so refreshing," she said, releasing me. "Lionel will be the one with the dreadful sash about his waist. He's English and apparently it is quite the fashion over there."

Father and I walked away from the Goulds at the same time and made our way into the crush. The place looked like Eden. Our rhododendrons were all in bloom along the sides of the enormous rooftop, and the grass along the path was clipped short. We'd installed a walkway beside the reflecting pool, which boasted pink blooming water lilies.

"I'm going to speak with Mr. Depew over there. We had quite a lovely political discussion last time and I'd like to resume it," Father said.

"I'll collect you in a bit," I replied.

I wandered past groups of strangers and acquaintances in cashmere and challis and silk. I knew who most of them were, the usual characters—the Webbs, the Coopers, the Kountzes, the Goelets, the Wilsons, the Astors—all people I'd met but whom I'd never truly befriended. They were the city set and I was only in the city once or twice a year. Even so, I'd have to say hello later, if only to make sure they knew our nurseries were behind this magnificence. The design had been Charles's idea, a masterpiece.

I picked up a crystal flute from a waiter standing at the mid-way point of the pool and took a sip. It was wonderful, fine sparkling wine with fresh crushed peach. As much as I didn't want to introduce myself to Mr. Reynolds, the introduction was inevitable. The faster I conversed with him, the faster I'd appease my father and be back home.

I passed a lone violinist playing Mozart and found Mr. Reynolds exactly where Mrs. Gould said I would. He was standing alone at the end of the reflecting pool, looking over the wrought iron balcony to the view of the Astors' and other mansions beyond.

"Good evening," I said.

He whirled around, looking a bit flustered, but quickly composed himself and smiled.

"Good evening to you," he said. Then he cleared his throat. "Lionel Reynolds." He took my hand and kissed it. "And you are?"

"Sadie Fremd."

"Ah, the famous Charlie Fremd's daughter. What a work of genius this is," he said, sweeping his hand across the garden. The man himself fit in well. He was handsome, fair with brown eyes and cognac hair. "Rhododendrons are my favorite."

"I can't take much credit for it, save the cultivation of the new variety, Arisaema candidissimum, the pure white in the back of the rows," I said. "My brother Charles designed the garden, and the rest of the varieties, from Abraham Lincoln to Jasminum grandiflorum, are grown at our nurseries in Westchester, just north of the city."

"I'm quite impressed you're so versed in horticulture, Miss Fremd," he said. "I've heard from both your father and others in the city that your nurseries are the largest in this part of the country and boast the most complete variety. Is your brother Charles here as well? I'd love to compliment him on the design."

"I'm afraid he's not. He's in Florida designing gardens for Mr. Flagler's Royal Poinciana Hotel. My father is here, however. He said he quite enjoyed speaking with you at the Whitneys'."

Mr. Reynolds smiled. His teeth were impeccable.

"Speaking with him was the highlight of my night. My family is, unfortunately, in the business of banking and I have no interest in it myself. It was quite refreshing to see a man who'd made a fortune doing the very thing my heart loves."

"I can't imagine doing anything else." I waited for him to balk at my participation, but he didn't. "I escape to the nurseries nearly every day. It is something remarkable to watch little seeds turn to such beauty."

"Indeed. I find it similarly remarkable that those seeds are ultimately able to turn a bland green space into a lush, flowering masterpiece." He paused. "This may seem quite forward, Miss Fremd, but another thing of beauty is watching your face come alive when you speak of the nurseries."

Behind us, it seemed the opera singers had relocated to the rooftop along with their orchestra and were now singing selections from *La Basoche*.

Mr. Reynolds reached for my hand. Perhaps it was the way he accepted my passion, but I didn't withdraw. Instead, I clutched his in turn. He looked over my shoulder.

"Dance with me?" he asked.

"Of course," I said.

He led me onto the verdant walkway next to the reflecting pond, joining a dozen others. His hand held my waist and I let my fingers dance on his shoulder.

"I can hardly believe I'm dancing with the most beautiful woman in the most beautiful place," he whispered in my ear as we turned. "I must admit that when I heard you might be in attendance tonight, I hoped you would be amiable. I had no idea you would be like . . . like this."

"What do you want from life, Mr. Reynolds?" I asked, ignoring his compliment. "What are your dreams?"

His eyes met mine.

"For as long as I can recall, my father has wanted me to help run the bank, but the truth is, the bank is not in a good way. It used to hold the funds of nearly the whole town but currently handles only our family money and that of a few others." He shrugged. "Anyway, the situation is good for me. I have an older brother who can handle Father's dealings without me, and I have every confidence I could break free of the bank if something else came along, something I'm passionate about."

"You're in the same position as my brother Freddie. He wanted nothing to do with the nursery business, so Father released him to explore politics."

Over his shoulder I could see Father still conversing with Mr. Depew, though his attention was entirely fixed on us.

"What of your brother Charles? Do you suppose he'll return to succeed your father?" Mr. Reynolds asked.

"No. At first I thought he would, but now I think he'll continue landscaping public spaces for people like Mr. Flagler. He doesn't particularly desire to stay in one place and enjoys the design element most. I believe he'll focus on the adventure of that and abandon the growing part."

"I see," he said. I thought of telling him about my intentions, but what did it matter if he knew them?

"Do you suppose you would want to start a nursery in England?" I asked. "Father started ours from nothing. I'm sure he'd be happy to explain how he began."

"I occupied him for the entire evening at the Whitneys' asking questions," he said. "I think he's designed the business rather effectively, although hiring so many men—some merely for the sake of charity—is honestly troubling to me. It's preventing true prosperity."

At once, any sort of enchantment I'd felt toward Mr. Reynolds was dashed.

"What do you suppose constitutes affluence?" I snapped, the memory of the rail village, of the slums fresh in my mind. I knew now how much I'd needed to see them, that before, I'd rarely thought of those outside of our circle. Though I still knew so little, the singular sight of families living in filth was enough to alter my perception forever. Opulence won by trampling the needy wasn't affluence; it was greed. Then again, so many of the fortunes dancing around us had been won this exact way. That was why the tenements were full and railroad slum towns existed.

Mr. Reynolds shrugged and spun me around, nonplussed by my tone. When I whirled back to face him, he drew me closer.

"For instance, if your father's business was mine, I'd let go of the dozens he says aren't essential. I'd utilize the excess funds to buy more seeds, to grow the nurseries larger. Within a few years' time, I'd groom the business to function on its own, perhaps even open additional locations convenient to the country's growth, and I would travel the world hunting exotic plants, finding seeds for growth and experimentation that I could bring home. The Himalayas are rich with rare breeds, I've heard." He let go of my hand, his other still steady on my waist, and touched my cheek. "Would you want to go with me?"

I stepped back. His response wasn't one of spontaneity. It was too specific. His earlier ignorance about my brothers and our business must have been feigned. At once it was clear— Father and the Goulds were conspiring to make us a match. Mr. Gould conversed with Father at least once each week about his gardens—both in the city and at his sister's at Lyndhurst— and he must have decided Mr. Reynolds would be a good match for me, a good replacement for Father. That was why Mrs. Gould had encouraged me to speak to him.

"I'm afraid I would not," I said. "I enjoy being home."

Mr. Reynolds's countenance hardened a fraction, but he grinned anyway.

"Perhaps both could be had," he said. "We could stay home in your town for some of the year and travel the other months."

"I apologize. I suppose I'm a bit confused. Excuse me," I said. In a matter of minutes he'd gone from speaking of vague scenarios to speaking specifically of our marriage and running our nurseries.

I walked away from him and toward the unoccupied bit of rooftop overlooking the city where we'd been before. I didn't want Father asking me about him, or Mrs. Gould either. My blood felt like it was boiling. Mr. Reynolds was presumptuous at best. So were Father and the Goulds.

I inhaled a breath of the air filled with the lily scent of blooming rhododendrons in an attempt to calm myself. I clutched the wrought iron railing and took in the scene below me. Some loved the panorama of endless buildings. It only made me feel claustrophobic. I wondered how those in the tenements felt, how Sam had felt. The constant sensation of bodies pressed to mine would drive me to madness. I palmed my heart, feeling it tighten.

"Miss Fremd, I didn't intend to upset you." Mr. Reynolds joined me. "But if I'm honest, I came to New York looking for a wife . . . and I've heard that you're looking for a husband. I'm due to go home in a week's time unless I make a match. We share so many similarities and I'm not interested in going home to the bank. With your brothers gone, your father will surely need a successor, and it would be my honor to be the next operator—with you at my side."

I wanted to scream. I didn't want him—or anyone else for that matter—taking the place *I* wanted at the helm of Rye Nurseries. I closed my eyes and tried to ignore him.

"Miss Fremd," Mr. Reynolds said, his hand covering the back of mine.

I opened my eyes and turned to face him, the truth of my intentions on the tip of my tongue.

"Marry me," he said before I could say anything at all. "I know I've known you for less than an hour's time, but I'll never find another woman like you, a woman who makes my heart skip and shares my interests. If I let you slip away, I'll regret it forever."

I flinched and pulled my hand from his. The vision of Sam on his knee holding a fistful of my favorite oakleaf hydrangeas flashed through my mind. I had barely let him finish his proposal before I said yes, before I threw myself into his arms and kissed him. We'd been in the planting fields in the moonlight, the place we first worked side by side digging dozens of hydrangeas for summer gardens. I could still smell his body, all earth and sun-kissed linen, and feel the way his mouth danced on mine.

"Mr. Reynolds, you're seeking a way out from under your family's thumb," I said, forcing the memory away. "It's only the nurseries you really want, not me. In any case I'm afraid you've misunderstood. My brothers might be elsewhere, but I'm still here. *I* will be my father's successor, Mr. Reynolds. Not you or anyone else."

He stared at me as though he thought I belonged in a madhouse, and then he laughed.

"In that case your nurseries will fail, just like the rest of the little businesses in your town," he said. "It's inevitable. It isn't proper for a woman to run a business, especially not an enterprise the size of your nurseries. No respectable man of industry would engage with a businesswoman voluntarily. Your father made no mention of your succeeding him when we last spoke. It would not surprise me at all if he will not stand for it. You're making a mistake by refusing me. I would allow you to work in the greenhouses. And I would love you. You would grow to love me. I know it. The way you felt in my arms, the way you leaned into me, I—" He reached for my face, but I backed away.

"No," I breathed. "For a moment I may have thought you handsome. For a moment I may have thought that you understood me, but you don't. You would take our nurseries from me; you would make them something I don't want or recognize. You would fire our employees for the sake of your own wallet. If you're capable of those things, I could never love you."

"No one with any sort of name or fortune will concede to marry a woman with such improper aspirations—aspirations that seek to trump his," he said, his voice a hiss. "Mark my words. If you ever find yourself in control of the business, you will fail. You will end up alone in a tiny, filthy flat somewhere remembering that at one time things could have been different. You could have had it all. It is much more bearable to start with nothing and end with nothing than it is to have everything and lose it."

At once I thought of Mrs. Griffith alone in her small apartment, her store, her home, her husband all vanished, and the faces of her employees too. Perhaps I was being selfish refusing marriage, risking the future of the nurseries on the belief that I could handle them. What if he was right? What if I would fail and our employees with me?

"Marry me, Miss Fremd," he said again, his face transformed from anger to pleading in a blink. "This is the last time I'll ask."

I stared at him, trying to imagine waking up to his face for the rest of my life, the face of a stranger. I could not. He had made me doubt myself, my proficiency. It wasn't as if Father would leave me alone to figure out the particulars if he conceded. Father would train me to take care of the nurseries like he did—most things I already knew how to do anyway. Mr. Reynolds was wrong. My leadership would be a success.

"Why don't you ask Miss Barbey?" I said, nodding over his shoulder to Ethel, standing next to her mother who was obviously surveying the party for a suitor. "She has a great fortune that will need managing, and it's rumored she enjoys watering her plants in her free time. Good night, Mr. Reynolds."

I wandered toward Father, my heart pumping fast.

"This will be your life's regret," Mr. Reynolds called over the music.

The doubt in the back of my mind said he was right, but my heart said refusing him was the smartest decision I'd ever made.

CHAPTER 7

The rancid odor of rotten meat stung my nostrils and, if I accidentally breathed too deeply, made me heave with nausea. Even Gene, typically a quiet horse, snorted and tried to back away from the iron hitching post at the corner of the street.

Mrs. Griffith's new living quarters were in the middle of town, down the alley from the meat market. The ground-level flat looked out on garbage—decaying carcasses from the market, piles of cartons, hangers, and broken furniture discarded from the department store's cleaning out by the bank—that wouldn't be disposed of until the garbage cart came around in four days.

I forced a small spade into the packed earth in front of the windows, thankful a bit of light from the nearly full moon evaded the shadow of the building beside so I could see. There wasn't much room to plant anything like we'd done for the man by the tracks, which ultimately was a good thing. Everyone knew Mrs. Griffith's favorite spring flowers were tulips—she'd ordered hundreds to be planted in big marble urns outside of the store— and I'd been able to transport a dozen of them in a small sack without having to hook up a cart. Even after watching Sam and Vincenzo the last time, I hadn't a clue how to do it myself.

I leaned down, clearing the dirt from the hole I'd just dug, realizing as I did that the hem of my white gown that I'd somehow kept mostly clean, save a bit of ash, on the elevated rail was now almost completely black with soil and soot. Father had been furious at my refusing Mr. Reynolds's hand. So angry, in fact, that he hadn't spoken to me the entire rail ride home. The man had been a solution to both of Father's problems—the need for a successor and my need for a husband—and I'd ruined it. I knew refusing proposal after proposal didn't endear me or my aspirations to him, but granting his request was impossible. It would mean my forever separation from the nurseries and from Sam. Instead of attempting to explain away Father's disappointment, I'd allowed the silence and turned my attention to Mrs. Griffith and the little garden I knew I had to plant for her immediately.

I dug another hole and cleared it. What would Mr. Reynolds have thought about his betrothed doing such a thing? He would probably gasp in horror and give me a lecture on appropriate charitable activities for a woman. He was ridiculous, nothing like my father. Then again, I wasn't broadcasting my traipsing around town under cover of night to my father either. I told myself it was because he'd think the hour of the night improper, but then again, there was a reason I hadn't asked him if I could take the flowers. Deep down, perhaps I expected him to respond like Mr. Reynolds.

I set the purple tulip in the first little ditch. My hand stilled on the mound of earth I was about to push over the roots, and at once I was six years old and it was Easter. The weather had been cold that year, the icy wind whipping over the hill and through the tall tombstones in the cemetery across from the nurseries. My aunt Jessie had just passed away, and while Father was busy delivering Easter lilies, Charles, Freddie, and I had joined Mother in front of her sister's grave.

Each of us held a tulip. Mother had chosen the colors. I could still see her face—wide eyes like Freddie's that always seemed a bit concerned, narrow nose and matching chin like mine, and thin lips that turned up at the edges like Charles's. Thinking of the similarities now, I was comforted knowing each of us inherited a small piece of her.

She'd pointed to me first that Easter Sunday.

"The purple will go right here in front," she'd said. When I knelt to dig the hole, she'd placed a hand on my back. *"To remind us that the Lord is King."*

I pushed the dirt over the roots and dug another hole, placing the second purple tulip for Mrs. Griffith beside the first.

"Red next, Freddie," I remembered Mother saying. Freddie had worn a new gingham suit for the service and hesitated to kneel on the dew-soaked grass. *"For the blood of our Savior."*

I reached behind me for the red lily I'd brought and planted it next. I didn't know if Mrs. Griffith would know the reason for the order—the succession of colors had been used symbolically for generations in my mother's family on the Isle of Mann—but even if Mrs. Griffith wouldn't, the progression still looked lovely.

"White now, Charles. How special to plant it today on Easter. It represents forgiveness, our salvation." I could hear Mother's tone. She'd always spoken softly, kindly. I wasn't gentle like her.

"And last, the yellow." She'd squatted then and placed her hand on her sister's name etched into the headstone before she put the last tulip in the ground. *"For eternal life in heaven. See*

you soon, dearest." She'd whispered the last words. Little had she known that "soon" would come only twelve years later. I was only eighteen.

Sam's father had done a beautiful job landscaping the cemetery the year Mother died, and in the wash of June flowers, I had almost been able to ignore the tombstones. I never fared well when confronted with grief or heartache. I didn't quite know what to do with it. In a way I was scared of the way it made me feel. So I did my best to push it down, to busy myself with various tasks to help myself feel happy, to make others feel happy.

I finished planting the last of the lilies, then stood and dusted my hands on my skirt. At least Mrs. Griffith would see something out her window other than decay—a metaphor I was certain she'd associated with her life. Perhaps now she would see hope, beauty sprung from a bulb that was once dead.

Gene stamped when I walked toward him and the flies buzzed noisily as I passed. I held my breath as I looped Gene's reins back over his head, then mounted and settled myself on the saddle. I thought about the ease with which Father or Sam or any of the other men swung across a horse's back, not worrying about a swathe of skirts. Father would argue that I needed to wear my habit each time I rode, but who had time to change in the moment?

"Come on, sweet one," I said to Gene before depositing my small shovel in the saddle bag.

We trotted through town toward Central Avenue. The streetlamps had all been extinguished hours ago, and with so many storefronts boarded up, it felt eerily like riding through one of those abandoned Western towns I'd read about in the papers. When we turned on Central, I urged Gene to a canter. We passed

Margaret's house and ten others like it, their iron gates scowling at the road, at any intruders who dared attempt entrance.

By the time we reached our drive, Gene's breath was labored and his coat was slick with dew. I slowed him to a walk, then leaned all the way back against him as we made our way under the tree-lined drive toward the barn. The new leaves were barely in this time of year, and the starry sky shining through the gnarled branches gave the illusion of a thousand blinking fireflies.

I righted when the trees dropped away but remained along the perimeter in the shadows in case Father happened to be glancing out his window in the middle of the night. When I reached the barn, the door I was certain I'd left open was shut. I dismounted and started to lead Gene inside when Sam called to me. He was in the field of roses, just down the hill, and started toward me.

My heart quickened. Even though I'd found Mr. Reynolds handsome, he didn't affect me the way Sam did. Everything about Sam made me yearn for him—for his touch, his love.

"Don't you suppose you should tell someone before you go riding off into the night?" he asked when he reached me.

"We live in Rye," I said. Nothing untoward ever happened in our town. "Not in the city and—"

"I'm aware," he said, taking Gene's reins from me. I hadn't intended to bring up the city, even though Father's words on the elevated train platform had haunted me all evening.

I touched Sam's hand.

"Wait. Father and I got turned around in the city this evening. He insisted on riding the Goulds' elevated train and we ended up among the factories and tenements."

Sam was looking down, his gaze fixed on his worn leather boots.

"I saw a family sleeping in a piano box, Sam, and the filth and the manure—the ash, it—"

I couldn't finish. What I'd seen flashed in front of me like a picture postcard. Before I could stop myself, I stepped closer to him and touched his cheek. His beard was soft under my fingers, not the rough feeling I remembered. Still, he kept his face turned away from me.

"I can't bear knowing you lived there, that anyone lives there," I said.

He looked at me then, his eyes filled with melancholy, and he gently removed my hand from his cheek.

"But you must. I *was* there," he said finally. "As I told you before, I'm glad for it, Sadie."

Gene pulled at the reins and Sam walked him toward the barn.

"When we were there, standing on the platform, Father said something. He said you'd lost—"

"I don't wish to discuss it," Sam said. I watched his free hand fist and immediately wished I could take it back.

"I'm sorry. It's only that I saw what you meant. There is no green there, not a speck of it. Yet Fifth Avenue looks like Eden."

Sam looked at me and appraised my dress then, his eyes drifting over my body, over the lace and silk and pearls. I wondered if he still found me beautiful, if he still wanted to hold me the way he used to.

"Speaking of Fifth Avenue, are you engaged?" The question shocked me. "To that Prince Reynolds your father's been speaking of for the past week?"

"The past *week*?" My response was uttered so softly he didn't seem to hear it. It was infuriating to realize Father had been speaking of my possible match with Mr. Reynolds to others for days, while I had been intentionally left unaware. I wondered if Father knew of Mr. Reynolds's specific aspirations with our nurseries—that he would let our employees go without a thought to their well-being so he could expand. I had to doubt it. In any case, the idea that Mr. Reynolds could swoop in and override me was preposterous. The idea that we would leave and travel the world without any sort of hand in the day-to-day business was asinine.

Sam and I stared at each other. So much remained unsaid between us, so much we refused to say, and suddenly, his question about whether or not I'd accepted Mr. Reynolds was irrelevant. It was about why I hadn't chosen us.

"I didn't want to leave," I said, my voice breaking. "I know I already told you this, but it bears saying again—I should have said something before, when I had the chance, but I suppose I didn't quite know how much I wanted an excuse to stay until I was about to leave."

I knew well that Sam would think what I'd said had to do with Mr. Reynolds, but it didn't. I wondered how long I would feel compelled to explain my abandonment each time I spoke to him. I'd made it clear the last time we spoke, and he wasn't asking for it now.

"I know," he said.

"I didn't want to leave the nurseries. Not because of the house or the niceties, but because plants are my heart. As much as you had it, so do the flowers." I felt choked and cleared my throat.

"I *had* it," he whispered, then shook his head. "And this prince of yours. He wants to settle here, to run this place? That is what you want, isn't it?"

"I told you. *I* will be running it." I tipped my head up and squared my shoulders reflexively.

"He'll never allow that," Sam said.

"He'll have no say. I refused him," I said, suddenly realizing I had yet to answer Sam's question. He stepped toward me. At once I thought he might embrace me, but he stopped. "And he is not a prince. He's an English banker who would like a way out of his family's business by way of our nurseries. He spent the first part of the evening telling me how beautiful I was and the second part telling me he would let all of our excess employees go and build the nurseries so large with the additional finances that we would stop running them altogether and travel the world."

Sam said nothing.

"Our employees are our family, and I don't want to hike the Himalayas," I said. "I just want to be about the business of flowers. They make people happy."

"If you can afford them," Sam said.

"I mean to change that. I saw the hopelessness the other day at the rail village and again today at the tenements and just a moment ago at Mrs. Griffith's place swarming with flies. I know I should have been aware of the need years ago, but I cannot alter the past. Now I know. I will not ignore it. If all it takes to breathe life into a person is a flower smiling from the earth, I want to plant them everywhere, and I want you to come with me to do it."

Suddenly I couldn't bear the distance between us. I closed the gap and stretched my arms up around his neck. He didn't stop me, but the feel of his hands on my waist remained only an echo. I let him go.

"If you're sure, there's another place we need to go," he said. "I know you've just returned from Mrs. Griffith's, but we don't have much time. We'd need to go now if you're able." His eyes searched mine and I nodded, trying my hardest not to let on that his not holding me back had crushed my heart.

"Mrs. Winder in Port Chester . . . Her hourglass is running out."

I'd never heard the name.

"Of course," I said.

We barely spoke on the way to Mrs. Winder's. Instead of conversation, my companions were memories—things Sam and I had shared and things we hadn't—and the acute awareness of the way Sam's free hand casually rested in the inches of space between us, his pinkie against my thigh.

The roads here weren't as familiar as those in neighboring Rye. Still, they looked mostly the same as the byways on the outskirts of town: Small clapboard homes dotted overgrown fields. An occasional clothesline flapped linen in the early morning starlight, and a crispness filled the air.

"We'll have to make haste at Mrs. Winder's," Sam muttered. "Your father will be up early readying for the Finks' planting tomorrow."

I nodded.

"The pink will be beautiful against the house and the sky and the ocean," I said. Mary Fink had decided she didn't want an Italianate design like so many of her peers but a color theme like the Goelets' blue garden. She'd chosen pink, a much easier collection to cultivate than blue, given that blue flowers didn't technically exist.

"When I visited the other day, Mary told me you'd been by before, that you'd asked if they needed a gardener."

"I did." He slowed the carriage and turned onto a narrow lane between two stretches of open field. "I asked everyone. I told you I didn't have a choice but to return."

"Were you so desperate to avoid me?" I looked at him, his eyes trained to the dirt lane in front of us.

"If the tables were turned, do you suppose you'd have been eager to see me?" he asked. I knew it was the truth, yet the reality of it gripped my heart. I had been the one to change my mind about leaving, and yet I'd been shattered. I couldn't fathom how I would have felt if I'd been the one standing alone on the train platform, realizing he wasn't coming.

"No," I said softly. "But I'm glad there wasn't something else. I'm glad you're here. I can't pretend I've forgotten you or that I've stopped thinking of you these past years. You've been every-where I've been. Sam, I've never stopped loving you. Not for a moment. I don't think I ever will."

Nerves riddled my stomach, but the tension I'd been carry-ing these past weeks swiftly disappeared from my shoulders. If Mr. Reynolds had the gumption to propose marriage after know-ing me only a night, surely I could tell the man I'd loved for years that I still loved him. He looked at me.

"Yet it wasn't enough." He was quiet a moment. "I've already told you that in so many ways I'm glad for it, for what happened." My insides wilted.

"There it is." He pointed to a shack up ahead. Paint protested the wood, curling away from it, and the front porch sagged. I swallowed hard, trying to forget his response to my love. I deserved his dismissal after all. The state of us was no one's fault but my own.

"I ran into her son in town the other week and he said she can't have anyone about, that her memory is gone and she believes she's five again. She doesn't recognize her children anymore, and meeting anyone new upsets her. All she does is rock on the front porch for hours, looking out at this lawn."

"Who is she? You never told me about her." I'd known all about his parents coming down from Rhode Island before he was born so his father could accept employ as the groundskeeper for another cemetery right over the border in Connecticut. I'd known that his mother left them when Sam was a baby.

"She was my nursemaid at one time. Although I wasn't in her care long. Perhaps only from age one to two, but she kept watch over me when Father was working. I owe my life to her," he said.

"Then I'm glad we're able to do this for her. At the very least she'll have something beautiful to look at." The cart rocked as we made our way up the long, uneven drive. I grasped the wooden seat to avoid sliding against Sam. The crickets were out tonight, singing their songs in the tall grass, and somewhere far off, a train whistle sounded.

We stopped in the drive a short distance from the house, and Sam swung off the seat. He came around to help me down, and then we silently carried the plants he'd chosen—two helenium, three geraniums, two globe thistles, a lily of the valley, a rock soapwort, and two blue sea hollies—to a little spot of bare dirt right in front of her porch.

A small window was open and a soft, steady snore provided a rhythm for our digging and planting.

"She'll have blooms now through fall," Sam whispered later as I planted the last geranium, then he started on the globe thistles to go beside them. "Add the sea hollies on the other side. It'll be a nice complement for the back. The helenium will go in the middle, then in the front, facing the porch, rock soapwort and lily of the valley."

He hadn't drawn the design on paper—we hadn't had time for that—but I could see it in my mind. It was textured and multidimensional, masterful, beautiful, something Father or Charles or I could have come up with. Sam had been trained up in plants too. Not necessarily to the extent we had, but landscaping was his father's job until he passed five years back. Sam had always had a natural gift for horticulture.

"When the wind blows, she'll have a little bit of fresh fragrance, and butterflies will come in the summer."

"You should apprentice under Father again," I said. My hands stilled on a sea holly root bundle. "This is clearly what you're meant to do, Sam."

He pushed a strand of hair back from his eyes and shook his head.

"It wasn't quite a true apprenticeship before," he said. "He was so focused on training up your brothers that he didn't have time for more than a few lessons here and there. Now it's clear his priority is grooming a successor, something I clearly am not."

"He told me he thought you more skilled than anyone else in our employ," I said. "And I suppose he hasn't formally taught me either, but I've learned just as much by following him around."

"He never seems to mind anyone doing that." Sam laughed under his breath.

"Not at all. He loves to talk plants with anyone who will listen." I sat back and looked at the garden, considering. "Do you suppose we should put a helenium slightly between the soapwort and lily of the valley to prevent them from spreading together?"

Sam patted dirt over the last thistle's roots and eyed the design.

"Yes, that's a good point. Do you suppose the ground is damp enough for the helenium? I recalled that the soil here tended to have a bit of woodland texture, so I thought they would thrive and encourage butterflies, but now I'm not certain."

We each dug our fingers into the dirt, then let it sift through them. It was good, dark soil, though slightly drier than the compost-like dampness of a forest floor. Neither of us needed to confirm our findings; we simply reached for the variety in question and began to plant them side by side. We had always been this way together, our minds on the same track.

Our fingers brushed as we swept the dirt between the two plants, and then Sam's comment about Father training up a successor struck me.

"What if the answer has been here all along?" I whispered.

Sam glanced at me.

"What if we told Father about us? What if we weren't supposed to go away together—what if we were supposed to stay? We could be together here. We could run the nurseries together, Sam. Surely Father would come to see that it's the right course eventually."

My heart was in my throat. Something about tonight had made me brave, something about the contrast of facing one man who didn't understand me and could never have my heart, then being with the man who understood everything about me. True understanding, true love was rare, and even if Father was angry at first, I hoped he'd come to see that my happiness meant more than a solid fortune.

Sam eased back on his haunches and his gaze met mine.

"Sadie, you know how your father feels about his children having any sort of relationship with his employees," he said softly. "The minute you told him, he'd terminate me and ship you off to your grandparents in Germany. And anyway, there's no 'us' anymore. There can't be. There's . . . there's someone else."

I couldn't breathe. Tears sprang to my eyes. He had forgotten me, truly. His indifference wasn't just a charade to guard his heart. Immediately I wanted to know everything—who she was, where she was, how they met.

"And even if I could have it, I don't want your father's business. I'm only interested in somehow making sure the poorest of our neighbors have a place they can go to rest in beauty, a place of solace, and he's not at all focused on that. As nice as these little gardens are, they're for one person. What about the others out there? Your father, like so many other men of power, has never even considered the need for such a space where all can go. Such men offer a little charity to others and feel good about that. Then they cease to do more, even though they *can*—and they *should*."

The combination of his rejection and his criticism of my father made me suddenly furious. Sam didn't know that the nurseries were in danger, that Father had taken on more employees than we could truly afford, that the thought of his bankrupt friends made him cry.

"And where do you suppose the plants for a park such as

you're suggesting would come from? Who would donate the land? It's a valiant idea, to be sure, but who would pay for it? Nothing is free, Sam, as much as we may want it to be. Our business cultivates beauty, and it's true that whoever is at the helm has the power to give or withhold it, but a business must also stay afloat to be charitable at all. You have no idea of the status of our finances. If our nurseries fold, all those in our employ will become jobless and homeless. Where do you suppose we would procure the flowers then?"

I was shaking and it had been an effort to keep my voice low. I pushed the soapwort into the ground with fervor and Sam rose to his feet.

"People like your father should donate them freely," he said as though he hadn't heard a word I'd just spoken. I looked up at him. His eyes were stony. "He obviously has enough. He just ordered a new Brewster carriage last week. You have *five* already. And that dress"—he flipped his hand at my gown, now dusted in layers of city ash from earlier and dirt from this venture— "how much did it cost? Likely more than a year's salary for most people."

"Perhaps we have a few fine things, but you know nothing of the true picture," I said, forcing myself to continue planting lest I scream. "We're hemorrhaging money just like everyone else, and every time a business folds it impacts us—there is one less estate to furnish and more unemployed families seeking work with us. Father is doing as much as he possibly can. You may accuse others of being heartless, but my father is not and you know it."

I pushed the soil over the lily of the valley and stood.

Sam said nothing, simply stared down at the garden we'd finished. Those were Father's plants too—plants he didn't know he was giving away. With only a rudimentary understanding of finances, even I understood that everything came attached to a price. I wished it wasn't so, but my wishing changed nothing.

"Is your new sweetheart of the same mind? Thinking ill of everyone—even those who are truly compassionate?" My words came out in a hiss. I marched past him toward the cart and pulled myself in without waiting for him to assist me. The thought of Sam with someone else made everything ache. He could criticize my father for plenty of shortcomings, but being callous toward those in need wasn't one of them.

He untangled the reins from the hitching post and climbed up beside me. I could feel his eyes on my face, but I stared straight ahead. When I got home I would crumple, I would weep, but not now.

"She's like me, Sadie. She needs me. And you . . . you never will. You can't. You'd never be happy with a man like me. I'm not enough for you." His voice was soft, and I hated it. This should be an argument—a screaming, passionate, horrible argument—one in which he realized how wrong he was and how much he still loved me.

"Perhaps you should take your father's advice and marry Mr. Reynolds. At least he loves the plants as you do. At least you could stay."

I looked at him then and something inside me broke. I now knew exactly how he'd felt on the train platform that night.

And he could see it, because he unexpectedly took my hand. My thumb drifted across his knuckles and his fingers tightened.

"Perhaps I will," I said, withdrawing my hand from his.

CHAPTER 8

I looked a fright despite Agnes's best efforts. Exhaustion and grief were a bad combination, and after sobbing over Sam I'd fallen asleep for a mere two hours before Agnes came with my coffee. She tried her best to remedy the bags beneath my eyes, swabbing them with green tea and then cucumber, but the swelling barely changed. I'd dressed in my white frock mechanically and barely worked up an apology as she plucked my filthy discarded ball gown from the floor and mumbled how fine fashion was lost on me.

Mr. Brundage was back, and he was planning to call again today—at least that's what Agnes kept saying—and I needed to look my best. In a way I was thankful I looked unwell. Perhaps he'd rethink his impending proposal.

I turned into the breakfast room and nodded at Mr. Cooper, who had been given the unfortunate task of cranking the Victrola. Brahms's First Symphony poured from the speaker.

"Good morning, Father, Mr. Cooper, Mr. Allison," I said

loudly. Mr. Cooper's assistant, Mr. Allison, hastened to my chair and pulled it out for me.

"Lovely morning, isn't it, Miss Fremd?" Mr. Cooper said from his post across the room. Though the day was sunny and beautiful, streams of water from a shower late last night rippled along the front drive. The Finks' planting would be delayed. Perhaps Mr. Brundage would be delayed as well.

"It is, Mr. Cooper. A rain shower and now sun. Food for the plants," I said.

Father didn't look up from the newspaper. Clearly he was still angry about Mr. Reynolds and didn't wish to speak to me yet.

Mr. Allison handed me a calling card.

"Old Mrs. Garner came to call last night and asked if you would come by today if you have a moment. She's having some Rye ladies over for tea this morning," he said.

"Thank you. I'll go by right after breakfast." Rather than going from one home to another visiting individually, attending Mrs. Garner's tea would provide a simple way to propose new gardens to several ladies at once. I was much looking forward to it.

He nodded.

"Very well. I'll have the new carriage brought around for you." The mention of the new carriage reminded me of Sam's words, and my using it now seemed greedy.

"No, the old single will work just as well," I said.

"As you wish." He deposited a halved grapefruit in front of me and a sugar dish to the side. Father must have already eaten his and was now on his second course—cracked wheat with berries and a strip of bacon.

"Cooper, have you read the paper this morning?" Father

asked. He plucked up the thin pages from their prominent display on the table and fluffed them upward so Mr. Cooper could see.

"A bit of it, sir," Mr. Cooper replied, still cranking the Victrola.

"Have you seen this article here about the gardens?" Father asked. "Apparently someone is going around town planting little arrangements for some neighbors who have fallen on hard times. What a delight."

At once my whole body flushed with heat, and I couldn't help but smile in spite of my nerves. He thought them a delight.

"I did see that story, sir, and found the idea charming myself. I wonder who is behind it," Mr. Cooper said.

"I'm not certain, but whoever the fellow is, he must have access to fine plants. He's done a rose garden in the railroad village and a tulip display outside Mrs. Griffith's place," Father said. I was surprised that the tulip garden had been included. I'd just planted it last night. Then again, the newspaper office was just down the block from Mrs. Griffith's, and the longtime editor, Joshua Martins, was known to make changes right up to printing at two in the morning. The garden in Port Chester would go undetected—at least for a while. It was too far removed from town.

"They've quoted the recipient in the rail village here: 'I woke up to a miracle. I've fallen on such difficulties this past year, I didn't know if I could go on, but now when I look out and see my roses—roses planted just for me—I allow my soul to hope again.' Isn't that wonderful?" Despite Father's foul mood toward me, my heart lightened with the knowledge of the man's response to my garden. I'd wondered how it had been received but couldn't find opportunity to sneak to the rail village undetected.

Father took a bite of bacon. "I wonder if it's the Rockefellers' gardener, Timothy," he said to Mr. Cooper. "We dug up all of those varieties when we went in last month, and he was quite reluctant to let any of the thriving plants go to the garbage." He continued reading.

I started to say something, to tell him it was me, but suddenly held back. Even if Father thought the idea of the gardens a wonderful thing, I had no doubt he'd find fault with me for taking the plants without asking or for going to the rail village without him.

"If it is Timothy," Mr. Cooper said, "it seems he will be quite busy off the job. Did you read that others are requesting flowers as well?"

"Yes, I can understand why. Flowers liven the most broken spirits," Father said without looking up. I always knew he felt that way about plants—that was why he'd dedicated his life to them—but hearing him say it now, after I'd been so confronted with the importance of natural beauty for those who couldn't see past hardship, made me hope he would understand what I'd been doing, that perhaps he'd even want to participate in developing a park like Sam had suggested.

I pushed my spoon into the grapefruit and took a bite, hoping to find the courage to speak up.

"It appears he may be in a bit of trouble, however," Father said. "Did you read the bit about Edward Garrison and Chadwick Horner being angry about it all?" Father laughed under his breath. "They're quoted here saying the gardener trespassed, and they can't afford to employ landscapers to keep up the designs, and more tenants now want flowers." He lowered the paper. "I don't understand why Garrison and Horner have to complain.

The gardens were presumably given free of charge. Garrison and Horner are near slumlords. Everyone knows it."

"Indeed, sir. They should accept the kindness and encourage more," Mr. Cooper said. "That paragraph below, where it says other families in the rail village and in town and even some out Boston Post Road are asking for the gardener to plant near their houses, is heart-wrenching. That poor family with the sickly child . . ." Mr. Cooper's eyes glistened. He quickly sniffed and withdrew his handkerchief with his free hand.

"It is heartbreaking indeed," Father said, still reading the article.

"Don't you suppose it's time to develop a public park here?" I'd found my voice finally, and Father looked at me. I cleared my throat. "There's been talk about the need for one. Everyone deserves to have a place of beauty to retreat to, and you must admit that right now only our clients, the very wealthy, have that ability. Think about how greatly it would improve mood and mental stamina—especially today when things are so uncertain. We could be a part of it, Father. It would mean so very much to me. Surely we could find a way to gift some of our plants."

"Seeing the slums yesterday has affected you deeply, and I know we're not immune to deep poverty here either," Father said. "In any case, who have you heard discussing the need for a park in this vicinity?" He snapped the paper shut. "Do you know how much funding would have to be given in order to develop a park? Of course, the scope would be much less, but when all was finished Central Park cost fourteen million dollars. Fourteen million.

"Even if our county developed a modest park, it would cost half a million. Someone would have to donate land and we would have to donate our plants. We would be giving away the equivalent of four gardens at least. We don't have the ability to gift even half of one fine garden without our business suffering, let alone four."

At once, my taking Father's plants gave me pause, but all in all I'd only taken a few. And I'd been right to say what I had to Sam. The idea of a public park was a valiant one, but nearly impossible right now in the shadow of the crash. I could see his face in my mind. His statement had been driven by emotion, by the desperate need to find a balm for the brokenness he'd seen, and he would insist upon it, despite it being impossible. Even so, I understood his sentiment.

"This is why it pains me when you refuse suitable proposals, Sadie," Father said. He sighed and folded his paper. "You say you want to run this business, but you are not rational in your thinking about it. You do not understand the finances, only the science and the romance, and in order to continue this endeavor, we must be about the business of figures *and* horticulture. One cannot exist without the other."

"I do understand the finances, Father," I said evenly. "It's not as if I am asking you to develop a large park on your own this minute. I know well enough times are hard. I only thought that we could help if a formal county proposal was ever presented. Clearly that could be years from now. Decades, even." I was backpedaling. I had to. I needed Father to see me as competent, not as a woman with unrealistic notions. "Perhaps in the meantime we could plant something small in town? Just a little area with a bench? We could sell one of the carriages to do it. We don't need that new one you just purchased."

Father grunted. "I'm doing all I can for the people of this town. There may come a time, sooner rather than later, when we will need to sell our assets, but that will only happen when we must do so to keep our employees and ourselves from disaster."

He sat back in his chair. "If you truly wish to help with such lofty endeavors, you should do as I've advised for years and accept the proposal of a man with deep pockets. These men aren't proposing for our money, they're proposing for your love, and a man in love will agree to about anything his wife asks of him." He took a sip of his coffee. "I am certain that if you wrote to Mr. Reynolds, he would find a way to forget last night's blunder. And if you can't see your way to that, perhaps you'll see your way to accepting Mr. Brundage—he said he's going to call soon, perhaps this afternoon." With that he unfolded the paper and went back to reading.

I swallowed hard. I didn't want to fall on the sword to win respite for those who didn't have it, but perhaps that was what Sam was suggesting last night when he told me to marry Mr. Reynolds. Still, I would be giving up everything, my whole life. Surely there was another way to win beauty for all while remaining true to myself.

"We will be able to accomplish it ourselves, Father," I said. "Perhaps not right now, but down the road. I am not going to swindle money from a man I don't love, and someday, when you see that I've helped win more accounts to the nurseries than Charles ever did, when you see that I know more about plants than Charles ever could, you'll know I'm the right person to hand this business to."

Mr. Cooper stopped cranking at that and silence permeated the room.

"Your carriage has arrived, Miss Fremd," Mr. Allison said as he emerged from the kitchen.

I stood before he could help me with my chair, leaving my breakfast unfinished.

"Good," I said. "I'll be back before the shipment is due," I said to Father. Our monthly shipment of imported varieties from our sister nurseries in Germany and Japan was set to arrive today, and nothing was as exciting as unloading species we had never seen before.

"That will suit well in case Mr. Brundage calls," Father said, not bothering to look up from his paper.

Mrs. Garner lived two houses down from my friend Margaret, near town. Her home was a Federal style, built in red clay her late husband had imported from a brick factory in his home state of South Carolina. Mr. Garner had been the founder of the town's first bank and left his widow an ample fortune with which to withstand the current downturn.

"Sadie!" Margaret called to me from the front steps. She was wearing the costume she'd ordered from H. O'Neill & Co. when I called on her last—a floral silk with a bell skirt and a flounce of lace around the bottom.

I waved and Mr. Green stopped the carriage and came around to unlatch my door. I ducked out, bending deeply through the doorway to avoid disturbing the fresh hyacinths I'd stuck into the velvet-and-lace trimming of my straw hat.

"Thank you," I said to Mr. Green. "Please come back around by one o'clock."

"Of course," he said.

I walked over to Margaret and looped my arm through hers.

"Lovely day for a tea, isn't it?" I asked as we walked through the limestone doorway and into a narrow entry that led to an atrium and out to the backyard.

"It is if we're celebrating," Margaret said, turning to look at me. "Rumor has it you were to have a proposal last night in town. Tempy said your father let it slip when he went over to pay the deposit on our garden yesterday." She lowered her voice when she asked, "Did it happen? And why didn't you tell me? You know we don't keep secrets, you and I."

"Yes. He asked and I said no." I thought of the countless secrets I'd kept from Margaret despite our childhood vow that we would tell each other everything. She didn't know about Sam or my aspirations with the nurseries. In fact, the moment we were presented it seemed our lives diverged. Finding common ground was a struggle at times. "I would have told you if I'd had any idea myself. I'd never even met Mr. Reynolds before. I was quite shocked."

Outside, four dainty wrought iron tables were set up around Mrs. Garner's fountain, which boasted a dancing cherub. The old English boxwoods we'd planted ages ago had held up quite well, but it was clear by the prominence of dandelions and goosefoot and prickly lettuce that the perennial garden Charles had so carefully planned had been given over to nature by the Garners' incompetent gardener. I'd have to speak to Mrs. Garner about having her beds redone.

Margaret sighed. "Lionel Reynolds is apparently one of the most desirable men in all of England—handsome *and* wealthy," she scolded. "What does it matter if you barely know him? You would get to know him eventually. You're going to wind up an old maid, Sadie."

I wanted to say that I'd rather end up an old maid than

settle, like she had—with boring Tempy Ridgeway no less—but I simply shrugged.

"Perhaps I will," I said as we made our way down the straight brick path toward the tables. The other guests hadn't arrived yet, and Mrs. Garner stood from her chair next to her longtime friend, Mrs. Hamrick.

"Good morning, ladies. Come on out here and have a seat," she crowed, gesturing to the table to her right.

"I don't understand how you haven't fallen in love yet, what with all these gentlemen asking for your hand and swooning over you," Margaret went on.

She would never understand my loving Sam. Like the rest of my peers, Margaret came from a long line of wealth and she passed by men like Sam as if they were irrelevant—like a park bench, perhaps, or a decorative vase. Margaret had been trained to see only wealth. If that wealth came with a fine face and an amiable personality, all the better, but neither was required. Father had tried his best to groom me into a version of Margaret. The difference was that despite his demanding I marry into prominence, he was never one to snub or ignore anyone but always insisted that all people should be treated with kindness and good manners regardless of station. I suppose that was what allowed me to fall in love with someone my friends wouldn't.

"To be honest, I find it mostly irritating," I said. "I just want to work with Father. If I fall in love, wonderful, but it won't be my life's ambition."

"Selfishly, I'm glad you declined the dashing Mr. Reynolds," Margaret said, ignoring my hint at ambition as we reached our chairs. "You know I want you to marry Mr. Bishop, and when he returns from his business in England, I'm sure he'll propose.

He and Tempy are so close, you know. We could do everything together."

"He's kind, but quite boring," I said, taking my seat. The truth was that he and Tempy had become friends because they'd been the dullest men in our primary school class.

"Do tell me you're speaking of your many suitors, Sadie," Mrs. Garner said, settling back in her chair. "I delight in hearing of these courtships. It takes me back to when I was a girl myself. I was quite the catch. William had to ask for my hand three times before I said yes." She leaned forward and snapped at her butler standing in the doorway. "Mr. Hogan! Do bring the tea. There's no reason to keep these ladies waiting just because the others are tardy." Mr. Hogan nodded and hastened into the house.

"We are speaking of men, but I'm afraid there's really nothing to tell," I said. "I believe your courtship with Mr. Garner is rather more famous than mine will ever be. Didn't he propose the last time in his family's English herb garden? Just looking about now, I wondered if you'd like to have one done back here. It would be a lovely memorial to him."

Mrs. Garner's eyes glistened and she smiled. "Yes, actually. That is a lovely idea. I'll never forget the way it smelled that night—sun-kissed rosemary and William's sandalwood cologne. You know, I'm not certain that I was ever *in* love with him, but I loved him fiercely. I miss him every day," Mrs. Garner said. "Do have your father call on me next week to determine the best design for it. In the meantime, enjoy yourself."

I watched Margaret fidgeting with her Medici collar. She'd never been a nervous person before, but it seemed bearing the Ridgeway name kept her in a constant flutter. To be fair, her mother-in-law would also be in attendance today and had always been most critical.

"Hmm," Mrs. Hamrick said softly, glancing toward the garden's entrance. "I suppose we are about to discover if your claim about your courtships being a bore is the truth, Sadie. Here comes Eleanor Brundage now."

I wanted to sink into the ground. I hadn't seen Mrs. Brundage since the unfortunate planting conversation on her patio.

"I told Eleanor that Harry should watch his pompous attitude, that it is a deterrent to women like you, Sadie, but whether he's heeded my advice is yet to be determined," Mrs. Garner said.

Thankfully Mr. Hogan came with the tea the moment Mrs. Brundage reached us, and I busied myself with situating my cup and selecting from the four varieties of tea available while she greeted the older ladies and took a seat at their table.

"Isn't it strange that Sylvie won't be here?" Margaret asked. She daintily dipped her tea bag into the water and reached for the silver sugar-cube claw. "It was always the three of us, and now she's just gone, never to be seen again."

"Surely you don't mean that." I took a sip of my tea, inhaling the vanilla and bergamot. "We'll see her again. She's our best friend. After a while, when their misfortune fades, she'll be back. I'm sure of it." Perhaps if I spoke optimistically, I could will it to be.

Margaret smoothed a lock of blonde hair that had fallen from her plaited coiffure and shook her head.

"No. I don't think so. I tried to write her the other week. Of course, not knowing her whereabouts in the city is a problem, but I guessed. I just wrote 'Lower Manhattan' as the address and it was returned to me."

I stared at her. Did I appear as out of touch to Sam as Margaret appeared to me? To think a postal worker could locate anyone at all in the crush of thousands in the manufacturing districts was preposterous. Clearly Margaret had never seen anything of the city beyond Fifth Avenue. Until last week, castle row was the only part I'd been subjected to as well.

"She should have accepted Aden," Margaret went on. "She could have been safe and comfortable just over on Post Road—and her parents with her."

Margaret's eyes met mine and I knew what she was thinking: that I could be next. I was tired of it. I was tired of my fate being seen as a liability. Yet in a way, she was right. The only safe fortunes these days were those captured ages ago, not based on today's commerce but from whaling and copper and iron won a generation past. Only a handful of those families lived in Rye—the Ridgeways, the Blankenships, the Brundages, the Finks, and the Bishops.

"Aden lacks Sylvie's intellect," I said. "He is not funny. He is not smart. He's a milquetoast, and—"

"Oh lord. There's my mother-in-law. And Mrs. Horner and that dreadful Molly Austin from Greenwich too," Margaret said, but I barely heard her. The image of the slums, of the piano-box home caught me off guard as I thought of Sylvie, and at once I thought that perhaps, despite Aden's unfortunate qualities, perhaps Margaret was right and Sylvie should have accepted him.

"Mrs. Ridgeway is wearing that beaded wrap with the jet fringe again. She's always after me when I wear a costume more than once," Margaret went on. She set her teacup down with a clatter and straightened her shoulders. "Hello, Mother!" she called out. I turned in time to see Mrs. Ridgeway nod before crossing to the opposite unoccupied table with the ladies she'd arrived with.

"Miss Austin, you're at the table with the young ladies," Mrs. Garner said, her fingers pinched to her teacup. Miss Austin, whoever she was, was one of the shortest women I'd ever seen. She had strawberry hair and naturally flushed cheeks that gave her a sort of innocent look I was sure men loved.

"Hello, I'm Molly," she said when she arrived at our table. Margaret simply forced a smile and said nothing.

"Sadie Fremd," I said, extending my hand over the silver tea service to take hers.

"Oh," Molly said, a look of panic playing on her face. Odd.

Mrs. Garner rang a little bell, disturbing the chatter, and rose from her chair.

"Wonderful for all of you to come," she said. "I was just wandering about out here the other day and thought the weather was finally amiable enough to orchestrate a little gathering. I do think my yard so lovely in the spring, despite the weeds. Miss Sadie, I suppose I'll have to call upon your father in short order." She laughed.

"We'd be honored, Mrs. Garner," I said.

"Just don't call upon that horrible mystery gardener the papers have been in a tizzy about. Whoever it is has been trespassing on our land and making Chadwick's life just dreadful as all of our tenants now want the land beautified. Flowers do not go with grime, and raising rent to hire a gardener isn't a consideration for them or us, and we certainly cannot give any more than we already do to those poor souls," Mrs. Horner said. I could still smell the stench of sewage and the piles of garbage that permeated the rail village. Charging people any money at all to live in such squalor was robbery.

"One would suppose a person in such dire straits would seek to save as much as they could and leave the place. Not plant flowers there. It seems frivolous and out of place," Margaret said.

I glared at her.

"I don't understand why it matters to any of you," I said. "The gardener hasn't asked you to contribute, Mrs. Horner, or asked any money of the tenants. And flowers are hardly frivolous, Margaret. They are a marvel and a testament that miracles are possible. Even if those people never move an inch and live in that rail village forever, they will at least see some beauty despite their hardships." I hadn't breathed and did so now. Everyone was staring at me. My cheeks reddened. I didn't ordinarily launch myself into societal controversy and I was certain everyone thought it strange.

"If it's your father's doing, Sadie, we—"

"It's certainly not Father," I said, cutting off Mrs. Horner.

"Well, I think what the gardener did for Patricia Griffith was just lovely," Mrs. Garner said. She held up her hand. "I know the Garrisons won't like it because it makes their building look shabby, but I'm sure those little tulips livened Patsy. They were her favorite."

I looked around, wondering if anyone else thought it strange that Mrs. Garner was speaking of her best friend as though she were dead. Apparently they did not. They also didn't think it strange that Mrs. Griffith obviously had not been invited today, despite still living in Rye a few blocks away. Money didn't only buy comfort, it bought friends, too, and despite not being at all contagious, poverty was clearly considered a plague. I looked down at the hand-embroidered napkin in my lap, trying to figure how I could leave prematurely. Being here around these people with their fickle loyalties was stifling. Being around Father lately had been stifling too.

"Enough talk of unpleasant things," Mrs. Garner said as though a word from the lips of a social darling would erase the existence of hard hearts and destitution. "Mr. Hogan will bring out the finger sandwiches and little napoleons in a moment, and, well, enjoy!"

"Miss Fremd," Molly said. I looked up and blinked back the emotion pooling in my eyes. "I think it best that I come right out and say it. I'm to be married to Stephen Bishop. He proposed in a letter yesterday and I have accepted. He was clear that for some time he'd had his heart set on you, but that was before he met me. I . . . I'm sorry if this comes as a shock."

Margaret gasped.

"Perhaps, though it is a happy sort of shock, Miss Austin. I admit I was not in love with Mr. Bishop, and I'm glad he's found a match in someone so lovely as you," I said.

Margaret's hand clutched her teacup so hard her knuckles went white. "I'm not happy about this at all," she snapped. "Stephen is my husband's best friend and Sadie is mine. Stephen promised Tempy he was going to ask for her hand when he returned."

Molly only blinked at Margaret.

"Dear Margaret, we'll always be friends," I said. "But even if he had asked me ten times, I would have refused."

"I can't see how you could," Molly said. "He's enchanting. And his estate on the water is just so lovely. To think I'll be mistress of it."

"It is a gorgeous scene," I said. "In fact, Miss Austin, if you plan to get married on the estate, perhaps you'd like the gardens done up for the occasion? There's nothing more romantic than a delicate garden full of peonies, camellias, roses, foxgloves, and snowdrops. The combination is striking and wonderfully fragrant. Margaret actually decided on a similar design for her yard."

"That sounds beautiful indeed. We haven't quite decided yet, but we're discussing a ceremony at home. I'll have Stephen call on your nurseries straightaway if those plans are solidified," Molly said. Pure joy, or perhaps it was relief, played on her face.

"Is that all you think about?" Margaret asked. "You've lost a suitor, the best one you had, and yet so long as your family gets to plant his garden you're happy with the loss of him?"

"It wouldn't surprise you so if you listened to me. I suppose I've never come out and said it plainly, but in a way, I've told you over and over again," I said. "It's the plants I love."

"They will never hold you. They will never give you children. They will never give you a home," she said, barely acknowledging Mr. Hogan's artistic display of sandwiches and desserts as they were set in front of her. "I can't understand you, Sadie."

I plucked a cucumber sandwich from the silver tray and ignored her pointed glare. I used to belong among these people. I used to consider them nearly as close as family, but now everything had been altered, my eyes opened, and just as she couldn't understand me, I could no longer understand her—any of them really. But it didn't matter. Winning gardens for my family meant financial soundness, and perhaps someday, financial excess. I would endure the callous society ladies and court them for their business forever if it rewarded the nurseries the funds to create a park for those our clients only pretended to help.

CHAPTER 9

"Can you urge him a bit faster?" I asked Mr. Green, who was letting Gene lollygag at the carriage's helm. I could hear the train whistle in the distance, the steady low hum of the wheels on the tracks, and felt myself liven with anticipation.

A carload of the Golden Chain Cytisus was coming from Germany—a handsome shrub with long, drooping racemes of yellow blossoms—and the gold-blotched Aucuba ash trees from Japan and Bleeding Heart peonies from England. I had never seen any of them before, only in the catalogs. I could hardly wait to see their beauty in person.

"You know Gene," Mr. Green said. "I can urge him all day long, but he'll only go faster if he wants to."

I laughed. "I know. I suppose I'm just a bit eager to get to the station. I want to see the new varieties before everyone whisks them off to the greenhouses and fields," I said. "I'm going to cross-pollinate a new deep red peony with a violet variety for Mother's birthday. She loved magenta, and peonies were her favorite. I thought I'd surprise Father."

I hoped the seeds would take. The last time I'd cross-pollinated a peony, I'd been with Sam, and we'd dreamed up the variety together—a pure white bloom with blush petal tips. It had been a successful endeavor—Sam and I were meticulous—and the variety, Summer Soiree, had proven one of the hardiest of our lot.

"That's a lovely idea," Mr. Green said. "Delivery day is a bit like a celebration for many of you, isn't it? I'll try to hurry Gene along to the house so you can dress in your gardening clothes, and then I'll take you directly to the tracks." He turned onto the drive, and I pulled my arms against my chest and shivered as the trees blanketed the sun.

"Don't you dare," I said, laughing. "Take me directly to the tracks. This is a fine enough gardening frock. You know I've been in the fields in my ball gowns before." Although I was telling the truth, I also knew Father was stuck with office work today since the Finks' planting day had to be moved, and I wanted to avoid the house to avoid him—him and his disappointment in my continual rejection of suitors, his callousness about my desire to plant a small community arrangement until larger plans could be made, his blindness in matters of my competence. He made it difficult to be polite.

"Much to your father's dismay," Mr. Green said, glancing back at me. Even so, when we reached the fork in the drive, he led Gene to the right, down the side of our land, past the greenhouses and to the tracks. "At least let me take your hat. It will be ruined otherwise."

"Well, I need something to shade my eyes and this will do." I sat up from the seat, watching as the train screeched to a halt, temporarily blocking my view of the barns and the planting fields and the employees' village beyond. Smoke rolled in a billowing cloud from the engine, disrupting the clear blue sky.

"Stop here if you will. I'll walk down." Mr. Green pulled on the reins and Gene slowed to a stop right between the last of the greenhouses and a square of green we kept uncommitted for unloading shipments. Already two dozen men and women were idling beside the train, waiting for the wheels to settle. I unlatched the carriage door and hurtled out on my own without waiting for Mr. Green to help me.

"Thank you!" I started out walking, but the moment the railmen swung down from their posts at the engine, I ran.

"Good afternoon, Mr. and Mrs. Sigallis, Mr. Rich, Mrs. Gibson," I said as I wove through the crowd of our employees toward the tracks. The heat from the train felt good in the chilly spring air. A railman wearing a pair of filthy Carhartt overalls slogged toward the latch.

"Which are you hoping to see first?" Sam stood beside me, his eyes trained to the doors too. "It feels like your birthday, doesn't it?" He pulled at the collar of his white linen shirt, looked down at me, and grinned. I smiled, too, the elation of excitement eclipsing the remembrance of our silence and my sorrow the night before.

"It's better than my birthday," I said. Each birthday Father reminded me I wasn't yet a wife or mother. Charles and Freddie never experienced the same attempted shame. "I don't care which I see first, though I suppose I've been most excited about the peonies."

"I owe you an apology," he said, lowering his voice and stepping a bit closer. I could feel his arm against my shoulder blade. "I'm sorry for my tone last night. I don't take back any of what I said, but my tone wasn't right. I was rude. To be clear, I appreciate your father, and I find no fault in you, Sadie. I only—"

Just then, the heavy doors were pushed open and a scream of metal against metal punctured the air. The peonies were in front. Though most were dormant, two were arrayed in glory—double blooms in shocks of deep red. Beyond them, the golden chains draped over their terra-cotta containers and the ash trees stood at the back. Everyone stepped forward immediately, hands outstretched, ready to do a swift job of unloading so they could start on the planting ahead.

"Father may have already told you, but peonies to greenhouse four," I said loudly. It occurred to me then that I'd only missed a handful of deliveries since I was old enough to help. My heart had always fluttered with anticipation the day we received new wonders, and hardly anything could keep me away from the tracks those days. In recent years I'd been the one directing the plants—Father and Charles were frequently out overseeing an installation, and oftentimes they didn't even ask, simply assumed I'd be present to point our workers one way and the other.

"Ashes and golden chains to the field. Trees on the left, row seven, and golden chains on the right, row two."

"Vincenzo and I have already tilled the field," Sam said to me. "The ground is still a bit wet from last night's shower, but not so significantly that the trees would mind." He reached into the car and plucked a peony and a golden chain from the sea of plants and handed both to me. "Are they satisfactory, Miss Fremd?"

For a moment, his eyes met mine, and then I blinked and looked down at the blooms in my hands. Everyone around me suddenly stopped their hustle and waited for my answer. I realized I was filling Father's place, that whether these new varieties were unloaded or sent back was my decision, and our employees respected me at the helm.

I tilted the peony bud toward my face and then the cascade of yellow blooms. They were exquisite.

"More than satisfactory. Wouldn't you say so, Angelina?" I held the plants toward Mrs. Sigallis's oldest daughter who had quite an eye for floral arranging. Father believed it was important to include others in the decision-making. Those in our employ were equally as responsible for our continued success as we were.

"Quite," she said.

With that, the crush pushed forward once more and Sam climbed into the car with Vincenzo, handing plants to waiting hands.

I deposited the golden chain in the area designated for field plants but kept hold of the peony. I wandered up the hill and let myself into the greenhouse that housed the roses and peonies and lilies and found the paper envelope holding the Royal Violet pollen on the storage rack beside the door.

I'd harvested the anthers and dried them to release the pollen grains a few days ago. Thankfully the tight buds on the Bleeding Heart were perfect for pollination today. I plucked a wax paper envelope from the storage rack and set the plant on the potting table. The Bleeding Heart petals were silky and bright red. I closed my eyes and thought about the mingling of the red and violet, the way the combination would create a deep magenta. Envisioning the creation before I attempted it had become a sort of ritual, something I always did in hopes that the ability to see it in my mind meant it could actually be possible. Most of the time it worked.

"What are you doing this time?" Sam asked as he entered the greenhouse.

"Making a new peony for Mother," I murmured, my imagination still fixed on the massive magenta double bloom. I would plant it at her grave and beside the porch where she always sat and watched the fields. She'd never been much of a hand at horticulture—like Freddie, she appreciated and loved flowers but didn't care to engage in the business of them.

"What color?"

I heard the slight clatter of pots settling behind me as Sam deposited the new varieties on the ground.

"Magenta," I said, opening my eyes. "Mother always liked deep colors." I swiped my fingers over the bud and gently began to peel back the layers. Sam plucked the discarded petals from the table beside me and held them in his open palm.

"These are gorgeous. It wouldn't surprise me in the slightest if people start to prefer peonies to roses. I certainly do," he said.

"I know. I do too. Our Summer Soiree is requested often." I knew in referencing one of our varieties, I was bringing us up again and I shouldn't. It would only bring me grief, remind me that he'd found love with someone else. Regardless, standing here together in the exact place we'd come for over a year to create dozens of new varieties of peonies and roses and irises and shrubs, I couldn't help it. I couldn't fathom how someone else could have stolen his heart from me.

We had spent countless days alone—Father was thrilled to obtain our creations and blind to the reason for our prolific imagination—dreaming up new colors and thinking of ways to make our plants stronger for this climate, while at the same time pouring out our souls to each other. I knew everything about Sam, and he knew everything about me. Each variety we'd created came with the memory of our discussions. When we created the Beaming Light Boxwood—a variety that could endure full sun—Sam told me about his father's continued heartache up until his death, how his mother's abandonment twenty years before still incapacitated him for days at a time and how, in those instances, Sam had been forced to care for him completely, even as a small child, doing all the cooking and cleaning, and occasionally working.

Another time, Sam had named a snow-white and bright yellow iris Sunrise—for me. I'd told him of my first cotillion when I was twelve. I'd come home from it devastated after overhearing Lane Snover comment that I was always dirty, too slim, too intellectual, and destined to be an outcast. Even though I knew he said those things mostly because I'd won the etiquette award over him, his words had remained with me for years. When I confessed this to Sam, he laughed. Not because he was discounting my feelings but because he thought Lane's comments so ridiculous.

"The first time I remember seeing you was at Mr. Fink's graveside service, and perhaps saying this gives me away, but I noticed your beautiful face and the way you didn't hesitate to kneel beside Mr. Fink's elderly mother the moment I helped her down to place the flowers, and suddenly the gray misty morning wasn't absent of a sunrise because you were there," he'd said.

Surely this new love of his didn't know him like I did.

"They're getting ready to bloom too," Sam said now, bringing me back to the present. He nodded to the corner where a dozen new peonies idled in galvanized pots.

I plucked the last petals from the flower and started removing the anthers. I checked my fingers for pollen and was heartened that it hadn't yet been otherwise pollinated.

"Do you want more than one for your sample?" Sam asked.

"I suppose that would be a good idea . . . if you have the time," I said. "I collected enough pollen for at least two."

Sam set another Bleeding Heart next to mine and began to strip the petals. We worked silently beside each other, our fingers deliberate and gentle as we laid the flowers bare.

"Here," Sam said, handing me the silver-handled magnifying glass when we were finished. I examined my flower, checking for anthers stuck between the carpels, and could feel Sam looking at me.

"Two are stuck. Will you hand me the tweezers?" I asked.

Sam reached for the tweezers and placed them in my hand, then took the magnifying glass and held it for me as I extracted the anthers. It had always been like this with us, a dance of equals—me, then him, then me again—our minds running the same race at the same pace. We had been perfect.

"Does she know anything about plants?" I asked, avoiding his eyes as I took the magnifying glass from his hand and he took the tweezers from mine. I held the glass over his flower as he examined it. "You say she's like you, but this, right here, is you, Sam."

He plucked an anther from a carpel and righted, setting the tweezers on the table.

"I doubt she's seen a plant in ten years," he said. Something inside me twisted at the likely horror of the slums his beloved was facing and the notion that perhaps all of his talk of parks was founded not on the fate of impoverished humanity overall but on the fate of a woman he loved—a woman who wasn't me.

"I'm sorry for that," I said. I wanted to ask him more

questions. I wanted to ask if she was still in the city. I wanted to ask why, if he loved her, he hadn't brought her back here. But that would only encourage him to leave, and I was enjoying him here with me, the way we used to be.

I opened the envelope and dipped my index finger in the pollen. Sam sneezed.

"A mighty gale has set out to thwart this transatlantic match today," I said, laughing.

"Well, of course," he said in his horrible English accent. "It's been rumored that the Royal Violet is only after the Bleeding Heart for his English title and the Bleeding Heart is after the Royal Violet for her dowry."

"Stop your complaining, will you? Your children shall have both," I said, liberally swabbing the stigmas with pollen. Then I sobered. Though I wasn't a Vanderbilt or a Goelet, I'd come close to a match like the one we were laughing about. Even facing it had sent me into a panic. I couldn't imagine the endless claustrophobia awarded Consuelo Vanderbilt or May Goelet or Minnie Stevens.

I handed the pollen to Sam and he doused his flowers, then we both covered the buds with wax envelopes.

"Have you heard much from Charles?" he asked. "I thought of him the other day when I was watering the palms."

"Only once," I said. "When he's gone, he's gone. I assume it's going well or he'd have returned by now. Even so, I should write him." Charles and I were close, but that closeness hadn't been won by constant chatter. Instead, we were brought together by our common interests and our penchant for seeking the other out exclusively in times of crisis. Not hearing from Charles simply meant he was faring fine.

"And Freddie?" Sam asked, a smile playing on his face. Before Freddie was cut free of the nurseries, he'd been known to follow Sam around, avoiding any sort of work and cracking jokes.

"You know well enough what Freddie's doing," I said. "Buttering up Mayor Harrison and trying to eventually win a seat in the government that will pay him to sit in meetings and nod."

"It seems like avoiding industry is work itself," he said.

"I can't understand it, and speaking of, we should get going. I suppose we should go see if the new plants need fertilizing."

I started to walk to the door, but Sam's hand caught mine, then released it as quickly.

"You've seen the article about the gardens and those who are asking for them?"

I nodded. There were four at least. Despite Father's words about the state of our nurseries, I couldn't stop now. I couldn't ignore the simple desires of folks who never saw their needs met. Father could pretend he couldn't do more, but I knew he could spare a small bit—especially the plants that would most likely end up discarded for their imperfections.

"We'll have to split up tonight if we're to grant all of the requests," I said.

"I don't think that's wise," Sam said. "Surely we can—"

"No one is about when we're out, and it would take us all night if we stayed together."

"I'll agree as long as you'll come find me when you're home safely," he said. The vision of me standing in Sam's doorway flashed in my mind, the way he looked in the starlight with no one else about. I swallowed hard.

"Very well," I said. "Let's go ahead and pull the plants now. We'll only take the ones Father would remove anyway—the plants that are still lovely but not perfect. We can put them in the seeding house. No one will be seeding today with the shipment just in and we can pull the carts around to it easily tonight."

"You haven't given it up, despite my criticism, despite my rudeness last night," Sam said. His face softened.

"I know how important it is," I said. "If you remember, you didn't ask me to start this. This endeavor was mine alone. And I know we can't possibly provide flowers for everyone. I know we need a larger place where people can go, but since that's impossible right now, I'm going to try my best to continue on. At least we can give a few people hope."

"I know," he said. "I know your heart, and I know you're doing the best you can." Just then, his stomach rumbled loudly and he glanced out the window at the sky. "I suppose we should hurry to select the plants, do the fertilizing, and then go on our way to supper. It's likely five o'clock already. Your father will be waiting."

"I'm not going to the house for supper," I said, walking out of the greenhouse. "Father is infuriating right now, and I can't bear to be in his company."

"You're welcome to dine with us," Sam said. "Mrs. Pratte is making spaghetti with bottarga and she always makes more than we can manage to eat."

I hesitated. Father allowed us to visit the village for Christmas and to deliver supplies when needed, but he'd always been clear that we weren't to mingle there. He'd read in countless business books that it was a fatal mistake of a businessman to interject himself into employees' personal matters outside of work, that it discouraged both parties' honesty in working relationships and caused chaos, resulting in lack of respect and ultimately tarnishing the reputation of the establishment. Father was always supportive, but a staunch noninterventionist in employees' personal lives unless he was needed. Because of his stance, I'd never been inside any of the village homes, though I'd long thought that sharing a meal now and again would endear both parties to each other while avoiding a sense of intrusion.

"It's all right if you can't, Sadie," Sam said, walking past me toward the greenhouse with the hydrangeas and irises. At once the thought that Sam knew how tightly Father held me, how much I compromised to appease him, made me feel small. It was true that my dreams would be won or lost by Father's perception of me, but I was starting to understand that I couldn't win by acquiescing to his every whim. Charles and Freddie had been allowed to forge their own way, to challenge Father when they didn't think him entirely correct. And right now I wanted to take supper with Sam.

"I would love to," I said.

Sam turned, his hand on the greenhouse door, and smiled.

"You won't regret it."

Everyone gathered two or three houses together for supper. Tonight, Vincenzo, his mother, his father, his brother, Libro, his sister, Pasqualle; Frank and Leonardo Russo; and Sam and myself were crammed in Sam and Vincenzo's tiny dining room. The space was simple—whitewashed walls and knotted pine floors and a table for four. Sam and I were seated with Mr. and Mrs. Pratte on account of my being a guest, while the others stood around us. Mrs. Pratte had just brought the spaghetti in from the kitchen—she'd boiled the pasta in a wrought iron pot over the chimney stove—and a mouthwatering steam smelling of garlic and parsley and salted mullet rose from our bowls.

"Thank you for joining us tonight, Miss Fremd," Mrs. Pratte said across from me. She dabbed a bit of sweat with her napkin and smiled. "It is an honor and I do hope you enjoy this humble meal. It is one of our favorites from back home in Positano."

"I thank you for inviting me. It looks delicious," I said. Despite the crowd of people in the room, it was quiet. I was certain it wasn't often like this. I had little doubt that supper was usually a noisy, boisterous affair celebrating the end of a workday. But I had come tonight and ruined it. One couldn't feel free around the boss's daughter, and that was unfortunate.

Vincenzo and Sam dug into their bowls, but Mrs. Pratte did not. Her eyes met mine and she leaned close.

"I am . . . We are thankful for your family, Miss Fremd," she said. "We have a good life here." Her eyes suddenly filled with tears.

"This spaghetti is heavenly," Sam said. Mrs. Pratte nodded at him and the racket of voices and forks against porcelain commenced.

"And now all of our family is here. That's what she's thankful for most of all," Mr. Pratte said, his voice low. "Your father gave Vincenzo a place here and it reunited us." He looked over my shoulder to where Vincenzo stood. "I thank the Lord that Sam got to know him in the city, that he found him and—"

"I haven't had spaghetti bottarga since before the boat," Vincenzo said, interrupting his father. "The bottarga is perfect, exactly like Nonna's. Did you cure it yourself, Mother?"

"Of course," she said proudly, tilting her lithe shoulders

back and sitting up in the ladder-back chair. "Papa caught it last September when the mullet were biting. Mr. Fremd went with him to a spot on the Sound where they get caught in migration."

"Really?" I asked. I'd never known my father to spend time fishing or doing anything for leisure for that matter.

"Oh yes," Mr. Pratte said. "He didn't stay to catch, mind you. He's too busy with the flowers for that, but he took me down and showed me. The next morning, he had the salt and oil delivered from your uncle's meat market."

I didn't quite know what to say. I knew my father cared for people, deeply sometimes, but I had no idea he did things like this.

"To work for a man, a family, of such generosity is a blessing indeed," Mrs. Pratte said.

I smiled, swirled my fork in the pasta, and lifted it to my mouth. It was perfect and I couldn't help but close my eyes as I chewed.

"This may be my favorite dish of all time," I said to Mrs. Pratte.

"Thank you. I'm honored to hear you say so," she said.

It occurred to me just then that perhaps they were complimenting my father to make me feel welcome, to let me know they were satisfied here. Perhaps they thought that was why I'd come, to check on the state of things for him.

"Surely my father isn't always considerate. Is there anything you suppose you'd like to see changed?" I asked. "And to be clear, I am only here to eat and have a merry time with you all. I have not been sent by him in any capacity, but I do care for all of you and want to make sure you feel as valued as you are."

Sam had barely looked up from his bowl since he started eating but did so now as though I'd asked the wrong question or said the wrong thing. Laughter burbled up around the room, first with the Russo brothers, and then it spread to Pasqualle and then finally to Vincenzo, whose deep chuckle practically rattled the walls.

"We don't mean to laugh at you, Miss Fremd, but we have all seen the likeness of the devil in our former bosses and landlords, people who viewed us like animals—and even animals are cared for here," Vincenzo said. "We have all lived in squalor, amid lice and feces and disease, before we came here, and some of us have more recent memories than others." He slurped a bit of his spaghetti. I noticed Sam had stopped eating altogether.

"I lived in a tenement next to the shirt factory and it was horrible. Lived five to a bedroom. I was considered lucky. Just a few streets over, Sam here was evicting people out of the Orchard Street Tenements for that imp Carl Freeman, and there it was twelve people to a thirteen-foot flat, and he lived in there too. There, when people were evicted, they just moved to the streets and Mr. Freeman knew it, so he'd often have the chamber pots emptied up the road from them so the excrement would flow down the street to where they lay."

Sam's face was pale, and he set his fork down on the table.

"Hush, Vincenzo. It's supper," his mother whispered, but Vincenzo didn't seem to notice.

"Eventually there was a cholera outbreak in that tenement and many lost their lives all on account of the evil of that man. So when you ask us about your father, Miss Fremd, you might as well ask us to criticize an angel. What did Mr. Foster say that one time, Sam? 'Our trees are rats and our flowers disease'? That about sums up our lives before this."

At once, Sam pushed back from the table, stood, and walked out the door.

"What? What did I say?" Vincenzo asked as Sam passed.

"Excuse me," I said. "I'll go speak with him." I tipped my head at Mr. and Mrs. Pratte, wove through the others, then went down the narrow hallway and out the back door.

"Sam?" I called. I walked down the steps and out onto the crushed-shell drive, then into the woods beyond. Late evening sunlight dappled the ground through the trees and I found him just beyond the first row of maples, staring into the gulf of ferns and rocks and moss. I thought to say something, but I didn't know what to say, so I just stood there beside him. Tears rolled silently down his cheeks. I could hardly bear it. I reached out and took his hand, but he let mine go.

"I hear him all the time, Sadie. 'Our trees are rats and our flowers disease.' I hear him when I wake up in the morning. I hear him when I go to sleep at night," Sam said quietly. "I met Mr. Foster in the tenement. He was in a wheelchair. He lost his legs to an accident in a mill that had since been shut down. He and his daughter were originally from Ireland. They'd had a farm there." He paused. Overhead a hawk called.

"They were the kindest people I had ever met. They invited me into their flat that they shared with ten others and it became my second home. When Roisin—" He choked on the name and my heart dropped into my stomach. "When Roisin would get home from the shirtwaist factory, she'd cook for us—even for me. They were my family."

We stood in silence for a moment. It wasn't my time to speak, no matter how much I wanted to comfort him.

"I told myself I'd find a way to get them out of there. One

day, though, after Roisin had been out of work for a few weeks because of an injury, Mr. Freeman handed me their eviction papers. I couldn't bear it. I couldn't let them live on the streets and there wasn't room in my flat—there were already eight of us. Roisin and Mr. Foster told me to leave them behind, that they would find their way, but I would not. I quit my job and found a post dyeing wool for a textile factory and immediately began work there. There was an apartment just around the block. It was still a tenement, but it was more private, reserved for a married couple." Sam wiped the tears from his eyes. The horror of his story made me ache. It sounded like a nightmare, like it couldn't possibly be true.

"I went home that night and asked Roisin to marry me," he said. My breath caught and I clutched the trunk of the nearest tree, sure I would collapse. "I told her and her father that if she did, we could move into the flat I'd found. She agreed. She said she loved me, and I . . . I didn't say it back. I suppose I thought she knew we were marrying for security, for housing, but she did not. The day before we were to marry, she said it again and I told her the truth. I said I loved her deeply, as a friend, as a sister, but nothing more."

He turned to face me then and his eyes held mine. He was going to tell me his heart was still mine. He was going to tell me he loved me. I was shaking—I could feel the tremor in my hands and immediately balled my fingers to stop it.

"After that, she took Mr. Foster and they went back to Orchard Street. They moved into a flat with more people and I moved across the street into a flat with nine. About that time, cholera started sweeping through their building. The moment I heard of it, I waited outside all day, hoping to catch Roisin or her father, and when I realized they could be dying, I went into the tenement myself, though Mr. Freeman had forbidden me to enter. I found Roisin, but Mr. Foster was dead." Sam began to cry again, and I reached out and embraced him. This time he didn't push me away.

When his shoulders ceased heaving, he stepped back.

"Right then I knew I could either leave the city or die in it," he said. He cleared his throat. "I begged Roisin to come with me. I told her I was wrong, that I loved her, that I'd marry her. She said she would think about it, that I should go and she would come behind if she chose. I told her I was coming back here, but she hasn't come, Sadie, and I feel deeply that she's gone too."

He pinched the bridge of his nose.

"If she and her father had only had a chance at fresh air and a clean place to stay, if they'd had a place, a park, they could have survived. They could have survived."

I swallowed hard, images of the life he'd lived without me playing out in my imagination.

"Come on then," I said. "We have to go find her. We have to bring her here. Surely she's not gone far from Orchard Street since you left."

The idea of Sam with another woman drowned my heart, but this was right. It was the right thing to do.

I turned to walk toward the house and the barn, but Sam caught my wrist.

"I've gone into the city every week to try to find her and I can't," he whispered.

"Together we will," I said. "You can't lose love twice. I won't let you."

He searched my eyes. "I've only lost it once," he said. He

pulled me close and his thumb ran across my cheek. My breath caught. "The last time I said it to her, I lied. I was desperate to save her. I loved her like I did my own flesh and blood, and I will look for her until my dying day, but when I gave my heart to you, I never got it back."

"I'm sorry," I started, but before I could say more, Sam leaned down and kissed me. I threaded my fingers around his neck and deepened the kiss, feeling the familiar dance of his lips, and his hands clasped my waist, pulling me against him with a hunger that burned like fire through us both.

"I love you," I said, when my lips broke from his. I kissed his neck and he drew a sharp breath. "I'm going to tell Father about us. I'm going to tell him I love you. He'll come around. He'll let us have this place once we—"

Sam pulled me away from him, his hands still gripping my waist.

"You can't," he said. "You can't." He looked down. "I love you, Sadie. I always will. But Roisin and I . . . If she comes to find me here and I've broken my promise . . ." He shook his head. "I've already lied to her about loving her, and that much I can't help. But if she comes and she needs me, if I'm the only way she's going to stay out of the tenements and the factories, I'm going to marry her."

"How long will you wait?" I asked. My heart was breaking all over again as I looked at him—at the eyes that loved me, at the lips that were my home. There would be no talking him out of it. Sam was a man of his word.

"I don't know," he said simply.

My hands dropped from his neck and I blinked back tears.

"There's no hope of us," I said. "Even though we love each

other. Even though we always will. Letting you get on that train without me is the regret of my life."

He cupped my face. "I started to believe years ago that I got on that train alone because I was supposed to, because if you had been with me, my love, I wouldn't have seen what I did and I needed to see it. It is enough for me to know you love me."

"It's not enough for me," I said. "It is a torture to have to pass you without touching you and act as though my heart is indifferent, when in fact it is bleeding."

"Should I go?" His question was asked gently, but it prompted a sob from my lips.

"No! Never. I would rather my soul be crushed with every glance than ever be away from you again," I said.

"Then so long as I can help it, I will never leave you," he said. "And if . . . if she never comes for me, I—" He stopped, leaned down, and kissed me gently. "I can't ask you to wait for me. I don't want you to."

"But I love you," I said. "Even if I end up an old maid, it would be worth it. How could I ever accept anyone else?"

CHAPTER 10

The sunrise washed the fields beyond me in pinks and yellows and reds as an ethereal haze rose from the earth. I rubbed my eyes and swiped my hand across the condensation gathering on the greenhouse glass to see the view more clearly. As lovely as the sunrise was, I couldn't keep this up. Missing so much sleep was taking its toll.

Sam and I had planted two gardens each last night and arrived back at the nurseries at five thirty. On my way home I'd glimpsed lamplight in Mrs. Griffith's front room and her draperies pulled back. She'd been sitting in front of the window staring out toward the flowers, though I doubted she could see them in the darkness. Knowing she treasured the tulips made my exhaustion worthwhile.

I yawned and pushed a strand of wayward hair back into its pin. After I'd settled Gene in the barn, I considered going in the house to sleep a bit and wait for Agnes to come to dress me, but Father often rose before the sun and I couldn't risk him seeing me. I hoped Agnes would simply assume I'd woken early, which happened on occasion, and that Father wouldn't notice that I hadn't changed. Wearing the same sort of white frock each day had its advantages.

I stuck a little brown stake into another pot, this time a hydrangea. The gardeners would start loading the Finks' pink varieties into carts in an hour or two, and though most had already been flagged for transport to the estate, the newly treated hydrangeas had not. We'd added lime to the soil a few days prior, but it took a bit of time for the aluminum to dissipate, which caused the flowers to be pink. In the presence of aluminum, they would be blue. After the Finks' plants were loaded, I planned to write to Mrs. Garner and remind her to call on us about her English herb garden. I couldn't let too much time pass or I was certain she'd forget.

Mr. Vicchialla tapped on the glass, startling me. He often rose before everyone else to water the plants.

"Good day, Miss Fremd!" he shouted, likely waking the entire village. "Today is a dream, isn't it?"

I nodded and smiled at him, but my mind was now on Sam, on what he said when I returned this morning. He'd been back for half an hour before I arrived, and he waited for me in the barn to unhitch Gene. When I saw him standing there in the dark, the memory of his confession that he loved me was too difficult to ignore. I'd kissed him, and he'd kissed me back. I could still feel the echo of his fingers in my hair, on my neck. But then he'd pulled away.

"Sadie," he'd said, his palm still on my cheek. "We can't keep this up. Not with what I've promised Roisin, not until we know that she's not coming for me." He'd paused and dragged a hand over his face. "I want her to come, Sadie. I want to know she's alive and *well. But I can't help but pray she's found another man to love her. Lord knows I'll never love anyone but you. This being here with you, working alongside you to do something greater, wanting you the way I always have . . . I can't keep my mind from thinking of you. Even so, we must stop this."*

I'd agreed with him then, but ultimately it didn't matter whether we kept kissing or not; even if he never kissed me again, my heart would shatter if he married someone else.

I yawned and lifted another hydrangea into place, next to the one I'd just flagged. I picked up the lime can and sprinkled a bit on the soil.

"Sadie, I must speak with you." Father burst into the greenhouse and slammed the door behind him. His face was red, and our account books were curled like scrolls in his hands. I froze. Was this the end? Were we folding despite my most ardent efforts? Was my dream about to dissolve?

I pressed a stake into the root ball to keep my hands busy.

"Stop that, will you?" he shouted. "We'll deal with it later. Someone is stealing from us!"

"What?" I turned to face him. His eyes were stony, his jaw set.

"I was just out on an early errand to your uncle Theodore's when I saw one of those gardens the paper mentioned. A Fremdeye ash was planted in the center of it," he said.

At once I felt faint. Father had cultivated the Fremdeye ash just two years back, a cross between the green and black ash trees with the look of their bark and leaves. The plants were unique and unmistakable. I hadn't checked the plants Sam selected, only my own. He must have included it, not knowing. He hadn't been here to see that cross originated.

"It must be a misunderstanding," I said when I found my

voice. I hoped Father couldn't hear it wavering. "It could have come from one of our account estates."

"No. It's too young," he said. "I need you to come to the barn. I've roused the village and I will get to the bottom of this betrayal." He started to turn away, but I grabbed his arm.

"Father, no. You can't do that. It's—" He yanked his arm free before I could confess and hastened out of the greenhouse.

"Father!" I called after him, but he wouldn't stop. I ran after him, down the hill, over the rail tracks. "Father, please," I said. I reached him before he got to the barn. Already most of our employees were gathered in the field between the barn and the village.

"Listen to me!" I pleaded. "It's my fault. It's not what you think." He only glanced at me, not hearing my confession. He shook his head.

"Stand over there." He pointed to the corner of the barn. "You've been keen to hear about the status of our enterprise. Now you and the rest will be privy to the whole lot."

He climbed up the stone mounting-block steps and unfurled the account books. His face was red and our employees took notice, whispering to each other, doubtless wondering what I had—was this the end for us?

"I have called you all here this morning because quite honestly, I'm furious." Father's voice boomed over us. My skin prickled with nerves.

"Father," I said again, hoping to catch his attention long enough to confess, but he waved a hand at me.

"*Wie konntest du das tun?*" Father yelled. *How could you do this?* The German was never a positive sign. He only broke into it when his passion overrode his rationale. No one would understand him.

I glanced into the crowd and found Sam standing in the middle next to Vincenzo. His eyes met mine and his face sobered.

"Yesterday Rye Jewelers folded. George Turner sold the last of his inventory to a store in the city so he could retain his home. There are now only two stores downtown. Two. The meat market and the five-and-dime, and when everyone is forced to depart this town, they will close too," Father said. The Sigallis family suddenly held hands in the front row, their eyes wide, as they waited for Father to tell them that we, too, were finished.

Father flipped open the account books.

"Twenty-nine thousand five hundred sixty-five dollars for employee salaries. Most of you are paid more than you would make elsewhere at $1.35 per day—nearly $500 per year—and your living expenses are taken care of without cost to you. The fee for our annual four thousand plants is nearly $24,000 and that doesn't include fertilizer and livestock and equipment. All in all, it costs me"—he jabbed his finger at a line in the account books—"$43,000 to run this enterprise each year, and that is a modest figure."

He ran a weary hand across his face, letting his fingers eventually come to rest on his beard. Then he flipped to the back of the book and began reading again.

"At the end of March we were running at a deficit of $21,000. The crash was at its height. Even now with the addition of the Finks and the Brundages and possibly the Garners paying $5,000 each, we are still down $6,000. Of course, our other properties will need upkeep, but those yearly retainers only add up to $2,000 at most, not enough to cover all of our expenses." He snapped the account books shut.

"Thankfully I am a frugal man and have secure savings, but my pockets are not infinitely deep, and they have suffered under the crash just like everyone else's."

"Are you saying we're closing?" Pasqualle Pratte's voice was soft and childlike, and she kept her eyes turned down to her toes when she asked.

"No, dear," Father said, his voice softening just for her. "But we are in danger of it, and it has come to my attention that someone in our company here is stealing from me. Someone here is the charitable gardener the papers have been yammering about."

A collective gasp rose from the crowd and suspicious gazes were cast about. None toward me.

"Father, if I may—" I started, but he cut me off, laughing under his breath and waving a hand at me.

"Whoever you are, I thought your gardens valiant at first. You've been clever. You've planted nondescript varieties until now, but when you planted the Fremdeye tree downtown last night, you made a fatal error."

He was back to yelling now. "Do you have any idea what you've cost us? There are now at least five *free* gardens about, and all in, the figures on those plants reach into the hundreds. You are sinking us! You are sinking yourself! And if I hadn't caught on, I'm confident you would have drained us of thousands . . . Thousands!" Father took a breath and straightened.

My heart skipped and my mouth went dry. I had thought the varieties we chose incidental. We threw away disfigured plants daily, and I'd assumed the small amount doomed to the garbage didn't matter. Then again, I hadn't witnessed the discarding for some time. Perhaps we were saving everything in these difficult days. Perhaps I was a fool, completely unfit to think I could understand the minutiae of business.

"If you come forward now, I will forgive your debt and refrain from calling the law. If you do not, I will relentlessly inquire of this bandit until someone breaks."

The silence that followed was palpable. No one moved. Finally, I couldn't take it any longer and I couldn't risk him interrupting me.

"It was me," I said loudly.

Father whirled, his eyes ablaze.

"I tried to tell you, but you wouldn't listen. I'm sorry, Father."

He swallowed hard and slowly turned back to our employees. I could see a vein pulsing in his neck. "I sincerely apologize to all of you. I am horribly embarrassed," he said. "Please forgive me."

I looked at Sam, whose eyes were fixed on Father. He had to look at me. I had to prevent him from confessing, too, because I knew in his soul he wouldn't be able to bear my falling on the sword alone.

"You weren't entirely wrong to accuse one of us." Sam's voice punctuated the air, and for the second time, the whole of the crowd tensed.

"I helped Miss Fremd, and I'm not sorry for it. Beauty doesn't only belong to the rich, Mr. Fremd, yet flowers and nature, the hope they provide, are withheld from the poor. Would you allow such people to wither away knowing you can afford to give those flowers away? We only chose imperfect plants, those you likely would have discarded. Despite the figures, you can afford it.

Look at your home and your carriages and Miss Fremd's fine dresses. You—"

"Pack your things and leave," Father spat. "Get out!"

"No, Father, it was my fault. I—" I stepped toward him, but before I could plead Sam's case, Father's hand clamped onto my wrist and he pulled me with him up the hill.

"I started doing it on my own," I said, struggling to keep up as we passed the greenhouses. My heart pumped in my ears.

"I met a man at the Brundages' who had fallen on hard times, a man who kept looking beyond the gates of the fine homes around here just to see a flower, to see hope. I didn't think it would hurt to plant a small garden for him, to give him strength to keep on. Sam saw me that night and didn't want me to go alone. Don't fire him, Father. He was only trying to keep me safe."

"I should have known," he hissed. "With all your talk of public parks and charity. With the countless refusals of perfect suitors. *He* has been in your head."

When we reached the porch, he let me go.

"That Sam Jenkins is nothing but trouble. *Und ich weiß, dass er dich liebt.*" *And I know he loves you.* He'd said it in German, likely so anyone who overheard wouldn't understand. His eyes bored into mine.

I took a breath and stood tall. "I love him too. He's a wonderful horticulturist and incredibly intelligent. Father, we could help you here; Sam and I could run the nurseries together," I said, my voice pleading. He'd already let Sam go. There was no risk to my confession now. "I know it seems like we've made an unforgivable error, but now that I know the true state of things, I wouldn't dare risk the future of the business again. I could discuss it with Sam; we would find another way to help—"

"You are both liars and cheats!" Father shouted. "You, my own daughter, stole from me—from us. You will never run the nurseries. You have proven your incompetence and so has your beau, if that's what he is. He has no idea of my figures, of the fact that I can only maintain this deficit for a year, that even if I sell the house and the carriages it won't come close to retaining this enterprise and our lives. And to think the two of you supposed I could fund a public park." He laughed.

A sob lodged in my throat. Why had Sam planted that tree? It was my fault. I'd insisted we do the gardens separately. "But, Father—"

"There are reasons I prohibited your close interaction with those in our employ, and this is one of them. Now I have embarrassed myself in front of our employees. You have fallen prey to dangerous notions. You have forgotten yourself. I forbid you to solicit accounts. I forbid you to set foot in the greenhouses. I forbid you to go anywhere but up and down the halls of this house."

I tried to take a breath but could not. His words stole the air from my lungs. I wanted to crumple, to faint and awake with this scene before me no more than a nightmare.

"I am going to send for Freddie and Charles. We will find a proper successor together, someone who will work alongside me in your brothers' stead to build the nurseries back up until I am ready to hand them over. It was an error to wait this long and allow your involvement in the business at all.

"You will select a suitable match—Reynolds, Brundage—I don't care which. If you do not, I will have you booked on the next overseas passenger ship and you will live with Oma and Opi in Stuttgart until you see clearly and accept your destiny as a woman of society, a woman of proper breeding. I will not lose the nurseries and your future to your schemes."

Tears filled my eyes and I didn't stop them from falling. Everything I wanted, everything my heart yearned for was gone. I would never have the nurseries. Father would never approve of Sam. I would never again give hope to those who had none. Compassion and business could not intersect here. Nor could love and business.

I would find Sam and go with him. Even if I lost everything, I'd still have love.

"I'm going for a walk," I said. At once the thought that Sam could depart without saying goodbye filled me with urgency. I needed to find him before he could leave.

"No," Father said. "You will not."

"I need to, Father. Everything you've said is too difficult to bear." I attempted to step off the porch, but Father clutched my arm.

"You will go inside to the kitchen where Mr. Cooper will watch over you until I can fetch Agnes. She will chaperone you day and night. She will sleep in your quarters. She will follow you through the house during the day," he said. "She will not leave your side until you are married."

"I don't love them, Father. Surely you know the importance of love. You and Mother were in love. *You* married for love. And I don't want to leave. This is my home and plants are my heart."

"Your mother and I were not afforded the luxuries you were. We were not accustomed to the life you now live. Love was our only option. You may not love these men, but they are amiable and they are in love with you. They will give you everything you could ever want and they will keep you safe," he said.

"I don't want safety. I want the nurseries and I want Sam," I said.

"You'll have neither!" Father barked. "You are young and naive and I have lived three decades longer. I understand life. If you want to stay here, you'll marry Reynolds. He said he would be willing to make this place his home, and despite a few of his ideas about our employees, he is a most suitable successor for me. Perhaps you can persuade him to finance your park."

I wiped my face and stared at my father. I'd always thought he loved me, that deep down, he would want me to be happy. Marrying Mr. Reynolds, watching him gallivant around the nurseries as owner in my place, watching him fight with Father to let our employees go, destined for the slums, would be a torture. Someone who could even think of dooming others to the fate of factory life for the benefit of their own prosperity would never concede funds for a public park. Eventually Father would understand why I had to leave.

"I think I'll go in now," I said, my voice barely a whisper. I crossed the threshold breathing in the familiar scent of old antiques and hyacinth, knowing well that these were my final hours of luxury, that within a day or two I may find myself in the city, buried in ash and grime.

Even so, I would be with Sam. I prayed I would be able to endure it, that we would find our way together.

CHAPTER II

Early the next morning, Agnes was still asleep in front of my door. I sat up in bed as the morning light filtered through my window and listened to her whistling snores. In the middle of the night, I blamed the noise for my insomnia, but the truth was that it was my captivity. Between Mr. Cooper and Agnes, I'd been afforded no time alone since Father's decree the previous morning. Even while washing I was given little privacy. The moment I saw Agnes, I begged her to let me go or to take a note to Sam if she would not, but she refused.

"He's gone," she'd said, and when I asked where, she only shrugged. "I don't suppose he told anyone." That, I knew, was a lie. Vincenzo would know; the Prattes would know. Knowing the conditions he faced in the city, they wouldn't allow him to disappear again.

I glanced at the window for the hundredth time in the last two hours. My room was at least eighteen feet from the ground. Would I die if I jumped or simply break a leg? The latter I was willing to risk.

I peeled the sheets off, situated my nightgown back over my thighs, and swung out of bed. The wood floor was cold on my toes as I crossed to the window. In the distance I could barely make out two figures by the barn. They were likely loading the carts for the second day of planting at the Finks' today.

I closed my eyes and inhaled slowly, imagining myself walking through the new garden. The heady scent of double bloom roses would mingle with the salty sea breeze; the noise of the sea and my boots on the crushed-shell path would be the only sounds; the shades of pink would be like a carpet of beauty rolled out before me. If I was afforded five minutes there, I knew I could figure out what to do now—how to dissolve the tension in my shoulders and the ache in my heart—but I was stuck, imprisoned in my father's house, waiting to become stuck and imprisoned forever in a loveless marriage or confined to a small German town where I knew no one.

"You're up, Miss Sadie. I apologize for sleeping so late. I'm unaccustomed to the silence here, I suppose," Agnes said as she rubbed her eyes and yawned.

"It's no trouble, but I would like to dress and then have a cup of coffee." I turned back to the window, hoping she would leave me and go down to the kitchen to fetch it. All I needed was a moment to slip out the back door.

"I'll ring Mr. Cooper," Agnes said. She leaned over the cot and extracted a large cowbell from below it.

"Heavens! Don't use that. You'll wake Father."

"He's the one who instructed me to use it," she said. "I'm not to leave you, even for a moment."

I sighed. "I am a prisoner and you my warden."

Agnes laughed. "Hardly, Miss Fremd. Your father is simply

ensuring your safety and that you end up quite where you belong."

I whirled on her. "He doesn't know a thing about where I belong. None of you do," I snapped. "I am twenty-two years old. I am not a child."

"Yet your sensibilities are not reflecting the woman you should be."

My fingers clenched. How dare she overstep this way. "Whatever do you mean? Do women not fall in love? Do women not aspire to make the world a better place? Do women not have dreams the same as men? I fail to understand how I am any less sensible than Freddie or Charles or Father, for that matter."

"You have stolen from your father, ruining your chances at realizing any sort of aspirations here. In love, you are simply naive. I've told you before that any sort of entanglement with Mr. Jenkins was a gaffe, but you would not listen. He is not of your class. He cannot give you security or comfort, and when love's fire cools those things are vastly important. Your father would rather risk your heartache than risk your life. You are a lady, Miss Sadie. You cannot forfeit your life to lie, diseased and dying, in the New York City slums simply because you love a man."

"Please help me dress. I've tired of this conversation," I said. "I'll have the black frock today, the mourning gown from when Mother passed."

"Miss Sadie, don't you find that a bit dramatic?" Agnes asked.

"Not in the slightest," I said. "In fact, a more suitable garment would be sackcloth and ashes."

One could occupy oneself with reading for only so long. As much as I adored Oscar Wilde and was captivated by *Lady Windermere's Fan*, nothing could keep my mind distracted from Sam or the plants, from wishing I could be with both. I needed to go to the greenhouse to check on my new peony. I needed to go sprinkle more lime on the hydrangeas. I needed to find Sam.

I ran my hands along the carved cherry arm of the rocking chair and pushed back the damask curtains of the library with my foot. A sliver of sunlight danced across my black leather boot. Agnes had closed the curtains a few hours before, complaining that the brightness hurt her eyes, but I couldn't bear the dark. It made me feel claustrophobic and exhausted.

"I think I'll go for a walk now," I said. I snapped the book shut and rose, not bothering to look at Agnes. If I led with the assumption that I was permitted to go where I wanted, perhaps she'd forget. I crossed to the opposite wall and shoved the book in its place.

"We'll go as soon as I finish this chapter," Agnes murmured. "Why don't you choose another book until then." She waved her hand around the room at the bookshelves lining every wall without looking up from *My Year in a Log Cabin* by William Dean Howells. Everything Agnes read was sensible nonfiction. She never bothered to dabble in fiction or fantasy. That was probably why her romantic notions were rooted in practicality instead of love.

"You don't need to go with me," I said. "I'm not going to get lost."

She looked up then. "Of course you would," she said.

I loathed that she knew me so well.

She went back to reading and I pushed the curtains open farther. The greenhouses were bustling today. Pasqualle Pratte was pushing a wheelbarrow of sod and set it down next to a pallet of spirea. I wanted to lift the window, to call out to her, but I knew she wouldn't hear me.

A dark green James Cunningham five-glass landau pulled into view and twin bay Clydesdales stopped abruptly in front of our house.

"What is Mr. Vaux doing here?" I asked Agnes.

"Mr. Vaux?" she asked, barely looking up from her book. "I couldn't say."

Calvert Vaux was the reason Father had started the nurseries. He hired Father out of the slums and noticed his eye for horticulture. Never mind that Father never had any sort of formal training. Mr. Vaux encouraged him anyway, ultimately advising that a high-quality nursery was needed in this part of the country. That one bit of encouragement changed Father's life—the rest of ours as well.

Mr. Vaux's driver swung down from his post and opened the carriage door. The coach was trimmed inside with dark green satin, the cushions lined with broad lace. It was one of the finest carriages I'd ever seen. Mr. Vaux emerged slowly, his gilded cane first and then his slight frame clothed in his signature gray. When he was properly situated on the ground, he pushed his small, round spectacles up the bridge of his nose and waved off the arm of his driver before starting up the walk much more slowly than he used to.

"I'm going to greet him. You can watch from the window," I

said to Agnes, then turned and walked from the library, through the drawing room, and out the front door before she could follow.

"Good afternoon, Mr. Vaux," I called as I stepped off the porch and down the walk to meet him.

He looked up, breaking his concentration on his footing, and smiled.

"Miss Fremd. How delightful to see you. I'm glad you're here. I was coming to call on your father and I admit I didn't have the foresight to telegram first," he said. "Do you know if he's about?"

"I haven't seen him yet today. It's our second day of planting a new garden at the Finks', so he's either there or somewhere around here," I said, looping my arm through his. It was one thing for him to refuse the help of his driver but another thing entirely to refuse my accompanying him up the walk.

"Oh, that will be lovely. They have the most magnificent backdrop," he said. Then he craned his neck and looked at my frock. "Has something dreadful happened?"

I glanced down at the dull black. The color was horrible to begin with, but it was especially horrible on me. It made me look sickly. Then again, it likely did that to most, helping along the impression that one should be somber for every moment of every day of the grieving period.

"No, thankfully. I'm only wearing it in a bit of protest." Vaux was a forward-thinking man. Perhaps serendipity had brought him here at the dawn of my despair.

"What are you protesting?" he asked. He grunted and sighed as he heaved his legs up the five steps.

"Calvert. Good to see you." Father materialized in the door-way. He looked at me and his eyes narrowed at the sight of my ensemble, but he wouldn't rebuke me. Not right here in front of Mr. Vaux. "I apologize that I didn't catch you at the road. I've been sorting out my books this morning."

"As we all are," Mr. Vaux said, shaking his head. "This is a hard time indeed, isn't it, Charles?"

"Certainly, but let's not dwell on it. I know that's not why you called. Let's get settled in the dining room and I'll have Mr. Cooper serve us a little luncheon," Father said.

Mr. Vaux stepped inside and I followed.

"There's no need for all that fuss," he said.

"I insist," Father replied.

"It's been lovely to see you, Mr. Vaux. I hope you'll call more often." I clutched his hand and he squeezed.

"Do join us, Sadie. I've been keen to compliment your gardens," he said.

I stared at him for a moment before we began walking to the dining room. Surely he didn't know. Not yet. I could feel Father's gaze.

"Word of it is all around the town. And that Sam Jenkins is now employed with Mr. Sanderson at the cemetery. Filled Lou Farley's spot—who left to go work on his family's cattle farm only last week. Circle of life, I suppose. His father and now him," Vaux said.

The nerves that had riddled my stomach at his mention of my originating the gardens suddenly settled with the knowledge that Sam was just across the street, not back in the city.

"He stole from me, Calvert. I can't say I'm thrilled at his fortunate role just next door," Father said, settling himself at the head of the table. Mr. Cooper materialized from the kitchen and held my chair out for me and then for Mr. Vaux as he sat next to Father.

When he was settled, Mr. Vaux cleared his throat. "I've come because Olmsted and I are going to need your considerable assistance in sourcing plants for a new public park in Newburgh. Downing Park it will be called, after Andrew," he said.

Andrew Jackson Downing was Mr. Vaux's and Mr. Olmsted's late mentor, one of the founders of American landscape architecture.

"It'll be quite nice, I think. Thirty-five acres. The land was given to Newburgh upon the death of a farmer in the area, and the mayor saw fit to make it a showplace, available to all, as you know Andrew would have appreciated," Mr. Vaux went on.

My mind flitted to the citizens of our town. Would any of them will their land to Rye for such a cause? The hope deadened almost immediately. Our town was a home for industrialists, most of whom had immaculate private gardens and therefore wouldn't likely think of gifting their land for public use. Newburgh was a farming community built on the backs of hardworking laborers who saw the advantages of such a project for common use.

"Of course you know we're good for it," Father said.

"It won't be for a year or so still, but you know we'll need thousands of plants, and that will take time. It's not the project Central Park was, of course, but quite an undertaking all the same," he said.

Mr. Cooper filled our water glasses and Mr. Vaux took a long drink.

"Of course, like Central, it'll be naturalistic, rustic. Off the top of my head, we'll need red oak, ginkgo, sycamore, American chestnut, maples, willows, and I want that rare yew tree you showed me in the catalog from Japan last year."

"We ordered a few and they're thriving," Father said.

"Good. Now the others will be easy—grasses and boxwoods and the like—but we want to do an ornamental daylily garden as well and obtain all the varieties we can find. Downing loved daylilies."

"We have over two dozen in our greenhouses just there," I said, pointing that direction. "And if you'd like a particular color, we've had great success in cultivating new varieties as well."

"You're a fortunate man, Charles, to have such a daughter," Mr. Vaux said, smiling at me. "Her passion for horticulture is obvious and her skill in it equally matched. I still can't quite believe you were behind those gardens, Miss Fremd. We passed a few on our drive in. The design of them is remarkable. Charles, I do believe you've met your match."

Father said nothing but busied himself with rearranging his napkin in his lap. At once, it occurred to me that I was sitting with the most renowned architect of public gardens in the world. If anyone could help me sort out adding a public space here in Westchester, it was Mr. Vaux.

"I appreciate you saying so, Mr. Vaux," I said. "Tell me something, will you? I know the Downing Park property was obtained by the city's inheritance, but where are the funds coming from for the plants? And for Central Park—how did the city obtain the land there?"

I could feel Father glaring at me, probably thinking that after being caught I'd surely given up the notion of a public park, but despite his wishing, I couldn't get the eyes of the man at the Brundages' gate out of my mind, nor the desperation of the rail village and the city slums.

"Andrew's widow donated the funds for the plants for

Downing. As far as Central goes . . . Ah, that is another story entirely," Mr. Vaux said. "The city utilized eminent domain in that case and took the land. The displaced residents were given only a fraction of the cost of their homes, and it was devastating to communities like Seneca Village, which housed mostly Black and Irish citizens. Many of those people were paid such a small sum for their properties that they couldn't find another piece of land to buy and had to resort to factory work in Lower Manhattan."

I recalled Sam telling me how the land for Central Park was obtained. Hearing it for the second time was equally perplexing—a park touted as a place for the public at the cost of the public.

Mr. Vaux continued. "Truthfully, I didn't know the true extent of it until the park was nearly finished. Neither did Olmsted. The irony of it was that our design was based on Birkenhead Park—the first publicly funded park in England. That park was built specifically to give respite to those living in poor conditions in the industrial areas. We hoped our Central Park would do the same. Unfortunately, we are not in control of the park we built, and it is largely occupied by only the Fifth Avenue set. Of course that set also donated millions for plants, so I suppose they think they own it in a way." Mr. Vaux shrugged. "With every new endeavor, our hope is to find a way to bring beauty to those who have none."

I smiled, but "millions" kept echoing in my mind. Millions. It cost millions to build a park, and I had nothing. The thought that I'd ever entertained the notion as possible now seemed utterly ridiculous. Father had never had that sort of fortune.

"Are you asking for a particular reason?" Mr. Vaux asked,

lifting a narrow cucumber sandwich from the blue willow tea plate Mr. Cooper had just set in front of him.

"She's been filling her mind with the idea of a public park here in Westchester. I told her it's impossible—especially in the midst of the crash," Father said. His tone was even, controlled.

"Every county should have one, but I daresay you're right, Charles. Unless some kind soul here donates land and there are people able to finance the planting, it is impossible. And alternatively, I would caution strongly against a campaign for the county to take land like New York did. To me, that quite cancels out the purpose of a park in the first place. If you give the poor a park but take away their homes, what good is that?"

"Surely there's a way for us to help. We're a nursery, after all," I said.

Father laughed, and Mr. Vaux shook his head.

"The way I see it, a person can be both philanthropic and business minded, but an enterprise cannot. Not truly anyway," Mr. Vaux said. He took a bite of the sandwich. "The enterprise exists to make money, and excess money can be used, in turn, by a person for whatever ventures he prefers. In your case it seems your father uses the excess to house his employees."

"I've been trying to tell her this, yet she cannot seem to grasp it," Father said.

His words irritated me. I did, in fact, grasp it. Even so, I wanted to find a way around it, to make things operate differently from the way everyone said they had to. If we grew the nurseries larger, we could finance more, but if the nurseries were overtaken by someone with Mr. Reynolds's sensibilities, the excess would be hoarded instead of given. Deep in my spirit, I'd sensed a shift since I planted that first rail village garden, a wrestling between what I'd always wanted and what I wanted now. If I couldn't create a space of beauty for everyone, perhaps I didn't want the nurseries after all.

"I do understand," I said finally. "But people are dying daily of hopelessness, of despair." Tears stung my eyes as the memories of the sewage smell and the lean-tos in the rail village and the garbage heap outside Mrs. Griffith's struck me. "Sometimes it might be cloaked in cholera or dysentery or diphtheria, but it is hopelessness all the same." I thought of Sam's Roisin and tears rolled down my cheeks. I didn't want her to come for him, and yet the thought of anyone wasting away for lack of fresh air and signs of life made my heart shatter.

"I know," Mr. Vaux said. His eyes were gentle and kind and he handed me his handkerchief. I wiped my eyes and settled. Next to him, Father swirled a spoon in his tea and avoided my gaze. "The best thing you can do is work with your father. Continue to grow this business until your excess can afford to be the remedy. You are a talent, Miss Fremd. I've seen testament to that."

It would take years, perhaps decades. And, of course, that was assuming Father would allow me to keep on, which was unlikely at this point. Still, I hoped he was hearing Mr. Vaux. I was an asset, a talent.

"Thank you," I said.

Mr. Vaux nodded and pulled his gilded watch from his pocket. "Heavens, it's late. I'm afraid I've got to be north this evening." He rose from his chair and Mr. Cooper hastened to gather his cane and hat from the doorway. "Do pull a list for me, will you, Charles? I know it's a year or so out yet, but we will need a master plan long before."

"Of course. I'll have it drawn up by the end of the week," Father said. He stood in turn as Mr. Vaux placed his boater back on his head and exited the room.

"Have a lovely day, Mr. Vaux," I called.

"You as well, Miss Fremd," he said.

The moment he was gone, Father sat back down and continued stirring his tea with fervor. I could feel his anger steaming. It made his face tight and his posture rigid.

"I only wondered about the parks," I said softly. "Mr. Vaux is right, you know. I could help you here. I *want* to help you here. I'm beyond proficient in—"

"Enough," he said under his breath. "I respect Calvert greatly, but in the matter of what is right for you, I cannot say I do. It is one thing for him to speak of how others should guide their daughters while he guides his a completely different direction. Helen and Julia—neither has even once shadowed him on-site. His sons, Bowyer and Downing? *They* are helping design the new park. Of course Downing should since he's named after the man, but either way, they are men about men's work, and they will eventually retain Calvert's interest in his business, just as Charles and Freddie were supposed to here. Helen and Julia are doing what?"

"They are married," I said. Both women lived in the avenues behind Fifth, close enough to walk to the park but not close enough to be considered New York aristocracy. Even so, they had married well and that was Father's point. "But, Father, Downing and Bowyer want to continue the work of Mr. Vaux. I know you were counting on Charles and Freddie, but they have gone. They have forged their own paths. I am here. I want to continue your work. Please let me. If I were a man, I—"

"But you're not!" Father practically shouted. "You are not a man. You are my daughter. I have gone over and over this with you. Your involvement is a risk I'm unwilling to take—especially with the market like it is and with your current sensibilities and dishonesty." He took a breath. "I promised your mother moments before she died that I would raise you as she would. I will not fail her."

"She would want me to be happy. She would want me to marry for love," I said, but even as I said it, I wasn't sure. Mother and Father had changed together. They had come from the slums and risen out of them, and that made a person cling to comfort like a life raft.

"She would want you to be settled and safe," he said evenly. "Tonight you will dress in the blush dinner dress just in from Wanamaker's and you will be charming. Mr. Reynolds and Mr. Brundage will be joining us for dinner, and you will select one of them. They are both keen to propose and I have told them that tonight you will decide. For the sake of all of us, you will choose. I cannot keep carrying this burden about. It feels like a millstone atop my shoulders. If you do not choose one, if you drive them away, you will be aboard the *Fürst Bismarck* next week, bound for Stuttgart. I've sent for your brothers too. They will be here in two or three days' time to help me find a suitable successor for the nurseries."

The blood drained from my face and my skin flushed cold.

"I . . . I can't believe Mr. Brundage and Mr. Reynolds would agree to such a thing. I thought Mr. Reynolds went back to England," I muttered.

"No. I telegrammed him the morning after the Goulds' party

and asked him to stay on here for a week or two if he was able," Father said.

"I can't love either of them," I said. "Please, Father." For the second time in the course of an hour, my eyes filled.

"Hearts are fickle things, Lily dear," he said. "Perhaps you believe that now, but over time your heart will warm to whichever man you select."

"I have loved the same man for four years. Some hearts may be fickle, but mine is not. I love Sam Jenkins and I always will."

I expected Father to explode, to throw his cup or yell, but he simply reached over and grasped my hand.

"I see that now," he said, his eyes filled with pity. "It is why I forbade you and your brothers from going to the village, but even allowing you to work alongside those in my employ was an error. You may believe you love him, but the two of you can never be together. You are cut from different cloths and it is impossible."

Much of what Father said echoed Sam's words. Perhaps he was right. Perhaps Sam and I would never be. Perhaps Roisin would come and they would marry and I would be left alone. Even so, I would rather risk loneliness than marry one of my suitors, but I didn't have that option. If I went to Germany, I knew my return wouldn't be for years, and by that time I'd lose everything. I'd lose my whole heart.

"I'm going to go now." I withdrew my hand from Father's and walked out of the room. Agnes was sitting in the hallway in a ladder-back chair, and the moment I emerged she stood to follow.

"Please," I said, my voice breaking. "Please leave me alone." Now more than ever I needed just a moment alone. I stepped up the stairs and heard her footsteps behind me.

For the first time in my life, I hated roses. Agnes had clipped a few sprigs of Cupid's Kiss—a miniature rose variety with a white petal base and a pink border—to adorn my pink lace décolleté and throughout the dinner both Lionel and Harry kept staring. It had been an awkward occasion to say the least. I'd barely spoken, save an agreeable nod when they asked to call me by my given name. The two men talked over each other, trying to impress Father as though he were the one whose hand they were contending for.

Then again, in some ways they were trying to win Father over. Lionel wanted our nurseries and Harry wanted to ensure that his wife was from a family that wasn't floundering. The fact that they found me pleasing to the eye was simply an incentive. Neither knew anything at all about me—what made me laugh, what made me cry, what I thought about their nonsense—and they didn't care to learn.

After the meal I reclined on the red velvet settee in the drawing room, watching the men select a cigar from Father's collection. I had come into the evening conflicted about my course, thinking that perhaps an engagement to whichever man I found less offensive would buy me a bit of time to win Father to my side and prevent him from shipping me off to Germany. I figured I could break the attachment before the wedding, but then, between the soup and the fish, I settled on the fact that a false engagement wasn't fair to them.

In the months of our attachment, whichever suitor I chose could miss his true match because of me. I loathed the possibility of being sent to Germany and what it would mean for my life, but it was the most honorable course—one that entangled only me, and perhaps Sam, in the snares of despair. Plus, Father was unlikely to change his mind about my becoming his successor or helping establish a park. I'd tried everything I could think of to convince him.

Perhaps it was time to give up.

"This row is Cuban, the middle is German, and the final row is American," Mr. Cooper said, holding the wooden box out to Lionel.

Lionel ran his thumb and index finger down his black mustache and then pointed. "I'll have the Cuban, please," he said. "If you're absolutely certain that lighting one in the presence of your daughter is acceptable, Mr. Fremd." Lionel was wearing the same sort of suit I'd seen him in at the Goulds', only a different sash was around his waist—a purple silk variety. He was handsome to be sure, but the line was drawn there. He wasn't witty or particularly interesting in any way, and even if he was, I wouldn't know it. I'd only conversed with him on the one occasion.

"You'll see in a moment that the Cuban is a mistake," Harry said, ignoring Lionel's concern about the impropriety of smoking around a lady. Harry had taken a seat on a tufted leather bench next to the fireplace to my left. "The depth of the American varieties are superior as of late, and I know Mr. Fremd is quite a connoisseur." He twirled his selection between his fingers.

Lionel shook his head. "I've already had an American and a German the past nights in town and thought I would expand my horizons."

"Sadie, why don't you play?" Father asked. I glanced at him as Mr. Cooper struck a match to light Father's cigar. Like Lionel,

Father had always found smoking in a lady's presence improper. This shift was quite unusual. Ordinarily, he would have the men withdraw to the smoking room adjacent to his office, but considering neither man had asked me a single question all evening, I was certain including me in this masculine ritual was his way of buying them time to woo me.

"Do you know Mozart's Sonata in C major, K. 521, Miss Fremd? I could play it with you. It's Mother's favorite," Harry said.

"I'm afraid I—"

"Or perhaps Beethoven's Fuge. That is a favorite of the king's and I have no doubt he'd be impressed if we played it for him at our next soiree," Lionel said. He doubtless knew most women would positively faint at the idea of being in the presence of the king of England in any capacity, but it didn't impress me in the slightest. Despite his title, the king was just an ordinary man beneath the pomp and circumstance.

"I'm afraid my proficiency in playing is limited to nursery songs," I said. I smiled sweetly but could feel Father glaring at me from across the room. I'd taken piano instruction since I was four. I could play either of the pieces the men mentioned with relative ease, but they were here to court a potential wife, not an entertainer, and I wasn't going to flounce about pretending my life's joy would be amusing my husband's peers at the piano bench.

"Sadie, don't be so modest. You've had nearly twenty years' worth of instruction in music—art and language too—and you just played the Mozart last week. I heard you," Father said, taking a draw from his cigar.

I took a breath, inhaling the sweet smell of the burning

tobacco. I understood why they enjoyed the cigars. They smelled comforting.

"I was about to say the same. Didn't you play Brahms's Sixteen Waltzes with Mrs. Ridgeway the other month at Mrs. Griffith's?" Harry asked. Smoke poured from his nose and mouth and his eyes met mine. As much of a dunce as I thought him, at least he knew Rye. At least he knew my friends and conversing with him was easy—though hardly a reason to accept engagement to the man.

"That was Sylvie LeBlanc," I said honestly. I hadn't played a thing at Mrs. Griffith's Christmas party. I thought of the thick swags of evergreen lining the grand stairway at Mrs. Griffith's home, the ten towering Fraser firs she'd ordered for the foyer and the drawing room and the ballroom and all of the bedrooms. Mrs. Griffith would never host another Christmas soiree, and Sylvie would never again sit on the bench of their shiny black Steinbach grand piano and entertain the likes of the Astors and Goulds and Rockefellers.

"Poor Miss LeBlanc," Harry said wistfully. I couldn't tell if it was sincere. "It's a shame her father couldn't manage his holdings. I feel for her."

"Do you really?" I asked before I could stop myself. Feigned sympathy made my blood boil, especially because before her father's misfortune, I knew Harry had his eye on her as well. "If you feel so badly, perhaps you should go find her in the city. Perhaps you should propose and save her."

Father gasped and Lionel chuckled, clearly thinking he'd won this round of the match.

"If you're speaking from a posture of jealousy, Miss Fremd, I can assure you there was nothing to the rumors of any sort of entanglement between myself and Miss LeBlanc. I've always had my gaze fixed on you." He took another drag of his cigar.

"Miss Fremd is captivating, Mr. Brundage. That much we can agree on," Lionel said as if I wasn't sitting right across from him. Then he turned to look at me. "From the moment we met, I kept imagining your portrait on our gallery wall at Exbury House, my Mitford family's estate, an estate I'll buy easily when I'm wed. Your countenance would be a jewel. We could remain here for most of the year and summer there in England. My family owns two thousand acres in Exbury and another five thousand in Cambridgeshire. Think of the gardens we could plant."

"Of course you know the breadth of my family's holdings, Miss Fremd, but to remind you, we have the estate here, the estate in Newport, the little townhome in the city, and the town my grandfather founded in Virginia. We would turn over all of the landscaping to your discretion," Harry said.

"Think of how much we could expand the nurseries you love so dearly," Lionel said. "I am willing to remain here for you."

I looked from Lionel to Harry and back again. Father's bringing them both here at the same time was a mistake. I had known it from the start. My hand was now a competition to be won on the magnitude of their estates. It was clear they had no idea of what made my heart soften. My mind had not been altered in the least. I couldn't choose either of them. I would have to accept my fate. I would have to go to Germany.

"If it's more land here you desire, I can buy you the Jay estate. Or perhaps beg the Parsonses' for Lounsbury or the Parkses for Whitby? Which do you want, Miss Fremd? Surely they would all be willing to part with the properties for the right price." Harry was pitched forward now, one hand clutched so hard around his knee that his knuckles were white. "There's Mrs. Griffith's too. My uncle has a contact with the possessing bank."

He kept talking, kept promising me the world, but all I heard was that these estates would be willing to rid themselves of their land. It was a convincing argument for marriage to Harry—in doing so I could win land to use for a park in the county—but I knew in accepting him I would also lock my own prison cell and throw away the key. Surely there was another way.

"Go for a turn around the grounds with me, Miss Fremd," Lionel said suddenly. He discarded his cigar in the crystal ashtray on the table beside him, rose, and walked toward me, his tall frame outlined by the moonglow coming from the panel of windows behind him.

This was my chance. I could come up with something on our walk, some excuse to wander away from him and find my way to Sam across the street at the cemetery. I wondered if he was living with the groundskeeper in the small house his father used to occupy.

"When you return, please join me by the fire alone," Harry said. "If it would be all right with you, Mr. Fremd."

"Quite," Father said.

I accepted Lionel's hand and rose from the settee.

"I've wanted to speak to you alone all night," Lionel whispered as I let him escort me toward the door.

"Just a moment," Father said. He plucked a little bell from the secretary and rang it. At once Agnes hastened into the room. "Miss Fremd requires a chaperone for a turn about our grounds." My hope suddenly deadened. Father had never assigned me a chaperone for a walk before. Now I was trapped, forced to endure a proposal I would decline.

I crossed under the doorway and crumpled the way I'd seen Lizzie Hudson Collier do in *A Gilded Fool* last year. I moaned and contorted my face into a grimace. Lionel and Agnes flew to my side.

"What's happened, Miss Sadie?" Agnes asked, her face full of fright.

"It's . . . it's my legs. They just gave out," I said. I gritted my teeth, pretending to be in a terrible amount of pain.

"Lily dear, what is it?" Father asked, joining Agnes.

"Her legs gave out," Agnes said.

I pinched my eyes shut and rocked back and forth, sure if I stayed this way long enough, Lionel and Harry would go.

"Miss Fremd . . . Sadie." Lionel's voice sounded close.

I opened my eyes to find him shifting behind me.

"Lie back against me here while your Father examines your leg," he said, his arm curling around my waist and pulling me against him. I twitched forward, wanting at once to rise to my feet and run away, but that would expose my lie.

Father knelt in front of me, and Harry came to my other side.

"Whereabouts does it hurt?" Harry asked.

"My shin, I suppose," I said. "The right one."

"Gentlemen, please do avert your eyes," Father said as he raised the hem of my skirt to my knees.

"Sadie, this isn't the way I wanted to do this, but I can't bear to wait any longer," Lionel whispered in my ear. "Will you be my wife?"

Nerves balled in my stomach. I whined and leaned forward, hoping the sudden jolt of fake pain would encourage Lionel to presume I hadn't heard him. What good was a feigned injury if it didn't stop the very action it was meant to prevent?

"It doesn't look broken or fractured," Father said. "I'll call for Dr. Robson first thing tomorrow."

"Thank you, Father," I said, whimpering.

"Mr. Brundage, Mr. Reynolds, I do appreciate you both coming, but I think it best I retire," I said.

"But, Sadie," Lionel said behind me, and then suddenly Harry clutched my hand.

"You know my feelings for you, Sadie, and I want you . . . I want you to marry me," he said.

"I've asked her too," Lionel said.

"She is in quite a state, men," Father said, surprisingly attempting to save me from having to dash both of their dreams at once. "Perhaps come by tomorrow and request an audience. She will be here." Father wrapped his arm around my waist and Agnes took my other arm. They hoisted me up, and I looked at Lionel, then Harry.

Both were still sitting on the floor, their gazes urgently searching mine for any sort of confirmation that I'd accept. As shallow as I thought their proposals were, it wasn't fair to string them along. I also had no desire to face another day of them pouring out their hearts to me when nothing they could say would change my mind.

"You are both wonderful men who have promised me more than any woman can dream," I said. "But—"

"Your father is right," Harry said. "It was unfair for us to propose to you now when you're in so much pain. I apologize."

"It's not that," I said. Father pressed his fingers into my waist, doubtless cautioning me to think before I spoke, but I'd already considered it all. "I cannot accept either of you. I've known my answer for some time, and it won't change tomorrow."

"You told me to remain, that her affections had altered," Lionel spat, glaring at Father. He rose from the floor.

"I'm sorry," Father said. "I had hoped."

"You can hardly blame Father. How would he know? Never once did you write to ask me," I said to Lionel. "I could have spared you a few weeks. I was clear that night at the Goulds'."

"You've wasted my time," he said.

Harry stood beside Lionel, his face clouded. "You have made a fool of me, Miss Fremd."

"I have made a fool of no one," I said, my tone sharp. "I told you both exactly how I felt and you ignored me. Even tonight, you barely spoke to me. To presume either of you love me is ridiculous. How could you? You barely know me." I sighed. "I'm going to retire. As of next week, I'll be residing in Stuttgart, so I do wish you both the best. You will find a match much more suitable than me."

Lionel muttered something under his breath, and Harry immediately turned and walked out the door with Lionel close behind. It slammed with a heavy *slap* that rattled the walls.

"I wish you would have chosen differently, Lily. It will be hard to lose you," Father said as we turned toward the stairs, my weight braced on his shoulders.

"Losing me is your choice," I replied.

Father shook his head.

"I wish you understood," he said.

I wished *he* understood.

CHAPTER 12

I saw no reason to prevent the world from knowing that my life was now over, so I donned my mourning dress again the following day. Agnes begged me to wear anything else—even the white linen costumes she had so criticized in the past. In a way it was freeing to know I could do no worse by Father.

Last night, after watching him from my window as he attempted to smooth things over with my suitors, I'd told Agnes I needed stationery to write some letters. She assumed they were farewell notes, but if I was to be shipped off with no return date issued, I had to do everything I could think of to further the notion of a public park in my absence. Ordinarily I'd think twice about being so bold, but Father was already beyond angry with me anyway, and my wish to run the nurseries was completely dashed.

I'd written to the Parkses, the Jays, and the Parsonses—all the estates Harry had mentioned he would try to obtain for me. Collectively they owned half of Rye. I told them of the plight of our neighbors and the need for a natural place of respite and asked if they would consider donating some of their land.

Then I'd written to Mr. Vaux. Of course, he wasn't a nursery man, but he knew others beyond Father. I told him of my aspirations here in Rye and asked if he would provide his expertise if the land were donated. Father would undoubtedly want to strangle me for writing such letters, but I'd told the recipients there was no need to reply, that I was being sent to Stuttgart and would provide my address when I got there, so perhaps Father wouldn't be aware for months.

"Do put up your parasol, Miss Sadie," Agnes said from behind me.

We were traipsing through the wooded part of our land on my second of two permitted walks for the day. I wondered at the bright spring sunshine beaming through the treetops and the delicate curled shoots of forest ferns emerging from the ground. I preferred to traverse the wilderness on our outings. Taking a turn around the nurseries' grounds without being able to check the new growth of my peonies or help orchestrate an order was a torture I couldn't bear.

"I don't need it. I have the trees," I said, gesturing up. I swung the folded parasol in front of me. The feathers along the edges fluttered.

"There's still a bit of sun, and that mourning bonnet isn't covering your face in the slightest," Agnes said.

"I don't have a parasol when I work in the nurseries." I lifted a hand to the soft ruche of lace and then the jet passementerie.

"Yes, but you wear a wide-brimmed hat, Miss Sadie." Agnes huffed behind me, and I tried not to laugh. "Even so, your skin is affected quite a bit. I do believe staying out of the nurseries and taking a leave in Stuttgart will be wonderful for your skin."

"Thank goodness," I said, feigned enthusiasm dripping from my words. "I should have given up horticulture and retreated to Germany long ago for the sake of my complexion."

We emerged on the drive that led back to the house, and I paused for a moment to stare into the next section of woods. One of my favorite walks was through the woods down to the edge of the village and back, but today, with only five days remaining at home, I thought perhaps I'd request something of Agnes that she'd be hard-pressed to refuse.

I pivoted to the right and started walking down the drive toward North Street. "I need to speak with Mother before I go," I said to Agnes.

She said nothing. Her hesitation told me she wanted to refuse me, that she knew well enough that in visiting Greenwood Union Cemetery we could happen upon Sam, but she couldn't forbid me from visiting my mother's grave.

Ordinarily I didn't make a habit of speaking to Mother at her resting place. I knew she wasn't there but with God. Even so, Mother had always thought it important to visit her sister's grave to ensure it was properly maintained, despite the groundskeepers at Greenwood always being nearly as meticulous as Father was with our operation. Sam's father, at Sam's suggestion, had always made it a priority to keep the departed's favorite flowers planted and cared for against their headstone, and that policy had been retained after his death.

"Are you certain? We could go tomorrow," Agnes said finally. "It may be a somber place today. You saw the news of Mr. Lucas in the papers yesterday, didn't you?"

"No. What's happened?" I'd been so distracted by everything with Sam and Father and Mr. Reynolds and Mr. Brundage and Germany, I hadn't read the papers. Mr. Lucas was the president of the town bank, a younger man of thirty-five or so who had inherited the position from his father.

"His heart gave out. They found him in the safe, just crumpled over, with the last hundred dollars in his hand," she said.

"That's horrible," I said softly. I'd had no idea the bank was folding too. I thought of Mr. Lucas's young children and his wife, now left penniless and without a father or husband. What would they do? Mrs. Lucas's parents lived in New Hampshire. Perhaps they would go there.

"I'm sure they will have him placed in the Lucas mausoleum today or tomorrow," Agnes pressed. "Perhaps we should wait to go to the cemetery until after."

I looked at her, trying to discern if she was truly concerned about encountering mourners or if she was using this as an excuse to reroute us.

"As horribly sad as it is, I don't believe we will be interrupting anything. Mother's grave is almost on the other side of the grounds. In any case, I'm dressed in the proper attire," I said.

We came out of the tree canopy lining our drive and crossed over North Street. The cemetery stood before us, awash in spring green. Gray stones and monuments and whitewashed family mausoleums dotted the rolling hills. Greenwood Union wasn't one of those spooky, horrid places where children went to tell ghost stories. The place was too lovely for that. There were streams and old trees with sprawling branches and always an array of blooming shrubs and flowers.

Agnes and I walked through a row of boxwoods and onto

the cemetery grounds. The actual entrance was down North Street a bit, but Mother's monument was on a little hill closest to us. The place was quiet. Mr. Erwin, one of the guards who kept the grounds free of homeless and passersby, sat as still as a statue on a bench in the distance. No carriages lingered down the way at the Lucas mausoleum. I could see their marble vault in the distance, beside the road.

There were, however, two figures next to it—an old man with silver hair glittering in the sun and a familiar sturdy frame. My breath caught when I saw him. They were planting annuals. A flat of what looked like snapdragons sat next to where they knelt. I wanted to be next to them, my hands in the dirt, my fingers brushing Sam's.

"Let's keep on," Agnes said, following my gaze.

I looked away and climbed the rest of the hill to Mother's resting place.

"Good day, Mr. and Mrs. Ryan, Miss Lowder," I said, tapping the traditional arched headstones with my fingers as I passed. "Auntie," I said, letting my hand linger on her square stone. Right behind her was Mother and Father's monument. Framed by magnificent ruby L'Eclatante peonies, the stone was elaborate, fashioned to look like some sort of granite Roman structure with two cathedral faux windows with Mother's name and dates etched into one and Father's name and birth date already engraved as well. I didn't like seeing Father's name there, waiting only for the death date to be complete. I knew feeling that way was silly, really, that despite not having a stone myself, my life read the same—all lives did.

I stared at the monument and Agnes stood beside me, doing the same.

"She was a wonderful woman," Agnes said.

"Yes," I said. "I would give just about anything to talk to her now. She would have helped me sort out the mess I've become entangled in."

Agnes suddenly reached over and held my hand. I wanted to pull it away. She wasn't a warm figure to begin with, and this display of affection felt strange.

"The first time we embraced, I felt as if I had stepped through the door to my home."

Mother's words about Father rang in my head as clear as the day she'd said them. Despite sometimes having trouble conjuring her facial expressions, I could still hear her voice. I was confident I always would. Perhaps because what a person said was a better expression of her soul than what she looked like.

"Mr. Jenkins is just down the way. I'm going to go speak to him about the arrangements I'd like planted here while I'm gone," I said. The desperation to speak with Sam seized me with a sudden ferocity, and I withdrew my hand from Agnes's and turned away.

She started to follow, but I stopped her. "Please stay here," I said. "You can watch me from this distance and verify that I'm not running away. Don't worry. Even if we plotted an elopement, you and Father are keeping me under lock and key. I wouldn't be able to go."

This explanation seemed to ease Agnes's fears, and she nodded. "Very well," she said. "I will remain until you've had your word."

"Thank you." I glanced down the hill at Sam and Mr. Sanderson still kneeling in front of the Lucas vault and started their way. I adjusted my bonnet as I went and bit my lips, hoping some color would bloom long enough for the blush shade to counterbalance the horrid pale brought about by my black ensemble.

"Mr. Jenkins, Mr. Sanderson," I said when I reached the bottom of the hill. Sam looked up from his planting and smiled, his eyes lighting at the sight of me, but then he noticed my dress and stood.

"Good afternoon, Miss Fremd," Mr. Sanderson said, not getting up. "What can we do for you?"

Sam reached me in an instant. He smelled like earth and his skin was bronzed from planting in the sun, making his hazel eyes look aquamarine.

"Sadie, what's gone wrong? Why are you wearing that?" he asked in a whisper, his gaze searching mine. His tone took me back to the edge of the woods, to his lips on mine, and I clenched my fists to stop myself from reaching for him.

"I do hate to disturb, Mr. Sanderson, but may I have a moment in private with Mr. Jenkins? I wish to discuss a few delicate items involving the care of my family's resting places, and though I know you are of the utmost competence, the Jenkins family has always handled the decorating of our plots," I said. I doubted he would think I was speaking the truth. What delicate items would I possibly need to discuss? The arrangement of flowers was hardly such a thing, but it was all I could think to say in the moment.

"Of course," Mr. Sanderson said, rising from the small bed in front of the mausoleum. "I've got to fetch a few more pallets from the shed anyway."

I watched him walk away, slowly at first as his knees loosened from the kneeling.

"Sadie. Why are you wearing black?" Sam asked again.

I squinted into the sun and then turned to face him. "Because my life is over," I said simply. "Can I plant those?" I asked suddenly, gesturing to the handful of pink snapdragons still idling next to the Lucas vault. I hadn't had my fingers in the dirt for three days. It felt like an eternity, especially when I was in crisis and expected that I'd never plant again—at least until I got to Germany. This was my only chance.

"I suppose. We're just doing a little border around the edge ahead of Mr. Lucas's internment tomorrow, but you haven't answered my question," Sam said. "What do you mean your life is over?"

I knelt and grasped Mr. Sanderson's spade before Sam could finish talking. The worn wooden handle was coated with small clumps of dirt, but I didn't bother to wipe it clean. I edged the point of it into the narrow bed, dislodging a few broadleaf plantain weeds. Sam knelt beside me, his spade, like mine, prying the weeds from the dark soil.

"Father is furious with me for the gardens we planted. He's sent for Charles and Freddie, and he's forbidden me to even walk through the nurseries." I grasped the base of the next weed and yanked it with unnecessary fervor. "My world has been upended and I cannot be among the plants. It is a misery."

"Yes, I know," Sam said simply. "I apologize. It's my fault you're in this dreadful mess. I should have come forward right away before you had the chance."

"And lose your post? The same post that drove you to the city slums when you lost it last time? No, Sam. I didn't want you to say a thing. I wanted you to keep working with us, to stay close to me. Surely you saw my face. I tried to meet your gaze, to tell you to keep quiet." My eyes filled and I looked at him.

"Sadie," he said softly, his fingers entwining with mine. "I'm here. I'm safe. When Lou left last week, Mr. Sanderson approached me and asked if I wanted his post. I came right over after your father asked me to leave."

I sniffed and he looked around and let go of my hand, likely thinking Mr. Sanderson could happen upon us and see.

I reached for a snapdragon and placed the bundle of roots into the ground where the weed once flourished. It was silly, but for a moment I felt sorry for the weed because in my eyes, Father had plucked me from the ground the same way and left me to wither away.

"The day you left, I tried everything to run away, save jumping from my window. I thought that I could find you, that I could run away with you, but I suppose I forgot you wouldn't go with me anyway," I said.

Sam stopped digging a small hole for the next snapdragon and sat up on his haunches. "You know how much I would want to, but—"

"Roisin. I know," I said.

"Yes, but I wasn't only speaking of her. Your father is angry now, Sadie, and he's keeping you from the nurseries to punish you, but sooner or later his anger will ease and you will be back in the greenhouses again," he said. "If we ran away together, you would never be able to return. I would never forgive myself for stealing you away. I know the truth this time, how much you truly want to stay."

A tear rolled down my cheek and I wiped it with a dirt-streaked hand, then pushed the soil around the snapdragon.

"You don't understand. He's not just angry this time. He told me that I either accept a proposal from Harry or Lionel or board a ship to Stuttgart in five days' time. He's already purchased my ticket. He said he regrets my involvement in the nurseries, that it threatened my feminine sensibilities, and he regrets not keeping me from . . . from you. He says my idea to plant the gardens was an idea born from your ideals. I tried to tell him it was not, but—"

"What are you going to do? Have you found either man amiable?"

I could feel his gaze on my face and I turned to look at him. My heart yearned to touch his cheek, to sink into his arms.

"Forget I asked," he said suddenly. "It is not my right to inquire this way, to act as though anything you decide is any of my concern. Our position is my own doing."

"How could I find any other man anything but completely unsatisfactory? Every moment in their company is agony, especially with their overtures of adoration for me when they know nothing about who I am. I will not marry either of them. I am going to Germany."

"No." The word whispered across his lips. "No," he said again.

"I don't have a choice. I don't know how long I'll be gone." I busied my hands in the digging of a final snapdragon hole. I could hear Mr. Sanderson behind me dragging the next pallet toward us. "I need you to know I wrote to the Chapmans, the Jays, and the Parsonses inquiring about them donating some of their land to form a public park. Hopefully they will write to me in Stuttgart, and if any responses are positive, I will write to you here and ask that you call on them in my stead. I've asked

Mr. Vaux for his services as well, if the land is acquired. I should have done this long ago, but back then, I had something to lose by disappointing Father—at least I thought I did. I'm sorry."

"Why did you do this? If your father finds out, he may never allow you to return. Sadie, please—"

"There are things more important than ensuring my own happiness, Sam." Until I'd started planting the little gardens, my life had been largely driven by selfishness meant to appease my ambition and happiness alone. Seeing the rail village and the slums had been a grace, a shattering of my naive entitlement. Gifts weren't given for the sake of our own solace but rather for the collective good of those we journeyed beside.

"And anyway, Father's response to our gardens makes me wonder if I want his nurseries anyway. If I can't make hope bloom for everyone, do I want to continue pressing on, planting for the wealthy who barely acknowledge the miracle of a bulb once dead, now alive in glory? Most have received too many miracles to notice the most obvious."

"I suppose I should give you a nickel for your work," Mr. Sanderson said as he joined us.

"Mr. Jenkins here claimed that the soil was quite well drained enough for snapdragons to prosper, but I had to check for myself." I flattened my palms around the stalk, burying the root securely, hoping I could savor the way the cool dirt felt against my hands and the sweet floral fragrance one was rewarded with when leaning close to a flower. "I'm off to Germany on Saturday's ship and can't risk Mother's place looking shabby while I'm away."

"How long will you be gone?" Mr. Sanderson asked. "Mr. Jenkins and I will personally check your mother's flowers daily."

"I'm not entirely certain. It could be a few months or a few years. I would appreciate you looking after her flowers," I said. "The peonies are lovely." I forced a smile and rose, wiping my dirty hands on my skirt. Mr. Sanderson looked alarmed at this action, as if I'd just destroyed a Worth ensemble.

"Certainly. Godspeed, Miss Fremd," he said. Sam stood and our eyes met. It occurred to me just then that the next time I saw him he could be married, he could have children, he might be gone forever.

"I'll escort you back up the hill to Agnes," Sam said suddenly, likely realizing the same thing I had, that this was our last moment. He stepped to my side and extended his arm. I looped mine through his and inched closer to his side, desperate to be near him to tell him without saying anything at all that I would love him always, that I would miss him greatly.

"As kindly as that sounds, Mr. Jenkins, I don't believe we have the time. Mrs. Lucas is supposed to come by at any moment and these need to be finished," Mr. Sanderson said.

"Look out your window at 3:00 a.m. Saturday morning. I have to see you one more time," Sam whispered quickly before releasing me. "I suppose you're right, Mr. Sanderson."

"Good day, gentlemen," I said, willing my voice to be steady.

I started up the hill toward Agnes, who had long since fallen asleep on the Rices' bench next to Mother, and felt Sam's gaze at my back and the dread of my heart entirely shattered ahead.

CHAPTER 13

My body ached from lying on the floor. Still, I pressed my right ear into the knotty oak and plugged my left, wishing Agnes would stop her idle whistling. I could only hear the conversations in fits and starts. Freddie hadn't said a word for hours. Only Charles and Father and the men they were questioning—the parade of unqualified candidates they'd dredged up in the last two days to succeed Father. The interviews had begun at eight in the morning, and it was now one in the afternoon.

"I shouldn't allow you to do that," Agnes said from her post by the door. She'd already crocheted half of a blanket.

"Please," I snapped, wishing I could do something to magnify the sound. So far, none of the men had made an impression. Three were seeking a nursery venture to run because they'd lost their own—something Father viewed as a fatal flaw—and one of them admitted that he was a banker by profession and knew nothing of plants.

"Do tell us, Mr. Jackson, of your experience in landscape architecture. Along with keeping our books tidy and the nurseries' supplies vast and well kept, we are often asked to serve as designers." Charles's voice was unusually loud. He was likely exasperated by all of this. He'd arrived home late last night on the eleven-thirty train and had been rather cross with Father for sending for him at all.

"*You've taken me from planting the north corner of the palm court. It's to be done in a week's time and those men haven't got a clue,*" he'd said the moment he walked in the door in his wrinkled linen suit. "*I do hope my being here is as necessary as you say it is. You and I both know we need my post now and possibly the check that accompanies it. If I am not about in Florida, if the palm court isn't satisfactory and I am let go, I will depart with no savings. I've not had enough time to obtain any. I won't be able to contribute more funds to the nurseries if you need a bit to fill in again, and I daresay my penniless presence here will hardly suffice to save us.*"

Father had reassured him that he would be returned to Flagler in short order, that he would never need to borrow money again, and that he simply needed assistance selecting a suitable man to apprentice under him and provide the hand that Charles and Freddie could not until he was ready to retire. I'd barely heard anything else. Instead, Charles's comment about contributing more funds kept ringing in my ears. The notion that I had caused Father to need Charles's money struck me in the gut. It also troubled me that I hadn't known he'd needed the help.

"I admit I am not a creative," the new man said in a normal tone. I strained to hear more but could only hear a bit of Freddie's quiet murmuring. I wasn't sure why Father had sent for Freddie at all. He'd never had any interest in horticulture and knew the least of the three of us. Even his attire spoke volumes. While Charles's boots were polished but dirt-stained, Freddie wore the tassels of a government man, his fingers callused on the pad of his thumb and the tip of his index finger from writing letters and legislation all day.

I heard Father's study door open and close and one set of footsteps fading down the hall. Another one was gone.

"We should be packing your trunks," Agnes said as I sat up from the floor and dusted a bit of pollen from my black dress. "Your things will fit in three nicely, I believe, unless . . . Do you suppose your grandparents' lady's maid is in possession of a set of curling tongs and horsehair brushes? The brushes must not be too coarse for your hair, Miss Sadie. And do you suppose she'll be proficient in doing up the Cleopatra for your ball gowns, or shall I write out instruction?"

I nearly burst into laughter. "My grandparents don't employ a single maid or servant," I said. "The town they live in, outside of Stuttgart, is tiny. Only fifty or so live there. Oma keeps house for a woman down the lane and Opi does nothing but tend a little farm out behind their home. There will be no balls. In fact, I have no doubt I'll be spending my days weeding and cleaning."

Agnes gasped and pressed a hand to her chest. "But I thought your father was sending you there to find a proper husband without the distraction of the nurseries."

"He is sending me there to teach me a lesson," I said, rising from the floor. Out the window I could see the seedlings being moved to the larger greenhouse and wheelbarrows of potting soil idling next to the planting shed. Ordinarily this was one of my favorite tasks—moving the thriving little plants we'd started as seeds to larger pots. It was a source of tremendous wonder. May's varieties were my favorite—anemones, lilacs, sweet peas, lily of the valley, and peonies.

I thought of the last peony I'd cross-pollinated with Sam, the ease with which we worked together. There was almost nothing as intimate as working in silence—knowing the needs of the task and performing them in tandem without a word. I thought of the brush of his hand, the way my arm felt wrapped around his just yesterday. Everything in me yearned for him. Not just for his touch, nor for the way my body wanted to melt into his, but also for his company, for the comfort of his love, for the sameness of his passion.

"And he's willing to let you wither there without a mate? You'll waste your precious childbearing years!" Agnes nearly shouted.

I laughed. "I'm not a stock animal," I said. The mention of high breeding, of my age in terms of fertility, always made me squeamish. "And I do believe he thought his threatening me with Germany would force me to make a match here. I don't think his putting me on a boat to Europe is what he'd want for me truly, but I won't give him his way, so—"

"I rarely say a word to your father, but I feel that I must given this information. Your mother would not have you go to be a helpmate to your grandparents right now. She would require a chaperone at every turn, of course. She would require you make a suitable match. But she would not have you waste your years."

"If by wasting my years you mean the years I'm not married, I cannot say the outcome would be different if I remained," I said. "I will refuse every proposal but one, and he cannot." I choked back a sob. The sudden emotion surprised me, and I cleared my throat.

"I only pray that your sensibilities ripen swiftly," Agnes said.

A knock at my door interrupted her, and she opened it.

"We're adjourning for a belated lunch on the lawn and Father wanted me to fetch you," Freddie said. His button nose, exactly like Mother's, scrunched and he tapped the brown felt fedora he'd temporarily removed against his leg—something he did only when he was considering saying something unwelcome.

"You look like that Mrs. Green on Wall Street," he said finally. "I know you wouldn't mind in the slightest being made a character in the funnies, but I'm your brother and a future congressman . . . at least I hope. Have some mercy on my reputation, will you?" He cracked a smile.

Mrs. Hetty Green was a Quaker and the wealthiest woman on Wall Street. She'd saved the entire city of New York multiple times. Even so, she had a horrendous reputation. Everyone called her a witch as a result of her black costumes and said she stunk on account of chewing raw onions and garlic to ward off illnesses. I admired her. She had never cared what others said and always remained true to herself.

"Do you suppose I'd still have suitors if I took up chewing garlic?" I asked, breezing past Agnes to the freedom of the hallway. I wondered, since my brothers were home and able to look after my whereabouts, if I'd be able to talk Father into letting me take a turn around the nurseries' grounds.

"Probably," Freddie said as we walked down the stairs. "You're pretty enough. They'd just order the household free of garlic once you promised them your life." He elbowed me and laughed. "But really, Sadie. I want you to know that I told Father I find it unfair." I took his arm and leaned into him as we wandered through the hall toward the front door. "I've never been bothered to settle, and I've certainly never been threatened with Germany."

"You're a man of industry and able to survive on your own," I said, rolling my eyes. Freddie's politics and standing had always been much more liberal than Father's, which was why they butted heads and he stayed away. "It seems Father doesn't feel the same way about me. He thinks I'm incompetent and is terrified that I'll end up occupying the slums if the nurseries fold."

"Perhaps you would. There's always the chance, especially in this downturn. But I feel that's your decision to make," he said. "I have to admit that your stealing the plants for the gardens was a bit naive, even if you were well intentioned. Surely you knew how Father would respond."

"I was thinking with my heart, Freddie. For once I wasn't thinking of myself or my own aspirations. I could think only of how dreadful I'd feel if the only thing I could see was the doom of what was and not the hope of what could be. I didn't think Father would miss the few imperfect plants we'd selected. You must see the desperation in Chicago as well."

Before he could respond, Mr. Cooper opened the door and beckoned us to the teak outdoor dining table and chairs set up under the Andromeda tree snowing white flowers. Charles and Father were already seated across from each other, leaning forward in what appeared to be a heated conversation. Charles's countenance was stony and Father's face was red.

"You're damn stubborn," Charles growled as we neared. He exuded a confidence upon his return he hadn't possessed when he'd left. Perhaps it was his post. He was out of Father's shadow, successful, in charge of several dozen men. Charles pounded his fist on the table, setting the crystal glasses filled with what looked like lemonade to rattling. I gasped and hurried toward them.

"Whatever is the matter? You're ruining a lovely luncheon and you're only here for a short while, Charles."

Charles glanced at me and shook his head. "Your attitude is remarkable," he said. "I've just been telling Father here that I cannot return, that Freddie will not return, and that hiring any of those men we've just spoken with as his successor will sentence the business to a swift death." He took a breath. "He needs a competent partner to help shoulder the immense amount of work the nurseries require while making them more profitable. None of these men have an ounce of the expertise our clients have come to expect. They would only be a hindrance and a drain, mark my words."

Father was fuming. I could feel his glare but chose to avoid it, focusing on Charles instead. Mr. Cooper pulled my chair out and I sat down and situated my skirt. It was unusually hot and I instantly regretted my black costume as sweat began to prickle my brow.

"I told Father that despite your misstep—and it has been significant, especially in this climate—you are our successor; you are the best possibility of our business staying as it is. There are nurserymen with no design acumen, there are businessmen with no horticulture background, and neither are satisfactory. You know more about plants than anyone, save Father. You have wanted this business since you were a girl—"

"And a girl is what she is!" Father shouted, suddenly breaking his silence. The yell tore through the trees and echoed loudly enough to temporarily paralyze the Mirani family on their way to start the afternoon watering. "She should be married well like her mother wanted. Not taxed with the particulars of an enterprise. She would be made a spectacle. Imagine—a spinster at the head of this business. We would lose our society clients. I would be deemed a terrible father." He quieted a bit and fanned his arm over the view in front of him.

"Our clients are already quite used to working with Sadie. We work with our peers and she is one of them. Times are changing, Father," Charles said. "If you don't believe me, think of Beatrix Jones or Ellen Shipman—both respected by society and studying with Charles Sprague Sargent and Charles Platt, clearly with the intention of making a profit from their efforts." He edged out of his linen jacket. He was right. I'd heard whispers that Beatrix and Ellen were training to become as famed as Olmsted or Vaux in the landscape architecture sphere.

"Miss Jones is of old Philadelphia stock and one of Mrs. Astor's four hundred," Father said. "Mrs. Shipman is married and from the Biddle family. They are hardly examples to compare to Sadie's lot. If their ventures sink, their fortunes will sustain them; society will still smile upon them. In any case they are considered artists, not leaders of industry. Their fathers and husbands aren't impressing upon them the burdens of their companies."

"Even so, Father, there are worse things to be than a happy spinster. Sure, she might be an object of interest for people to gossip about, but what has Sadie ever cared about that?" Charles asked. He looked at me as if gauging whether what he said was okay.

"And if Sadie fails? If she's left penniless?" Father asked. "She would be alone. All alone. You will be in Florida, and you will be in the city," he said to Freddie. "If the nurseries fold and all of our assets are lost, neither of you will have the funds to pay her debts and save her from the perils of bankruptcy. Even with your considerable salary, you would be rendered destitute as well if you helped her, Charles."

Charles was silent then and Mr. Cooper deposited the cucumber sandwiches while he had a moment's peace. Father dabbed at his forehead with his napkin. I thought of what it would be like with Father and my brothers gone, what it would feel like to have this place to myself, alone. But I wouldn't be. The image was clear. I would be with Sam. I would beg him. I would promise Roisin a job and a dwelling forever and then Sam and I would be together. He could help me.

"I wouldn't fail," I said, tipping up my chin. "The nurseries would thrive in my care. You have to admit that Charles is right. I am a capable designer, a skilled horticulturist. I've secured several new accounts on my ingenuity alone. Besides that, I wouldn't have to be a spinster to be your successor, Father. That's what I've been trying to tell you all along. I could marry if I chose, and my husband could help me if he wished."

"Perhaps, but a man of our ilk will have his own career, Sadie. There's not one I know who is idling about waiting for a calling," Charles said. "Isn't that why you've had a difficult time accepting a proposal? Because you wish to stay."

"Lionel Reynolds was willing to move here, and Sadie denied him," Father said.

"He wanted control of the nurseries and to dismiss many of our employees, and I wouldn't allow it. He knows nothing about how this is run. He wanted to build it and leave it to someone else to manage while we spent most of our time traveling around the world," I spat. I plucked a sandwich off the stack and set it forcefully on Mother's blue willow china. "I will only marry if I will be at the helm and my husband will work alongside me, as a partner."

Freddie laughed. "I must admit that's unlikely, as much as I want to agree with you, dear sister."

"Perhaps it's implausible if the man I choose is a man of fortune," I said. "However, if the man I love has no fortune at all—"

"I will say it again—you will not marry Mr. Jenkins!" Father nearly shouted. "He is a thief and a liar, and his sensibilities would further tarnish yours until the finances were depleted for the sake of philanthropy and our employees driven to the factories and this place left nothing but a field of weeds. Both of you live with your heads in the clouds without any concept of how to run a business."

Charles's eyes were as round as saucers and Freddie's mouth was agape.

"Don't you two understand it now?" Father went on, looking from Charles to Freddie and back again. "All you see is her proficiency with plants, but in business, she is not fit. We must choose the best of what we've seen today, and Sadie will go to Germany. When she returns, she will undoubtedly be ready to assume her role where she belongs."

"Mr. Jenkins?" Freddie asked, apparently not hearing anything else Father had said. "Sam Jenkins?"

I nodded and Charles blinked at me. I was sure Father had told them. Clearly Charles knew about my planting the little gardens; I assumed he knew about Sam too.

"I love Sam," I said to my brothers. "I have for some time." I turned to Father. "I made a mistake in taking the plants, Father, but I will listen now. I will learn from you, and I will grow our business to the point of thriving again, and then I will find a way to cultivate the park Sam and I have dreamed of too. I know it's all possible. And you've heard Charles. You must know I'm the most suitable person to follow in your footsteps."

"Sam Jenkins," Charles murmured, still fixated on my confession.

"How can I trust you when you're still speaking of that park?" Father asked. "You are too easily swayed. Our nurseries are barely surviving. I've had to ask Charles for a loan to compensate the grower in Japan. I've hired every unemployed person I've been able to, and you are still insisting that we give more. You are not fit and you do not understand. My word stands. You will go to Germany."

"I wasn't meaning that the park would be a possibility now but rather in the future, when we are thriving again," I said, but he didn't hear me. "Please, Father."

"I don't envy the predicament you're in, Sadie," Charles whispered beside me as Father tossed his linen napkin to the tabletop, stood, and began walking back toward the house. "You cannot have what you wish in any direction. However, I can't say I blame Father for his reluctance to hand off his daughter to a man who cannot support her and his nurseries to a woman whose love intertwined with her business has cost him dearly."

"The gardens were my idea and my idea alone," I said. "Sam only agreed to help me because he understands how desperately those who have no money, no hope, need to see the miracle of a bloom. I should have realized how even a little could impact our finances deeply, but I did not. It is my fault, but it is not a fatal error. I can learn from it, Charles."

"In politics they say that in order to reach an agreement, it is often prudent to leave the elephant at the circus," Freddie said.

"You knew how angry Father was about the little gardens and you mentioned them anyway. Charles was trying for you, Sadie, but I'm afraid that was the final attempt. You'll be off in three days' time, and three days is not nearly long enough for Father to soften again." He took a bite of his sandwich and shook his head.

"What can I do?" I asked. My throat felt tight and I pulled at the black lace collar.

Freddie shrugged. "I don't suppose I know. Marry Mr. Reynolds and remain here? Accept your fate as a spinster without command of the nurseries? Run away with Mr. Jenkins?"

Charles elbowed him at the final question.

"Sam won't marry me. Not right now anyway," I said.

Freddie nearly choked on his lemonade. "I was speaking in jest," he said, his eyes serious. "You cannot. Regardless of love, you must know—"

"I have thought of everything," I said.

Charles cleared his throat. "We should go to Father before he telegrams that horrid Earl Wescott," he said to Freddie.

"Yes. If it must be one of them, it must be Reginald Andrews," Freddie said.

Charles nodded and they both stood.

"We'll discuss your situation later," Charles said, leaning down to kiss the top of my head.

A sense of finality settled in my mind, and my fear of loss, suddenly realized, released anger and tension to pick up sadness. My shoulders slumped and my eyes blurred. Only Germany was ahead.

CHAPTER 14

The offer had been extended following our lawn lunch this afternoon. Reginald Andrews, a man who failed at maintaining his father's ironworks business but still possessed a moderate amount of money to his name and who knew a decent amount about plants, would be the next owner of Rye Nurseries. He would move into Charles's quarters and begin following Father about next week. I wouldn't meet him until I returned home, and by then I was sure Father would be altogether disengaged from the business.

My brothers and I sat on the front porch watching the evening rain slap the ground and the lightning shock the sky. Mr. Cooper had brought us tea half an hour ago, and though my cup had mostly cooled, when the wind blew the earthy-sweet storm smell across us, a bit of bergamot still joined.

"I find it unbelievable that you two can simply give this place away. You had everything I've ever wanted right in your palms and you tossed it out," I said. Deep in my soul I was angry, but the words came out in a gentle tone. Father felt the same. I knew it because after sending the telegram, he'd retired to his bedroom and hadn't emerged since. He'd only gone to bed in the afternoon one other time, the day Mother died.

Charles sat forward in the teak chair Mr. Cooper had returned to the porch. He shook his head and finally rested his chin in his hands, elbows on his knees.

"As much as you've wanted to remain, I've wanted to leave," he said. I thought of the years of *National Geographic* magazines still riddling his desktop and the ship and train schedules he'd collected over the years, starring the most interesting routes. "Palm Beach has confirmed that it wasn't just the allure of what I didn't have. I crave the wonder of new landscapes, new projects, new cities, new plants." He sighed.

Thunder cracked overhead and a jagged streak of lightning seemed to strike the woods just beyond us. Freddie started counting next to me and at thirty-four the next rumble of thunder sounded.

"Close. It's a wonder the woods have never been set aflame. We always seem to be the recipient of the weather up here on this little hill, blocking it from the rest of the town," Freddie said.

"Believe me, Sadie, the guilt I feel about all of this is insurmountable," Charles said, ignoring Freddie's talk of the weather. "If I would only put my selfish wants aside, Father wouldn't need another hand at the business, we wouldn't be selling, and you could remain as long as you wanted—"

"We need the security of your salary in some capacity it seems, so your venture in Florida isn't selfish. And even if you returned and agreed to succeed Father, I wouldn't have the nurseries," I said. "I could help you and I could stay here, but all the things I've dreamed of doing would have to be approved by you and done under your thumb. I want the freedom to order the varieties I wish and to design our clients' spaces to my liking and find a way to make a public park a reality."

Charles was like Father in so many ways—kind, remarkably so, but also calculating. Perhaps he would appreciate my suggested innovations if they profited well, but he would not support the park, and the future park had been intrinsically tied to my want for the nurseries from the moment I planted the first garden in the rail village. All of it was futile to think of now anyway. Mr. Andrews had already been telegrammed and Charles and Freddie had forfeited their chances.

"Perhaps when you return you can get on with Mr. Platt as Mrs. Shipman has. Clearly he's amenable to a woman of your interests," Freddie said, fiddling with his cuticles.

"I don't want to simply plan gardens and plant them. I don't even want to be at the helm of another nursery. This place is so special to me because it is ours, something Father and Mother built from nothing, and now look." I flipped my hand at our view. The clouds flashed gold, lighting up the greenhouses and planting field.

"But it is only a place," Freddie said. "A home is less about the land and the buildings and more about the people you love. I think you're restricting yourself, Sadie. You're tying yourself here and ignoring what could be. You could love a well-suited man if you allowed your heart to see anyone but Mr. Jenkins. You could accomplish much of what you wish elsewhere if you would remove your blinders and see the world beyond this place. I know. Because though I feel for Father and I feel for you, I have found purpose on my own and . . . and love too."

"What?" I jolted forward and smacked his arm with the back of my hand. "Love? How could you keep this from me, Freddie?"

He shrugged and grinned. Charles laughed.

"It's unlike men to discuss matters of the heart until we're sure. When we tell you we're in love, it's not a possibility but a certainty," Charles said. "Which should tell you much about the feelings of the men who have asked for your hand."

"So you've not found love yet, Charles?" I asked. He shook his head. In so many ways I wasn't surprised. Like his business aspirations, Charles always seemed to appreciate the chase, the adventure, but not the idea of settling, of marriage. "And you can say a confession means love, but I don't believe the society men who have proposed to me love me in the slightest. An ardent declaration is one thing, but these men are after either my looks or our business and can't possibly be in love with me. They never took the time to know me. I know . . . I know the difference. I know what love is and . . ." I trailed off, recalling the look in Sam's eyes when he proposed. His question had been asked in desperation, in need. He hadn't just wanted me. I hadn't just wanted him. We *needed* each other.

"Like you, I thought I couldn't love anyone else after Father found out about my flirtation with Emma, but in time I realized he was right," Freddie said, following my thoughts. "We weren't as alike as I supposed, and in time, when I saw less of her and after she married Luca, I understood that we weren't destined for each other."

"I thought you only found her attractive, Freddie. I had no idea you loved her," I said. When Charles told me of Freddie's entanglement with our former maid, Giulia's daughter, I hadn't thought of love as a possibility. Giulia had only worked with us for a month's time before Father put a stop to Freddie's seeing Emma. In my mind it had hardly been enough time for love. Then again, it hadn't taken long for me to fall for Sam.

"I did. But when I see her now, I don't feel anything at all. I haven't for years," he said.

And that was where we were different. Perhaps distance had allowed my thoughts to stop fixating on Sam; perhaps in a way, my love had been simmering coals instead of a flame in his absence, but the moment we were face-to-face again, my heart was a wildfire.

"In any case I met a woman in Chicago. Frances Maynard. Mr. Harrison is quite good friends with her father, Isaac, who is a judge in the New York court of appeals," he said. "She's beautiful, with auburn hair and the most glorious freckles you've ever seen along the bridge of her nose. She's smart, too, and knows nearly as much about politics as I do. She's convinced me that I'm in the right place and I must agree. Though businesses may falter, the need for a public servant will not."

I supposed he was right, though no amount of security in the world could convince me to run for any sort of office—even if I was permitted to do so. There were always two sides to every feud, and the public servant was always tangled in the middle. It seemed like a horrid place to be.

"I'm so thrilled you're happy," I said. "Perhaps when I'm back home I can meet her. Don't get married until I return, will you? I'd be so dreadfully sad."

"I thought you said you were to ask Mr. Maynard for her hand when you wrote last week," Charles said.

Freddie removed his fedora and turned the brim around and around.

"So you'll tell Charles but not me?" I asked. "Why? I'm just as suitable a confidant."

"Only because I wanted to know the opening dates of the Royal Poinciana in hopes we could visit on our honeymoon tour," Freddie said. "And I was to take the train to New York and ask him over dinner at Delmonico's last night, but of course I was beckoned here and delayed." Freddie rolled his eyes.

"I'm sorry," I said.

"I can't promise we'll wait until you're home, Sadie, but I will tell you the moment I know the dates," he said.

Suddenly a sound like rapid cannon fire erupted over us. I fell to the porch and instinctively covered my head. Charles and Freddie laughed.

"It's just hail," Charles yelled over the noise. "But my goodness, have you ever seen any that size? Take a look at that."

I stood and looked over the railing to find the grass riddled with hail the size of the snowballs we used to make as children. A cool breeze filtered over us and when that was settled, the air felt warm again, but the hail continued in torrents, pounding the roof. In the distance I could hear glass shattering—the greenhouse windows. I thought of the field of trees and roses and started down the steps.

"Where do you think you're going?" Freddie asked, pulling me back. "One hit to the head and you're gone."

I stepped back under the roof but stared out toward the field. "It's going to ruin all the plants! The impact has already taken several panes from the greenhouses and—"

Suddenly the hail stopped. The wind stopped too. The sky darkened to an eerie green-black and Charles drew a sharp breath.

"Freddie, get Father, Mr. Cooper, and Agnes if she's inside and get in the cellar. Now," Charles said hurriedly.

"The cellar?" Freddie asked, scrunching his nose. "There's likely snakes and bugs and—"

"Now!" Charles said. He jumped up and ran down the steps to the walkway and then toward the greenhouses. "If there's anyone in the field, anyone at all, run for cover! Come up here!" Charles shouted as loudly as he could.

I ran after him, echoing his words. I didn't understand, but at the same time comprehended plainly: something was coming. He glanced at me but didn't tell me to go back as we ran through the greenhouse alleys and down toward the field. Trees and roses and shrubs lay flattened from the hail and at least one pane was shattered in every greenhouse.

"A twister is imminent!" Charles shouted as we circled the barn and careened down the hill to the village. My heart dropped to my stomach. A tornado. Tornadoes happened in the South, in the Midwest, in the desert. Not here.

"Take cover! Take cover!" we yelled. My voice was hoarse, the sound of it an inaudible screech, but I continued to scream to the vacant land.

It was eerily silent as we ran past the field and toward the greenhouses. And then a roar, a rumble, and a high-pitched whine like the continuous blast of a train whistle. I looked back, certain I'd see the dusty shadow of the engine coming up the track, but the rails were vacant.

Charles clutched my wrist and yanked me forward, around the side of the house and into the cellar where the rest of my family huddled in a small corner in front of the dusty jars Mr. Cooper had prepared from our summer fruit last year. Charles forced the wooden door shut over our heads and said our names under his breath as the rumble and the whine split my ears.

"Agnes, Mr. Cooper, Sadie, Father, Freddie."

"What's happening?" I asked as the door above us began to rattle. The hinge jostled and slapped up and down.

"Kneel and cover your heads!" Charles shouted.

I fell to my knees, feeling the damp soil seeping into my skirt, very aware that less than half an hour before Charles and Freddie had been laughing at me in this very same posture.

Now the door was trembling, the wood crying, and at once I felt a tremendous *whoosh*. Charles's hand was hard on my back, pressing me into the dirt.

"Stay down!" he yelled. Overhead the wind now sounded like a loud hiss. Above the constant noise, trees groaned and glass shattered. Something huge fell to the ground near us, the thud shaking the earth.

"Lord, calm the storm," I heard Father murmur.

I reached out and clutched his hand and as I lifted my head, something sharp struck it and everything went black.

"The gash isn't great and the presence of the lump is promising so we know the impact didn't cause an internal bleed, but we must keep her under eye. She's undoubtedly had a concussion," I heard Freddie whisper. "When the doctor examined Leonardo that time the plow prongs fell atop his head, it looked the same and that's what he said."

I opened my eyes to a clear, cloudless night and Charles's face leaning over me. Apparently I'd made it out of the cellar.

"Is everyone all right? Is the storm clear?" I asked. My voice was gravelly, sounding as though I hadn't used it for days.

"Stay still," Charles said. He shifted his knees beneath my head just slightly and my equilibrium waned. I lifted my hand to my head and my fingers brushed a large goose egg on my crown before Freddie snatched my wrist and gently forced my arm down beside me.

"Answer me or I'll touch it again," I said. I tried to find our house in my peripheral, but my vision didn't reach that far. The only things I could see were the roots of Father's favorite hickory right in front of me, the ball of veins crooked like a Medusa head in the shadows.

"Yes. Everyone is all right, thank God," Freddie said. "Mr. Cooper and Father went down to the village and found that the barn and homes were spared entirely. It seems the twister was a small one, relatively, and only sustained across the top of our hill just here."

Charles didn't say anything, and in the silence, I understood. We had been blessed to live, incredibly so, but we had lost much.

"A piece of roofing slate struck you," Charles said finally, looking down at me. His eyes were weary. "I told you to keep your head down. We thought we'd lost you at first."

"I'm sorry," I said. "Would you care to help me sit up?"

He hesitated at first and then nodded. I grimaced as I pulled my body upward and Charles applied pressure to my back. For a moment all I felt was dizziness and a heaviness in my head, and then my vision settled. Slabs of slate riddled the lawn and a few boards had peeled back from the house and snapped. Still other bits of siding were half withdrawn, curling away from the frame.

"Where's Father?" I asked, squinting beyond the house toward the greenhouses. I gasped. Even from this distance I could see the destruction. Naked iron frames stood bent and gnarled in the moonlight like doomsday ghouls. The sparkle of earthen stars atop the greenhouse glass was absent.

"In the field," Charles murmured.

"I'm going too." I started to rise despite the way my swollen brain protested every small movement.

"No, you're not," Freddie said. "There's nothing you could do besides. He's just looking to see all that's gone."

I shivered and my teeth started to chatter, as much from fear as from the bite of spring chill. The prospect that we'd lost everything in a matter of moments was shocking. I imagined our entire field of greenhouses flattened, the seedlings and tropical plants and peonies and roses scattered and trampled. If my little gardens burdened the nurseries, I couldn't fathom the impact of this storm.

"My head hurts, but I have to see it myself or I'm going to go mad with imagining the worst," I said. I stood quickly, before Charles or Freddie could stop me. I stumbled and Freddie caught my arm.

"I'll go with you," he said.

Immediately I was brought back to the night I decided to go to the rail village. Sam had said the same, that he'd go with me.

"What of the cemetery? Is it all right? Is Sam hurt?" I asked, my chest suddenly gripped with urgency.

"I went down the drive to check the land for Father when the storm cleared and looked across. It appears nothing else has been touched. There were a few fallen limbs, but otherwise it seems the twister originated here and stopped here," Freddie said.

I heard him and believed him, but my heart still raced. I walked slowly around the side of our house. I reached out and touched a curled plank. The nail was still embedded in the wood.

"The velocity of the winds can do some terrifying things," Charles said. "Flagler told me the warning signs of a twister the moment I arrived in Florida and showed me a photograph of one as well. An early summer storm two years back wiped out his work on the Hotel Ormond and nearly killed a whole crew. The saving grace was a fellow from Kansas who recognized the stillness and encouraged cover in the hotel's recently dug sewage trench."

"And now his warning has saved us through you," I said. "We'll have to write him and thank him."

I reached the front of the house and a sob burst from my throat. The warped iron remains I'd seen weren't only the skeletons of two or three greenhouses; they were the remains of all of them save one, and that one only boasted three unshattered panes. Even from my position on our lawn, I could see it all—the field laden with broken glass and petals and palm fronds and planters and tree branches. Father stood in the middle of the destruction, hands on his hips, facing the barn. He turned slowly and then shook his head and made his way toward us.

"You shouldn't be on your feet," he said to me as he passed us. He walked up the steps and into the house.

"Father!" I called and immediately regretted the force of my voice. I clutched my head and Charles reached for my arm. "I'm fine," I said. "Is the house safe do you suppose?"

Charles nodded. "The storm pulled the slate, but not the roofing boards."

"Then let's go to him," I said. Charles took one of my arms and Freddie the other, and I walked as quickly as I could up the steps and into the foyer.

Father was sitting in the dark on the red velvet settee in the drawing room. He'd just lit a cigar and was twirling a lily of the valley sprig between his fingers. The smoke swept the room, encouraging a rich, loamy smell that reminded me of all we'd lost and made my eyes tear. I edged free of my brothers, who hesitated at the door—both had inherited Father's resistance to emotional turmoil—and walked toward him.

I lowered myself to the floor and sat at his feet like I used to do when I was little. Back then, he'd told me stories of his adventures as a child and imagined tales of my own quests. Perhaps it was his fault after all that I aspired to what I did. It was only within the last five years that stories of freedom and wonder were replaced by reminders of expectations and rules.

The cuckoo clock tweeted on the wall behind him, and the bird chirped nine thirty. Until that moment, I'd thought it well into the morning—two perhaps.

After another moment's silence, Father spoke, his voice low and detached. "We will announce our closing in the morning paper. I will keep the house and sell the rest of the land. I'll wire Reginald to tell him there is no nursery to overtake and Vaux to inquire of a post I can fill doing landscaping with him."

Goose bumps prickled my arms and I blinked, sure I would suddenly wake from this nightmare.

Father looked down at me. "I told you I wanted you well situated and you ignored my pleas. I never could have fathomed this tornado, but otherwise, I saw a storm coming." His voice rose just slightly, and a tear trickled down my cheek. "We have lost so much. Thousands in plants. Thousands in damages. I will pay our dues to the nurseries overseas, and when we sell the land, I will split the funds among our employees and hope they can find suitable posts elsewhere. I'll have to figure where I can write them recommendations."

He ripped his rumpled bowler from his head and took a long drag of the cigar. "You should have learned from Sylvie's plight and taken Brundage or Reynolds while they were keen. Now you'll have nothing. No more suitors, no business to contend for. Pray I'm able to get on with Vaux. If I do not, I'm afraid the house will be the next to go. *Herr hilf mir.*" *Lord, help me.*

"I'll have Flagler forward my pay," Charles said from the doorway. "Don't fret about the house."

"You will not!" Father barked. "It is shameful enough I was forced to ask you once. I will not accept funds from you again. A man must make his own way, and if he fails, he fails alone. I will not take nourishment from the pocket of my child again, even if it means I must go back to the factories."

Father blew a cloud of smoke from his mouth in a tremendous sigh. I was now a burden, only an extra expense for Father to worry over. I had been selfish all along—looking after my own wants and my own happiness, ignoring the bleak possibilities before me. Now it was too late.

The acrid stench of the sewage, the dusty dim from the factories, suddenly overtook my senses. If I had married Harry or Lionel, the slums would never again be a reality for Father. Their reputations wouldn't have allowed for their wife's relations to be swallowed into poverty. Despite Father's greatest protests, they would have forced their support upon him.

I glanced at Charles standing in the doorway, his lanky frame overshadowing Freddie's slightly shorter build by a hair. Mr. Flagler paid him well, but he was paid contractually. He, too, was counting on the nurseries' pockets to be a reinforcement until the contracts drew together and became consistent.

Freddie made little with Mr. Harrison—barely as much as one of our gardeners.

"I had an opportunity to help mightily and I dashed it," I whispered.

"Yes." Father extinguished the cigar on the crystal ashtray on the tea table and stood. "It is time to retire. All of you. Fred, I trust you'll keep watch over your sister. I told Agnes and Mr. Cooper to go rest. By morning light, I will notify the papers and start the rounds to our clients. They have been loyal to us and should be told in person."

I watched Father go, disappearing up the stairs. In a matter of hours he'd aged decades.

"Come along, Sadie. My stamina has run dry," Freddie said.

"Would you rather I sleep by her?" Charles asked.

Freddie shook his head and started up the steps before him. I rose slowly and wandered reluctantly toward where Charles waited for me. I might lie down but I knew I wouldn't sleep.

"I've ruined us all," I said when I reached Charles. "You told me to marry, Father told me to marry, but all I could see was my happiness extinguished forever. I was selfish. This is all my fault."

Charles took my hand and we started the climb to our quarters. "No. Freddie and I insisted on our own paths too. We are all to blame," he said.

I nodded and forced my mind blank to avoid imagining what was to come. "Perhaps there will be a miracle," I said, letting his hand go as he disappeared into his room.

"Perhaps. But we've had so many in our lives already; I don't suppose selfishness awards more."

CHAPTER 15

The hairline plaster cracks on my ceiling looked like either a bunny or a dragon depending on the way I tilted my head. I hadn't slept—in part because of my headache but mostly because of worry. Freddie, who was occupying Agnes's cot beside me, hadn't either. We hadn't spoken at all, but every time I looked his way he was staring at the ceiling too.

"I suppose we could get up now," I said.

"Yes," Freddie said, his voice gravelly. Then he turned on his side toward me and jabbed an arm under his pillow to fluff the feathers beneath his head. "Tell me the truth. Should I stay? I could forfeit the position with Mayor Harrison and attempt to help Father build us back. I could try to forget about Frances. I don't know that her father will find me a suitable prospect anyway with my inheritance now dashed."

"Father seems positive that we can't rebuild." I sat up slowly and rubbed my head. The quilt pooling around my middle now made me too hot and I flung it back and got out of bed. "And surely Mr. Maynard knew you weren't an Astor. It's not like your inheritance was going to win you and Frances a mansion in Newport."

"No, but he saw me as a reliable choice."

"You still are," I said, forcing my wardrobe door open. "You still have a viable career in politics. You have been distanced from the nurseries for quite some time. I doubt he'd even bat an eye at the nurseries failing."

"Perhaps he won't, but he should. I am paid little. When the time comes for me to find appropriate lodging for a family, I won't be able to afford it now. I suppose I was counting on Father."

I reached into the wardrobe and selected the last clean mourning frock I had. It was a hideous hand-me-down from Margaret Ridgeway, faded nearly gray from the amount of time I'd worn it in the sun, and the hem was full of snags.

"Must you wear that?" Freddie asked as I held it up by the collar and beat the wrinkled skirt with my palm. "Father already knows we're in a sort of mourning and now he must face the way you'll look in rags too? It's too much."

"Agnes has packed almost all of my good costumes for Germany," I said.

"Almost all—there's a yellow gown just there."

"It's a dinner dress from six seasons ago," I said.

Freddie shrugged. Then he heaved himself off the cot and tousled his mop of mahogany hair. "I still think it a better choice." He departed, leaving me with the option of an ornate yellow silk ensemble lined with Brussels lace and ornamented with lace flowers at the décolleté or a veritable potato sack.

"Let's hasten your dressing," Agnes said as she breezed into my room without so much as a tap on the door as a warning.

"A visitor has requested an audience." She snatched the yellow gown from my hand and lunged for my corset still hanging on the hook on the wardrobe's back wall.

"With me?" I hoped it wasn't Harry or Lionel. As much as I knew I could alter our future with a simple yes, I wasn't ready to say it yet. Then again, after last time, I doubted either would try again. If they did, I had to applaud their perseverance.

"With all of you," she said, threading my laces.

"Well, who is it?" I asked as she finished my corset and held the dress out. I stepped into the skirt and turned my back to her once more so she could do up the pearl buttons.

"I'm not at liberty to say."

I rolled my eyes. "Agnes, if you're about to entrap me with one of my suitors, I'll—"

"Sit so I can do up your hair."

I complied and she eyed the low neckline. "A soft pompadour arranged in three loose coils at the back. Whimsical and swift," she said, hurriedly jabbing a dozen pins between her lips.

"At least have the decency to warn me, dear Agnes," I attempted as she forcefully teased my hair and twirled and prodded my scalp. I bit the inside of my lip to keep from wincing.

"It's not an unwelcome guest, Miss Sadie, but I've been sworn to secrecy on the matter, and I cannot in good faith break a promise," she said.

For a moment I wondered if it was Sam come to save us, but Sam's saving us was impossible. He could save me, that was obvious, but my family? Not a chance. Even so, Agnes's insistence on my beauty in this moment was perplexing if the visitor was not a man of my age.

"You're finished. Come along. Your father and brothers are in the breakfast room waiting for you," she said.

"Why are they waiting? Surely they could have gone ahead of me to the study."

I took her hand and stood. Despite the gown being inappropriate for breakfast and years out of style, I felt good in it, powerful even. Yellow was eye-catching and the shade made my olive skin tone and raven hair sing.

"The audience is requested out of doors, and it is required that all of you are in attendance." A grin pulled at the sides of her mouth, but she quickly squashed it.

I reached out and took her hand as we walked down the hall. "I know you see me as an awful nuisance at times, but I'll miss you when I've gone away, Agnes. Before, I thought I'd see you upon my return, but now, with the nurseries ruined . . ."

I couldn't say the rest of the words, that all the people who had worked alongside us to make our nurseries the most acclaimed in the country would now be left with hands empty.

"Don't worry about us, Miss Sadie. We will find a way," she said.

When we reached the bottom of the stairs, Agnes called for Father, Charles, and Freddie. Father stumbled, stone-faced, out of the breakfast room. I could smell the sticky, rotten scent of alcohol on his skin as he passed me. Charles's eyes shot to mine and he shook his head. Freddie shoved a bit of bread in his mouth and followed Charles.

"Out the porch and to the left," Agnes instructed.

I was last to emerge from the door, but I watched as my family turned and stopped one after another as though bewitched by something in front of them.

I crossed the threshold and walked into the balm of spring sunshine. I was barely across the porch, about to turn my head and look, when I heard his voice.

"You're all here now." Sam stood in the front of a crowd of people nearly one hundred in number. He was smiling the sort of smile that made his eyes spark and my heart race. Behind him were our employees, our neighbors, the man from the rail village, and strangers. Sam's eyes met mine and lingered.

"What is this?" Father asked when he found his voice. My eyes began to tear.

"Mr. Martins at the paper reported early this morning that the nurseries were to be closed, but we cannot let that happen," Sam said. "Without them, what will be left of our town? Without them, what will become of us? Without them, what will become of the family who has treated us like their own?"

"But we haven't. Not always," I said before I could stop myself. Either way, it was the truth. I waited for Father to defend himself, to challenge me, but he didn't. He kept his eyes fixed on the ground.

"Close enough," Mr. Pratte said from somewhere in the back of the crowd. "We have a lovely little home and a beautiful view. We are valued and we know it."

"I could do better," Father said softly. "But I'm afraid all is lost. We have lost thousands in plants, my friends. And in structure." He swept his hand across the tableau of the shattered greenhouses. "To see you all here supporting us brings tears to my eyes, but it is all lost."

"We will help rebuild for free." The man from the rail village looked at me and pointed an iron contraption in his hand my way. "This lady here saved my life."

I shook my head. "I only planted a few flowers."

"I saw the miracles and knew that someone cared," he said. "That was all I needed. I'm a welder on the rails and I can fix those greenhouses."

"Among us there are architects, welders, glaziers, laborers, and horticulturists. Give us a chance to rebuild this place. We feel it is as much our home as it is yours. We don't want to lose it," Sam said.

I swallowed hard. I wanted to run to him and wrap my arms around his neck. I wanted to tell him that this would always be his home—this place and me—that his initiative now meant everything.

"I appreciate what you all are trying to do, but I'm unable to purchase the supplies," Father said. "Not to mention the plants to replace the ones we lost."

"Chadwick Horner agreed to give us the old windows he's been collecting for years for who knows what," the man from the rail village said. "They're piled up by the hundreds behind my barn. All we'll need to do is get one of the glaziers here to cut and reshine them. Name's Robert Deal, by the way."

"Thank you, Robert," I said, heartened to know his name and completely shocked that Chadwick Horner, the greedy landowner of the rail village, had agreed to part with anything he owned.

"Where will the glaziers fire the glass? We don't have a furnace, and I don't believe we know anyone who does," Charles said.

"Don't have a way to melt the iron frames either," Freddie said.

"Milford Glaziers has a furnace and the owner is my uncle. He'll help," a large man with a bushy mustache said.

"And Mr. Reid down at the railroad said we could use the clay oven," Robert said.

I felt hope bloom in my soul and looked over at Father. Surely he would launch into a symphony of thanks, but he just stared out at the ruined greenhouses.

"I'm certain there are some plants we'll be able to save," Sam said, his gaze following Father's. "The twister couldn't have ripped all the root balls. If we can locate the planters, we can salvage many."

"I've walked through the ruins three times now, and I don't think you'll find but a handful," Father said, his voice barely audible. "As touched as I am, as grateful as I am, I don't want to waste your efforts. You all have families and some of you still have posts. I would feel terrible indeed if you spent the weeks or months to help us and we still failed."

Some of the crowd began to whisper, but Sam spoke up. "We will not fail. Have faith in us," he said.

Then he turned to the group he'd gathered and started his instructions, sending some to the barns—which, thankfully, had been unaffected by the twister—to hitch a carriage to gather the windows, some to the woods and the ruins to gather as many plants as could be salvaged, and the majority of the men to the iron remains of the greenhouses.

"We'll have another carriage hitched and idling in the drive just here. Let's bend the iron if we're able—it's fairly thin—and fit as many pieces as possible in the carriage," Sam instructed.

"Why is he doing this?" Father whispered. I turned to him to answer but realized he wasn't speaking to me.

"Because he loves Sadie," Charles said from Father's other side. "And he knows this is the place she loves the most."

"No. He's doing it because he can't bear to see people suffer," I said. "If the nurseries fold, it's not only us who will crumble. Our employees' families will too."

I smiled at Alessandra Brambilla clinging to her mother's skirts. Everyone had come to pledge their support, even the children.

"I know, and the knowledge is a heavy weight. It's been a heavy weight since the start of this blasted panic," Father said. "I'd do anything to keep them here."

"Then let this crew try," Freddie said, leaving Charles's side to follow the group of men heading toward the iron frames.

By noon half of the greenhouse structures had been broken down. It was a strange view without them, a flat, barren field, and the contrast between the growing field below—still dotted with a few mature peony and iris and rose blooms—and the muddled dirt where I stood, reminded me of my mood. I found myself vacillating between hope and despair, not only because of the nurseries themselves but also because of my ship to Germany porting in two days. Father hadn't changed his mind about my leaving—at least, he hadn't said anything—but I wondered if that was simply because he hadn't had time to consider it.

"Look here," Elena said from the edge of the woods. She held up two little birch pendula laciniata saplings, her face triumphant. The weeping birch had been one of my very favorite new varieties this year. In addition to the gorgeous weeping branches, it had the most exquisite silver-white bark. It looked like a tree one would find in an enchanted forest.

"Oh! I'm so glad," I said, walking over broken clay pots mingled with clumps of planting soil to get to her.

"And it looks like another set of iron planting rows as well," she said, pointing in front of her.

The planting rows—little contraptions that looked like small bread molds linked together in a set of ten—had been flung quite a distance, but all fared well.

I leaned down to pick it up and found a battered cucumber magnolia seedling as well. I held it in my hand and rubbed the dirt away from the stem and roots. They had been severed. I tossed the plant into the woods and wiped my brow. We had grown sixty cucumber magnolias and only one had survived so far. They were a favorite of the Goulds because they were interesting—tall trees with creamy yellow flowers and large fruit resembling a cucumber when green but changing to bright scarlet and crimson as they ripened. Three dozen had been ordered by the Goulds for delivery next week at a fee of seventy-two dollars. I couldn't help but add up the losses as I found them. The Norway spruce saplings, crushed in the fall of glass, fifty-four dollars lost; the Japanese hydrangeas, punctured and crushed by their clay containers, one hundred thirty-two dollars lost; the new peony variety I attempted to create for Mother, snapped in half.

My boots rustled through the old fall leaves as I kept walking down the edge of the woods next to the greenhouses and toward the hill that led to the growing field. Healthy palm fronds waved in the slight breeze to my right, and I plucked the whole dwarf palmetto up from the ground and set it on the edge of the woods. When we were finished combing the forest we would come back around to collect and repot the plants we could salvage.

"So this is what the Rockefellers see every morning when

they look out their window," a deep voice said. "I've never seen such a thing. It sure is pretty. I don't know what half of these plants are."

I glanced through the trees to find a man my father's age standing on the edge of the hill overlooking the field, one hand on his waist, the other holding a rusty pair of pliers. Though the winds had snapped and scattered most of the blooms and caused the stems to lean so far east that the roots were nearly exposed, the field was in relatively good shape otherwise.

"Must be nice," another man, perhaps his son, said back as Father walked past them toward Charles, Freddie, and Sam, who were attempting to take down a frame.

"Select a plant to take home," Father said to the men. "Any sort you want from down there."

I was stunned. Clearly he'd heard the older man's comment, and it prompted him to give despite his whole enterprise being laid to waste.

The older man whistled. "I think I'll take one of those pink bushes home to my wife."

"Whatever you wish," Father called as the iron frame screamed and gave way. I looked toward the noise and felt my cheeks burn. Unlike my family's insistence on wearing overcoats during manual labor, Sam wore only a simple linen shirt. He'd rolled the sleeves to his elbows and I paused, unable to look away from his forearms as he hoisted the freed iron on his own and tossed it into a heap beside them.

"Do you suppose you could lend us a hand with this disassembly?" Sam called to the men standing to my right.

"Sure," they said and turned away from the blooms to help Sam pry a bolt away from the middle of an iron strip.

"Iris bulbs," Pasqualle Pratte said, startling me. She smiled and walked past me to deposit the bulbs at the edge of the woods. "How are you faring in all of this?" she asked when she turned back.

"I'm not certain," I said, realizing she'd been the first to ask.

"Me either," she said, shaking her head. Her dark hair was done up in a simple braid and wisps had come loose while she worked. She looked years older than seventeen. "Rosalina, my friend from the meat market, came up to see if I was all right the moment she heard, and when she asked how I was faring, I couldn't give a response. I'm afraid I'm operating like a clock pendulum."

We walked together to the edge of the hill, our eyes scanning the leaves and moss and our feet scuffing the ground.

"It was kind of your friend to check on you," I said. Margaret was supposed to be my closest friend and she hadn't bothered to come up. Neither had any of Father's friends or Charles's or Freddie's for that matter. The people rebuilding our nurseries were ordinary folk with remarkable loyalty. We didn't deserve them.

Pasqualle nodded and then laughed. "Yes, but Rosalina doesn't have anywhere else to be otherwise," she said. She reached and squeezed my hand. "I know you're suggesting that your friends are negligent, but perhaps you've forgotten the date in all the commotion? The Finks' pink party is this evening."

"Oh! Yes, I forgot entirely." Even without the tornado, I wouldn't have remembered. Banished from the nurseries and sentenced to Germany, I didn't think Father would have relayed my invitation, and I hadn't been involved in the normal preparation of declaring a garden finished—the week of walkthroughs, the substitution of plants that had withered, the final day of trimming and insecticide spraying—a variety Charles had developed from a mixture of pyrethrum, soap, tobacco, lime, and sulfur.

"I wonder if there is any pink left to marvel at or if the winds stripped the petals from the stems there too? I suppose one of us should go check, though even if the entire garden is in shambles, there's nothing we can do. We certainly can't replace unsatisfactory plants when we have none."

"Perhaps the winds were less severe five miles from here," Pasqualle said. "I imagine it will be a lavish affair regardless. The rumor in town is that Mrs. Fink ordered a crate of flamingos imported on the train from Florida, and I don't suppose she can hold on to them until her garden is perfect." She giggled.

"I'm sure that would be impossible," I said. It was strange how trends were set. First the Tiffanys with the hummingbirds, and now everyone had to have some sort of exotic animal in attendance or their soiree was considered a terrible failure. "I doubt Father has had a single thought about going over and finishing the garden before tonight." I knew I was fixating on the party unnecessarily. A company's reputation couldn't be ruined when it ceased to exist. Still, I couldn't let the memory of Rye Nurseries' final arrangement be one of complete shambles.

"If you need to go, Mother and Elena and Rosalina and I can start repotting the plants," she said. The idea of my going to the Finks' now, while everyone else cleaned up the destruction, seemed a bit selfish, but the idea of the quiet, of being alone in possibly the last garden we'd ever plant, was heavenly.

"Only if you're certain," I said.

"We are." She flipped her wrist at me to go.

I walked out of the woods and into the sunlight, wiping my dirt-streaked hands on my skirt.

Groups of men were working on three other frames, but I didn't see Father. I wandered down to the field and over to the barn, and then I heard their voices.

"I want to apologize for it all," Sam said.

"There's no need," Father replied.

"Yes, there is," Sam said. "For so long, all I've been able to see is the horror of the slums and what the absence of greenery, of plants, of hope did to me and those I loved."

My heart shriveled at the last word. Roisin. Even though he said he hadn't loved her like that, a part of me wondered if he was telling the truth.

"I was angry and in a way it felt like you were withholding life from people who so desperately needed it when you denied the help for a park, when you let me go for helping Sadie with the gardens. I started to see you the way I saw my boss at the tenements and my boss at the factory." Sam paused.

"But this morning I was awakened by your employees, my friends, telling me the news. They were adamant that you had helped them; you had sustained them and this whole town, really. In that moment my vision cleared, Mr. Fremd. You were doing much. You were doing all you could—for me, for them— and I'm sorry. I took your kindness for granted. You even hired me back after I left, and—"

"Thank you, but you are forgiven," Father said. "And I must apologize for my tone toward you. My feelings were mingled with many things, but your character is pure and honorable, and I have always seen you as my most promising gardener. Surely you know that."

"I do," Sam said simply.

I stood outside the door waiting for them to continue talking, but they did not. I waited for the conversation to turn to me, but it did not. Finally I opened the barn door. They were both busy tacking up Admiral and Gene for the iron transport to the rail station.

"Mr. Jenkins, Father," I said in greeting. "I'd like to go over to the Finks' to see how their garden fared. It is the day of their party."

"I suppose that's fine, though we have no plants to supplement if they're needed," Father murmured, busy with the reins. "While you're there, tell them the news, that we're likely finished. They've read it in the paper by now, I'm sure, but it's imperative that we tell them personally as well."

"Don't," Sam said. "Mr. Fremd, surely you can't be so pessimistic. Look at the progress made so far today. Give us a week at least until you begin to further spread the news of your closing."

"Yes, please, Father," I said, though all I could think of were the numbers—of the plants broken and the funds owed.

"Very well. One week," he said. "There's a container of insecticide just there, Sadie, in case their garden still stands." He pointed to the wall where a large glass container sat under an open window beside ten of the same.

I started toward it and grinned. Whether it was a slip of his memory or an intentional grace, Father had just permitted me to participate again, and my hope multiplied. Surely those bound for Germany weren't given mercies like these.

"Let me lift it into your saddlebag. It's heavier than it looks," Sam said, suddenly beside me. He clutched the lid of the insecticide and lifted the container in his palm. He looked around at my father, who was still occupied with Gene's tack, and then his eyes met mine and he leaned toward me until his lips were beside my ear. "Your father can say what he will, but I will not allow this place to falter," he whispered. "Don't worry. Trust me."

"I do," I said. I wanted to ask after his change of heart, but I'd already overheard it in his apology. Faced with the closing of the place that had sustained so many, he now understood its importance.

CHAPTER 16

I didn't bother to notify Mary Fink that I was about. I wandered along the serpentine pathway that had been laid on both sides of the drive and bent down at each new bed, sprinkling Charles's insecticide along the plant bases.

The flowers arranged on the back side of the house, above the Sound, had been completely stripped of color, but here in front the plants were mostly untouched. All I could figure was that the expanse of the Finks' home had somehow shielded the garden from the most severe elements. Of course, a few petals here and there had been scattered, but almost everything was still blooming in full glory—the deep pink-red of the Japanese maples nearest the brick garden wall followed by pink rhododendrons and the coral-white of the Notre Dame du Rosaire roses and the rose-pink blush of the Mons Paillet peonies. Primroses and corabells and hyacinths edged the front closest to the path, and the honey-sweet scent of the hyancinths nearly overwhelmed the salt-tinged sea breezes drifting up from the sea beyond the house.

As I stood in this garden, all the confusion and upheaval of the last days and weeks seemed to ease. The possibility of Germany and the calamity of the nurseries seemed distant. The idea that the nurseries would be saved and Father would come to love Sam and everything would be perfect seemed within reach. As naive as it might have been to grasp that hope, I did. Fiercely. I had to.

"Good day, Miss Fremd. The garden turned out lovely indeed. Mrs. Fink is absolutely tickled," Mr. Wilson, the Finks' butler, said from the limestone steps. Some of the Finks' servants were polishing silver lanterns next to him, while others worked to rig up a canopy made of pink silk streamers over the end of the drive. The canopy looked like an awful lot of work. The servants had tied hundreds of strips of silk to a tall pole set up in the grassy middle of the circular drive and were affixing the far ends to smaller poles arranged around the perimeter.

"I'm so glad she's pleased," I called back.

"I must assume all of Westchester County will be knocking on the nurseries' door after the party this evening," he said. He hadn't read the papers. Perhaps preparations for the party had occupied him.

The image of the current state of our nurseries flashed in my mind and my hope from moments earlier seemed to dissipate. All of Westchester might not have a door to knock on.

I forced a smile at Mr. Wilson and continued sprinkling the insecticide. A butterfly skimmed and soared over the blooms beside me, and I watched it land for a second on the tip of a primrose blossom. Both the flower and the butterfly were miracles, and I believed, truly, that miracles were real, that they could occur. I couldn't lose sight of that reality when things became difficult.

"Mr. Wilson, would you mind—"

The heavy iron door opened and Mary Fink's voice interrupted mine. "Sadie Fremd, is that you?"

I looked up and nodded. Mary hastened down the steps, the train of her sage silk dress in her fist. As she neared, I could see the sympathy in her eyes and I braced myself to speak of the tornado, of the devastation, without sobbing. She turned to scowl at the sun, yanked the brim of her straw hat over her face, and started up the path toward me.

"I didn't send you an invitation to tonight's festivities because I thought you'd been sent away," Mary said. She reached for me, gripping my arms. "Margaret said just a few days ago that your father had sent you to Germany. I thought how dreadful, how horrid."

"I'm to sail in two days," I said. I'd written Margaret a letter to tell her the news rather than visiting in person—my being chaperoned to visit my best friend like a prison ward hardly seemed fair. She hadn't responded for days—she'd been back and forth to the city of late, having costumes prepared for Newport—and when she finally did, she berated me for not choosing a husband from two suitable matches and begged me to reconsider. I hadn't bothered to respond.

"May I ask why? You are twenty-two years old, and being sent away at this age is a terrible risk indeed. By the time you return all the men of any worth or interest will be paired off and you'll be stuck with the old widower set." Mary scrunched her nose. Surely she already knew I'd rejected Harry and Lionel. She avoided my gaze and looked over her garden. The edges of her mouth pulled up. I was glad she was so delighted by it.

"I've declined all five proposals that have been extended in the past three years, and Father is keen to encourage me to be less particular. I suppose he thinks if I live in a tiny town with no prospects for a few years, I'll be thrilled to make the first match offered upon my return," I said. Mary didn't need to know that was only part of the reason. She wouldn't understand the others.

"Why are you so particular?" she asked, twirling a thin brown strand of hair. She pursed her lips. "I mean, it is rather peculiar to decline so many men, you must admit. A few have been less than handsome, though not offensive looking—like Harry Brundage—and a few of them have been downright heavenly in appearance—Lionel Reynolds, especially."

"I don't want to move away. I don't . . . I didn't want to leave my home and our nurseries to run a household with a man I don't—"

"Love," she said, snapping her fingers at me. "Love. You are in love with someone else. Who is it?"

The question took me by surprise and I shook my head, but my cheeks burned. "It's the nurseries, truly. I have loved plants my whole life, Mary, and I can't imagine living somewhere where I can't be immersed in the business of them," I said, hoping my insistence on this fact would both distract from the truth of her statement and root my hope that the nurseries would recover after all.

"Well then, marry Harry Brundage," she said. "He's in Rye and you could go over to your father's whenever you please and wander through those greenhouses or wherever it is you go for solace."

"I can't. They're gone," I said. "Did you read in the paper of the tornado last night? Our greenhouses were flattened, and almost all of the plants ruined. The slate was torn from our roof."

Mary's eyes widened and she shook her head. "No, of course not or I would have said something straightaway." She flattened her palm on her chest as though the news was horrific for her as well. "I admit I've been preoccupied with preparations for this evening. Of course we heard a bit of wind along the ocean and saw a little rain, but nothing of a twister's force was felt here."

"It was small. It touched down nowhere but atop our hill, I suppose. I'm glad for the town being spared, but as small and brief as it was, it devastated us. Nearly a hundred men showed up this morning to repair what we've lost, but as hopeful as I am, I also know there's a possibility that we won't recover, that we've lost everything."

"Oh." The word came out in a whisper. "Not you, too, Sadie. Not your dear family as well." Mary's eyes welled and she looked down at her kid-leather boots. "I will pray right now that everything is salvaged."

"Thank you," I said. "But be assured that your plants will all be perfect for your party and beyond. I'm just going to finish sprinkling the insecticide and—"

"You must come tonight," she said.

I laughed. "Thank you, but I'm afraid with the tornado and my ship coming in a few short days, I don't have the time. And in any case, all of my gowns are already in my trunks for the voyage," I said. It was true that I could locate a ball gown and attend, but I wasn't at all in the merrymaking mood, and no one enjoyed a grouch at a party.

"All the more reason to attend. If all is lost, you may no longer be in Rye when you return, and surely you'll need the memory of one last fine party. I know I would. You wear a thirty-six-inch bust, forty-one-inch skirt length," she said matter-of-factly. "I can tell by looking at you. You and I are the same size. I will lend you a dress. Come on. You can choose one to take. I expect to see your father and your brothers too. I heard they're both in town."

I wanted to decline, but as silly as it seemed and as much as I thought myself above the need for fine things, she was right. I would cherish the memory of being served champagne in crystal flutes and a full orchestra playing Mozart over the soft lapping of the water on the shore. I would be able to close my eyes and dream of the night in the pink garden with the view of the sunset over the sound. I would remember myself as a sort of rose, too, done up in the splendor of fine silks and imported lace.

"I think I know just the dress," Mary went on as I set the bottle of insecticide down and followed her. "I told all the women to wear pink, and this Worth gown I had shipped over last year will look stunning with your complexion. It's a pink damask satin woven with the most darling bearded irises and swags of rose ribbon. I had them inset the sleeves with tulle panels and diamanté studs."

"That sounds lovely." I nodded to the servants as I started up the stairs behind her, thinking of the black soot–stained garments on the ladies I'd seen in the city. If the nurseries weren't to be, if Father couldn't get on with Vaux, then the city was a reality we were facing.

One final night of magic, of flowers and loveliness and laughter, would be melancholy but worth it.

By the time I arrived back home, the greenhouse land had been cleared and the men had gone. Three small rows of salvaged plants stood in place of the buildings, a symbol of all we'd lost. I rode down to the barn, Mary's ball gown covered in old sheets and draped across Gene's neck. Father, Charles, Freddie, and Sam sat in the dirt beside the barn, their backs propped against the wood. They were clearly exhausted—my brothers' suit jackets, long discarded, hung from the plow handles, Father's face was red with exertion, and Sam's linen shirt was soaked through.

"How did it look there?" Father asked when he saw me.

"The arrangements on the ocean side were completely stripped of petals, though they all remain intact. The garden in front of the house is nearly perfect, though," I said, dismounting and heaving the dress from Gene's back. "We couldn't have timed the blooming better. It will be like a dream."

"What do you have there?" Freddie asked. "We didn't lose the plant covers in the twister. They were in the barn."

"It's a ball gown Mary Fink insisted I take. She wants us all at the party tonight."

"I don't think I can muster the enthusiasm," Charles said.

"I'll go with you, Sadie. I need a little merriment about now," Freddie said.

"You should reconsider, Charles," Sam said. His eyes met mine and I looked away, sure my family would notice us staring at each other. "I went by the estate on an errand for the cemetery, and it is spectacular. The evening will be lovely. Perhaps it would distract you a bit from the calamity of today."

"You helped plan most of it—you and Sadie," Father said to Sam, leaning his head back against the barn and closing his eyes. "You should attend with them."

I glanced at Father. Either the statement was a rude jest or something in the last day had completely altered his mind.

Sam laughed and shook his head. "Imagine that, will you? Sam Jenkins, the man who once begged to be employed as the Finks' gardener, now appears, uninvited, to their party. It would be a scandal," he said.

"Not really. I mean, I suppose people would talk, but if you attended with us, there would be nothing left to say. And in any case, Rye society has dwindled of late. How many are in the whole lot now, Sadie? Thirty?" Freddie asked.

I stared at Sam, imagining him standing under lantern light, among the hundreds of blooms, in a tuxedo. He would be stunning, captivating, and I wouldn't be able to resist him. I wasn't able to resist him now.

"Regardless, there is still the need to be invited. Formality is still alive in this little town," Charles said, interrupting my daydream.

Charles's eyes met mine. Though Father's walls seemed to have crumbled in the tornado—that he saw our loss of fortune as my loss of prospects along with the funds to sustain us—Charles was looking beyond today, and it was clear he saw regrowth, and in it, the reestablishment of the rules ingrained in us since we were young.

"Don't worry, Charles, I wasn't intending to go," Sam said. "There's much work to be done at the cemetery, and in any case, I don't have a fine suit."

"That's sensible, I suppose, if you have business to conduct," Father said, suddenly awakened from the tornado's trance by Charles. I could see the hard stare return to his eyes and wished Charles would have kept his mouth shut.

"I do. And speaking of that, I'll depart for the day. Good evening." Sam stood and dusted off his canvas trousers. "Promenade pretty," he whispered as he passed me. "Perhaps it's not too late for you to attract a fortune and save everyone and the nurseries after all."

I whirled around, a retort on my lips, but his tone was confusing. It wasn't sharp or angry. It was quiet, matter-of-fact, as if he believed if he and I chose selflessness, I alone could remedy everything. Fire coursed through my veins. I wanted to run after him; I wanted to punch Charles, but I did neither. Instead, I swallowed the ball of fury lumped in my throat and faced the reality of his words.

Despite how awful I felt at what he'd just said, it was the truth. If a man of fortune still wanted me, knowing my family's new calamity, I would have to consider it. I would have to consider the sacrifice of my life and heart for the sake of the people I loved, for the people who would be cast out in the absence of our nurseries.

The pink party was to take place in the twilight so the blooms could be enjoyed both in the sunset and under the stars' twinkle, but as our new Brewster & Co. carriage—still smelling of new leather and shining with silver fixtures—lumbered under the pink silk streamers that now canopied the entire drive, all I could think of was the woman I'd just seen wandering along the side of the road on our way.

She was new in town—at least I'd never seen her before— and clearly without a home. Her cheeks were hollow with hunger and her old dress was threadbare. I'd wanted to stop the carriage, to give her something to help, but what could we give now? Our hands were already empty and soon enough this carriage and our others, anything fine we could sell, would be sold and the funds divided to pay our debts to our source nurseries. Any extra we had would be given to our employees.

The thought that all of them—that all of us—were one unfortunate step away from the woman on the side of the road was a harrowing reality. I wanted to believe that Sam and the others who had come to help would fix everything and save us after all, but with the greenhouse field now empty, with nothing left but three pallets of plants, the thought that we could continue on seemed unlikely. I knew my family felt it too. I'd watched the way Father looked out at the vacant field, his face haggard and his eyes dull, the way Charles had finally turned away and murmured that they'd done all they could, despite his earlier optimism.

"Well, isn't this fine?" Father asked. His eyes lit up as our carriage lingered for a moment in the drive behind a line of others. I was glad we'd been able to convince him to attend despite his reservations. "I can't say I've done a color theme very often, but with the plentiful varieties of pink, this looks quite lovely."

Father was dressed in his traditional gray evening suit with the copper filigree buttons he'd ordered from H. O'Neill's earlier this year. Freddie, ever the government man, was wearing a traditional black set with a pink bowtie, and Charles was in his Palm Springs attire—a light linen suit—with a bowtie that matched Freddie's.

I smoothed the pink silk dress and stared out the window at the blooms dipping and righting in the sea breeze. I regretted being here. We didn't belong anymore. We were pretending. We were gold plate—a glistening shimmer on the surface, but worm-eaten wood beneath.

"It is exquisite," Charles said. "Did you say Jenkins designed it?" Charles lowered his eyeglasses and squinted out the window.

"We did it together," I said. "Layered textures and serpentine paths. Whimsical—that was what Mary wanted."

"I daresay it looks good," Freddie said. "I mean, I've always known of your skill, Sadie, but it rivals something Father or Charles would do."

"I designed the Brundages' as well," I said.

"And it is the talk of the town," Father said. "As much as I regret involving you, I'm glad you had the chance to conduct a few landscapes. I know it's your passion and rightly so." His eyes met mine and that softness I'd seen in the tornado's wake had returned. It was almost as if, stripped of the society-man mantle, his true heart was laid bare.

Father sighed. "Sam was an asset to me as well, and in my anger I alienated him. Not that my anger was misplaced at the time, mind you. Now I suppose you know how much we truly couldn't afford to be more charitable." The coach lurched forward.

"He's an immense talent," I said, but no one responded. What could be the reply now anyway? Father certainly couldn't ask him back. Still, I wondered if perhaps Father's heart had softened toward our love for each other now that our fortune was already dashed. I bit my lip, the thought of Sam and me, finally married, finally together, flushing my cheeks. It felt within reach.

But then I remembered Roisin. It wasn't only Father standing in the way of us.

I could hear the orchestra playing Brahms, and out my window I could see the older set had already arrived, situated in willow chairs around a glass table displaying a cherub ice sculpture. Margaret stood behind Mrs. Ridgeway in a palest pink costume. The shade was nearly a match with her skin tone. The only way to determine she wasn't naked was the paste diamonds shimmering in the sunset light along her bodice. I wasn't in the mood to speak to her, to hear the pity in her voice, the same tone she used when she spoke of Sylvie.

"My goodness. Is this the whole of who's left?" Charles asked, following my gaze. "The average age of the Rye elite is now near seventy? As beautiful as this party is, it will conclude by eight."

Mr. and Mrs. Garner sat at the head of the glass table next to the Bishops and Mrs. Ridgeway. Mrs. Horner, the Blankenships, and Mrs. Hamrick occupied the other side.

I laughed. "Of course not, Charles. That's just the older group. Though, I admit, the younger set has dwindled with the crash, as you know." I was heartened to see that the Brundages weren't in attendance—at least not that I could tell.

As our carriage started around the needle-nose part of the drive, Freddie pointed out his window and laughed. "There are the others. Already dancing. We should have known. The Finks are always the first to show off their waltz."

The lanterns the servants had polished earlier were now gleaming silver atop stakes situated in a large rectangular pattern between the start to the gardens and the house. The flames were turned up so high that the small blazes licked the tops.

Mary and Phin were in the middle of the crush of our one-time peers. Her gown was a coral with a ruched silk skirt, and Phin's suit was a shade of the same. Even from this distance, I could tell she was happy—her head tilted toward her husband, a smile on her lips. Stephen Bishop and his fiancée, Molly, were dancing as well, while Ida Horner, Minnie Blankenship, and Emma Hamrick—girls nearly five years my junior—ogled a group of men who appeared to have no interest in leading anyone out to the dance floor.

Edward Melsom raised a crystal glass high and quite nearly smashed it into Harry Brundage's, who had only raised his a hair. I balked at the sight of Harry. I didn't want to face him, not after his hurried proposal that seemed driven more by his desire to be the victor over Lionel than by any desire to win my hand. Then again, he'd been pursuing me for quite some time now. Lionel's proposal had seemed more disingenuous.

"Miss Hamrick is looking lovely," Freddie said as our coach stopped.

"If Brundage is keen to propose again, even after our certain calamity, hear him, Sadie," Charles whispered beside me. Our eyes met and instead of offering a retort, I nodded. Harry had been clear the night of Charles's send-off that he wouldn't marry a woman in need of his fortune. As much as I desperately wanted to help those I loved, I was hoping I would be suddenly undesirable to him. Because if he proposed again and I declined, knowing the needs of my family and our employees, and if Sam's efforts to resuscitate the nurseries failed, leaving those who counted on us homeless and hungry, I couldn't bear it. If Harry proposed again, I would have to accept.

"Stephen Bishop isn't wed yet either," Charles went on. "I know he's engaged, but he hasn't seen you since the night of my departure and he was quite taken with you then."

"I won't intentionally separate him and Molly," I said. I would do what I could, but not at the expense of another woman—or Stephen's happiness.

"I would find an advantageous match myself, but I'm afraid my intentions would be too obvious to win one at this stage. Freddie's too. Our absence has awarded us no entanglements and now it might fall upon you. I'm sorry for it, Sadie, though I've told you before that a match like this, where you can find yourself settled, would be best for you," Charles whispered.

"Oh, good. Jenkins decided to come after all," Father said.

My heart stopped and I clutched the window frame.

"What? I thought we said it wouldn't be polite," Charles retorted.

Father shrugged and pursed his lips. "I had Cooper come by and inquire whether the Finks would see fit to have him attend, considering he was one of the designers. They agreed and I sent Cooper down to the cemetery with a suit and a carriage in case he decided he'd like to come. It was the least I could do to express my appreciation for all he's done. Lord knows I've made many blunders when it comes to him, and I'm ashamed. He's a man like I was before I came into this life, but I suppose I'd been keen to forget that man."

"I think you made a mistake," Charles said sharply. "Everything is hanging in the balance, Father, and to encourage him knowing Sadie—"

Freddie or Father must have stopped his tirade. I didn't see how, nor did I care. Sam was here and my father had invited him. My gaze swept over the guests lingering at the glass table and then out the other window to the dancing set. Finally I found him alone on the garden path, bent low over an azalea. He righted just then, as if he could feel my eyes, and looked at the drive, finding our carriage. The sight of Sam in Father's double-breasted indigo pinstripe suit stole my breath. He was stunningly handsome in his work clothes, but now, with his beauty outfitted in finery, he was absolutely striking. He adjusted the deep-pink necktie, and then suddenly Ida Horner was by his side. She fiddled with the curl hanging loose at her nape and let her hand sweep her décolletage as they spoke, but Sam's gaze was trained on our carriage.

Mr. Wilson finally opened our door and held out his hand. I edged around Charles, ignoring the proper way to exit a carriage—which was to let any elders emerge first.

"Miss Sadie Fremd," Mr. Wilson bellowed. His hand released mine in the direction of the orchestra, but I hastened behind the lantern rows and down the shell path.

"Sam," I said, breathless, when I reached him. His eyes met mine over Ida's head, but there was a coolness in his gaze, a resolve I couldn't understand.

"Oh, hello, Sadie," Ida said. "Of course you know Mr. Jenkins. He said he worked with you on this design." Ida kept chattering on, attempting to explain the casual way in which I'd addressed the most stunning man she'd ever seen. Saying so wasn't an assumption. It was a fact.

"You look lovely, Miss Fremd," Sam said finally, a strange formality to his voice. "But I'm afraid you must excuse me. Miss Horner here has just asked me to take her for a turn at the start of the next waltz and it's just begun. Perhaps you should locate Harry Brundage. He's been asking for you."

Sam took Ida's gloved hand and they stepped around me. He glanced at me once more, hesitating for a moment when he saw my eyes fill. He let Ida go for a moment and leaned toward me. "I thought to refuse to come, but then I considered. We must get used to this. We must get used to seeing each other with someone else. You must do whatever it takes to keep the village intact, the nurseries in business for your family and for them, for the town. I didn't want you to come here, with opportunities all around you, and refuse them because you were thinking of me at home—what I wanted, what I thought of all of this. I'm here, and I want you to understand that you cannot . . . you should not love me. I want you to marry a good man who can help everyone we love—and I don't have the pockets to do so. That's someone else."

I opened my mouth to speak, but nothing came, and in that moment he took Ida's hand once more. "But you are helping. Your efforts are going to work," I called. "We have a crew of nearly one hundred."

Sam looked back.

"Perhaps, but we don't know for sure," he said. "And as your father said, we can replace the structures, but the plants will have to be ordered again, and . . ." He shook his head, not wanting to further discuss the particulars in front of Ida. "You cannot risk it when there's something to be done that can work, something that is a guarantee."

I watched them go, watched as Ida's fingers rested on Sam's nape and not his shoulders, watched as he smiled at her and leaned closer. He thought being here, letting me know he wanted me with someone else, would help me make the decision to accept if someone proposed.

It did not. All I felt was a deep ache, an acute longing that made my knees weak. I knew his dancing with Ida was harmless. He wouldn't marry her or anyone else with the possibility of

Roisin hanging in the balance, but still, though we had danced around despair for months, tonight he had shut the door in my face.

I wandered back down the path, away from the dancing. I didn't want to watch him with Ida, and I wasn't in the mood to be asked to dance myself. I walked under the ceiling of ribbon, watching the distant lantern light start to flicker in the impending dim.

"Could I interest you in an oyster?" one of the Finks' servants asked, holding out a silver tray of half shells. Though popular and quite convenient to soirees, oysters had never been a favorite of mine. They were much too slimy, and without an oyster fork one was forced to tip the shell into her mouth and hope the oyster fell out—an action one couldn't do without looking quite silly and undignified.

"No, thank you," I said. "I have my eye on one of the pink ices on that tray just there." I pointed toward the glass table to the spot where Margaret still stood solemnly beside her mother-in-law. I didn't understand why she hadn't come over. Surely she'd seen me arrive or heard me announced.

"Yes, you'll be glad you had one," the servant said. "It's lemonade mixed with a strawberry puree and shaved ice."

I wandered over and took one of the silver goblets and a spoon, an action that forced me to stand in the center of the older set. Father and my brothers had been detained in the grassy center of the circular drive by Mr. Fink.

"I'm sorry to hear what happened," Mrs. Garner warbled. "It's a terrible tragedy."

I looked at her sitting there in her rose silk gown—adorned in diamonds on three necklaces, enormous teardrop earrings, and rings on every finger—and thought how ridiculous her apology was. The sale of one of her diamonds could have helped her former best friend, Mrs. Griffith, enormously—and given the Garners' fortune, no sale would have been necessary—but the Garners hoarded money and were never ones for charity.

"Thank you, but I don't believe you truly care at all about our disaster. You certainly haven't cared about others' of late either," I said calmly, then spooned a bit of ice into my mouth. It was quite good, and it felt wonderful to say something cross. I was angry about the twister, angry about Sam's words and the truth of them.

A collective gasp rose from the group, but no one said a word lest they begin a disagreement. Disagreements were frowned upon. It was a mark of the highest pedigree to keep one's temper cool.

"Let's go watch the dancing, shall we, Sadie?" Margaret said, suddenly emerging from the shadow of her mother-in-law. "What were you thinking?" she whispered pointedly as she grasped my elbow and pulled me back under the ribbons toward the orchestra.

"Everyone's so terribly sorry, but no one of this set lifts a finger to help anyone," I said, taking another bite of my ice. "This is my final party, Margaret. Unless a miracle happens, the nurseries are to be closed. I'm sorry to say, but you will be alone now, three dwindled to one."

"Perhaps if your father hadn't hired so many people, he could have saved more income," she said, her voice void of any sort of sympathy. Obviously she heard this bit from Tempy or one of the older women. Margaret hadn't any idea about business. Her father was an heir to a rail baron and her husband an heir to the copper business. No one had been required to have any sort of business acumen for three generations.

She continued her lecture. "You should have learned from Sylvie. You should have accepted one of the wonderful men who proposed, though I should say that—" She stopped abruptly and elbowed me, grabbing for my ice cup. "Here he comes," Margaret practically squealed, her earlier scolding replaced by excitement. "He's been asking for you all evening, and I don't want to assume why, but—"

"Miss Fremd . . . Sadie."

I sighed and turned to face Harry, who was suddenly in front of us on the walk. I didn't know why he'd been asking for me or why anyone believed he would humble himself a third time and propose again. If anything, I assumed he was here to gloat, to tell me that our misfortune served us right, that I should have accepted him.

"Good evening, Mr. Brundage," I said. Margaret disappeared from beside me, leaving us alone.

He was wearing a pale pink suit with a gold bowtie, a combination that screamed flashy Fifth Avenue and not at all sleepy, elegant Rye. Before I could stop him, he snapped a peony from its stem and handed it to me. I accepted it, though irritation burned in my chest. Surely he knew you didn't pluck blooms from someone else's garden.

"You are more beautiful than every flower here—other ladies included," he said. His typically pompous tone was strangely absent, replaced by something softer. "I've been away, but I told myself the moment I returned I would beg an apology from you for the manner in which I conducted myself that evening at dinner."

People were watching us. I could feel their stares. I hoped Sam was looking, too, that his heart was gripped at the thought that I could be promising my life, my love, away.

"It's quite all right," I said. "I suppose you're heartened it went the way it did, what with the recent calamity befalling our fortune." I knew I shouldn't have said it so openly, but I didn't care. He had been adamant about ensuring I was worthy of the Brundage name, that I wouldn't be deemed some sort of fortune hunter if we became engaged.

"Not at all," he said softly. "Would you walk with me to the front, to the terraces?"

He held out his hand and I was stunned when my fingers complied, curling around his palm. I looked straight ahead as he led me around the lanterns, through the enormous shadow of the stucco mansion, and into the sunset's orange-gold light beaming across the Sound and onto the four terraces.

"Can we sit for a moment?" he asked when we reached the bottom terrace. I nodded and sank onto a wrought iron bench along one of the curved edges and he sat beside me. In front of us the ocean was still violent from last night's storm, the waves crashing in angry sprays that glittered the sunset view.

"It's a beautiful evening," I said, simply to break the silence. I was acutely aware of Harry's leg brushing against mine, the way our hands rested only inches apart.

"I can't stop thinking of you," he said suddenly and took my hands. His thumb ran slowly across the back of mine, and I immediately wanted to pull away, but I stopped myself. "I've tried. I've tried to convince myself that I belong with Miss Harris of New Jersey or Miss Clark . . . anyone else, but I cannot. You have the loveliest face, an intelligence that rivals mine, and though you sometimes speak to me with contempt, I deserve it. I wanted to despise you after that night at your house, but I found that I could not. You were right to deny me. You have never fallen over me for my fortune like the others, and I—"

"I am penniless," I said. "I don't know that you understand the extent of our catastrophe, but the twister last night has sent us into possible bankruptcy." The thought of the tornado's strike being exactly a day prior was at once incredible. It seemed like a week had passed. I lifted my hand reflexively to my head, and also found it remarkable that I hadn't had any pain since the morning.

"I know how important it is for you to find someone who does not need your fortune, but that can no longer be me, Mr. Brundage."

"Harry," he said, his fingers tightening around mine. "Surely you still feel able to call me that after all we've been through."

"Of course," I said.

He was still staring at me, though he didn't say more. I'd just told him I was worth less than one of his maids, yet he wasn't letting me go.

"I know the extent of your misfortune. When I saw the papers, I found myself in tears," he said. "That's when I knew I didn't care if you had nothing, if I'd met you as a beggar on the streets. I still would . . . I would still be in love with you."

Everything inside me froze, and I had to ask. "Why? What do you love about me, Harry? I—"

He let go of one of my hands and brushed a wisp of hair from my cheek. "I have been enamored with your beauty ever since Sylvie's fourteenth birthday party. Do you recall it? It was St. Valentine's themed and we were to shoot arrows at the various hearts for prizes. I watched you in your pink lace dress and floral crown as you hit each target with ease. I can still see you—a raven curl springing loose from your braid, the pink of your cheeks when you were declared the victor." He sighed.

I wanted to pull away, but I couldn't. Sam's words echoed in my mind. *"I want you to marry a good man who can help everyone we love."*

"From then on, I told myself you'd be my wife someday," Harry said. "But you haven't made it easy on me, and I suppose that's one of the main reasons I've come to love you so. You are like me. Unyielding to your own standards, stubborn."

I was yielding now, though, bending severely like a sapling in a storm.

Harry laughed. "Which is why we have found it so difficult to see eye to eye," he said. "Sadie . . ." He looked out at the water and then back at me and leaned in. His fingers twined in my hair and his lips found mine. I wanted to stop him, but I didn't. Instead, I opened my mouth, I kissed him back, and my heart felt hollow. When our lips parted, he remained close, his forehead tilted into mine, his index finger tracing slow figure eights on my arm.

"What do you want most in this world, Sadie Fremd?" he whispered. "Name it and it's yours. I'll give you anything, if only you'll be mine."

"You know what it is," I said softly. "I've told you before."

He pulled away just slightly and shook his head. Of course he wouldn't remember. Men like him intentionally forgot the parts they didn't want to hear.

"The nurseries. I want to keep them. I want them to thrive again," I said. "You know how plants enliven me, Harry."

"Yes. Yes, you'll have them. I'll buy them and they will be yours, ours. Your father can still run the business, and—"

"When Father retires I will run it, and we must keep on all of our employees," I said sweetly. I waited for the prospect of his future wife entangled in business notions to outrage him, but he simply nodded.

"Yes, of course. Anything," he said.

He touched my leg as he leaned in to kiss me again, but this time felt worse than the last. This time, as his lips asked mine if I loved him, too, the reality that I was selling myself, that I was about to agree to a lie for the rest of my life, permeated my spirit. Just up the hill, I could hear the orchestra striking up another Mozart waltz and all I could think of was that the love of my life would never be mine.

"I'm going to ask your father for your hand again and to buy the nurseries in tandem," Harry said. He had finally distanced himself a bit, though his hands were still wrapped around mine. "Tomorrow morning. Will you be about? If he agrees, I can't bear to wait, Sadie. I'll race to your side and propose straightaway."

His proposal would be delayed until the morning. I wondered if between now and then I could retain the strength to accept it. It would be a marathon. Perhaps at home, in view of the state of the nurseries and in front of the possible peril of those we loved, I could muster the courage.

"Does your mother know of your plans? Surely your parents will have some objection to me now," I said.

"I have no doubt, but they are well situated, and I am a man of twenty-four years," he said. "Perhaps they will put up a bit of a fuss now, but all will be forgotten when they hold their first grandchild."

I could force myself to stomach his kisses and his overtures of love, but the thought of bearing his child made me want to throw up on his boots. I wondered how easy it would be to feign some dreadful disease after the wedding, something that would make my proximity entirely undesirable.

"I suppose we should get back to the party," I said.

"Are you certain we must? Aren't we all that matters now?" he asked.

"We haven't danced together in years. I'd like to see how we do," I said. At least while dancing among the other guests he wouldn't try to kiss me again.

"Very well, my darling," he said. He stood and extended his hand, helping me rise in turn. "After tomorrow, we shall be promised, and you will forever be mine. I can scarcely believe it."

I forced a smile and realized, as he led me back around the house and into the dancing throng, that though he said he loved me, that he wanted me, he hadn't asked me if I felt the same or even if I would accept him. He simply assumed it when I let him kiss me.

Harry pulled me against him and held my waist tightly as we danced. Father and Charles, standing on the edge of the dancers, took notice and stopped their talk with Tempy to stare. I looked away and instinctively reached up, my hand searching for a nape nearly a foot taller than my own, and my fingers grazed the top of Harry's bowler.

"Where shall we honeymoon?" he whispered. "Shall we do a tour of Europe or perhaps Alaska?"

I barely heard him. Over his shoulder Sam was dancing with Minnie and his gaze met mine and lingered. Harry's words, that tomorrow I would be bound to him forever, kept repeating in my ears, and all I could feel was the pain of a love that would always be and the ache for his arms that would never ease.

My eyes filled with tears and I let them fall onto Harry's shoulder. Sam stepped back from Minnie abruptly, his gaze still fixed on mine. He ran a palm across his face and as Minnie tried to catch him, he turned away and walked quickly up the Finks' drive and into the darkness.

I sniffed, swallowing a sob, and Harry looked at my face.

"I'm sorry," I said, but he only smiled.

"Tears of joy are welcome," he said, not bothering to brush them from my cheeks. "Tonight, my dear, we have finally settled. Tonight, my Sadie, we have saved each other."

CHAPTER 17

I took a sip of my morning coffee as I sat on the front porch watching the thin stream of vapor drift into the morning chill and Mr. Cooper and Mr. Allison yank my trunks from the carriage they'd prepared in advance of my departure. I wasn't going to be banished to Germany anymore. Instead, I would accept Harry's proposal to become Mrs. Sadie Brundage. The mere thought of it, regardless of the circumstances that would encourage my swift acceptance, seemed preposterous.

I'd told my family of Harry's offerings in the carriage on the way home from the Finks'. They'd all been heartened to learn of his willingness to save us, and though they tried to cloak their joy for my sake, I could see the relief in their eyes.

"It will take me all day to put your things away," Agnes grumbled, interrupting my thoughts. She was sitting next to me in a matching wicker chair sipping Irish breakfast tea. She twirled the metal tea ball in the china cup with fervor.

"I'll help you," I said.

Everyone was in a foul mood this morning. It wasn't

necessarily the inconvenience of my staying that was the problem—though it was a fine scapegoat. Everyone's nerves were frayed on account of not knowing if the nurseries would sink or swim. Father had been very clear that he doubted, despite everyone's best efforts, that we would survive the fallout from the twister, and because I hadn't yet accepted Harry's proposal, we didn't feel at liberty to share the news of our certain salvation.

"No, you won't. You can't. Didn't you say you're expecting Mr. Brundage?" she asked, eyeing the backs of my hands.

"Yes," I said and raised my free hand for her inspection. "They're not bruised like you thought they would be. And if they were, that's what gloves are for."

I'd made her take a nighttime walk with me to the cemetery when I returned home from the Finks' last night. Despite Father's declaration that I'd be staying in Rye, he hadn't communicated to Agnes that she was free from chaperoning me, and so she refused to leave my side until she heard directly from Father.

She'd tried to keep me trapped within the nurseries' grounds, but I told her I was going to find Sam and nothing could stop me, that she could either accompany me or go back home. I'd been able to think of nothing but Sam's face since he saw me crying, and I needed to find him. I needed to know if he'd changed his mind—if he would forfeit the notion of Roisin and the insistence that I marry to save the nurseries.

Agnes had followed me across the street and down to the groundskeeper's quarters. It was only nine, but the lanterns were put out and the windows darkened. She started to turn around when she saw it, likely assuming I'd do the same, but I went to the front door and began to knock. She tried to stop me, saying

I'd wake Mr. Sanderson, but I told her I knew he'd given the cottage to Sam and had moved in with his daughter in town.

When Sam didn't answer my knocks, I began to yell his name and pound harder on the door with my fists until the hinges whined. Agnes was horrified, and finally, after several minutes of begging me to stop, she'd come up behind me and pinned my arms to my back. I crumpled to the floor then, right there on the threshold, and I told her everything. If Sam didn't answer, if I didn't have a chance to tell him goodbye, I would never be able to. I could be engaged to Harry by morning.

"Mr. Brundage is a good man," Agnes said, bringing me back to the present, but echoing her sentiments from Sam's porch last night. "To offer to care for you, for all of us that way. I know you don't love him now, but you will, and as time passes, when Mr. Jenkins is married off, too, this love you feel so deeply will be merely a pleasant memory."

I swallowed the tension in my throat and stared out at the field. The older generation could say what they wanted. I might be young, but I was wise enough to understand that most people settled for a marriage of circumstance. Most people never knew a love like mine and Sam's.

The village was staring to wake. Vincenzo and Rosalie ambled up the hill with full watering cans, and the Sigallis family was weeding the growing field, dropping down every few minutes to snatch a variety that didn't belong. Father, Charles, and Freddie had gone to the bank to speak about the state of our accounts.

Ordinarily, knowing Harry's visit was imminent, I'd disappear, encourage Father to linger in town, but Agnes's sentiments were everyone's and who was I, really, to refuse him? My sacrifice, the sacrifice of one for the good of sixty-seven, seemed right, despite how wrong it felt to my heart. Perhaps the greater community never would have the park we'd dreamed of, but at the very least, I could help salvage the well-being of my Rye Nurseries family.

"You look beautiful. He's going to have quite a difficult time finding his words," Agnes said.

She'd extracted one of my trunks from the carriage herself in the early morning hours and chosen my ensemble—a marquise costume made of lavender satin lined with silk, veiled at the sides and back with ivory sprig net and edged with lace. It was a soft, delicate look, an appearance Agnes insisted was irresistible to a man. I told her I rather felt like wearing sackcloth and that at this point I doubted Harry cared at all what I wore, but she'd ignored me and spent nearly an hour doing my hair in an elaborate figure eight adorned with Cecile Brunner roses, a light pink fragrant variety that survived the twister in the growing field.

One of the carts we'd lent out for the glass yesterday came into view on the drive and I sat forward in my seat, shielding my eyes with my hand to get a better look at the driver. I'd begun to wonder in the middle of the night if Sam hadn't ignored me after all. Perhaps he hadn't been home.

"It's only Micah Greenwell, the glazier, and his men," Agnes said. "Surely you know Mr. Brundage's carriages by now."

Harry and his mother had matching Brewster & Co. broughams, though Harry's was silver-plated and always pulled by a team of white Percherons. I had no doubt that deep down he fashioned himself a royal.

Mr. Greenwell, a man my father's age but who looked at least eighty, was helped from the cart by his men and, carrying a measuring tape, walked slowly to the only standing greenhouse. My heart sank. I knew things took time, but I'd hoped for something more—even a single new glass emerging from the cart would have felt like progress.

"Robert Deal coming to meet us?" Mr. Greenwell shouted to one of his men standing idly beside the cart. "Can't exactly get the dimensions of the glass right without knowing how thick he's building the frame."

"Yes. Saw him just minutes ago in the rail village. He's going by the station with Jenkins and then he'll be here," the man yelled back.

My heart skipped and I stared at the drive, willing Sam to appear. I only needed a moment.

"Have a scone, Miss Sadie," Agnes said, plucking a small blueberry pastry from the plate and holding it out to me. "You're looking quite pale. A bit of something in your stomach will settle you."

"I don't think it will," I said. Just then, a second cart appeared, making its way toward the house. I flew from my seat, barely taking time to set my cup on its saucer. "If Mr. Brundage comes while I'm gone, please have him wait in Father's study," I said hurriedly.

I heard Agnes call after me as I gathered my skirts in my hands and ran down the walk and onto the drive. Gene had just been stopped by Mr. Deal and I caught his halter and edged around to the seat as Sam was stepping down.

"I need a word with you," I said.

"Sadie," he breathed, startled at my presence. He wiped dirt from his linen pants and then looked at me. "You . . . you look—"

"Good day, Miss Fremd. The sun is shining and the wind is

light—a perfect day to start rebuilding," Mr. Deal said, not at all noticing the way Sam and I stood staring at each other.

"Indeed it is," I said. I couldn't keep my eyes from Sam's. His were tired, bloodshot, haggard, and yet I'd never seen anything more beautiful. "Mr. Jenkins, would you mind terribly helping me get Gene back in the barn? He's quite old and needs to be watered more often these days."

"I'll go on down with Mr. Greenwell then. Just meet me after you're through," Mr. Deal said to Sam.

"Yes," Sam said mechanically. I watched the way his fingers hurriedly unhooked Gene, the way his eyes kept darting to the drive. When Gene was freed from the harness, Sam started walking to the barn, his gait long and swift. I could barely keep up, and he didn't wait for me, nor did he say anything.

We walked into the barn, under the roof's shadow. Sam led Gene to the trough and then, finally, faced me.

"You're not in white or in mourning," he said. "That's a proposal gown." His eyes drifted from my face to my toes in a slow appraisal that sent shivers up my spine.

I stepped toward him until we were inches apart. I reached for his hand and his fingers twined with mine. "Harry will be here any minute to ask Father for my hand and to buy the nurseries for me. He's promised to let Father and me run them and to retain all of our employees. Directly after he speaks with Father, he'll propose," I said. My voice sounded foreign.

Sam nodded, his jaw tight. Once more, my eyes filled and I looked away, but Sam took my chin in his hand and gently tilted my face toward his.

"I knew what this meant last night," he said, his voice low. "I knew this emotion meant that you'd done the honorable thing, the thing that would save so many, the thing I'd asked for, and yet—" Sam's voice broke then, and I sobbed, pressing my face into his chest. His arms wrapped tightly around me and held me. When I composed myself, I pulled back just slightly to find tears on his cheeks.

"I walked around our whole town three times after I left the Finks', 'til morning light, trying to figure out another way. But I could not, and even this morning at the rail station . . . They said it would take two months to build the frames. I know your father doesn't have that much time."

"I don't want to marry him," I said. "I'll never love him."

"Then don't," Sam said, his palm on my cheek, his fingers tracing my nape. "As honorable as it would be, how can anyone ask you to lay down your whole life? I thought it would be the right thing—for you to go on, to forget me, but last night I realized how selfish I was to say that to you. I was asking the impossible. I know because, though I'd have to go on, I'd never forget you."

"I am only one person. I can't let everyone suffer, knowing I could have done something to help," I said. A tear broke from my eyelid and Sam wiped it away. "It is better that the suffering strike just one of us than—"

"Two," Sam whispered. "Two of us. But you're right."

"I thought if I declined for love, no one would fault me, that perhaps that wasn't so selfish, but you will never be mine truly, will you? Even if the twister had never happened, even if I was free." My voice rose in an angry pitch, and I punched my fists into his chest, fury and despair finally spilling out. Tears poured from my eyes, and I tried to back away from him, but Sam grasped my fists, still pressed against him, and pulled me close.

"I'm sorry. I'm so sorry," he said, his eyes pooling. "I wish I hadn't proposed to her. We are standing here, together, and yet we're both locked away." I could feel his heart beating against mine, and I sighed and lifted my hands to settle around his neck.

"I need to hear you say it," I said. "Just one last time."

"I love you," he said swiftly. "I love you," he said again. "And I always will. I . . . I won't interfere. You'll be another man's wife, but I'll never stop loving you, Sadie, I—"

I pulled him down to me and kissed him. His lips were slow and soft, and as the kiss intensified, as my tongue swept his and his teeth gently bit down on my lip, I knew this was the last time.

"I love you, Sam," I said when it was over, when all that was left was an echo, a memory.

"One more for goodbye," he said. His lips whispered across mine and the barn door squealed open. Sam's arms jerked away from my body and he stepped back.

"Mr. Jenkins, Miss Fremd," Agnes said behind me.

Sam's face paled and I turned.

"This woman here, just in on the rail, says she'd like to have a word," Agnes said. A small, beautiful woman with strawberry hair and milky skin stepped around her. Chills rippled my skin.

"Roisin," Sam said.

He said her name the way he'd just said mine. The affection was the same. As he walked toward her and took her hands in his, I wondered if he'd been lying all this time, if perhaps the promise he'd made hadn't been given in an effort to protect her after all.

I whirled away from them, walking quickly past the horses and out the barn's back door. I couldn't bear to see them reconcile further. I lifted my hands to my lips, then pressed my fingers into the bags beneath my eyes and pinched my cheeks. Down in the village Mrs. Pratte, Mrs. Sigallis, Mrs. Ciuzzo, and Mrs. Pompero were hanging laundry to dry. Mrs. Pratte waved and I waved back, recalling what she'd said when I joined them for dinner—that living here had saved her family, especially Vincenzo. Absent the tasks that needed doing at the greenhouses and for our clients, all of our employees were gathered in the growing field fertilizing, weeding, watering—likely anything to resuscitate the place they loved, the place they called home.

Suddenly it was clear. Roisin appeared at this exact moment for a reason. My heart was shattered, pulverized so severely that I felt nearly numb, yet my purpose was obvious. Sam had been taken away forever, and now, with him gone, there was no hesitation.

I would accept Harry. I would trust his kindness in buying the nurseries. Perhaps, as time went on, I would even grow fond of him.

"We're nearly through measuring here, Miss Fremd, and we'll be ready to start the iron firing later today," Mr. Deal said from around the other side of the lone greenhouse.

"How wonderful," I said, though my enthusiasm was lacking. I cleared my throat and forced a smile. "We truly appreciate everything you all are doing," I said. The men shouted an array of welcomes and happy-to-do-its.

"Are you quite all right, Miss Sadie?" Agnes asked, catching up to me as I crossed the greenhouse field toward home. I glanced at her, willing myself not to look back down the hill at the barn where I knew Sam and Roisin were getting reacquainted.

"No," I said.

She stopped me and smoothed my hair, then licked her fingers and wiped a few salt lines from my cheeks.

"Sorrow may last for a night, but joy comes in the morning," she said.

Her gesture was so like Mother that I nearly began to cry again. Instead, I was interrupted by Harry's carriage making its way out from under the tree canopy. The silver gleamed in the morning light. Mr. Cooper hastened out of our front door and down the walk, his black coattails flapping behind him.

"Your father and brothers are back from town and situated in his study," Agnes said. "I must say that they returned in jovial spirits."

"I can't imagine how unless this match is heartening them," I said.

Agnes clutched my hand. "Last night, we were all discussing what would happen to us, where we would have to go. We were wondering if we'd starve, if we'd be forced to the factories, if we'd catch disease. And now, thanks to your incredible heart, we will be saved. We will never forget your kindness." She paused. "Those that are leaders, those that are followed, don't only think of themselves. You are a worthy successor, Miss Sadie. We'll follow you anywhere."

Harry's coach stopped and Mr. Cooper opened his door. I watched him step out in a beige linen suit. His gaze swept me and stopped. Even from this distance, I could see him smile. When he lifted his hand to wave at me, I waved back, finding that though the prospect of Harry as my lover still disgusted me, the prospect of Harry as a friend, as my husband, didn't fill me with dread any longer.

I was to be Mrs. Brundage. This time the thought didn't make me recoil in disbelief. My heart had accepted my fate.

Father's deliberating with Harry lasted longer than I thought it would. I'd been idling in the drawing room pretending to read for nearly two hours, and the waiting was agony.

Not that I wanted Harry suddenly, but the thought of Sam keeping his promise, the way he'd gone to Roisin and left me, had marred me. He was still here but truly gone forever. I wondered which was worse—his absence or the torment of encountering him every day with her, knowing that despite his being in reach, he wasn't really. He could never be mine.

I hoped desperately that the news of my engagement would travel quickly to the village and make Sam extraordinarily jealous. But what if it didn't affect him at all? What if he was happy for me? The questions were mere whispers across my mind, but they haunted me. He could have lied. Roisin could have been a captivation, not just a friend.

"They're still at it?" Freddie came through the front door and swiped beads of sweat from his brow. Then he crossed to the bookshelves and busied himself pulling out volumes and pushing them back in. Something was bothering him.

"Of course," I said, setting Conan Doyle's *The White Company* on the tea table. "I'm going to be married and Father is giving away Rye Nurseries."

"I shouldn't think turning the nurseries over would render much discussion. He was planning to hand them over to someone in a few years anyway. As it is, he'll still be able to manage the business and it will be saved from extinction," he said.

"Yes, all of that is wonderful and true, but it will no longer be Father's. It will be taken from him—in a way—earlier than he'd planned. He'll mourn that. As he should," I said. I did wonder, despite Harry promising me the world, if we would come to regret selling to him later. Regardless of his overtures, I knew Harry well enough to know he could be shrewd. I had to hold to the hope that he would keep his promises.

"I understand, but it's nearly a certainty that we'd have to close otherwise. As valiant as the men are who have volunteered, it'll be a slow-moving rebuild. Even Sam has already stopped his progress for the day to escort a woman around the town." Freddie turned from the bookshelf slowly and his gaze steadied on mine. That was why he'd come into the house in such a state.

"That woman is Roisin Foster, his . . . his fiancée," I said. My fingers grasped the velvet cushion in an attempt to thwart the emotion in my chest.

"Oh," he said. "You knew of her?"

"They met in the city and in an attempt to get her out of the slums, he proposed," I said. "She declined at first because she was in love with him and his proposal was one of benevolence, not passion, but he begged her to accept when cholera broke out. She would not, but he promised that if she ever changed her mind, she could come here and he would marry her, take care of her."

"And now he's upholding that pledge. Of course Sam would," Freddie said. He shook his head. "When you're a child, everything seems simple, straightforward. That's not how life is, though, is it? I'm sorry for you, Sadie . . . not that the two of you would have found yourselves together now anyway, but—"

"It's easier this way, really," I said, even though, strangely, it wasn't. I suppose deep down I always thought Sam would remain unattached, and me as well, that we'd always have this love affair. "Now I can accept Harry knowing love is impossible."

"But that's not—"

Freddie was cut off by the sound of the study door opening and slamming. The particular clipped cadence of Father's steps came down the hall, and then he stood in the doorway in front of us, his eyes worn, his shoulders slumped, despite the smile he was wearing.

"It's all settled. Mr. Brundage will purchase the nurseries at the price of their current state—one-third below the value of what they're worth. I will remain here, as will our employees, and he will rebuild. I will receive a stipend of $5,000 yearly for my management and I will go through his finance man to request funds for each order I place for supplies. Our employees will receive the same funds," he said. He scuffed his boots along the floor and sighed. "Sadie, when it is time for me to retire, you will take over at the helm."

As much as Father's losing control made me incredibly melancholy, the idea that Harry was truly going to support my involvement was both a shock and a joy. Even so, now was not the time to express my excitement about it.

"I'm sorry, Father," I said. "I wish it didn't come to this."

"Me as well," he said. "It feels like I'm saying goodbye to both you and another child." He shook his head. "I knew we were going down this path anyway with Mr. Andrews, but selling to him was my decision. Now there's nothing to sell him but debt, and Brundage, I'm absolutely certain, is the only charitable sap willing to take it—and that's only because he's in love." Father glanced at me. "He's requesting you join him in my study. I'm going out for a bit." With that, Father walked out the front door and Freddie followed, practically running across the room to catch up with him.

I took a breath and stood, then began to walk out of the room, but suddenly felt unsteady. My heart raced and my pulse throbbed in my temple. This was it. My final moment of freedom. It occurred to me that we hadn't discussed where we'd live. Certainly not here at the nurseries with Father when Harry's veritable palace was but a few miles away. I made my way to Mother's secretary beside the door and unlatched the hinge. A little satchel of lavender sat in the drawer where she'd kept her pencils, and I grasped the silk bag, pressed it to my nose, and inhaled.

"Strength," I muttered under my breath. "Give me strength."

I thought of the crowd gathered on our lawn after the twister. I tried to think of all the faces of the people who had worked alongside us for so long. I conjured an image of me walking through the nurseries as an older woman, fulfilled from a life of doing what I loved, even if I didn't love my husband. I thought of Father, elderly, safely rocking on the front porch while I worked, away from the despair of the slums. This was for them; this was for me. I could manage if I could keep it all front of mind.

I put Mother's lavender satchel back in the drawer and closed the secretary. Then I looked at myself in the small hall mirror. The blotches had gone from my skin, the bags from my eyes. I pinched my cheeks and watched the rose color them. I was ready.

By the time I reached the study door, my heart had calmed. I knocked and Harry answered and before I knew it, I was standing in front of him, my hands in his. He was gaping at me, then suddenly remembered himself.

"I . . . I'm embarrassing myself," he mumbled. "There's so much I want to tell you, so much I want to say to you, but first." He lifted my hand to his lips and kissed it, then dropped to one knee.

"Sadie Christina Fremd, I didn't want to love you. I thought it weak. But I couldn't help wanting you. I thought that was all it was, an obsession, because you look like a goddess, because you wouldn't concede and fall into my arms like every other woman."

I barely kept myself from rolling my eyes. Even now, in the midst of a marriage proposal, he thought it necessary to remind me that he'd chosen me from hundreds.

"When I heard of your calamity, I thought I would rejoice because you'd bruised my pride, but I did not. Instead, my heart broke, and I realized then that this wasn't an infatuation. This was love, pure and simple. Strangely, my love didn't care that your fortune was gone, but it cared deeply that you could go away. I want you to marry me, Sadie. I want you to be mine forever. Will you?"

There was the familiar pause, the way my mind reeled and backpedaled.

"Harry, I . . ." My hands loosened on his and my eyes broke from his gaze. The word *forever* repeated in my thoughts and my knees felt weak.

"I need to sit down," I mumbled. Harry stood hurriedly and grasped my elbow, leading me to one of Father's matching leather chairs in front of his desk. As I settled on the seat, I caught sight of my father's ledgers open on the desktop. Even from my chair, I could see the sixty-seven lines, the people we employed, and my strength steadied.

Harry was crouched next to me, the barely-there smell of his just-smoked-cigar breath tainting the air, his eyes searching mine. His pale skin held a tinge of red, as though with any hint of a refusal from me, he would erupt. He plunged his hand into his coat pocket, withdrew a matchbox pack of Sen-Sen breath perfume, and deposited a tiny black candy in his mouth.

"I've just had a celebratory smoke with your father, and it occurred to me that I didn't freshen after," he said, as though his offensive breath was the reason I was hesitating. He shifted in front of me, still on his knees, and reached up to my face.

"Perhaps you don't love me like I love you, and I don't mind," he went on. He rose slowly and his hands came to rest on the chair back right beyond my shoulders. "But we have something, darling. You can't deny it," he whispered. He leaned in and kissed me. This time it was urgent, hurried, his tongue thrusting and tasting of licorice and mint, his mouth pressing hard into mine. I closed my eyes and tried to imagine it was Sam I was kissing, but nothing of this kiss was like the way our lips danced. When Harry withdrew, he was panting.

"Say something," he said huskily, his face still against mine. "Please."

I glanced at Father's desktop one more time. My stomach churned and my head spun, but I nodded. "All right," I whispered. It was the most I could muster.

"What . . . what does that mean?" he asked. The corners of his mouth lifted.

"It means I agree. I'll marry you," I said.

With that, he groaned and fell on top of me, his lips sweeping down my neck and then capturing my mouth once more. "I don't suppose you understand how elated I am," he said against my cheek.

"I imagine I can tell," I said stiffly, and he stood abruptly. He cleared his throat.

"I got carried away. I apologize. I was quite out of sorts, but we can't blame ourselves for this display, not after all this time," he said. Despite his apology, his grin was wide and victorious. He thought my passion for him had thrown my caution to the wind as well.

"You love me," he said wistfully. I wondered how he'd convinced himself of a truth I'd never uttered. Then again, I was engaged to him, I was kissing him. Of course he would assume I was fond of him. "Shall we marry next month?" he asked. "At the church or in your beautiful rose garden at our home?"

"As quickly as possible," I said, mainly because I was afraid he'd change his mind on the nurseries if we lingered too long.

"I agree. It is irresponsible to continue to court with a passion burning as deeply as ours," he said. "In two weeks' time then, in the rose garden. My parents will have moved out by then and the staff will have time to do your quarters in any sort of fashion you prefer."

I recalled that day on the terrace with Mrs. Brundage, the way I had adamantly sworn that I didn't love her son. I hadn't been lying then and I wasn't now, and yet I was to assume her position as the new Mrs. Brundage, lady of the manor.

"That will do nicely," I said, forcing a smile. "And you're sure you're satisfied if I involve myself with the nurseries at a later date? It is quite an undertaking and a commitment."

"A week ago I would have thought it was deeply improper and the thought of my wife toiling away would have horrified me, but now I don't care what you do so long as you marry me," he said. "You have my word."

"And the staff. They cannot be fired because you tire of the idea," I said. The notion that he wouldn't have made such a concession only a week before made my insides swim with nerves.

"I said you have my word."

"Next week," I said. "I want to marry you next week."

He took my hand and pulled me up to him.

"Very well, my darling. Let us not delay."

CHAPTER 18

People did unusual things when their lives were in upheaval. Father's peculiar response to the nurseries' sale and my impending marriage was to turn everything with any sort of basin into a planter. My parents' blue willow wedding china teacups, filled with Areca lutescens palm seeds and Cocos weddeliana palm seeds and Cycas revoluta palm seeds, lined the length of the drawing room windowsill.

Vincenzo Pratte had come by the evening before, on the heels of Harry's departure, with a large envelope of palm seeds he'd found in the branches of the Indica azalea on the far side of the growing field. We'd lost nearly all of the palms in the twister and Father was heartened to see the seeds. We grew the palms for all of our clients but specifically for the Goulds' palm court at Lyndhurst. Miss Gould requested new varieties nearly once per month, as her father had before her, and we were happy to deliver, but now we risked losing their business. We couldn't have that happen on the heels of Harry's investment if we could help it. We needed to press on as strongly as we could.

"Charles, use the Waterford candy dishes for the abutilons," Father called from the dining room. I could hear the crystal clatter as he rummaged around, and I had to laugh despite the situation. Who in their right mind would ever encourage someone to plant a Chinese bellflower in crystal? I tried to imagine how Mary Fink or Edith Gould would react if they wandered in and witnessed this scene. They'd positively faint. But in this house, plants had always superseded anything else.

"Would you please be still, Miss Fremd?" Laetitia Allaire, a French seamstress with the House of Worth, rapped the leather tape measure on the wooden plant crate I'd fashioned into a dressing stand. "It is difficult enough in this . . . this environment," she muttered.

I'd told Harry I would wear Mother's wedding gown. That was what I wanted. He'd laughed and shaken his head. *"No,"* he'd said, not hearing at all that I *wanted* my mother's gown. *"You're a Brundage now, darling, and you'll have the best. I'll telegram Worth's operations in the city and Mother's seamstress will be up on the train to fit you by lunch. It will be quite an undertaking to have a gown as fine as a Worth sewn in a week's time, but I'll pay her enough to make it worth her while. Miss Allaire is world renowned. Your gown will be the talk of the papers."*

I bent my knees just slightly to keep them from buckling. I'd been standing for two hours while she measured and pinned, and I was becoming quite tired.

"Je tel'aidit! Restetranquille," she snarled, still in a whisper. *"Je ne peux pas croire que je suis ici. Sa mere vous deteste."* I barely kept myself from gasping out loud. She was complaining about being here, saying that Mrs. Brundage hated me. Not that I blamed her for that, but to speak so openly about it in front of me was

entirely unprofessional. Clearly Miss Allaire thought me a simple flower girl with no fine training in languages.

"*Peut-etre qu'elle le fait, mais elle ne m'epouse pas,*" I said. *Perhaps she does, but she's not marrying me.* I expected her to respond, but she did not, only kept measuring with fervor.

I tried to ignore her and stared past the palm seeds out the window instead. Mr. Deal and his men had been working on installing one steel beam for the last four hours. It wasn't so much the difficulty of the task, I didn't think, but likely the tension radiating among the workers. They'd had three arguments already. I'd seen them all from the window. Twice Mr. Vicchialla walked away and once Mr. Sigallis. It was all because of the uncertainty lingering over everyone like the threat of another tornado.

I'd begged Father to go down to the village last night and tell everyone the news, but he hadn't been in a state to celebrate giving up the business he'd created. He went to bed at six, long before the sun went down, and in his absence, Charles, Freddie, and I decided that if Father didn't inform the others today, we would have to do it ourselves.

I dreaded that idea. I didn't want to go down to the village at all, with everyone whispering about Sam and Roisin and me and Harry, knowing full well that Sam and I were still in love. It didn't matter that Sam and Roisin likely wouldn't be there—I hadn't seen them since she arrived in the barn, and I knew Sam had work to do at the cemetery too. Even if they were absent, they were close enough to merit gossip. Sam was just across the street, though I had no idea where Roisin would be. Perhaps Mr. Sanderson found a place for her to stay until she and Sam married—or perhaps they already were.

"The base will be a gold mulberry silk we've just had in from Japan. It's difficult to find and rare, of course, since the silk is spun from the Bombyx mori moth," Miss Allaire said. "The neckline will be portrait, trimmed in small white pearls, accentuating your long neck. Inside, the corset will be steel-boned and outside, the bodice will boast a gold filigree threading that will continue down the front of the skirt. The train will be five feet, a modest length for a ceremony out of doors." She scrunched her nose at that, and I was suddenly thrilled Harry had decided on the rose garden. "The veil will match this length and will be made entirely of white Leavers lace."

"That's not necessary," I said. "Surely Brussels will do fine." Leavers lace was the most expensive and sought-after lace in the world, imported from northern France. I knew Harry had what appeared to be pockets without end, but to insist my dress have mulberry silk and Leavers lace simply because he could afford it was asinine.

"Mr. Brundage's telegram was clear. The gown is to be made of the finest fabrics we can muster," she said. "I will not go against his wishes and lose the respect of his family."

I nodded. Although I was used to fine things, spending these past weeks worried about the nurseries' future and the needs of people who had nothing at all, had changed me. I wasn't going to fit in with Mrs. Brundage's insistence on finery and hoped that perhaps when she was away, living in her city townhome, I could convince Harry to my side. Perhaps he would even come around to donating funds for a park someday. His buying the nurseries was a clear sign his sensibilities could be altered.

"After your wedding, I'll be by the estate to fit you for the summer season. It is important to Mr. Brundage that you look your best," she said. Her eyes drifted down my white cotton dress. It wasn't high fashion, but it wasn't rags either. One couldn't exactly wear Worth to tend a garden.

"Of course, though I'll need some sensible gowns too. I am going to be here quite a bit working with Father, and frocks like this one are wonderful in the heat and clean nicely," I said.

Miss Allaire threw her head back and laughed. "Mr. Brundage said the same thing, that you will need gardening costumes," she said through her laughter. "You are both so naive. I work at nearly every fine home in this state, and you should understand that for much of the next ten years you will be reclining on a tufted sofa, with child."

The back door flew open, slapping the house with such enthusiasm that it rattled the walls in the front.

"Father! Father! It's time," Charles yelled, pacing through the house. He passed the drawing room in his linen Palm Springs suit, his cropped brown hair slicked back with exertion. "Where's Father?" he asked me, nearly breathless.

"I don't know," I said, Miss Allaire's words ringing in my mind. She was likely right. That was the way it seemed to work with new marriages in society. Then again, Margaret wasn't with child yet and it had been over a year.

"Vincenzo and Roberto nearly killed each other just now on account of Vin thinking Roberto stole his rake," Charles said. "And I've heard them whispering about the possibility of your union, but since nothing's been said, and you've declined so often, I—"

"Father's probably down in the cellar looking for more containers suitable for seeds," I said, stepping down from the box. "If we see him on the way down, we'll call for him, but if not, I'll deliver the news myself right now."

I eyed Miss Allaire, who looked from me to Charles and back again. "Thank you, Miss Allaire. I trust I'll see you again soon. Mr. Cooper will bring a carriage around to take you to the train." I stepped past her, knowing how rude it was to depart without escorting her to the carriage, but this fighting among our employees was a spark waiting to explode, and I couldn't let it. Not when I could so easily provide a dampener to extinguish the flame.

I took Charles's arm and we made our way down the walk and across the drive.

"I'm sorry it has to be you," he said as we crossed the greenhouse field. It looked nearly like a battlefield—with holes where stakes had been dotting the landscape and grass unearthed by the twister's path leaving large swaths of dirt.

Charles continued, "If I had any prospects, any at all that would fit the bill, I would take your place. Arabella Williams married, as you know, Miss Brown lost her fortune, and Miss Shelton and I haven't spoken in nearly a year. It would be quite obvious as to why if I began to court her again." He cleared his throat. "And Freddie says Miss Maynard hasn't returned a single telegram since he arrived."

"It's all right that it's me," I said. "And I'm sorry for Freddie that Miss Maynard is put off by our misfortune. At least one of us could do something to help." I suppose my soft tone wasn't convincing, because Charles grasped my hand that was looped through his arm.

"Regardless, I feel awful about it. You are my favorite person on this earth, Sadie, and to know that you'll be sad forever on account of us is nearly more than I can take," he said.

"Then I have a remedy," I said. "I'm not doing this for you or for Freddie. Without the nurseries, you would still have Flagler and Freddie would still have Mayor Harrison. I've agreed to this union because of Father and because of the people who depend on us. There is little other work in Rye. I could not live with myself knowing they were all working in the city factories and I could have done something to prevent that fate."

Charles stopped me on top of the hill next to the lone steel beam—one greenhouse required six—that Mr. Deal and his men had just erected. Below us, the field was busy with pruning and fertilizing, watering and transplanting. Mr. Deal and the others who'd been helping install the beam were huddled in the barn's shadow to escape the heat. Mr. Deal mopped his forehead with the hem of his shirt and leaned in to grab the shared metal canteen from Mr. Sigallis.

"One more thing before you tell them," Charles said. "What will you do about Mr. Jenkins?"

"Nothing," I said. "I will love him forever, but he promised himself to another woman when he was in the city, and she appeared here yesterday. I suppose they'll marry, and I'll marry, and we will bury our love for the rest of our lives."

My eyes started to itch and I took a deep breath. "Even if he wasn't promised to someone else, what would change, really? We would still be here, the nurseries and our employees hanging in the balance. I would still choose to marry Harry." Even as I said it, I wondered if I was telling the truth. If Roisin hadn't interrupted us yesterday, would my heart have allowed my selflessness?

"I see," Charles said finally. "I don't envy you. I wish I could lighten your load somehow."

"But you cannot," I said. "Come along. Let's tell them before the guilt of a murder that could have been prevented weighs forever on our consciences."

By the time everyone had been rounded up and gathered on the village green, it was nearly sundown.

Father, who finally emerged from the cellar, said he would communicate the news in my stead, but I had declined. If I was to manage the nurseries on my own someday, I needed to find the courage to speak things both hard and joyful to those we employed.

While Charles and Freddie quieted everyone, I climbed up on the Prattes' small porch. Father followed and stood beside me. I was glad it would be me informing everyone. As much as I thought Father's spirits improved in the last couple days, they were still withered, and I doubted he could make it through the speech without sobbing.

I looked out at the faces that had, days ago, been light with optimism, led by Sam's charge to rebuild. Everyone was haggard now. Their shoulders slumped, their faces hardened, and the children, sensing the anxious shift, huddled closer to their parents. Surely most thought this meeting was to herald their calamity.

"Good evening, everyone," I called out. I tried to smile for them. This was good news, after all, melancholic only for my heart. Vincenzo muttered a greeting in response, but he was the only one. The rest just stared. Some wrung their hands, some looked at the ground. I noticed Mrs. Sigallis staring at her little clapboard house across the semicircle. Her longing wasn't about the house, of course. It was about what this village meant—security and safety. It meant home. Some had lived here since the beginning, since 1870. Twenty-three years.

"Right away I want to say that we won't be closing, and your jobs and your homes will remain just as they are," I said. I'd listened to railroad barons and Wall Street financiers make speeches, and they loved to draw out the point—likely because they enjoyed seeing the fear and dependence in the eyes of those they controlled. On the contrary, I could hardly stand to see anyone suffer that way, especially if I could alleviate it swiftly.

"Thank you all so much for your kindness in helping us rebuild. I know it was everyone's hope that we could do it alone, and I am confident that if we had enough time, we could have done just that."

I expected cheers. I expected relief, but they all just stared at me.

Finally Agnes pushed to the front of the crowd. "I think what everyone wants to know is . . . how do we know that for sure? At least, that's the question I keep hearing. The wallpaper plant closed, Griffith's closed, the upholstery shop closed, LeBlanc Stoneworks closed. How are we able to be spared?"

Murmuring started in the crowd and then silence fell as they waited for my answer. Of course Agnes already knew it, but it was likely no one believed her. Who would blame them, really? Though they hadn't been privy to every detail of my many proposals, they knew I'd refused them all.

I cleared my throat. "I . . ." I suddenly couldn't say the words out loud. The memory of Harry's mouth on mine, the way my stomach revolted when he pressed against me, made me wonder if I could go through with marrying him after all.

I looked around at the houses, at the magnolia soulangeana with its cup-shaped white and purple flowers blooming next to the Castanzos' house, the Japanese quince with its profusion of bright scarlet flowers like a ribbon of flame beneath the Russos' porch, and the cherry carmine of the Marshall P. Wilder roses growing along the side of the Pomperos'. Everyone had put down roots here just like I had. They deserved to stay. So did I. If it came at the cost of my heart, at least I could retain the part of it that would always reside here.

"Harry Brundage will be purchasing the business from Father, and his fortune is secure," I said finally. "He has promised to keep everything as it is, including retaining all of you as employees. You will remain in your current situations. Father will continue managing operations, and when he retires, I will succeed him." I could discuss the business arrangement without feeling as if I were going to faint or vomit. Father took my hand and squeezed. The crowd began to prattle among themselves again, and Father leaned in against me.

"You are the most selfless person I've ever known," he whispered. "You deserve to succeed me. I suppose you deserved it all along."

The sentiment startled me.

"I'm sorry I couldn't accumulate more, that it didn't allow you to marry whoever you wanted," he went on. "I only wanted you safe. At least you'll be safe now."

"Why?" Mr. Sigallis shouted over the chattering. "Why would Mr. Brundage have any interest in this place? He just hired the nurseries a few months ago and is hardly a regular customer."

Beyond Mr. Sigallis, the sun was setting in oranges and pinks and reds, dipping behind the row of houses. I shaded my eyes with my hand.

"Shall I say it?" Father asked me.

I shook my head. "Because I am engaged to him," I said. "We are to marry next week. He knows how much I love it here and how important the nurseries are to me and to the town. He said he couldn't bear to see them shut down forever."

That last bit was a lie, but without heart, it would seem like he could change his mind at any moment and the nurseries would cease to exist. At once the urgency to marry him rose again. If I hastened to uphold my end of the bargain, Harry would be swift with his checkbook, I was sure of it. His deciding he wouldn't save the nurseries after all was my most acute fear. He could still change his mind after we were married. The thought passed through my mind and paralyzed me. I felt the blood drain from my face and I reached out to clasp the wooden railing. I would be trapped then, truly trapped, but I didn't have a choice. I had to risk it, to trust that once we were husband and wife, he would do anything to make me happy.

Just then I realized no one was celebrating. No one was running home for celebratory wine or insisting that everyone come for torta della nonna.

Instead, I saw Mrs. Pratte, her hand pressed to her soil-streaked shirtwaist, a tear rolling down her cheek. Rosalie, standing next to her, hugged her close.

"Miss Fremd, you cannot do this for us," Rosalie said. "I know what I'm saying is forward, but—"

"This is a cause for celebration!" I said, forcing a smile. I ignored my own tears. Perhaps no one would be able to see them from here. "We will all still be together."

"Nothing will change at all except for the person writing the checks," Father said finally. "Mr. Brundage has sworn to it. I will still reside right there." He gestured up the hill to our house.

"And what of you, Miss Fremd?" Vincenzo asked. His gaze was pointed, as if he were asking me something else entirely. What that was, I wasn't sure.

"Mr. Brundage and I will occupy his estate on Post Road, though I will be here daily," I said. Even as I said it, I knew Harry would not be delighted by that arrangement, but I didn't care. I'd been clear about my desires, and if he wanted to dispute my intentions, he'd had time to do so.

"Everyone knows you can't keep Sadie from the plants. Father's tried for years," Freddie said, laughing. He threw an arm around Vincenzo's shoulders. "Come on, let's dip into a bit of champagne, shall we? Father's got plenty in the barn."

Everyone seemed to liven at the thought of a nip, and the women started for their houses for glasses while the men followed Freddie and Charles to the barn.

"I think I'll go take a rest," Father said to me. "I'll understand if you join me instead of feigning merriment." He walked down the steps and up the hill, tipping his hat to his friends as he went. It was unlike Father to wallow, but I couldn't blame him. Soon enough he would accept this new arrangement and return to himself. I supposed I would as well.

I reached the bottom step at the same time as Mrs. Pratte. She clutched my hand and shook her head. "Mr. Brundage will not allow you to come here," she said. "He may say that now, but he will want you at home, with him."

Over her shoulder Freddie had returned with the first of the champagne. He held it over his head and pulled the cork with vigor. Bubbles poured from the bottle and cheers rang out from the village.

I grinned. "Perhaps you're right, but I don't have a choice but to trust he'll stand by his word," I said, squeezing her hand.

"Have you come to love him at least? That way, if you cannot be here, you'll at least be happy."

I didn't say anything. I wanted to tell her the truth, but I didn't want it going around for decades that I'd married without love, only for money—though I was certain the fact would always be whispered.

"You're willing to close your heart to Sam Jenkins?"

"No," I said, blinking away the tears that immediately came, not bothering to deny that I loved him. By now everyone knew, even if we'd never said it. "But what choice do I have, even when it comes to him? He's gone, too, stolen away by—"

"Ladies, would you like a glass?" Charles appeared next to us with two champagne flutes. I didn't know where he'd procured the glasses, but they were caked with dust.

He pressed a flute into my hand before I could answer. "Perhaps you might not be celebrating, but a few sips may ease the nerves," he whispered.

"Come along, Mother. Everyone is collecting their goods for a dinner on the lawn," Pasqualle said, appearing from the side of her house with a nearly empty flute. She blushed when she saw Charles. "Excuse me, Mr. Fremd, Miss Fremd." She took her mother's elbow and led her up the stairs. "You're welcome to join us, of course. Both of you," she said when she reached the threshold.

"You and Freddie will stay, won't you?" I asked Charles when Pasqualle and Mrs. Pratte had gone inside.

Charles took a sip of champagne and shrugged. "I wasn't exactly planning on it. I need to figure out my train tickets and do a little designing. I've neglected everything since I've been here, and Mr. Flagler will be quite impatient to get the indoor Poinciana grill design set and completed," he said. "The grill will be in a sort of atrium with a glass roof. He wants it to be an extension of the outdoor landscape—all of the palms, some fiddle-leaf figs, a few wandering shrubs of which I have yet to choose the variety."

I'd known Charles was going back, but I suppose I'd forgotten. Soon enough, I would be married and Freddie would be back in Chicago and Father would be alone.

"Are you sure you shouldn't stay instead?" I asked.

Charles's nose scrunched. "And do what, Sadie? Help Father and have your husband pay my wages too? Not a chance," he said. "Even so, I'm thrilled to go back. I've loved Florida, and Mr. Flagler's even spoken of another hotel farther south."

"I'm happy for you," I said.

Charles sobered, a stark contrast to the merriment on the green behind him. Mr. Sigallis, Mr. Russo, and Mr. Pratte had emerged with their instruments—an accordion, violin, and small drum, respectively—while little Peppino Castanzo began to sing "Funiculì, Funiculà."

"I wish I was happy for you," he said.

"Could you stay for just a bit longer?" I asked him. "I know it would mean much if our family celebrated alongside everyone, and I long to stay myself. If I could feign gaiety right now, I would, but I've already been asked if I love Harry and if I've stopped loving Sam. I cannot fall apart and ruin the day."

"It's the least I can do," Charles said. "And it looks like we won't have to convince Freddie to join in."

I laughed. Freddie was standing in front of the makeshift band arm-in-arm with Vincenzo and Guiseppe.

"I suppose we won't," I said. I wrapped my arms around my brother. "Thank you. Good night."

"Will you come visit me in Florida?" Charles asked after our embrace. "You could come for a few weeks, a month even, and escape from Harry."

"I'm sure I'd love that." I walked away toward the barn and the field, then up the hill to where the greenhouses had stood. Charles was worried about me, worried about Harry with me. I could see it in his eyes.

As I walked across the barren greenhouse plots, I glanced to my left, toward the drive that led to North Street, to the cemetery, to Sam. I started toward it but stopped myself. What was I hoping to find if I went to him? He couldn't be my comforter, my home, my love anymore, and if I saw him in Roisin's arms, a husband to another woman, I'd crumple. It was best to force myself to be strong, to accept my plight and revel in the good that my match would bring.

"Come here, Lily," Father said. He was sitting on the porch in one of the wicker chairs, his bowler on his knee.

"This is a hard season, Father," I said, reclining onto a matching chair next to him.

"Yes. But sitting here just now made me consider that there could have been stronger storms," he said. "We could be looking down the future at living in a tenement, working in a factory, breathing sooty air and sewage. We could have found ourselves living in the dirt beneath the pole barn like Mr. Deal. We could have found ourselves starving or diseased."

I knew all of those things. I knew how fortunate we were, and yet all I could see was a prison ahead. For now, its bars were open, but the warden could close me in at any moment.

"I found this when I was looking for bowls earlier," Father said, reaching into his pocket. "It was your mother's wedding gift from her parents, sent from the Isle of Mann. I never met your grandparents." He placed a small marble figure in my hand, a cherub holding a fistful of lilies of the valley.

"I thought you should have it. I suppose your grandparents gave it to your mother because of the meaning behind the flowers—motherhood, purity, sweetness. It suited her. Those were all the things Jane was to me and more. I started calling you Lily, though, because I came to love them as a boy when I'd walk in the forests. I remember just stopping and staring at them and marveling at the miracle of the tiny little bells and the fragrance—green and sweet with a hint of lemon.

"You've always reminded me of myself—curious and stubborn and loyal—and early on, when you were just a little girl, I remembered the adventure of walking the woods and seeing the flowers. I saw the same spirit in you as you wandered around these grounds." He laughed. "It shouldn't have surprised me in the slightest that you would be the child most taken with the flowers. Charles and Freddie always humored me—Charles more so than Freddie—and Charles loved the plants, too, but he wanted to see the world. You saw the wonder right here."

I turned the cherub over in my hand and ran my fingers down the cascade of flowers it held.

"I'm sad, Father," I said softly. "A bit angry and scared too." I looked at him. "But we will have the flowers and we will have our friends. Without them I'm afraid I would be hard-pressed to get out of bed."

"Blessings abound," he said.

In the distance the accordion wailed to the "*Tarantella Napoletana*" and laughter shifted in the wind.

"You might be much of me," Father said as he put his hat back on his head and stood with a sigh. "But your heart, your compassion, is your mother's."

CHAPTER 19

"What has changed?"

I looked at Mrs. Brundage standing beside me as her servants stretched yards of lace and silk and velvet down the expanse of the crushed-limestone path that led to the reflecting pond in their new garden. I would marry Harry under the newly constructed arbor at the top of the circular pool, and Mrs. Brundage had insisted that her servants lay out a variety of fabrics for my selection as an aisle runner.

"I've been dying to ask, but the servants have all been within hearing," she whispered. She ran her fingers along the delicate pleats of her turquoise-blue silk surah with a matinee waist. "Last we spoke, you were not in love with him. You said it at least twice and seemed quite determined the fact would never change. I told Harry such."

"When we spoke at the Finks', I saw a bit of him I hadn't before. He was kind and his love for me was evident. It wasn't cloaked in pretension," I said. It was the true and honest answer. I couldn't tell her I loved him too.

"Eliminate the point de Paris lace, please, Miss Sweeney. It looks cheap," Mrs. Brundage crowed, pointing to yards of a cream lace that would inevitably blend in with the path anyway. Miss Sweeney, a girl at least five years my junior, hurriedly balled up the lace and hastened away.

"And your sudden change of heart had nothing to do with your family's misfortune occurring just a day before?" Mrs. Brundage turned to face me. Harry had her hooded brown eyes and thin nose but his father's full mouth—a blessing that saved him from his countenance always appearing shrewish like his mother's, even when she was happy.

In this case, however, it was clear she was suspicious and upset and wanted to protect her son from a woman who was conceding to the match because of what he could give her, not because of who he was. I didn't blame her.

"I told him from the beginning that he was to find a love match, a woman of a family similar to ours who needed nothing from us, who would accept his proposal because of her affection," she said.

My chest clenched and I glanced up at the monstrous limestone-and-brick mansion behind us, wishing Harry would suddenly emerge from the glass doors and call to us from the porch, but he was in the city.

"I understand," I said finally. I avoided her eyes, instead watching the servants watching us, their hands clasped tightly to the ends of seven different types of fabric, undoubtedly wishing I'd hurry and decide. "I think I'd like to have the gold silk," I said loudly, pointing to the middle option. "It won't interfere with the deep red-pink of the American Beauties on the sides."

"A practical choice," Mrs. Brundage said, but her eyes darted to the white velvet, and I knew she thought it more elegant.

"I've changed my mind. The white velvet might be a bit more eye-catching," I said. She already knew I didn't love her son. The least I could do was make the wedding process a bit more agreeable.

"Yes, that was my preference too," she said. The edges of her mouth turned up, but then she doubtless remembered the woman she was standing with and ceased any sort of merriment. "Mr. Coulter, take the length in and have it steamed, pressed, and hung up," she ordered. At once the fourteen servants disappeared in a flurry of black livery and white aprons and we were left alone.

As much as I didn't want to answer her earlier question, it had to be addressed. I couldn't live my whole life with my mother-in-law presuming I was a fortune hunter—though in so many ways, that was exactly what I was.

I pulled in a breath. The garden smelled divine—the new green scent of the boxwoods, the sweet old-rose fragrance of the American Beauty and the Wichuriana, the spicy-soft scent of the Madame Alfred Carriere and the Souvenir de la Malmaison.

"When we plant roses like these, the soil must be perfect," I said. I walked slowly along the path, the slight train of my porcelain-blue taffeta chine gown disturbing the crushed limestone. "Too much clay and it chokes the roots; too much sand and the soil will drain before the roots can get enough to drink. The clay and the sand must come together to create a perfect loam." Mrs. Brundage had remained where I'd left her, arms crossed over her chest.

"It's a bit like Harry's and my agreement," I said. "We are both giving something and receiving something in—"

"I told him he shouldn't have offered to buy the nurseries," she snapped. "It's the only reason you accepted."

"It's one of them." I stopped at the first turn of the reflecting pool. The sun and the pinks and reds and yellows of the closest roses were mirrored in its face. It was perfect and I had designed it. Pride welled up inside me despite the tension with Mrs. Brundage. Roses and boxwoods and beauty surrounded me, nearly an acre of glory. If I had to be mistress of a fine home, I suppose I was glad it was this one.

"What are the reasons otherwise?" she asked. "If we are to go on, if we are to be cordial, if you are to be my daughter, I need to know them. Why Harry and not that Lionel Reynolds or Stephen Bishop?"

The truth was that Harry had been the most persistent, but I dared not allow that admission.

"Mrs. Brundage, Harry found me in a horrid place that night at the Finks'," I said. "We had just faced the possibility of losing everything, but my own calamity or even Father's wasn't the reason my heart was wrung. I couldn't bear the thought of the families who worked for us having to face homelessness or factory work. They counted on us, and that night it seemed like we had failed them. The twister was no fault of ours, and yet the inability to repair what we'd lost was—in a way."

Mrs. Brundage's face was blank. Of course she didn't understand.

"When Harry came to speak with me that night, he could tell I was distraught, and he knew why. He had the ability to ease my pain and he did so because he loves me. Perhaps I am the charitable match you worked so hard to forbid, but isn't all true love about charity? We give up much to be the healing balm for those to whom our hearts call out."

At once I thought of Sam. My walking away would allow him to heal, to be the man he'd promised Roisin he would be, and in the process of my marrying, the forfeiting of our hearts would win the well-being of those we loved.

"What are you giving my boy back?" Mrs. Brundage asked. The question was a hard one, and her voice was small.

"The promise that I'll love him forever," I said.

"Can you truly promise him that?" she asked.

"I learned from my parents that love is as much will as it is passion." If Harry continued to be kind, I knew I could become fond of him. I knew I could love him, but in a different way than I loved Sam. Harry and I would never experience the desperate infatuation that came from the intertwining of two souls, but he could become my family, my confidant.

Mrs. Brundage walked toward me and took my hands. Clearly something about my promising to love Harry eased her fears, though my words indicated loving him would be something of an effort on my part.

"If you promise you'll love him until the day he dies, I will be content," she said, her eyes searching mine. "He loves you with a fervor unlike anything I've ever seen. If even half of his passion for you is returned, he will be satisfied, and so will I." She smiled. "When he came to tell me you'd accepted, he was alight with joy. He said he had never wanted anything so much in his life."

"His proposal was a tremendous relief to me too," I said, though my relief was won by something else entirely.

"You will make a perfect match. The two of you will be

envied by all—the new royalty of Rye," she said. "My great-grandfather was English nobility, you know."

I nodded. I knew. Mrs. Brundage's ancestry was one of her favorite topics at dinner parties.

"We're of more noble birth than that Lionel Reynolds too," she said.

"I was never taken with Mr. Reynolds or Mr. Bishop either," I said. Even though it was mere days until the wedding, my indecision was known in town, and I had no doubt Mrs. Brundage fretted about me changing my mind.

"Very well, dear Sadie," she said. It was the first time she'd addressed me with any sort of affection, and it felt quite nice. Perhaps I'd like having a mother figure again. "Let us take a turn around the garden and discuss the rest of the ceremony." She kept my hand in hers as we walked.

"The guests will be gathered on the verandas. Our families will be seated in darling wicker chairs I'm having shipped in from Wanamaker's. We'll line up down the aisles adjacent to the reflecting pool, leaving only you and Harry and Reverend Price at the arbor."

I nodded and adjusted my fancy braid poke hat to shield my eyes from the sun.

"I've asked Reverend Price to come by to speak to both of you about the service tomorrow at teatime. Are you available?" she asked.

"Of course," I said, though my heart longed for my last free days to be at home. Mr. Deal was installing the final iron pieces of the first reconstructed greenhouse today, and I was keen to see everything being made new again.

"Mr. Christianson has begun preparing your marital suite,

which is quite easy considering Mr. Brundage and I haven't occupied it in some years. We will be fully removed to the city on Thursday, though I imagine there may be a few things left for me to retrieve from your quarters after the wedding. I do apologize," she said.

"It's quite all right. I know we haven't given you much time," I said.

She laughed. It was almost a giggle. I'd never heard anything so merry come from her lips. "I would have been satisfied with a day," she said, patting the back of my hand. "And truth be told, I imagine you won't be in your quarters very much at all those first few days to notice my lingering belongings." She whispered this last bit, and I felt my cheeks flush.

As determined as I was to marry Harry, I couldn't think much past the vows. The thought of his skin on mine made any fondness I felt when I thought of him completely disappear.

"Then, of course, you'll be on the boat off to England and on to your honeymoon tour of Europe. Oh! The memories will last you a lifetime," she went on. "You'll absolutely love Morocco. Have you been? Jacob and I had the most romantic time in Essaouira." Mrs. Brundage rattled on about dips in the Mediterranean and trying b'ssara and tagine, but I barely heard her.

We were reaching the end of an aisle, and at once I could see him—linen shirt plastered to his strong chest, his ocean eyes on mine. Sam had returned just before we planted the rose garden here. I could still feel the nerves in my stomach, the way my heart yearned to reach out and touch him.

I blinked and stared at the blooms in an attempt to dislodge the memory. The roses were all thriving—the Eugene Verdier with its silver-pink and fawn foliage, the enormous full-blossomed deep red of the Paul Neyron, and the blush Baltimore Belle running up the storied brick walls. I'd never seen such success in the first year. Ordinarily the blooms improved over time as they adapted to the soil. I reached out and touched a Madame Hoste. They'd bloomed lemon-white. I'd only ever seen them display in a canary yellow.

I breathed deep, and doing so settled me. Perhaps I would be happy here like my roses. Perhaps I simply needed to allow myself to be planted.

"Let us go to the gate and see about the post. Ordinarily I have Mr. Chamberlain retrieve it, but I imagine he'll be delayed on account of his many to-dos today," Mrs. Brundage said.

I walked with her to the iron gate. A coach lumbered past, but otherwise, the road was quiet. I thought of Mr. Deal, of how much his words had changed my life. Even so, my efforts hadn't been enough. I'd not been able to realize a park.

Mrs. Brundage extracted a skeleton key from a planter along the wall and unlocked the gate. She ambled around to the gold post box affixed to the brick.

"Have you ever considered leaving the gate open?" I asked. Perhaps I could convince Harry to leave it open, to invite anyone to take a stroll among the flowers.

Mrs. Brundage reappeared with a solitary letter. She laughed and closed the gate, then locked it.

"Heavens no, my dear. Post Road is a main thoroughfare and our residence a constant spectacle to those passing by. Can you imagine what sort of people we'd have traipsing through our gorgeous gardens?" She patted my back. "There could even be some who would risk breaking into our home. Harry wouldn't take kindly to jeopardizing your safety."

I wanted to argue my case, to say that an open gate would bring so much joy to others, but there was no reason. Next week, this estate would be mine and I would find a way to convince Harry to keep the gate open.

Perhaps there was hope for an alternative park after all.

CHAPTER 20

Harry's carriage was in the drive when I returned home. His horses stamped and tossed their heads as though they'd been standing for hours and were ready to get on with it. He was supposed to have been in the city all day on business. I wondered why he had come by. If Mrs. Brundage knew he was in town, she hadn't mentioned it.

Mr. Green pulled Gene to a stop beside the glittering silver carriage and nodded at Harry's driver, Mr. Bucard, who, unlike the horses, didn't move a muscle—didn't so much as look our way.

"I suppose you'll be trading us for much finer service all around," Mr. Green mused as he swung down from his seat.

"That could never be true," I said. "I'd rather employ a friendly face any day than a man who can't so much as smile at a greeting." I said the latter a bit loudly and Mr. Bucard's eyes drifted toward me.

"Mr. Brundage has instructed me to stay stock-still, to say nothing," he whispered.

"When I am his wife, that will change," I said.

Mr. Green appeared at my door and clicked it open. He was a bit older than Father and wore a hardness won by years of factory work, but today his countenance was nearly cheerful, his cheeks even a bit flushed.

"Did you see, Miss Fremd?" he asked as I took his hand and stepped down onto the cobblestone path. "The greenhouse is finished and I daresay it looks even more handsome than the others used to."

He stepped to the side and I nearly began to sob. Though I'd known Mr. Deal was to put in the iron frame today, I had no idea the glass would be back from the glaziers to complete it. The new greenhouse stood in the same spot as the first one Father and Mother had built—on the top left side of the field. The sun sparkled on the new delicate swirls in the glass, and already someone—likely Father—had filled the building with our china containing the newly planted seeds.

"We're going to be okay after all," I whispered, mostly to myself, but Mr. Green nodded.

"I have to admit that it heartened me mightily to see it, Miss Fremd." His lips pressed together and his eyes squinted just a bit. "I only pray you'll be able to be about the grounds as Mr. Brundage promised. I know you're most happy here."

I nodded and unpinned my braided hat from my hair.

"So do I," I said.

Agnes wouldn't be happy with me for disturbing any part of the careful swirling of braids and curls and twists she'd spent nearly two hours styling this morning, but the hatpins were pinching my scalp and I was home, after all.

"He will do anything Miss Fremd wishes. He is absolutely

infatuated with her," Mr. Bucard said softly, now apparently a friend to conversation regardless of his employer's adamant demands.

"I'm sure there are limits, and we are not yet married," I said. "Perhaps once we are, he'll change his mind." I spoke calmly, my voice not letting my fear reveal itself in the slightest.

Mr. Bucard laughed under his breath. "When you are married, I imagine his obsession will only deepen."

"I suppose we'll both see in time," I said.

I stared out at the greenhouse for a moment longer and let my heart fill with warmth. Everything was going to be all right after all.

I walked around the horses slowly, stroking their faces, taking my time getting into the house. The andromeda—one of Father's favorites—was blooming along the porch in trusses of white thimble-shaped flowers, and the long, narrow hickory leaves were fully uncurled, casting shade over the walk.

Harry had known I was at his estate and he hadn't come home to see me there. He was here to see Father. I hoped it wasn't a tense discussion. Perhaps he had come with the necessary papers required to buy the nurseries.

At once the front door burst open and Harry appeared. He looked disoriented, furious, and even when his eyes met mine, it seemed as though he didn't see me. He walked down the steps and brushed past me. Only then did he stop.

"Sadie." He turned back to me, blinked a few times, and ran a hand across his face. "I . . . I didn't see you."

"I've just come from being with your mother." I smiled but could feel the blood draining from my cheeks. Something was wrong, but it couldn't be. Perhaps he had pulled out of the deal. He couldn't. Not when he'd given us so much hope.

"We've worked out the details for the ceremony," I went on, but Harry barely seemed to notice. Instead, his gaze hardened and his hands curled to fists. "We'll have a white velvet runner as an aisle and an arbor of roses to stand beneath. It will be lovely, Harry—"

At the mention of his name, Harry reached for my arms. He led me under the hickory, his hands gripping my elbows, his chest against mine.

"Your father arranged a meeting last night for late this morning. I came as soon as I was finished with my business in the city so we could sign the papers for the purchase," he said, his voice a low growl.

"Now he said he would not sell, and—actually, your brothers *and* your father were clear—that you don't love me, that you don't care for me in the slightest, and that it would be in my best interest to dissolve the promise of our union."

I felt faint. My knees began to buckle, but Harry's hands held me firm.

"Why? Why would they say that?" I whispered. It was unfathomable. They were going to ruin everything—and for what? The nurseries would fold, our employees would have to go, and then what would become of our town? It would evaporate like a cloud.

"I was well aware that you never said it back to me, that you never told me you loved me too—not in word—though when you kissed me and said yes, I couldn't help but assume." His hands were shaking now, his fingers still holding my elbows as though he could will a confession from my lips.

"I . . . I am fond of you. I . . . I do care for you," I said.

Before I could stop him, his hands lifted from my arms and threaded in my hair. He pulled my face to his and kissed me hard. His mouth was hurried, desperate on mine, and when he pulled away, it was only just slightly. I could feel his heart skipping wildly against my chest.

"Tell me you love me," he said. I hesitated and he gathered me close. "Tell me you love me," he said again.

"That's enough." Charles's voice came from the porch over my shoulder. "You are a fine man, Harry, but she does not. She never will. Let her go."

My eyes filled with tears. What was Charles doing? Why was he throwing everything away? We had a plan that was going to work. We had a plan that was going to save everyone and everything we loved.

"Is it true?" Harry whispered. "I cannot only hear it from them and believe it. Surely our engagement wasn't only because of what I could give you. Surely you love me, even a little."

At once I was ashamed. It was wrong, terribly wrong, to have accepted him.

"I feel for you. Otherwise I wouldn't have agreed to a lifetime in your company," I said. That was as much truth as I could say, but it wasn't what he wanted to hear. His eyes filled with tears, and he sniffed and looked away. "And I could have come to love you. If I'd stood at the altar and promised I would, I would have found a way."

"You would have 'found a way'?" He released me and glared at me, his eyes still glassy with tears. "Do you know who I am? Do you know how many fathers have begged me to marry their daughters? But I love *you*. Out of hundreds of women I could have chosen, I chose you. I would have given you everything I have, all of—"

I placed my palm on his chest. "If I could choose who I love, I would choose you," I said. "And I'm sure if you could choose, you would not choose me. You'd choose someone easier, someone better suited. But we can't choose, can we?"

Harry shook his head. "I knew you didn't love me the same. It would have been all right if you loved me less. I just needed to know you loved me a little. Your family was clear that you don't love me at all, and now it's been confirmed. I'm moving to the city and my parents will remain here. Don't come looking for me. Goodbye, Sadie."

I tried to grab his hand, to tell him I knew he would find love, but he stepped away from me and hastened down the walk toward his waiting carriage. I stood under the hickory and closed my eyes. Who was I to tell him he'd find love when I knew there was no guarantee, when I knew very well that I'd never love again? My heart felt hollow and I pressed my fist against it. I wanted to cry out, to collapse in the unrequited love that had left us both broken.

I heard Harry's carriage roll away and I wiped my cheeks and opened my eyes. Charles was looking at me from the porch, a wide smile on his face.

"What could you possibly find merry about this?" I snapped. I started up the steps. "You've just ruined us—all of us—and broken his heart in the process." I turned the brass knob and pushed the heavy front door open. "I had made peace with the sacrifice I was making. I was glad for it."

Despite my anger, I stopped abruptly at the foyer table where a Strelitzia was displayed in a crystal planter. I'd never seen the bird of paradise except for in one of Father's catalogs from a source nursery in Hawaii. The brilliant royal-blue and bright yellow flowers were displayed in a horizontal inflorescence, like a bird perched on a banana leaf.

"Lovely, isn't it?" Charles said from behind me. He shut the door and I refused to look at him.

"Father!" I yelled. When no one answered, I tried again. "Father!" I stormed into the drawing room and then back into the hallway and down to the dining room. When I found that vacant, I walked down the adjacent hallway and into his study. He was sitting at his desk, sobbing, a letter clutched in his fist.

Freddie was standing by the window, a small trunk at his feet.

"Oh, hi, Sadie," he said. "You've come just in time to see me off before I take the train to Chicago."

I looked from Freddie to Father and back again.

"What's happened?" I asked. "I just saw Harry out on the walk, and he said you wouldn't sign the papers to sell and that you were all adamant that we dissolve our engagement, and now I find you going"—I gestured to Freddie—"and Father in such an emotional state that I fear your leaving."

"You've been set free," Charles said as he walked into the room.

"I don't understand," I said. "I cannot be free, not with the fate of the nurseries and our employees hanging in the balance. It is selfish and horrible to even consider it. I'm going to go beg Harry to take me back. I'll promise to make him deliriously happy. I'll promise to soothe his heartbreak, and I'll set my mind to loving him." I started to walk out of the room, but Charles blocked me.

"Mr. Flagler sent the bird of paradise," he said.

"It's lovely," I replied. "Now, if you'll please move."

Charles stretched his arms out, filling the doorway. "It came this morning on the rail with a note," he said, tipping his head toward Father. "There was also a check for far more than we will need to repair what we've lost."

Goose bumps rose on my arms, but I didn't fully understand.

"'Dear Fremd family,'" Father read, his voice shaking. "'Charles telegrammed of the natural disaster so horribly contained to the finest nursery in the country and asked for a bit more leave. I am no stranger to the devastation of such a calamity. We have endured the cost of fires and hurricanes and twisters—as is the risk of building in the tropics—and we understand the hole it punctures into an otherwise thriving enterprise. It has occurred to me more often than you might think that I am fortunate for my major interests to be beneath the ground, in oil, removed from the threat of the winds—unlike my hotels or your nurseries. This endeavor allows me the luxury of deep pockets, the ability to help my friends—and you are my friends.

"'Please accept the accompanying check. Cash it and thrive as you were. I do not want repayment or thanks, nor will you ever be in my debt. The survival of Rye Nurseries is as much in my interest as in yours. I expect a wide array of palm varieties and tropical plants at Charles's disposal for the outfitting of the Ponce de León. The nurseries in these parts are quite loyal to the ordinary, and, of course, I am not. I trust I will see Charles back in short order and the whole of your family and your nurseries back to health in no time. Sincerely, your friend, Henry Flagler.'"

I sank onto the leather chair in front of Father's desk and laughed as tears rolled down my cheeks.

"We got the letter at eleven this morning, and I've not stopped reading it since," Father said.

"Harry arrived right after the letter and Father told him he wasn't going to sell after all. Harry started demanding that he sell, claiming that he loved you and you wanted the nurseries, and he'd buy them for you no matter the cost. He became quite irate and disrespectful, and it slipped out that we thought it best for him to walk away, that you didn't love him," Charles said.

Despite the lightness I felt, despite the joy in my heart, I imagined Harry falling apart in his mansion, perhaps to his mother, whom I'd just told I would love her son. I hated that I'd caused his sadness when he'd done nothing to deserve it. He'd only loved me. I wished I could take away his pain.

"You don't love him, do you?" Freddie asked, likely wondering at my silence.

"No," I said. My thoughts suddenly fixated on Sam's face, but my new freedom did nothing to bring us together. If anything, the idea that he was married and I would not be seemed worse. "I'm not proud of myself for entrapping him in a false engagement, but I would have been true to him if we had married—"

"Love matches are rare among our sort," Charles said flippantly. "Don't fill yourself with guilt over agreeing to his engagement. Marriages are more often a gambling chip for the social standing of parents. Think of it honestly, Sadie—do you know one match made for love among your peers?"

I couldn't think of a single one. The moment an engagement happened, the two were suddenly deeply in love despite the constant disassembling of every suitor's shortcomings the week before. Even Margaret had found Tempy an utter boob before they were married. She probably still did secretly, though on the surface Tempy was her heart's passion.

"I suppose you're right," I said.

"Don't get me wrong," Father said. "I would be overjoyed if you loved him, Lily. This gift of Flagler's is a generous one and we will return to what we were, but our fortune isn't nearly as stable as the Brundages', and the thought that you could some-day be in this precarious spot again isn't an impossible sort of worry."

"I'm willing to risk it," I said.

Father sighed. "I know. And I will not force you to re-consider, nor will I send you away. It was wrong to threaten it the last time. I see that now," he said.

"I suppose I should begin gathering my things if I'm to depart tomorrow," Charles said. He looked around the room wistfully, but I could tell in the way he was tapping his left foot that he couldn't wait to leave.

"Yes, I imagine Flagler will be delighted to see you," Father said.

"I may collect my things in Chicago and return," Freddie said suddenly. His face displayed a heaviness I couldn't place. "Not to work here at the nurseries," he said, raising his hand to clarify. "I will work for Uncle's mayoral office here. I just can't fathom living in Chicago now. It seems almost surreal that I was to propose to Miss Maynard. She hasn't responded to one telegram, one letter. I know she's heard of our misfortune and abandoned me."

"You should go see her before you conclude that," Charles said. "Perhaps she's been away."

Freddie looked at Charles but didn't immediately respond.

"I'm going into town to telegram Mayor Harrison," he said finally. "I'll catch another train. I'll postpone gathering my things for a few days yet."

My brothers started to walk out of the room and I followed. I didn't quite know what to do now. Should I apologize to Harry? Should I change and spend the afternoon in the nurseries? There was certainly much work to be done.

"Sadie, stay a moment, will you?" Father asked.

I paused, my hand resting on the top of the leather chair. Father watched Charles and Freddie disappear down the hallway and then gestured for me to sit back down.

He cleared his throat and spread his hands on his desktop before looking at me. "When your mother and I became a family, we swore to each other that you children would always be protected, that you would never experience the hardships of the life we knew before. It was a gift we thought most important to give.

"Your mother was especially adamant about you. Less than an hour before she died, she made me promise that you would be well matched, that I wouldn't allow you to be swept into destitution. She said she knew Charles and Freddie could forge their own way, but that you were a woman who had been raised in prominence. We hadn't encouraged the steel soul of a working woman in you. Instead, we had nurtured the softer side of a society woman. We had filled your mind with art and music and languages and manners. These were the things we wanted for you, things your mother planned. She was supposed to be here to walk you through this, to help you find someone suitable. It was clear before she died that she thought your future depended on a correct and proper match, that you wouldn't survive anything less, and I—"

"But, Father, I—"

"I loved your mother with all of me. I could not go against her wishes for you. And if I'm honest, I was convinced she was right—that nothing but a proper match could make your well-being a certainty. But I've always known that despite the finishing schools and the music lessons and the fine clothes, you are me made over. You have always had a passion for our plants, a love for them far beyond that of your brothers. Your mother saw it in you—the determination of two penniless immigrants—and at times would come back from her afternoon walks after seeing you dirt-covered and filthy and tell me you needed to learn Spanish or cello or poetry, anything to keep you indoors and away from the greenhouses."

Anger burned from my heart to my head and I felt as if I were about to explode. I loved my mother, too, but Father had just told me I didn't have to marry Harry, that he wouldn't send me away either. Was he about to change his mind again?

"I love Mother. I always will. But this is my life, Father. Not hers. If she were standing right here, I would say the same. I have appreciated the luxuries afforded me. I will forever be thankful that I was not subject to the slums. But I am a woman now. If I choose to risk my livelihood for the sake of my happiness, that is my decision to make," I said.

"Her wishes for you were perhaps her wishes for herself," he said. "She had a gentler spirit, much like Freddie's, and even after we had been free from the factories for decades, she couldn't bear to recall the memory of it. She thrived in managing our social calendar and caring for the three of you and playing the piano and writing poetry and needlepointing. She often remarked how fortunate you all were, to be able to live your whole lives this way. She was tender and she tried to force that upon you, though you have always been spirited and strong-willed."

"I'm sorry I'm not what she expected," I said. My anger had now dwindled to sadness. I was a disappointment. The dying wish of my mother had been to see me married well. Perhaps it was my responsibility to beg Harry back regardless.

"You misunderstand me," Father said. "You were your mother's greatest joy. Her desire for your life was based on the fear of her own. A timid soul satisfied with domestic life was easier and safer. Stability was your mother's balm. Lively women are prone to taking risks, more likely to find themselves penniless." Father paused and his gaze held mine. "The danger of bankruptcy will always accompany you like a shadow."

"I can't alter who I am, Father. I want to honor Mother, but I cannot do it this way. I cannot marry because she wished it. I wouldn't if she were still here."

"The twister changed my thinking," Father said. He smiled. "In its aftermath you abandoned yourself. You were willing to promise your life away for the sake of our employees. When you did that, I began to see that I'd lost a bit of myself. I thought of your little gardens with shame. I was telling the truth when I said planting them risked our enterprise, but the spirit behind them, the spirit of love you had, was one I'd often told myself I embodied too."

"You do. Look at what you've done. You've employed five dozen people, kept them fed and housed. You've kept the town afloat when everything around us was closing," I said.

Father shook his head. "Yes, perhaps you're right, but I'd become self-righteous about it. In any case I saw you for the first time after the twister, Sadie. For so long you've been my little girl, and I your protector. I watched as the people you gifted those flowers to showed up to help us. I watched as Sam Jenkins, a man I'd offended and discounted, came to our rescue. I watched as you fell atop the sword for us." He yanked the top drawer of his desk open and extracted a new green leatherbound notebook. "I know your mother would have quite a bit to say, but I know she would be proud of you." He patted the top of the notebook. "If you would still like to, I would be honored if you would succeed me, if you would take this book and fill it with your plans and ideas."

Instantly I started to cry.

"I have withheld this from you for far too long," he said, coming around the desk. I stood and he wrapped me in a hug. "You are more than proficient, more than able. Forgive me for only realizing it now."

By the time my tears dried, Father's gray lapel was saturated nearly black.

"Of course I want the nurseries," I said, sniffing, finally answering his question. Father grinned and handed me his white handkerchief.

"It might take a while to rebuild to what we were, to have extra equity to provide the funds for the park you've been dreaming of, but perhaps in the future—"

"As long as we're working toward it," I said. My spirit was light, so light that I felt I could lift out of my body. I smiled at Father. "This is a dream. I'm certain I'm going to wake and find it all gone."

Father shook his head and walked back around his desk. "Do you need me to pinch you?" he asked, laughing.

"Perhaps," I said. As ridiculous as it was, I dug my thumb

and index finger into my arm and squeezed. When I let go, I was still in Father's study, still his successor.

"There's one other thing I was wrong about," Father said. He was looking down now, pretending to scan his account books. Of course, they were all wrong, done before the twister. "Before, I couldn't understand it. I suppose I didn't want to. Now, I see no match more suitable. If you still love Sam Jenkins, Lily, I give you my blessing. The two of you can have this house upon your marriage, and I will build a little cottage down the way. Your shared passion for horticulture, your shared passion for each other will be a sustaining gift."

I stared at Father, sure I was hearing things. I'd known he'd softened to Sam over the last few days, but all of this, all at once, was shocking.

He looked up at me. "He is loyal and smart. Your equal in so many ways."

Despite Father's words, my heart remained still. Sam wasn't mine.

"You have my permission to speak to him about these developments," Father said, plucking his pencil from the desktop and scratching notes on a blank sheet. When I didn't move, he sighed. "Go on."

I shook my head and swallowed the lump in my throat. "He's likely married by now. His fiancée came to fetch him the other day."

"Fiancée you say?" Father set his pencil down.

"A girl he met in the city," I said softly. I thought of Sam's last kiss, the way his lips had felt against mine, and forced the memory away. I had just been given the nurseries. I had just been freed from Harry Brundage. I couldn't let the half of my heart wallowing in pity drown the half of it alight with elation.

"Nevertheless, I will be more than all right, Father. Thank you for allowing me to follow in your footsteps. I doubt I'll truly believe it for quite some time."

Father grinned at me. "Go take a turn around the grounds. Feel the truth of it and dream of what we will become," he said. He handed me the new notebook and a sharpened pencil. I accepted them.

"I love you, Father," I said.

"I love you, too, Lily."

Laughter burbled up inside me as I turned and walked out of the room. I clutched the notebook to my chest and hugged it. Finally.

"Check on the salvaged peonies down in the barn," Father called out from the office. My work had officially begun.

"You haven't told us which varieties you'll want for your wedding bouquet," Mrs. Pratte said. She drained the rest of the water from the galvanized watering can into a cracked clay pot housing a scraggly looking Summer Soiree peony that had been flung into the woods by the twister.

I considered the two remaining bulbs on its stalk, glad I wouldn't have a wedding bouquet constructed from the peony I created with the man I actually loved. I was even happier I wouldn't have a wedding bouquet at all. Mrs. Pratte set the watering can on the ground and examined the bulbs. Perhaps they would blossom with the blush color only on the tips of the petals or splashed farther down onto the white. That was the one thing Sam and I overlooked when we concocted that variety. Sometimes the light pink was barely a hint and other times it nearly eclipsed the white background.

"I don't suppose we have much choice with the peonies. We only have these three Summer Soirees and two Bleeding Hearts. Not nearly enough to create something as magnificent as what you'll be wanting." She met my eyes and then looked away, almost apologetically, as though my lack of options was her fault. "But the roses have all maintained their blooms, and the varieties are plentiful. In fact, just last night, Vincenzo came home with a bouquet he'd clipped that looked much more beautiful than what the Astor girl had at her wedding last week—at least according to the paper's description."

Mrs. Pratte flittered around nervously, inspecting each bulb and root and plant. Everyone had suddenly gone from thanking me for accepting Harry to discussing my wedding. I knew why. They were worried that if they didn't continually bring it up, I'd somehow forget how much it meant to them and deny him. I knew the compulsion well.

I tied the burlap bag of miscellaneous roots and bulbs we'd collected to store until we could find planters and stood, wiping my dirty hands on my white frock, not at all concerned that it could stain. I had no one to impress now. I'd already wooed my love and won.

"I won't be needing a bouquet, Mrs. Pratte," I said.

She whirled around to face me. Even in the barn's dim light, her face paled. I watched her swallow, alarm playing across her face.

"Of course. Of c-course not," she stammered. "You d-don't love him. How could anyone expect—"

I stepped toward her and grasped her hand. "I would have married him for all of you, for the nurseries, but that's not necessary anymore." I smiled and the reminder of Flagler's generosity and Father's words filled me with happiness once more. "A . . . a friend has given us a second chance. He's given us enough to go on alone, and Father has agreed to train me to lead upon his retirement."

Mrs. Pratte squeezed my hand and then leaned in and kissed my cheek. "Thank God," she whispered. "I knew we had no choice but to accept your kindness, but the thought of your sadness for the sake of the rest of us kept me up at night."

"I know Father will likely make some sort of announcement, but I see no harm in telling others if you'd like to . . . primarily so they will stop inquiring about my floral arch or my bouquet or the wreath for my veil."

Mrs. Pratte laughed. "As you wish," she said. "Was Mr. Brundage very angry?"

"Very sad would be more accurate, I suppose." I loathed this part, the hurting part, the part that had lumped him into our scheme. Despite Charles's insistence that it was normal, an engagement made solely for advantage seemed wrong—especially when a heart was involved.

"Yes, I could see that. Though he will recover when he realizes the woman he loved wasn't actually you," she said.

I stared at her, confused, and she shook her head. "We try to keep to ourselves, but we all see your interactions, your flirtations."

My face felt hot.

"Mr. Brundage looked most in love with you when you refused him and when you were done up in finery. That night at Charles's send-off, the night after your dinner with Mr. Reynolds. You were like a rare diamond he couldn't obtain, and that made him rabid to have you." She shook her head. "He is the sort of man who is accustomed to winning, accustomed to being fawned over. He could hardly stand it that you, the loveliest flower in his kingdom, wouldn't yield to him. Even when you did, he knew it wouldn't be entirely or always. He was in love with your beauty, with a woman who would challenge him."

"And that isn't me?" I asked, removing my hands from hers. Even though I didn't want Harry, the idea that everyone thought he hadn't really loved me was a difficult concept to reconcile.

"No," she said. "You are stubborn, but only with those who don't truly understand you. You are beautiful, but more so among the flowers with a soil-stained white skirt and your hair affixed in a simple knot atop your head."

I laughed. "I'm unsure I would attract anyone at all with that description, though I suppose it is correct." She was right about it all—about my penchant for ruining gowns and abhorring conflict. I would speak my mind, that much was certain, but I craved understanding and peace. I craved a love that preferred me most in my passions.

"After a few weeks of marriage, Harry would have tired of me climbing into his gilded carriages arrayed in filth." I smiled, yet a bit of melancholy floated through me. I would be blissfully happy here, but I would be alone.

"There was someone who loved you most when you were

planting, when your eyes and your soul were alight with bliss," she said.

I closed my eyes and turned away from her. I didn't understand why she'd bring him up. She knew about Roisin. She must.

"Come. Let's gather the palm seeds from the house and move them to the new greenhouse. The Goulds and Mr. Flagler alike are keen to have a large variety to choose from, and right now we have none."

Mrs. Pratte nodded and followed me out of the barn. Evening was coming quickly. The growing field was awash in gold, and with the haze of cool air mingling with moisture from the ground, the remaining long, drooping racemes of yellow blossoms hanging from the few Golden Chain Cytisus and the handful of swaying old roses in pinks and crimsons and the sphere-like white oakleaf hydrangeas appeared dreamy. The smell of woodsmoke and onions drifted in the air from the village. It was dinnertime. I'd kept Mrs. Pratte too long.

"We can move the ferns tomorrow," I said, nodding toward the village. "I didn't realize the time."

"You've had quite a day," she said, taking my hand once more. "Perhaps you should go rest yourself."

"This is my comfort and my rest," I said, tipping my head at the new greenhouse. "But I suppose I must go in as well. Charles is leaving tomorrow. I imagine a fine farewell dinner is waiting."

"Ah yes. Chicken Vienna-style?" she asked.

"I'm certain," I said. Charles had requested the same meal on birthdays and special occasions since he was a little boy.

"If it is disappointing, you're always welcome to join us. Martina Sigallis is making risotto alla Milanese tonight."

"Another time?" I asked, and Mrs. Pratte nodded.

"I couldn't be more thrilled about the news, Miss Sadie," she said, letting go of my hand.

"We're of the same mind, Mrs. Pratte," I replied and started up the hill to the new greenhouse.

When I reached it, I ran my fingertips over the smooth new glass as I passed. I could hear Mother's scolding in my mind, saying the surface would have to be cleaned again, and grinned. She had always been strict about the upkeep of everything on our property.

"Stop your toiling and come along!" Charles called from the porch steps. "Dinner's almost ready."

I waved at him, but he was looking beyond me. He walked down the steps and across the drive to meet me.

"Turn around," he said when he was by my side. I turned to find the most glorious colors on the horizon—fire and tangerine and honey. "What a masterpiece. Sometimes it takes my breath."

We stood there, in the middle of the greenhouse field, the bare rectangular spots now dappled in a surreal saffron hue.

"Do you suppose you'll come visit?" he asked. "Now that you're free? I'd like you to see what I've built. It was a mound of sand when we started and now it's shaping up to be an oasis of sorts—a tame jungle."

"I suppose I could make the time," I said.

"Very good." I could tell he wanted to say more. Perhaps he wanted to apologize again or to explain why he couldn't stay, but he didn't. I was glad for it. Either would have been unnecessary.

"There's a letter for you that's just come in today's post." He reached into his pocket, extracted a small envelope, and handed it to me. "I was going to put it in your room, but Cooper's dinner call prevented me."

I didn't recognize the insignia on the return address. The initials swirled together in a fancy design that would only serve to confuse the mail carriers if the letter were to be returned. I broke the seal and opened it to find a note written in an elaborate cursive hand.

Dear Miss Fremd,

I admit I have never received such a forward correspondence as yours. It seemed urgent and hurried and demanding. I am not a man who yields to demands. Requests of this nature typically come with some sort of preamble—a fine dinner, a shipment of Scottish whiskey—a favor for a favor, if you will. Yet your proposition interested me.

My work in the law has exposed me to much, and I am aware of the conditions you have described. I happen to agree to the cure of it. I am quite close with Dr. Thomas Story Kirkbride, a doctor of psychiatry. Perhaps you have heard of him. He believes in open air for healing, that it is essential to the well-being of every soul. I have also strolled Birkenhead Park in London with the laborers, heavy with soot and soil from their day's work, who traverse the paths. They are not light of foot by any means, but I notice that they are light of face.

My travels make my time at home scarce, and when I am home, I admit I do not mind the town like I should. I had no idea of the conditions in Rye—of the failing companies that sent men and their families to live beneath discarded sheets and in cast-off crates. I suppose I assumed such a life was far away from Rye, a misfortune only of the places with towering smokestacks and tumbledown slums.

Upon receipt of this letter, I solemnly swear to give the town of Rye forty-five acres of my holdings to be used as a public park and $5,000 with which to ornament it with whatever horticultural endeavors your nurseries see fit.

Please accept this hastily written letter until I have the time and occasion to write comprehensively. I know you said not to trouble myself replying to your return address as you might be in Germany, but I am about to board a train to California and thought I'd chance sending it in case you might be about and would receive it much faster than if I put it in the post from the opposite coast. If you are in Germany, I assume your mail is being forwarded as mine is when I am abroad.

Sincerely,

John Parsons, Esq.

I could barely breathe. I stared at the letter and read it again. In the midst of calamity, I'd forgotten all about the letters I wrote.

"What is it?" Charles asked.

"I have to go." I started to run down the drive, not bothering to fold the letter.

"But your dinner will be cold!" Charles called.

"So be it!" I yelled back, clutching the paper to my chest as I ran.

No longer would they be held back by iron gates, no longer would they be kept away from the proof of beauty, from the proof of miracles.

CHAPTER 21

My hairline was damp with exertion and humidity by the time I reached the cemetery grounds. I held my skirt balled in one hand and kept hold of the letter in the other.

The sky was getting dark, the last rays of the sunset barely visible over the hill where Mother was buried. I gazed at her monument in the distance, fleetingly wondering if I should stop and turn back, if perhaps she was watching me running past with a sense of immense disappointment. I knew the notion was ridiculous, but I was certain I could feel her scrutiny. I hadn't done what she'd asked. I hadn't married a rich man. Instead, I was to be a woman of industry, a woman she'd been once and loathed. Then again, she'd been a seamstress in a factory and the role had confined her to the slums. Industry was different when one was at the helm.

I looked away, scanning the valley of tombstones and columbarium to my left, searching the wooded areas to my right for any sign of movement, for any sign of him. Leaves rustled in the forest and I stopped, only to find a squirrel emerging. Owls called and screeched overhead. I slowed to a walk. It was a good practice anyway, slowing.

I couldn't just come upon him in a passionate flurry anymore. I couldn't allow my joy to overtake my sensibilities as I often had before. I knew I would find him with Roisin. I would have to deliver this news with the delighted detachment of a colleague or acquaintance while my heart exploded with both elation and sorrow. I thought of Mrs. Pratte, of the way she spoke with me—warm tact, that's how I would tell him.

I read the letter again as I walked. The park would have a stream running through it; the babbling sound would be a balm. The surface of the water would be awash with blooming water lilies all coral and green. Maples—the Japanese Colchicum rubrum with its dark crimson leaves and the Thalictrum dasycarpum with its shiny silver leaves—would be interspersed to provide shade. I breathed deep, imagining the heady scent of English boxwoods and jasmine and honeysuckle in the background, though all I could smell were the snapdragons in bloom in the valley beside me and lily of the valley in the forest.

Sam and Mr. Sanderson had truly made this place a sanctuary in which to pay one's respects—the grass was lush and thick and something new was always blooming. That last bit was important. A cemetery should be a place of hope, not a place of despair—as it often seemed—and being met with dead flowers would only remind mourners of what they'd lost.

I wandered past the Lucas vault and onto the main carriage drive that led to the gated entrance. As the gates came into view, I turned left down another wide lane, and my heart quickened. An iron lantern hung flickering on the stoop of the gatekeeper's cabin, casting shadows on the stone entry and chimney and lighting the white stucco. Woodsmoke drifted in the air and plumed a thin gray cloud into the darkening sky. I took a deep breath and steeled myself to face him, to face her.

I walked up the two stone steps and stood in front of the door. It was an old door from the Presbyterian church—a thick mahogany with ornate swirls and grapevines carved in the center. The bottom was rotting slightly, a given considering the door had graced the vestibule to the choir loft in its previous life. It hadn't been conditioned to endure the change of harsh winter to warm summer. I felt sorry for it as I stood there. I, too, was mostly whole, mostly solid, with a bit of brokenness.

I knocked. The muffled sound of plates rattling met my ears, the thumps of footsteps, but none my direction. I knocked again. This time I heard him. His gait was unmistakable—unhurried, his height buying seconds between the floor's groaning.

At once I couldn't do it. I turned and walked down the steps, but I wasn't swift enough to disappear. The latch clicked and the door opened.

"Sadie," he breathed, and his voice hooked my heart. I heard him close the door behind him and I faced him. Our eyes met, his playing ocean green in the lantern light. He'd just put his shirt on—the linen hung open and loose across his chest—and I tried to ignore the implication and the jealousy that rippled through me.

"What are you doing here?"

I swallowed hard and glanced at the closed door behind him. He hadn't wanted her to know I was here.

"I . . . I . . ." I thrust the letter toward him and closed my eyes for a moment, attempting to compose myself, attempting to channel Mrs. Pratte. "I wanted to show you this," I said evenly, forcing a polite smile. "I thought you'd like to know."

He walked down the steps toward me and took the letter from my hand, his thumb brushing my fingers. I pushed my hand into my skirt and grasped the fabric as he read.

When he finished, he looked at me, his eyes filled with tears, and smiled. My heart was crushed at the sight of it, at the grin I'd fallen in love with.

"You did it, Sadie," he whispered. "No longer will the poor be locked away from the proof of miracles and beauty. No longer will they have to search the mud and filth and soot for hope. They will see the flowers; they will breathe the sweet air and know that . . . that they are loved, that there is hope." He reached for me reflexively but stopped. He ran a hand across his face and looked down at his boots.

My heart was racing, the whole of me calling for his touch. This was the moment we had been dreaming of. This moment was supposed to be ours.

"We did it together," I said softly. "Without you, I would have been blind; I wouldn't have seen the need. I came right away. I . . . I thought you deserved to know as swiftly as I did."

Sam handed me the letter and I folded it and put it in the pocket of my skirt. His beard had grown a bit longer over the last week and the ends of his dark hair curled just slightly. I had always thought him the most beautiful like this, a bit disheveled. Perhaps because it was such a contrast to the other men I knew, who counted on silk-trimmed suits to make them handsome.

"Thank you for telling me," he said finally. He lifted his eyes to mine, then scuffed his boots on the ground and looked over my shoulder at the moon. We were holding back. The silence was earsplitting.

"Did you set a date for the wedding?" His question sounded choked, but he forced his lips into a smile anyway. When I didn't answer, he shook his head. "I'm sorry, I shouldn't have asked. It's not my business."

Before I could stop myself, I grasped his hand. I knew I should pull away, but his calloused fingers threaded swiftly through mine, his palm warm against the chill of my own.

"I'm not marrying Harry. I can't."

At once Sam let my hand go, confusion playing on his face. "What will happen to you then? To your family? To the others?"

His jaw locked and his fingers fisted at his sides. "Is it me? Is it me who's ruined everything for you? I've tried to stay away these last days, but it's not enough, is it?" He shook his head. "It's not enough for me either. Years, a lifetime of distance, wouldn't be enough, would it? We are forever entwined and it is my doing, a curse I've brought upon you. I never should have let my heart open to you, Sadie. You never should have let your heart open to me." His voice was low and angry. He turned away from me and stared at the closed door. Despite his fury, butterflies fluttered in my stomach. I wondered if Roisin was close enough to hear.

"A friend of Father's has saved the nurseries. He's given us enough money to rebuild and then some," I said quietly. "I told Harry no because I don't love him, because the state of the village isn't dependent on his love for me anymore." I watched Sam's back, watched his breath rise and fall. I wanted to run my fingertips across his broad shoulders. I wanted to feel his skin against mine. But that was another woman's treasure now.

I cleared my throat. "Father told me he wants me to succeed

him regardless, that he was wrong to deny me before. It was all because of Mother's wish to see me settled with a fortune, to ensure I'd never see poverty as they had, but Father understands that, given the choice, I choose to risk ruin. I choose my heart over her fear.

"Sam . . . I . . . When he told me the news, when it settled in, I kept thinking of you, that I wanted you with me." The moment the sentiment passed my lips, I regretted it. There was no reason for it. There was no happy ending to it. Perhaps I simply wanted him to know I still loved him. "I know it's not fair for me to say it. I know you have Roisin now and you will be loyal to her, but I—"

"Roisin is married," Sam said. He faced me, then walked toward me until he was so close I could smell the echo of soil and grass on his skin, mint tea on his breath. "She only came to apologize for being so cold to me before, to tell me she was safe and healthy, married to a man she met in the city. They live in Connecticut now." His words cascaded from his lips and only when he stopped did I realize I hadn't breathed. I did so now, feeling tension stretch across my chest.

Roisin was gone. Sam still loved me. I looked into his face and let my hand rest on his chest. His fingers wrapped around mine.

"Father said he'd been wrong about you, that if we loved each other, he saw no reason we shouldn't be married. He gave his blessing," I said. Sam was trembling. I felt the slight tremor under my palm.

"Regardless, I'm not the man your parents wanted."

"Father understands now, and even if he didn't, I don't care. I can't care. I love you. I'm always going to love you. You understand my whole heart, the way it longs for the flowers, the way it longs for you. Sam, I—"

He kissed me. His lips were warm and soft and I wrapped my arms around his neck and pulled him harder against me. He answered, his mouth pressing into mine, his hands gripping my waist. I didn't want him to stop. His lips drifted down the curve of my jaw and his teeth closed lightly on my earlobe. I gasped and pulled him back to me, letting my hands trace the skin at the hem of his shirt as I kissed him. The fire between us now raged. Father wouldn't smother it, and Roisin couldn't extinguish it. Sam was finally mine and I was finally his. Sam's fingertips traced my collarbone and I shivered under his touch.

"Will you have me?" he asked suddenly, his lips leaving mine. "I just realized I haven't asked." He dropped to his knee and kissed my hand, my wrist, my palm. "Will you marry me, Sadie?"

"Yes," I said without reservation, and he stood and picked me up. My legs wrapped around his waist, my skirts bunching around my thighs. He kissed me and I returned it with equal passion, holding on to him, feeling the long muscles along his shoulders and the strong arms bearing my weight.

"Tomorrow," I whispered against his neck as he tilted his head to the sky and closed his eyes. "Will you be mine forever tomorrow?"

"I've been yours forever since the moment I saw you," he said. I threaded my hands in his hair and he planted another kiss on my mouth. "But if you're asking if I'll swear to be your husband tomorrow, the answer is yes. I never told you, but I bought a ring last time. I still have it. I couldn't bear to let it go.

It's only that I wonder . . ." He stopped and put me down, his gaze training on my hands holding his.

"I'll not change my mind. I'll not leave you standing alone again. I promise you, Sam. Letting you go that night has been the biggest regret of my life," I said.

He nodded once. "I know."

"Come home with me," I said. "In the morning I'll have Father call for Reverend Price and he can marry us wherever we like—in the house, on the grounds. It will be your home now, too, if you'd like us to live there, of course, and—"

"On the hill overlooking the field," Sam said suddenly. "That was where I first saw you. You were wearing the same sort of frock you have on now, and you were carrying La Reine roses up to the greenhouse. I remember thinking that I'd never seen a person so suited to the roses, more beautiful than the blossoms she held."

"I can think of nowhere more perfect," I said. Sam tipped my head up to his and kissed me again.

"Let's go home then, shall we?" he asked, offering me his arm.

I hadn't slept. I'd tossed and turned all night, often glancing at Mother's wedding dress, which Agnes had hung on my armoire hook, just to remind myself that this was real, that I was to marry Sam and have the nurseries too.

Father and my brothers had taken the news of our engagement and sudden wedding with joy, and Freddie had immediately squired Sam to his quarters to find a proper suit. I'd retired then in hopes that I'd meet my wedding day rested, but that was not to be. I was too overjoyed.

News had reached the village around eleven last night. I could tell because about that time the noise began—hammering and chatter and laughter seeped through my window. I thought to peek outside to see what they were about, but I knew well enough—they were preparing for our ceremony.

"Are you certain about this marriage?" Reverend Price asked me.

I surveyed my reflection in the window. "I've never been more certain," I said as I ran my hand down the white satin bodice of Mother's dress. She'd made it herself and it fit me perfectly and was still so lovely. My favorite part was the deep flounce of Honiton lace—lace she'd incorporated into the dress from her mother's veil.

I hoped Sam would find me beautiful today. Agnes had summoned me out of bed at dawn and spent the next two hours curling the length of my hair and coiling half of it into elaborate braids. Then she'd affixed Mother's veil—handmade with Brussels lace appliquéd on dotted cotton tulle with designs of lace rondelles and cabbage roses—to the top of my head.

"I only ask because—"

"Because I was engaged to Harry Brundage just yesterday," I said, meeting Reverend Price's gaze. I smiled at him and hoped he'd smile back, but he did not. Our previous pastor, Reverend Wright, had been a jolly sort of fellow. Not so Reverend Price. It was clear, even by looking at him, that his emphasis was on piety. He always wore a faded black knee-length jacket with tarnished brass buttons and a frown.

"You must admit it seems a bit peculiar. I'm called before break of dawn to officiate a ceremony for a woman I was supposed to visit at the estate of her fiancé today—and that fiancé is not the man she is marrying." He pushed his Bible into his chest and cleared his throat. "You do comprehend that marriage is a lifelong commitment, do you not? A promise to your husband and to God."

"I have loved Sam Jenkins for years," I said evenly. He would not alter my elation. "Yesterday I was set free, Reverend, suddenly permitted to marry for love." I looked out the window at the bright late-morning sun and thought of Sam waiting for me at the altar. "I think Harry Brundage is a fine man, but I don't love him. I would have upheld my promise, but it would have been an effort. I have no hesitation with Sam. He's had my heart for some time and he'll have it forever."

"I see," Reverend Price said. "I suppose—"

Father appeared in the doorway and stopped. His eyes filled when he saw me, and he extracted his handkerchief from his black double-breasted suit pocket.

"You look like her today," he said. "The flush of your cheeks, the curve of your smile. That was how she looked when I saw her walk toward me that day. I was assured of her love for me in a glance, and that image of her has remained with me always."

He came toward me and opened his palm to reveal Mother's diamond necklace and earrings. "These are exquisite. From Turkey. I bought them for her when we had been married ten years. Would you like to wear them?"

I nodded and leaned forward for him to clasp the necklace at my nape and attach the earrings to my lobes.

"Everyone has worked through the night and made it all heavenly," Father said. "Margaret has just arrived with Tempy. Would you like her to stand with you at the altar?"

"No," I said. "Sam and I will stand alone."

Margaret didn't understand us. I knew it without speaking to her. I'd sent Mr. Cooper over with a message, mostly out of obligation—she was my oldest friend, after all—but I knew well enough she'd be silently furious for the rest of our lives. I was supposed to marry Harry or Stephen or Lionel—someone who would accompany me to the balls and soirees, someone who would buy me a mansion in Newport, someone like Tempy. These past weeks, my closest friends had become our employees—people who had struggled alongside us and held fast.

"We're ready," Charles said, walking into the room. He held three rosebuds—The Bride, a pure white variety with a divinely strong old-rose scent—and one perfect Summer Soiree peony. This one was immaculate. The petals were white with a dark wash of pink at the tips, exactly the bloom Sam and I had envisioned. Charles handed the peony to me and I twirled it gently in my gloved hands.

"Everyone wishes there were more, Sadie," he said.

"There will be someday soon, but today one is perfect."

"Sam has one, too, affixed to his jacket," Charles said. "We thought it appropriate for you two to wear them since you cultivated the variety together."

The mention of Sam dressed in wedding finery made goose bumps prickle my arms.

Charles took a pin from his pocket and attached a rosebud to Father's lapel and then another to Reverend Price's. Then he handed me his. "I can't have it crooked for my sister's day," he said, smiling. I held the rose against the black silk lining and slid the pin through it.

"It's perfect."

"No. That word belongs to you today, dear Sadie." Charles

pulled my veil straight over my shoulders. "I'm sorry I tried to convince you to accept any other man but Sam. It's clear now, with everything in the open, how ardently you love each other. It was wrong for us to interfere, even if our interference was prompted by love and concern."

"All is just as it should be now," I said. "All is forgiven."

"I suppose we should make haste," Reverend Price said, clicking open his pocket watch. "It is 11:24." He tipped his head at me and walked out of the room to join the others at the place where we would meet again, where I would swear my life to the man I loved.

"I'll see you after," Charles said, kissing me on the cheek and following him out.

At once it was silent. Just Father and me.

"I'm proud of you," he said. "I know I've not made it easy on you, but perhaps in the hardship you've become who you were intended to be."

I nodded and blinked away the tears. I couldn't cry, not now.

"Shall we go?" he asked and held out his arm for me. "My father always said, 'Wo man liebe sat, da wachst freude.' I know it to be true for you. It means—"

"'When you sow love, joy will grow,'" I said as we walked down the hall. "I haven't lost my German, Father." I smiled as we passed a small portrait of Mother. Unlike the typical fashion, Mother's mouth in her portraits was never stern but always turned up in a slight grin.

Father opened the door for me, and I gasped. A runner of crocheted linen flanked by rose petals of various colors lined my long walk from the porch, across the greenhouse lawn, to an arbor done in an assortment of green branches and blooms, where Sam waited alone. Even from this distance I could see him, his broad shoulders atop his tall frame, outfitted in Freddie's tuxedo, his black hair trimmed short. Perhaps Mr. Sigallis had been his barber last night.

"Who fashioned this runner?" I whispered to Father as we stepped off the porch and onto the first bit of crocheted fabric.

"Late last night the women decided you needed one, that you might stain the hem of your gown on the grass if you didn't have one, so they got out all of their tablecloths and napkins and blankets and spent the whole of the morning attaching them together," he said.

With each step I thought of them, of each family who by giving their precious possessions had demonstrated their love and support for us.

The moment we crossed the drive, a violin began to play from somewhere far away, and after a few seconds, a chorus began to sing my favorite hymn.

"All things bright and beautiful, all creatures great and small."

I glanced around, wondering where they all were, where the sound was coming from, but saw them nowhere.

"Each little flower that opens, each little bird that sings; He made their glowing colors, He made their tiny wings."

We were close enough to Sam now to see the tears in his ocean eyes, to see the way the white oakleaf hydrangeas, delicate palm fronds, and tiny cream-colored star jasmine highlighted his beauty. Nerves tumbled in my stomach like butterflies as we reached him, and then he smiled at me. I vaguely heard Father agree to give me away. I barely registered my hand escaping the crook of his arm, and then Sam and I were facing each other, hand in hand.

Everything quieted suddenly. I held Sam's gaze, acutely aware of his touch as he slid the simple gold ring onto my finger, and my soul emerged and tangled with his as we swore to love each other forever. When he leaned down to kiss me, when his lips, soft and sweet and mine, parted my mouth, the music began again, this time just the instruments, but louder, as if played in testament to love's victory.

I pulled Sam closer, feeling my heartbeat, feeling his, and when we finally parted, our hands still clasped, I looked out over the growing field and began to sob.

Standing among the beauty—the trees and the flowering shrubs and the roses—was our family. All of our employees. Mr. Russo sat on a stool in the corner, his head crooked to his violin. Even Margaret was there, standing with Tempy next to my brothers.

"I love you, Sadie," Sam said and gathered me close, his hands resting on my hips. I leaned back against his chest.

"This is a marvel, all of it, all of us," I whispered. "Are you sure it's really happened? Are you sure it's really us here, married at last, with the nurseries saved and a park on the way? I can hardly believe it."

Sam plucked the peony from his lapel and held it in front of us. "Surely you can believe it," he said softly. "There are miracles everywhere. Look at the care, look at the wonder of these blooms."

I curled my hand around the back of his, holding the flower

as Mr. Russo concluded the final notes of the hymn. As his bow lifted, everyone cheered and threw bits of colored fabric like streamers in the air.

Sam turned me around to him.

"You are my favorite in all of creation," I said.

"May I always be worthy of your love," he said and kissed me one more time as the whine of Mr. Sigallis's accordion and the tap of Mr. Pratte's drum joined the violin, heralding the start of a celebration, of "*Ciuri, Ciuri.*"

"'Flowers, Flowers,'" Sam said, grinning. "Appropriate. Suppose we should join them?" Before I could reply, he took my hand and pulled me down the hill. I ran after him, the surprise of what my life had suddenly become burbling up in joy so overwhelming that, as he twirled me, tears rolled down my face.

"It is like a fairy tale for all of us," Mrs. Pratte said as she materialized next to me. "Though I shouldn't have been surprised. Despite the hardships of this life, I've found it true that love never fails."

EPILOGUE

"Vincenzo, have you counted the Oreodoxa regias? They need twenty-three!" I shouted, weaving around the crates and plants waiting beside the idling train to meet him in the doorway of the fourth open-air car we'd loaded today. Charles was just about to finish the Royal Poinciana's palm court and needed a last shipment of a few varieties.

"I've situated twenty-four just here, Mrs. Jenkins," he said, panting and wiping away the sweat along his forehead with the edge of his linen shirt. "In case one of them doesn't make it. They're hardy, of course, but I thought it prudent to—"

"Yes, wonderful." I turned back to the loading deck and eyed the dozens of palms. Mr. Sigallis and Mr. Russo stood behind them, their hands shoved into the pockets of their canvas pants as they waited to instruct their men and women.

"Latania borbonica in the fifth car with the Phoenix reclinata. Four dozen each," I said, pointing first to the broad-leaved fan palm of the first and then to the curving, wide-spreading fronds of the latter. I leaned down to pull a pot slightly away from the one next to it and noticed I'd dirtied the grass-green satin bow at the hem of my yellow silk skirt where it was appliquéd with white lace. I brushed the dusty dirt from the material and shrugged. Margaret knew well enough what I did day to day, and a bit of dirt wouldn't be a surprise to anyone in our circle.

Everyone in Rye was used to my involvement, and now that it was heartily endorsed by Father, no one treated me any differently than they had Father when he was running the nurseries alone. Their acceptance made the transition to my sharing the lead easy. Those outside of Rye had seemed rather skeptical about dealing with a businesswoman at first, but when it was clear their peers trusted my judgment, the hesitation to work with me diminished.

"Perhaps you should go on up and meet Mr. Jenkins on the drive," Mr. Russo said as he watched me trying in vain to expunge a smudge of soil now evident on the white lace. "We've been loading two varieties in each car, ensuring room between each plant. Is that how you'd like us to continue?"

I nodded and lifted a hand to my forehead. It was clammy with sweat. I had no doubt I'd ruined my hair by now. The light, wispy curls Agnes worked on for hours were now likely lying flat in a damp mess. I should have known I wouldn't let the shipment go without overseeing it. Not that I mistrusted the others to do it for me, but the plants were almost like my children—I'd seen them through the start of their lives. It was the least I could do to see them situated correctly as they went off.

"Thank you, Mr. Russo. Just ensure that the Cocos

weddeliana and the Kentia belmoreana are situated toward the middle of the car. Their fronds are so delicate I fear they'd snap in the wind, even with the protection of the ceiling," I said.

"I'll have Libro and Pasqualle look everything over before we give the conductor the go," Mr. Pratte said. He'd just come down from the greenhouses, whose new glass sparkled in the sunlight like stars in the afternoon. He pulled his cap down over his eyes and gestured to his children, who were currently wandering around the pots with buckets of soil, filling any that seemed low.

"Wonderful. I'd appreciate that very much," I said. Over the past year, in the wake of the economy's rally—with businesses new and old emerging or returning to Rye—and our rebuild, I'd continued my quest to call on the ladies of fine homes all around the region, and we'd been busier than ever before. The increase in business meant we'd needed to organize our staff into specialists over several varieties and functions—a recommendation of Sam's. Vincenzo's siblings, Libro and Pasqualle, had been assigned to the growth and care of the palms.

The shrill bleat of a carriage horn startled me, and I looked up the hill to see Sam standing in the carriage in his Palm Beach suit, gesturing to me. He looked like he should be in a fashion magazine—his black hair and tanned skin a contrast to the light blond of his suit. Even so, Margaret and Tempy—probably all of the old society set—would loathe his costume, though they all had eventually come to love Sam. The Ridgeways would find the suit too casual for the reveal of their butterfly garden and the thousands they'd spent on our plants and design and the caterpillars they'd had brought in from all around the world.

I'd mentioned the error in dress to Sam, but he only shrugged and reached for the accompanying jacket. *"If it's good enough for*

Charles and Mr. Flagler, it's good enough for the Ridgeways," he'd said. *"And in any case, it's light, and by the feel of the day, it'll reach ninety. I'll be comfortable."*

"I suppose I actually should go now," I said to no one. They were all bustling around me. I bunched my silk skirt in my hand and began the walk to meet Sam.

I glanced into the full greenhouses as I went, a rainbow contained in glass. Gladiolus, hydrangeas, geraniums, fuchsias, dahlias, chrysanthemums, azaleas, peonies, roses, and every kind of fir seedling we could procure for a future Christmas tree planting.

"You're looking lovely, Mrs. Jenkins," Mr. Deal said as he appeared from the planting shed, his arms from fingertips to elbows covered in black grease. We hired him last year to oversee maintenance, and he'd taken to nursery life well, even striking up a bit of a romance with Frank Russo's sister, Bella.

"I appreciate the compliment, Mr. Deal, but I fear I've done it again—disobeyed Agnes—and now I suppose I'll be repaid with laughter at my expense at the party."

He shrugged and chuckled. "I suppose you come by it honestly. Last week, moments before your father left for Florida to visit Charles, he saw Vincenzo digging out a lime tree incorrectly and ended up down in the field. The knees of his slacks were covered in dirt."

"The perils of horticulture," I said.

"Enjoy yourself." He tipped his straw hat at me.

I walked past the barn and climbed the little hill to the greenhouses and then crossed to the drive where Sam now sat against the carriage's tufted leather seat, a grin playing on his lips.

"I suppose I owe you a nickel, Mr. Green," Sam whispered

loudly. Mr. Green, perched on the driving seat, winked at me and then nodded, his hands wrapped around the reins that were strapped to an impatient Admiral who snorted and stamped.

"Whatever for?" I asked, smiling.

Sam stood and stepped down from the carriage, meeting me at the door. He wrapped his arms around my waist and pulled me to him. I lifted my hands to his neck, letting my fingers trace the hairline at his nape as our lips met and we sank into each other.

"You can't distract me from asking again," I whispered in his ear when his mouth broke from mine. "No matter how handsome you are or how much I forget everything but wanting you when you kiss me."

"I suppose I'm out of luck then." He grinned. "Mr. Green, we've been found out."

Sam stepped away and held out his hand. I took it, climbed into the carriage, and sat back against the leather. When Sam was situated beside me, his fingers tangled in mine, Mr. Green slapped the reins, and I waited.

Sam's dimples deepened, though he kept his mouth straight. "Each time we go anywhere, you depart before me, saying you'll meet me at the carriage," he said finally. "And each time, I get to the carriage and find you vanished. I suppose since we were a bit tardy today to begin with and considering both of us gave detailed instruction about the freight order to the others, I assumed you would be there upon Agnes finishing your hair. I even wagered a nickel with Mr. Green because I was so certain that you weren't at the carriage only because your hair wasn't done yet." Sam laughed. "It was Mr. Green who spotted your sunshine gown down next to the rails."

"I . . . I'm sorry." I hadn't realized the pattern of my behavior. I always assumed I had just a few minutes' time to check on the nurseries, but those few minutes turned into half an hour at least.

Sam's hand squeezed mine and he brushed an ebony strand from my face. "I didn't want to go to the Ridgeways' anyway—even if we did design and outfit the place. I'll pay the nickel every time for the sight of you absorbed in what you love," he said.

"I suppose the moment I see the object of my affection—whether that's the flowers or you—I want every moment I can get away with," I said softly so Mr. Green couldn't hear.

We made our way down the drive, past Father's new bungalow—a little white house tucked into the trees—and onto North Street.

"Yes, and I can't express how thankful I am for that," he whispered back, and then his lips brushed the hollow of my neck.

"The Brundages' still looks splendid," Mr. Green remarked as we turned onto Post Road. Beyond the iron gates, the roses were in full bloom. I recalled the last time I'd walked that garden, the desperation hollowing my heart, the way it had felt like the iron gates had absolutely trapped me.

"Yes, the original design has held up quite well. I wouldn't expect any less from Sadie, of course, but we've only had to replace a dozen roses this year," Sam said.

Despite my previous entanglement with Harry and his heartbreak over me, the Brundages had kept us on. Perhaps it was because Mrs. Brundage now thought us water under the bridge. According to the papers, Harry had set his sights on debutante Amy Bend during the winter season and hadn't come home from their townhome in the city since.

"Perhaps it's the mild weather we've had? The Finks' garden has behaved too," he went on.

"Regardless of the reason, this year has served us well," Mr. Green said. "To think last year we were almost capsized is unbelievable, really, considering the success of this year. How many gardens have you done since? How many thousands of plants have you shipped all over the country on freight?"

"Thirty-two gardens," I said. I'd just looked at the books this morning when I wrote down another request from the Goulds to design a topiary garden on the grounds of a mansion still in design on Lake Carasaljo in New Jersey. We'd traveled hundreds of miles over the last year, following design requests—everything from an English rose garden for the Berwinds in Newport and an Italianate for their neighbors, the Westmores, to a moon garden for Emily Vanderbilt Sloane at her family's triple palace in the city, to a tropical greenhouse garden for the Garners and the butterfly garden for the Ridgeways.

"Over fifty thousand plants out on freight to Vaux and Olmsted and Flagler just this spring," Sam said.

"Remarkable," Mr. Green mused.

I leaned into Sam's chest, knowing full well the gesture could further ruin my hair, but I couldn't help it. He was the most perfect partner, the most perfect husband, and at times my love for him overwhelmed me. He stood alongside Father and me at the helm of the nurseries, his direction a perfect mix of Father's tendency to focus on figures and my tendency to run with my dreams.

"I don't suppose I could love you more," I murmured, and I felt the slight tremor in his chest as he laughed.

"I can't believe how fortunate we are, how unequivocally blessed."

His arm wrapped around my waist and drew me closer, and it occurred to me as my heart skipped that his love for me was a wildfire displayed in a touch, in a whisper.

"The park is a popular place today," Mr. Green said, slowing the carriage slightly as we passed Parsons' Park. I sat up and stared at the crush of people gathered around the pond at the start of the serpentine path that led nearly a mile through lush green shrubs and trees and a kaleidoscope of blooms. Along the walk bordering the small creek were stone benches for one to rest or read, and at the back of the park was an open grassy knoll for children to run and play. Since its opening in April, the park had attracted the whole of the town—poor and rich alike—and it wasn't uncommon to see Mary Fink occupying a bench with a book across from Peter Skelton, who lived in the rail village.

"Should we stop for a moment?" Sam asked, doubtless sensing my longing.

"That's all right. Let's keep on and go tomorrow," I said, though I wanted desperately to say yes.

Mrs. Griffith appeared from the tunnel of jasmine growing on an arbor at the start of the path. She wore a white work frock, like mine, only hers was always perfectly white despite her immaculate groundskeeping. She placed her hand on the back of a man wearing soot-stained overalls, said a word of greeting, and then glanced up at the road.

I waved as we passed, and she smiled and lifted her hand. She lived in a small cottage toward the back of the grounds now, hired by the town to maintain the park.

"Look at them," Sam said, his eyes trained to the crowd of shoeless children and women in Worth gowns. "From all different walks of life and yet drawn here, together. Perhaps it's not only the flowers that are the miracles. See? They are all speaking, and someday soon they will begin to understand each other; someday soon they will see that though some may be cloaked in ordinary shrubbery while others are cloaked in the majesty of roses, they are all souls worthy of beauty. They are all the same. When that truth is finally realized, perhaps the slums will disappear, perhaps the rail village will be swallowed up by suitable houses."

I sighed and squeezed his hand, letting my spirit soar with hope because as implausible as his dream sounded, I'd seen this park materialize from what had once seemed a preposterous fantasy.

"I pray you're right," I said. "I pray that loveliness will flow from this place in waves." I breathed deep, inhaling the sweet scent of honeysuckle blooming nearby, and Sam planted a kiss on my forehead. "Of all the pretty places we've designed and have yet to design, this will always be my favorite."

AUTHOR'S NOTE

I want to say right off, if you've flipped here first, ahead of reading the story, don't read further. This note contains spoilers and it's not at all fun to read a story when you already know what's going to happen.

For those of you who are familiar with my previous work, it will come as no surprise at all that this story is largely based on my ancestry. I continue to be enraptured by true stories of daring women in my family tree and find that writing about them, getting to know them in this way, is a unique gift.

My first attempt at a novel (no, you'll never see it—ha!) was set in Rye, New York. Despite never having lived anywhere remotely close to this magical small town, I have long been drawn to it—likely because it was home to generations of my family—and have often dreamed about what it must have been like to live among such beauty at the nurseries. I grew up hearing stories from my grandmother—whose maternal side was the inspiration for *The Fifth Avenue Artists Society*—who lived at Rye Nurseries until she was three years old and grew up in Rye, as did her father and grandparents and great-grandparents, who started the nurseries in 1870.

Charles Fremd, my great-great-great grandfather, immigrated from Stuttgart, Germany, and landed in New York City around the year 1860 knowing four languages (none of them English). Prior to his immigration, he earned a degree in horticulture with a concentration in the study of trees, but because of the language barrier, finding work was difficult.

During his time in the city, he met my great-great-great grandmother, Jane Clague, from the Isle of Mann, and they fell in love. She taught him English. As soon as he was proficient in the language, he became employed with a prominent landscape architect in New York. We aren't sure exactly who he worked for in real life—whether Vaux or Olmsted or someone else entirely—but we do know he worked on large private-estate gardens. Over time his skills as a horticulturist were recognized by his employer and clients, and someone suggested that a fine nursery was needed in this part of the country and urged him to go into business.

Within a few years, Charles purchased twenty-five acres of land on North Street in Rye—occupying both sides of a railroad track. When he married Jane in 1865, he expanded his property by forty-five acres and built a large home on the property as well. The nurseries were finally started in 1870 and quickly developed a fine reputation for having an expansive and exotic variety of plants from the United States, as well as imported varieties from Yokohama, Japan; Boskoop, Holland; Stuttgart, Germany; and others. The business became the sourcing nursery of choice for many notable landscape architects in the area—likely including Olmsted and Vaux, based on the gardens we know the nurseries were involved with. Throughout the nurseries' life, the business also provided landscape architecture services and often both sourced and planned large gardens for notable Gilded Age families.

From its inception, Rye Nurseries was committed to hiring immigrants, particularly Irish and Italian immigrants who, in the late nineteenth century, were experiencing discrimination in the city and were often refused quality employment. Charles provided housing in a little community next to the nurseries and would often pay for certain family members to travel back to Ireland or Italy to retrieve the rest of their families.

Charles and Jane had three children—Charles Jr., Sadie, and Freddie. Charles Jr., an expert in trees like his father, was originally slated to take over the nursery business but instead accepted a post with Henry Flagler and was the landscape architect for several of his hotels. Charles Jr. stayed in Florida the rest of his life and started his own pesticide company along with continuing to provide landscape architecture services.

Freddie became a town leader along with his cousin Theodore Fremd, who held countless offices, was a staunch supporter of women's rights, and was ultimately dubbed the "Grand Old Man of Rye." In the story I position Theodore as Freddie's uncle for narrative purposes, but in reality, Theodore was his contemporary and was drawn from Stuttgart to Rye by his uncle, Charles Sr., after his parents' passing. Along with Freddie's community endeavors, he helped his father run the business side of the nurseries for years. In the story I chose to focus on his political endeavors to differentiate his interests from Charles's. He married and lived on a large prerevolutionary farm in the nearby town of Purchase.

Sadie, my great-great grandmother, married the love of her life, Sam Jenkins, the son of landscape architect Robert Jenkins who was, in fact, in charge of Greenwood Union Cemetery. Despite Charles Sr.'s original hope that the nurseries would fall to one of his sons, Sadie's love of horticulture won, and she ultimately became the owner of Rye Nurseries—one of the first businesswomen in Rye. Sam and Sadie were always very much aware of the need for natural beauty for all and did as much as they could to ensure that others—regardless of their economic status—would be able to enjoy the hope of flowers. They were instrumental in designing and donating plants to several small public gardens, including New Haven Station Park (though the first official public park wasn't opened in Westchester County until 1927), and also employed as many people as they could as the economy dipped and steadied and dipped in the years leading toward the Great Depression.

Parsons' Park is a fictional park I created to suit the timeline. I decided to include John Parsons—considered the most successful lawyer of his time—as benefactor because he and his family had a country home in Rye and ultimately donated a large amount of land to the town, including a piece of property that would eventually serve as a nature center.

The story I set out to write at first was solely about the nurseries, but as I researched developments of late-nineteenth-century landscape architecture and horticulture related to Sadie and the nurseries, I kept coming across newspaper stories about large public parks—Central Park and Downing Park, among others. Right next to those stories, sometimes within the span of a page in the same newspapers, were articles about tenement catastrophes and the happenings of the Fifth Avenue set in Central Park.

I already knew the park had been primarily utilized by the social elite as a promenade, but seeing these articles side by side brought to my attention a distinct similarity: many of the plagues of tenement life—namely disease, pollution, and despair—were absent in the presence of clean air and natural beauty. This realization prompted me to further investigate access to natural spaces and public gardens for the average person, and I was stunned to find that, unlike today, public spaces were seldom designated for the entire public to enter and appreciate the miracle of flowers.

The public park movement wasn't really started until the 1830s, when cemeteries began moving from cities—where they were often public health hazards—to the outskirts. With more land available on the edges of towns, these new cemeteries were sprawling and lush, awash with flowers. Soon they became a place for people not only to pay their respects but also to sit in peace away from pollution and collect their thoughts amid natural beauty. Over time, people began to use these landscaped cemeteries for leisure as well—for walks and games—igniting the desire for city parks.

Like landscaped cemeteries, the first city parks were often found on the peripheries, away from factories, tenements, and industry. They also usually required a train ride or carriage commute, preventing those without the income to obtain a ticket the ability to seek refuge from disease-ridden tenements and smog-infused air. This worked quite nicely for the upper crust, who often campaigned for the construction of large city parks for their own use and for the increase in property values a park would guarantee—never mind the fact that these parks weren't essential to their well-being since they had access to their own elaborate private gardens. Outwardly, cities falsely proclaimed that the parks would be constructed for all to enjoy, despite often obtaining land for the endeavor by claiming eminent domain over property owned by immigrants and minorities. In the beginning, city parks were ultimately not at all the places of refuge and natural contemplation for the weary that they claimed to be.

By the very late nineteenth century, this fact was obvious, and some, realizing the desperate need for hope and access to nature for all, attempted to build parks near tenements and factories—where the people who needed them actually lived.

Though Rye in 1893 was hardly a factory-riddled town, I wanted to keep the story as local to the nurseries as possible. Many who worked for the Fremds—and Charles and Jane themselves—began their time in America in the factories of New York City and would have settled in the town still hungry for natural beauty. The Panic of 1893 affected everyone—rural and urban citizens alike—and I knew the destitute and homeless would naturally live in Rye as they would anywhere else.

Rye also boasted a large number of industrialist Gilded Age estates with elaborate gardens landscaped by Olmsted, Vaux, and the Fremd family. Disparity of economic status was everywhere, as it is today. I imagined a man, just let go from the railroad in the midst of the panic, lingering at the gates of an estate to see the hope of a flower and recalled the compassion Sadie and Sam were known for in real life. Back then, though green space and trees would have been plentiful, gardens in towns like Rye truly would have been restricted to the confines of Gilded Age mansions. I thought about how hungry people must have been for nature and decided that was the story I needed to tell.

Rye was not affected by the Panic of 1893 in the way I portray it in the book. Of course some businesses struggled, but the town was never truly on the verge of complete collapse. The wealthy families on the periphery of the Fremds' circle—the Finks, the Brundages, the Ridgeways, etc.—are all based on real industrialists who either lived full-time or summered in town, though I changed their names to suit the fictional narrative I gave some of them. I allowed Mr. Flagler's and the Goulds' names to remain because the family had true relationships with them—though the closeness of the Fremds and the Goulds is unknown and might be exaggerated for the sake of story. However, the names of the nurseries' gardeners I used are all accurate, pulled from census data from the nurseries. I thought their contributions should be acknowledged.

In real life Sadie and Sam ran the nurseries together for many years. They had six children, one of whom was my great-grandfather, Fred Jenkins. Fred and his wife, Winifred (the daughter of Mae, really named Alice, in *The Fifth Avenue Artists Society*), were given the reins to the nurseries upon Sadie's retirement. By that time Sadie and Sam were living away from the nurseries' grounds in a home that still stands on Central Avenue.

Fred and Winifred started their family in the original Fremd family home. My great-uncles Bruce and Peter were born at the nurseries, and my grandmother, Alevia, lived there until she was three years old. In the late 1930s, amid the fallout from the Great Depression, Rye Nurseries was forced to close its doors.

On a recent trip to Rye, my dad and I drove around the area where the nurseries once stood. It's difficult to picture the enterprise being there at all. A soccer field and a car repair shop are there now, and the interstate runs through the middle of what would have been the growing field. However, some echoes of the gardeners' village are still present. Some buildings look like they could be original to the era and a church still stands that my grandma says was built when the nurseries were in their heyday. Despite knowing Rye Nurseries was mostly a memory, we drove up and down the streets a few times anyway.

Sometimes magical things happen when I write about my family, and I was certain I'd find a clue about where a greenhouse stood or where the big white farmhouse I'd seen in photos once loomed, but we found nothing. At first I found the disappearance of the nurseries to be a bit melancholic. I wanted so desperately to see our family photos come to life. Then I thought of the flowers. Perhaps the nurseries weren't as important as the legacy they left behind. My family's passion had been filling spaces with blooms that flourished for a time, died, and then blossomed again in another spot, on another stem. Sadie and Sam, Charles Sr. and Jane, and Freddie and Charles Jr. were like flowers themselves, beacons of hope for many in the time and place they were needed most. Now it's our turn to carry on their legacy, to bloom, to bear evidence of miracles to a hurting world.

Sadie Fremd Jenkins

Growing fields at Rye Nurseries

ACKNOWLEDGMENTS

I'm not much of a gardener, but I greatly appreciate flowers. They are miracles, evidence of a hope that can only be given by God, and when I stop to really examine them, I'm amazed at the craftsmanship displayed in even the smallest petal. I'm thankful for that.

If you looked at my family tree, you'd notice a few gifts seem to be prevalent, passed down from generation to generation. Writing is one and gardening is the other. My mom inherited the appreciation and gift of horticulture from Sadie, and my parents' yard is spectacular. It's one of my favorite places to browse the flowers. My cousin, Abby, also inherited that love and her pre-revolutionary farm in Rhode Island is magnificent. I think these gifts shared with our ancestors tend to bridge the generations a little and allow a person who lived hundreds of years before us to teach us something. I'm thankful that I get to learn from them.

Thank you to my mom, always my first reader, for the support and for assuring me that I seemed like I knew what I was talking about—despite knowing little to nothing about plants.

ACKNOWLEDGMENTS

One of the most challenging things about writing this book was getting into the headspace of a woman whose father (initially) didn't want her to go into business or use her gifts. My dad, a business owner like Charles Fremd, has always been one of my biggest fans, always encouraging me to go for my dreams. Thanks, Dad!

This book (and *The Fifth Avenue Artists Society*) wouldn't have existed without my grandma, Lee. She has always captivated me with the stories of her childhood and of her parents and grandparents and great-grandparents. I'm honored that she shared them with me and can't wait to hear more!

Thank you to the rest of my family—Jed, Hannah, Reece, Josh, Bethany, Elise, Mady, Diana, Johnny, Jeremy, Momma Sandra, Aunt Cindy, Bill, Samantha, Jamie, Jancis, Porter, Mauve, Uncle Jim, Uncle John, Uncle Billy, Janine, Blair, Davis, Camden, Aunt Sarah, Richard, Ellen, Jeb, Keith, Britt, Jeremy, Ryan, Lori, Randy, Rochelle, Tim, Alice Jean, and Becky. I love you all so much and am incredibly thankful for you.

Thank you to my BFF4L, Maggie Tardy (Drew, Ava, and Claire, too) for always supporting me and always being there. You're the inspiration for every good friend and every sister I'll ever write.

I couldn't do this job without my friends. Thank you to Jessica, Mindy, Amanda, Carolyn, Brittany, Julie, Ronni, Megan, Elaine, Jodie, Katie, Shea, Court, Hollie, Laura, Sanghee, Joy, Michelle, Liz, GraceMarie, Christine, Kasey, Alice, Rena, Rich, Jim, Carrie, Sarah, Arden, Caitlin, my Avondale family and my Park Crossing family for understanding when I pick up the kids from the bus looking like a cave dweller, for all the coffees and chats, and for just being there.

ACKNOWLEDGMENTS

Thank you to my fellow writer friends Cheyenne Campbell, Kim Wright, Marybeth Whalen, Erika Marks, Kim Brock, Lauren Denton, Leslie Hooten, Brenda Janowitz, Erika Robuck, Kristy Woodson Harvey, Sarah Henning, Lauren Edmonson, and Meredith Jaeger for always being willing to hop on the phone to go over a story problem or just commiserate over the crazy fun career we've chosen.

It has been so wonderful to get to know some amazing bookstore owners and booksellers over the years. I know how instrumental they are to any book's success and I'm just so thankful. Thank you especially to my instant friend for life, Olivia Meletes-Morris, and Wendy Meletes from Litchfield Books, to Sally Brewster and Sherri Smith at my hometown bookstore, Park Road Books, to Kimberly Daniels Taws at The Country Bookshop, to Shaye Gadomski at New Chapter Books, to Ashley Warlick at M. Judson Booksellers, to Karen Schwettman and Gary Parkes at Foxtale Book Shoppe, to Jill Hendrix at Fiction Addiction, to Dan Carlisle at Taylor Books, to Ashley and Mandee at Booktenders, and to Dawn Nolan and Dawn Hylbert at Cicada Books, and to Marlene England at WordPlay.

Thank you to all the fantastic bookstagrammers, bloggers, and podcast hosts who take time out of their day to read my stories and spread the word! I'm looking at people like you Annissa Joy Armstrong, Francene Katzen, Renee Blankenship, Julie Chan, Valerie Souders, Cristina Frost, Lisa Harrison, Brenda Gardner, Courtney Marzilli, Cindy Burnett, and many others I'm forgetting here. You all truly make a difference and know how to make an author smile. Thank you also to the countless book clubs who have selected my books and invited me into your homes and meetings to get to know you and celebrate the uniting power of stories.

It goes without saying that a great agent in an author's corner is absolutely vital. Thank you so much to the incomparable Kate McKean for the guidance and friendship—couldn't do this without you!

Thank you to my fantastic publishing team at Harper Muse who have become good friends—Kimberly Carlton, Amanda Bostic, Kerri Potts, Margaret Kercher, Jodi Hughes, Nekasha Pratt, Jere Warren, Taylor Ward, Becky Monds, Laura Wheeler, Caitlin Halstead, Savannah Summers, Patrick Aprea, and Colleen Lacey. I am beyond fortunate that my books are in such expert hands.

Finally, and so importantly, thank you to my husband, John, and my children, Alevia and John. You've been subjected to lots of takeout and many days of watching me hole away with my laptop. Thank you for always loving me, encouraging me, and standing beside me. I love you all so much. The story we're writing together is my favorite one.

DISCUSSION QUESTIONS

1. *All The Pretty Places* is based on my ancestry, on stories I've heard from birth. Do you have any family stories or figures that have captivated you? Why?

2. Sadie starts out wanting to run the nurseries simply because it is her passion, but later she realizes her dreams could also serve a greater purpose. Has this ever happened to you?

3. If you could choose the professional path of Sadie, Charles, or Freddie, which would you choose and why?

4. What surprised you most about the book?

5. If you could transport back in time and visit the Brundages' rose garden, the Finks' pink garden, or the Goulds' rooftop garden, which would you choose?

6. At one point, Sadie must decide to forego her own happiness for the sake of others. What does it take to make such a decision? Have you ever had to make a similar choice?

7. What is your favorite flower or plant? Why?

8. Nature has a profound impact on our well-being. Why do you believe that is?

9. Why do you think Sadie was slow to notice how much natural beauty was restricted from the poor? What do you think truly caused her to take action to make gardens accessible for all?

10. Who was your favorite character? Least favorite?

From the Publisher

GREAT BOOKS

ARE EVEN BETTER WHEN THEY'RE SHARED!

Help other readers find this one:

- Post a review at your favorite online bookseller

- Post a picture on a social media account and share why you enjoyed it

- Send a note to a friend who would also love it—or better yet, give them a copy

Thanks for reading!

ABOUT THE AUTHOR

Photo by Bethany Callaway Photography

J oy Callaway is the author of *The Fifth Avenue Artists Society*, *Secret Sisters*, and *The Grand Design*. She holds a BA in journalism and public relations from Marshall University and an MMC from the University of South Carolina. She resides in Charlotte, North Carolina, with her husband, John, and her children, Alevia and John.

joycallaway.com
Instagram: @joywcal
Facebook: @JoyCallawayAuthor